"It's too late."

"What the hell are you talking about?"

Her gaze darts to a tattered book in the midst of what appears to be an altar. The edges are degraded. A symbol I've never seen before stamped into its center. "There's no redemption for what I did. But there's still time to stop me."

I stare at the aged book. Its blackened pages bear writing in an alien language.

That sick mother of a feeling chews at my gut. I refuse to acknowledge it. "Whatever you did," I say, voice low. "We can fix it. Just tell me where you are."

"I can't." Manda shakes her head, tears dwelling in her fiery emerald eyes. "I won't."

Anger strikes like a damn rattlesnake. "What do you mean, you won't? You brought me here for a reason, didn't you?"

"I did."

"Then tell me how I can find you."

"I can't."

Patience is for the strong, not the ones on the brink of maximum fear. "Amanda," I yell. "Stop playing games. This isn't funny."

Bitter laughter crawls up her throat. "No, Alex. No, it's not." She sighs. "That's why I need you to promise me that when time comes you won't hesitate. Finish what you started the day you learned what I was."

Realization hits like lightning. "Are you asking me to kill you?"

She musters a smile. "I'm asking you to save me."

Praise for Nadine Nightingale

Karma (Drag.Me.To.Hell.Series, Book One) won 3rd place Paranormal Romance Guild, Reviewers Choice Award.

~*~

"*Karma* is probably my favorite paranormal book that I have reviewed in a very long time."

~*SBR Blogs*

~*~

"*Karma* is a fun, exciting, and phenomenal story that I can't get enough of! I definitely can't wait until the next installment."

~*Bookalicious Babes Blog*

~*~

"I haven't read such an amazing paranormal/UF book in a while. [*Soulmates*] had it all: action, humor, suspense, romance and more."

~*Betul, Silence is Read*

~*~

"I loved every word. I have been mesmerized by this story from chapter one of *Karma*, and let me tell you, Ms. Nightingale does *not* disappoint with *Soulmates*! You will want to join Manda and Alex on this crazy and exciting journey!"

~*Tiffany, BookRelations*

Fate

by

Nadine Nightingale

Drag.Me.To.Hell. Series, Book Three

Fate

Cover Art by *Debbie Taylor*

The Wild Rose Press, Inc.
PO Box 708
Adams Basin, NY 14410-0708
Visit us at www.thewildrosepress.com

Publishing History
First Black Rose Edition, 2018
Print ISBN 978-1-5092-1905-6
Digital ISBN 978-1-5092-1906-3

Drag.Me.To.Hell. Series, Book Three
Published in the United States of America

Dedication

Dad,
Thanks for making me a fighter.
I love you.

"Fate is for those too weak to determine their own destiny."

~Kamran Hamid

Chapter 1

Alex

Lightning cuts through the graphite sky, a blazing shock of white, forking quietly to the flooded streets. The mighty *boom* follows quickly, rippling through my marrow like the shockwave of a damn explosion. Mrs. Munch, our old Sunday school teacher, used to call lightning storms the wrath of God. "Hear that, Alexander?" she said to me once. "That's God and he's mad at you." I'm still not sure I believe in an old grumpy dude with a white beard sitting up there on his throne watching us screw up his creation. But if he does exist and Mrs. Munch was right, he's beyond pissed.

Pissed I'm alive when I should be rotting in hell.

Pissed the demon didn't claim my soul.

Pissed the damn hellhound retreated as the clock struck midnight.

I know it sounds crazy. Why would God be ticked off because I wasn't deported to hell, right? He should pull a John Bender, throwing his mighty fist up in the air. I did after all; score God one, Satan zero. Fucking shame it doesn't feel like a win. I made a deal with a demon, sold my soul for…Well, it doesn't matter why. The thing is my soul should be on its merry way to the infernal regions where hellfire and torture are the daily dish, garnished with the prospect of eternity.

Why the fuck I'm sitting in the passenger seat of my beloved Mustang is a mystery to all of us, including Bonnie. Queen B, as she likes to be called, is Amanda Bishop's—she's my lying, runaway ex, by the way—best, extremely neurotic, mamba friend. On normal days, I'd put a bullet between her gorgeous cognac eyes. I'm a hunter after all. My prey? Witches like B and Amanda. Sometimes other creatures too—vamps, succubuses, wendigos. You name it I killed it. The urge to off supernatural abominations runs through my hunter DNA. But Queen B isn't just any witch. She stuck with me when I needed help, tried to save me despite my heritage. And although she drives me nuts most of the time, she kinda grew on me the way Richard Gecko, one of the protagonists of *From Dusk Till Dawn*, grows on you.

Still assaulting her phone, she watches me in the rear-view mirror. Her heart-shaped face painted with worry and suspicion alike. The mamba knows better than anyone hell doesn't just give up on a soul. "That's impossible," she said as the dog-like creature with the red glowing eyes merged with the night, leaving me completely unharmed. "Anna wasn't your soulmate. The smoke… It was black."

For anyone who doesn't speak witch it translates to: Bonnie performed a ritual to determine if Anna, an ex-flame of mine, was my soulmate. Why? Because according to the Bishop grimoire—one of the oldest and most powerful spell books in the world, belonging to my lying ex's family—there's only one way to get out of a deal with a demon. Find your soulmate, ask her to claim your soul, and exchange hell for fated love. It's why we—Bonnie, Jesse, Manda ('til she ditched us in

Winter Harbor for no other reason than being the selfish witch she is), and I—spent the past nine days roaming the country, trying to find every girl I ever liked. Needless to say, the Find-Alex's-Soulmate mission was a complete flop. Neither Anna nor any of the other girls on the soulmate list was *the* one. It wasn't a rude awakening or anything. I *liked* those girls. They were nice, kind, and good. But I didn't *love* them. My heart doesn't dig good girls. It has sick, masochistic tendencies, beating only for the rotten apples. You know, the ones that screw you lovingly and leave you desperately. What can I say? I, Alexander Ethan Remington, am a sucker for the I-ruin-you-forever chicks.

So, why the fuck didn't the hellhound tear me apart even though we never found my soulmate and no other way out of this deal existed, according to the witches? Nobody knows. Not even Queen B, the mamba, who likes to pretend she's omniscient.

Letting my head melt into the leather seat, I focus on the pouring rain while we wait for Jesse to book us a room in the Westminster Motel. Any other day, the sound would calm me. Maybe even help me make sense of all this madness. Today, however, it stirs up the restlessness in the pit of my stomach. A constant, unpleasant flutter, screaming at me, "This isn't right. You should be dead."

B is just as edgy as I am. "Amanda," she barks into her phone, eyes on me. "If you get this, call me back." Voicemail number two-hundred-seventy-eight. The mamba isn't a quitter. She's been trying to get a hold of Mrs. I-promised-to-fight-Satan-over-your-soul-just-to-walk-away-when-you-needed-me-most for over an hour. Unsuccessfully.

"Where the fuck is she?" Must be a rhetorical question because she knows damn well I have no clue where Manda is. The witch called half an hour before my hellish-deadline ended, told me I was never more than a good fuck for her, and hasn't been heard from since. Yup, that's Manda. Never cares about anyone other than herself. Not sure why I thought she'd give a shit if I lived or died. Blame it on wishful thinking.

"Amanda Caroline Bishop," she yells, close to pulling her wild curls out. "Call me! Now!" I sorta feel sorry for the mamba. She deserves better than a BFF who leaves her hanging with two witch hunters.

Another flash of too bright light lights the dark sky. Thunder rumbles, bouncing off the ground with an anger that makes us both jump in our seats.

Across the parking lot, under the safety of a small roof, is Jesse. He waves us over, keys dangling from his fingers. He got us a room. Finally.

B and I run through the icy rain. The street is a muddy war zone. Buckets full of water turned snow and soil into a slippery death trap. We make it to the other side without breaking our necks. But not without being soaked, head to toe.

"You okay?" Is the first thing my brother asks.

I have no fucking clue how many times I've heard that question today, but I'm getting real tired of it. "I will be if we ever get out of this shitty storm." Violent winds level even the mightiest trees behind the motel. Staying outside is suicide.

We—two hunters and a mamba, natural born enemies—march into room number 237. Two king-sized beds, shabby carpet, and a small kitchen—

Westminster Motel is just like any other rat-hole we've slept in over the past few years. But thanks to Stanley Kubrick's adaptation of *The Shining,* I'll probably dream about a rotting, old woman, trying to seduce and kill me. Fun times.

Under Jesse's scrutiny, I kick my shoes off and take up the bed on the right. I hate the way he looks at me. Like I'm fragile and broken.

"Alex?" Reluctantly, I meet his gaze. "Are you sure you're okay?" I get he's worried. For all he knows, hell could come barging in here any second, reversing their little mistake. But enough is enough.

"Ask me again," I mutter, flinging myself onto the hard mattress, "and I'll give you a taste of how *o-kay* I am." Hey, he's my little brother and I love him. Doesn't mean I can't lovingly beat the crap out of him every once in a while.

"Amanda!" B pushes past Jesse, throwing her bag onto the left bed. "Last chance. Call me back, or I swear I'll donate your dildos to the Salvation Army." Can't believe she's still calling her. Someone's gotta tell her how pathetic she is. Manda walked away. She doesn't care about us.

When the mamba dials her again, I can't take it anymore. "It's pretty damn obvious she doesn't want to talk to you." That came out harsher than intended. It's Manda's fault though. She's got that certain something. It turns me into an asshole every time I think about her mesmerizing emerald eyes. The clinical term for my disease? I believe it's called Having Been Screwed Over By Amanda Bishop syndrome.

B snaps her head my way, piercing holes in my soul. "Don't remember asking for your opinion."

"Hey." I shrug out of my wet leather jacket, dropping it on the chair beside my bed. "Just trying to make sure you don't lose your dignity."

She slams both hands on her well-formed hips. "Says the guy who doesn't even know how to spell dignity."

Jesse's face slips into a major frown. "Guys," he grumbles, tired as hell. "Can we not fight?" The whole my-bro-should-be-in-hell-but-isn't business still messes with him. He fears the demon will realize the glitch in the system and come back to drag me to hell. I have the nagging feeling he won't.

"Look," I say, hands up in defense. "I'm not trying to be an ass—"

"You don't have to try," B cuts in.

I ignore her hostility, for now. "All I'm saying is you're wasting your time." Like I wasted my hopes. Fuck, I want to bang my head against the wall for even considering a girl like Manda—a goddamn witch— could be my soulmate. Yup, for the fraction of a second, back in Winter Harbor, I thought Amanda Bishop might be *the* one. Never mind she's a witch and I'm a hunter destined to kill her. Forget the lies and hurt she brought into my life. When she loved me the way I thought she could only ever love herself, I believed the illusion she sold me. The fairytale of a dark queen and a white knight riding off into the sunset together. Pathetic, huh? But can you blame me? Manda has perfected the art of manipulation to a point where she believes her own lies. Buying her bullshit, when she moaned my name as if made for her lips, was easy. Too easy.

Anger flashes across B's eyes. "You do realize

you're talking about my best friend, right?"

"Best friend, huh?" I don't think Amanda is cut out for that. I hear friendship is a give and take relationship. All she knows is how to take—your heart, your brain, your fucking life. "With friends like these—"

"What's the matter with you, Alex?"

"Hey, I'm just looking out for you."

"No, seriously. What the fuck is wrong with you?" She cocks a brow, ogling me like a true killer witch. "When you came barging back into her life, half dead and doomed for hell, she left everything behind she worked so hard for to help you. Fuck, she took a goddamn bullet for you in Bakersfield. Yet here you are, acting like Amanda is the queen of darkness?"

I don't think Manda is the queen of darkness, more like the queen of selfishness, but I never get to correct B. "Maybe," Jesse interferes, casting me a warning glance. "We should give Manda some time. For all we know, she thinks you're in hell." Jesse shrugs. "We all grieve differently."

Grieve? The girl gives a shit about others. Especially me.

Even B doesn't buy my brother's lame excuse. "Time?" she barks. "Are you kidding me? I've known her most of my life and I'm telling you something is wrong. I feel it in my bones."

When it comes to Manda nothing is ever right. Why can't the mamba see she's the definition of wrong? "C'mon," I say, starting a last attempt to take off her pink glasses. "We all know this isn't the first time she ran." Won't be the last either. It's kind of her trademark.

Remember the expression on Voldemort's face

moments before he whacked poor Cedric? That evil half-smile, paired with unspeakable darkness in his eyes? That's pretty much how B stares at me. "*You*, Alexander Remington, don't know shit about her." There's so much confidence in her voice, I almost believe her. Almost.

"I know she claimed she'd fight Lucifer over my soul." Yup, a guy doesn't forget when a chick tells him she's ready to rumble with the ruler of the infernal regions for him. "Then she steals JJ's car a day before I'm supposed to go to hell and leaves us all hanging." I shake my head, nails digging into my palms. "Sorry, B. That's exactly the Amanda Bishop I know. Selfish. Careless. Unreliable."

The mamba's light brown eyes catch fire. "What about the Malleus Maleficarum Order?" She blows out some steam. "They're gunning for her, remember? So, what if she didn't just leave us *hanging*? What if she…" She trails off.

"What, B?" I raise my brows. "What if she what?" Secretly, I want her to give me a reason to believe in Manda. Despite everything she did, I always thought there was goodness underneath that armor of bitch-attitude—a damn heart inside her thorny chest. After last night, I'm not so sure anymore.

It looks like even her best friend can no longer find reasons to justify her shitty-act. "I don't know, okay." She throws her hands in the air. "I don't know why she stole the damn car, or why she said all those things on the phone. She had to have had a reason, though." B's gaze darts to me. "I'm telling you, she cares about you… More than you think."

No, she doesn't. And as hard as it may be to admit,

she never did.

Tired and drained, we sit on our beds. Awkward silence wraps the gloomy room in an uncomfortable blanket of unspoken accusations and unrequited feelings. None of us—neither B, nor I—is ready to give up our prefabricated opinions. And Jesse? Well, I think he's just glad B and I stopped fighting.

Flashes of lightning illuminate the room, accompanied by deafening thunder, rolling through the night sky like a damn bowling ball. I'm so focused on the storm, I don't immediately hear the buzzing of B's phone. Only when she jumps to her feet like a damn rocket, do I recognize her ringtone "Crazy in Love" by Beyoncé.

"Amanda?" she yells into the phone.

My pulse races faster than my Mustang at full speed. Jesus, what a traitorous, ungrateful mother my heart is. Never mind the countless times Manda shattered it. The hollow, muscular organ doing backhand springs in my chest is eager for more. More pain. More lies. More tragedy.

Judging by the grim look plastered across the mamba's face, I won't have to fight another Love Her, Hate Her battle just yet. "Are you serious?" B hisses through gritted teeth. "She left JJ's car at *your* place?"

Who the hell is she talking to?

"In Salem?" B goes on.

I'm guessing Melinda, Amanda's sister.

"No way." B paces the room like a tennis player on steroids, her sexy dark complexion paling. "She'd never—" She clenches her jaw. "Bullshit, M."

You don't have to be a witch to tell something bad is cooking.

"Just tell me where she is," the mamba demands with a force that's rather impressive. "What do you mean you don't know?"

Jesse cups B's elbow. "What's going on?"

She pulls back, ignoring him completely. "I'll be there as soon as I can. And M...when I get there you better tell me the truth before I share a certain secret with a certain someone."

Share a certain secret with a certain someone? God, why do witches always speak in damn riddles? Do they suffer from some kind of speech impairment? Or do they get off on annoying the shit out of people? A combination of both, I assume.

"Got it?" she asks. "Good."

Arms crossed, my little brother draws to his full height. "What is going on?"

B heads straight for her bag, tossing her phone in it. "I gotta go."

"Go where?" Jesse inquires, half worried, half pissed, totally unhappy.

"Salem."

"Now?" Jesse narrows his eyes, pointing at the ugly orange clock hanging above the bed. "It's the middle of the night, B."

"So?"

His eyes soften. "So, let's get some sleep and leave first thing tomorrow morning."

Did he just suggest we'd drive her back to Salem? What the hell is wrong with him? Did his Queen B obsession corrupt his damn brain cells? "I ain't going nowhere," I clarify.

They both glare at me as if I sacrificed a damn puppy. I don't care. I'm done with Manda. She wanted me out of her life and I'm finally ready to honor the deal we made back in Bakersfield. I won't bother her again. Ever. It's what she wants. It's what I need.

"Alex!" Every fucking argument Jess and I ever had started like this. Him barking my name. Me grinning. This one is no different. "I know you're mad at her, but—"

"I'm not mad," I assure him, calmly. "I'm just done."

"Of course, you are." B curls her small hands into ironclad fists. "I mean, now that you didn't go to hell you don't need her anymore, right?" The wicked grin on her lips scares the shit out of me. "And you dare to call *her* selfish?"

How is it Manda walked away and yet I'm the boogeyman? Doesn't matter. I don't need to justify myself. Not when Amanda was the one who put a nail in our coffin. "Exactly," I say, standing taller than ever. "I don't need a witch like her in my life. For all I care"—I shrug—"she can go to hell." Not literally. Even Amanda "Queen of Selfish" Bishop doesn't deserve an eternity of demonic torture. Still, it wouldn't hurt her to get a taste of her own bad medicine, for once. Karma, if you will.

B might be pissed, but that's nothing compared to my little brother. He crosses over from anger to burning wrath in a nanosecond. "Are you fucking serious, dude?"

Am I serious about never wanting to see the witch again? About never wanting to feel the pain she caused me when she said I was just another one of her lucky nights? "Yeah," I assure him. "Yeah, I am." My heart won't survive another game of Love Me, Hate Me. Not when I was ready to give up everything I am just to be with her. Not when she left me, *again*.

B has heard enough. Without another word, she marches to the door. Her grip on the doorknob is so tight it turns her knuckles white. "I can't believe"—she catches some air—"she almost died for a guy like you." That said she walks into the stormy night, never looking back.

Disgust with a hint of shame is what I see in Jesse's eyes. He hates me a little, right now. But that's okay. I hate myself as well.

By the time he realizes I won't change my mind, he rushes outside. "Wait," he yells after B. "I'm coming with you."

If he thinks I'll follow him, he clearly doesn't know me.

Leaning back on my elbows, I enjoy the chilly wind wafting through the open door. The rain beats against the roof, the wind howls, and in the midst of all those noises I hear the love of my life, a black '65 Mustang roaring to life.

This has got to be a joke. He'd never—

Nope, this isn't a joke. I'd recognize the sound of that engine anytime, everywhere. I spent years working on that car.

Jumping up, I grab my stuff and run outside. They're halfway out of the parking lot. I almost break my damn leg getting to them.

"Stop," I order, yanking the backdoor open.

Jesse grins like a mother. "Changed your mind?"

"No." Feeling like a drowned rat, I hop in. "But my car isn't going anywhere without me."

Chapter 2

I've never given much thought to climate change. All that fuss about rising sea levels, expansions of deserts, and heat waves don't sound half as threatening as a striga, a wendigo, or Amanda Bishop. Plus, there's no way in hell I'd give up my beloved Mustang just because it blows out more exhaust fumes than a calumet. But staring out the window from the back seat of my car I come to think the whole we-are-fucking-up-the-world mythos might not be a mythos after all. In a little less than two hours, we drove from a murderous thunderstorm right into a damn blizzard. It's snowing so heavily, you barely see a mile ahead.

"Think we're passing by Westford," he says, eyes on the road signs.

Isn't that just fan-fucking-tastic? In about forty minutes—maybe more if the snow keeps obscuring my brother's sight—we'll be in Salem. Jesus, why the hell did I get in the car again? Oh, right. I refused to let my brother drive the love of my life without being there to protect her. Now that we've almost reached our destination, I'm not sure that was such a great idea. Coming face to face, eye to eye with Manda *never* is. I mean, what the hell am I supposed to say to her? Thanks for using me? I'd sound like a damn girl. Or how about, you're a goddamn liar. Why did I ever believe you cared about me? Nope. Still sounds like a

13

chick suffering from the unrequited love syndrome. *Why say anything?* I'm just going to stay in the car and wait 'til B is certain witch-bitch is all right. Then Jesse and I can go back to our old lives, the one where we kill witches rather than fall for them.

Meat Loaf's "I'd Do Anything for Love" blasts through the speakers. B, as agitated as ever, changes the station. Judging by the way she glares at my radio, I'd say she's not a big fan of the "Bat Out of Hell" singer. Or maybe she just hates nineties love songs. Whatever it is, she desperate tries to find another song. "What the actual fuck?" she murmurs when the same song plays on every damn station.

"Weird," Jesse admits, maneuvering the car over the slippery road.

Yup, especially because the same line—the one about him running into hell and back for a chick—plays simultaneously on every station.

B slams her thumb against the "off" button, but the radio has a mind of its own. It keeps playing. "I think it's broken," she says, more to herself than anyone else. How do I know? She hasn't spoken to us since we hit the road. Even ignores Jesse, though he was the one who didn't think twice before offering her a ride to Salem.

"Hold on." Jesse pushes one of my old cassettes in. "That should do it."

Takes me less than two beats to recognize "Sympathy for the Devil." It's one of my favorite Stones songs. There's something about Mick Jagger's smoky voice and the lyrics that gives me goosebumps.

B blows out a long, frustrated breath and leans back in her seat. Gazing at the trees flying past us, she's still on edge. Has been ever since she got that call from Melinda. I admit, it's weird Manda voluntarily went back to Salem. I saw the way her sister treated her when we barged into the Bishop residency, looking for a way to save my soul. Manda wasn't welcome. Worse, her family went to great lengths to erase the witch's existence from their memories. There wasn't a single picture of Manda. All right, there was one, but I have a feeling the only reason it survived the purge was the fact Melinda was in it, too. Selfish witch or not, you don't treat family like that.

So, why did she go back?

The question still echoes through my mind when Mick Jagger's voice is cut off by static, white noise. At first, it sounds like a woman screaming for help. Then the static sound fades and Meat Loaf's "I'd Do Anything for Love" is back on. Same line. Same old "I'd barge into hell for you" nonsense.

Jesse's gaze darts to the radio. He doesn't say anything, but I'd bet my Beretta we think the same: *What the hell is going on?*

B pales to a point where she resembles Manda, in the morgue, back in Bakersfield. You know, when the spirit of little Isobelle—one of Francoise and Walter's victims—killed her. "Please," she pleads. "Just hurry." My brother speeds like a bitch in a damn blizzard. Any faster and my beloved Mustang turns into the Weasly Family's flying Ford Anglia. Or worse, we hit a tree.

"We're almost there," he promises her, but it doesn't calm the mamba. Instead, it makes her more restless.

B isn't the only one who feels the heat. Remember that unpleasant flutter in the pit of my stomach? Well, it's back to send chills down my spine. "Always trust your gut," was my dad's advice when he heard Jesse and I would join the family business, hunting witches, saving innocent. The thing is, right now, my gut screams "trouble" louder than ever.

****

Half an hour later—that goddamn song continues to torture us, but at least it stopped snowing—Jesse pulls into the Bishop driveway. Like Melinda predicted, JJ's car is parked near the First Period Colonial house with the ivory façade. Still can't believe Manda gave up *this* for a life on the road. The mansion is breathtaking, inside and out. On the other hand, money can't buy everything. Sure as hell couldn't buy Manda the love and appreciation of her family.

Jesse hasn't killed the engine yet when B yanks the door open and jumps out of the car, running toward the massive wooden door.

"B," he yells after her, pulling the key out of the ignition. "Wait." He's out of the Mustang and next to her in a damn heartbeat. He *so* likes that chick more than he should.

Needing to stretch my legs, I get out and lean against my love. I will stay right here until Jesse gets back. No way in hell I set foot in that house again.

B's expression is an odd mixture of being pissed, worried, and happy we made it to Salem. "Thanks for the ride." She crosses her arms. "I can take it from here."

"I'm coming with you," Jesse insists.

"Amanda is *my* friend. *My* responsibility." The mamba's fiery eyes dart to me. "Go, take your brother and get out of here. I'm sure you guys want to celebrate his out-of-hell experience at the next strip club."

Jesse rarely gets mad. He's one of those guys who believes in love, peace, and sex. Only a handful of people can push his get-out-of-his-way-or-die-a-cruel-death button. Me? I'm one of them. So is B, apparently. "Manda is *my* friend, too."

Friend, huh? I laugh. What a lot of crap. Amanda Bishop is so much more than *just* a friend to my brother. The instant he laid eyes on her in that alley he adored her. Don't ask me why, but Jesse loves Manda. Truth be told, there were days when I believed his feelings ran deeper than brotherly-friendship. The way he looked at her, the spark in his eyes when she gave me hell—it made me wonder if maybe he, too, fell for her wickedness. Soon I came to realize how absurd the idea was. Jesse Remington has never been, and will never be, a one-lady type of guy. Just the word "settle" turns his stomach into knots.

"Is she now?" B barks, voice sharper than my hunting knife.

The muscles in his arms flex, expanding his tight shirt. "What the fuck is that supposed to mean?" he shoots back, raw anger poisoning his vocal chords. *Congrats, B. You really do know how to push his buttons.*

The mamba doesn't back down. "One"—her index finger comes up—"you're a hunter. Two"—middle finger follows—"you're a guy."

"I have no fucking clue what you're saying." Wow, mad and confused. This should be good.

Bonnie shrugs a lazy shoulder. "Guys never do anything out of the goodness of their hearts. They play the long game, always wanting something in exchange." She cocks her head to the side. "And hunters?" She laughs. "Dude, you kill our kind. Don't even try pretending you care about what happens to us *witches*."

One: B has a problem with men.

Two: She really does hate hunters.

"Listen." Jesse moves in on her, lips inches from hers. One move and they get it on, right here, in the driveway of the Bishop mansion. "I have no idea what sorta guys you let into your life, but I don't play any games." True. He might be a younger version of Hugh Hefner, but he's never been a player. He doesn't have to be. Chicks dig him so much they'd do anything for a night with him. Even when they know it's a one-time ride.

Their gazes collide. Jolts of pure attraction fly through heavy snow clouds, electrifying the air. "Manda is the closest thing I have left to a sister," he goes on, voice heavy and thick. "So excuse me if I don't give a fuck about what you want right now."

Bonnie's brows fly up. Witch or no witch, she didn't see that coming.

"And about the hunter thing," he adds. "I don't remember pulling my gun on you or Manda. Ever." He blows out some angered steam. "Now, I'd greatly appreciate if you could get over yourself, so we can check on *our* friend."

For a second there, the mamba is rendered speechless. I don't think anyone has ever given her that kind of attitude. And Jesse isn't quite done yet. "You just gonna stand here and grow roots, or can we move on?"

"Whatever," she murmurs, spinning toward the

entrance.

I'm pretty damn sure those two are another tragedy in the making.

"Alex," Jesse shouts across the driveway.

Why the fuck is he mad at me? I didn't do shit. "What?"

He stares me down, murder on his face. "You coming or what?"

The way I see it I have two options. Holding my ground and directing all his anger at me will probably result in a fistfight and for once, I'm not sure I'll come out on top. Or going against my new I-never-want-to-see-the-witch resolution and beating myself up for it.

"Alex," he yells.

Yeah, I think I would like to live some more. Besides, I am dying to know what lies Manda will throw at us. Maybe it'll help my heart to get over the witch once and for all.

"Fine," I grumble, pushing myself off the car. "Let's hear the cheap excuses."

Chapter 3

The pregnant cloud tailing us since Westford gave birth a while ago, covering most of the driveway with a thick layer of fresh snow. It's like eleven degrees out here and I'm freezing my nuts off.

Why's no one answering the fucking door?

B has been knocking so hard, her knuckles are torn. If Melinda doesn't let us in soon, we'll all make a trip to the next ER for frost boils, pneumonia, and in Queen B's case, a broken hand.

"Melinda," she yells like a lunatic. "I know you're home." Her gaze shoots to the black BMW parked in front of the garage. "Your fucking car is in the driveway."

Unlike B, I'm not eager to come face to face with any of the Bishop sisters, but I get why she's acting like Dwayne "The Rock" Johnson on meth. She assumes the worst. Why? Because Melinda Bishop isn't the kind of woman who leaves anyone outside to catch death.

"I'm going to kill her," B barks, close to kicking the door down.

"Hey." Jesse cups her elbow. "Maybe she's running an errand. Let's wait in the car." He's not half as concerned about losing his nuts to the cold than he is about Queen B's torn knuckles and neurotic behavior.

She jerks her arm away, casting him a killer glance. "An errand?" She shoves her phone under his nose.

"It's four in the morning. Who hits a grocery store in the middle of the night?"

Jesse and I do. It's kind of our thing after a successful hunt. Yeah, yeah, I know it's lame. You'd expect guys like us to hit the next bar, right? What can I say? Real life isn't half as glamourous as the movies. Killing witches is exhausting. It's why we look for an open twenty-four-seven, grab our favorite stuff—Reese's and OJ for my brother, chips and soda for me—and fling ourselves in front of the TV. Still, Bonnie has a point. Melinda has a little boy. I highly doubt she'd leave the house in the wee morning hours for diapers, or snacks. The woman is way too Martha Stewart to pull a stunt like that. So, the question remains. Why isn't she answering the door?

Bang! Bang! Bang! The mamba is going to wake the whole damn street. "Melinda! Open up! Now!"

All right, enough is enough. "Turn it down a notch," I order, leaning against the porch railing.

"Shut up," she hisses, assaulting the door further.

"Fine. If you fancy a night in prison"—I shrug—"then by all means, carry on. Just don't say I didn't warn you." Frankly, I hope she doesn't dig prison. When the cops show, and they will if she keeps this up, she won't be the only one wearing silver bracelets. Last time I checked, I was still a fugitive. Carter, my boss at the FBI's Paranormal Analysis Unit aka PAU, has no clue I'm alive and kicking. I doubt he put much effort into fixing the Francoise dilemma. The bokor who turned my brother into a real-life zombie—not the brain-eating kind, the brainless kind—and assisted pedophile Walter, abusing little kids, died in a private visitor room in prison, while I sat across from him. He called me, told me he'd help me out of my deal. Thanks to my little brother's persistence, I was dumb enough to agree to a meeting. Next thing I know, he drops dead. Someone, or should I say *something*, snapped his neck right in front of my eyes. Since there was no one but me in the room, the guards added one and one, believing I offed the bastard. After everything he did, to Jesse, those kids, and Manda I would have loved to send him to hell. But I swear by my sister's empty grave I didn't touch the asshole. Nevertheless, I was arrested. Jesse broke me out after the hellhound tore me apart. Now, we're both wanted men. So yeah. The cops are the last thing we need.

Seems like the mamba doesn't fear tiny, windowless boxes, or uncomfy cots. She keeps banging and yelling like one of the *Crazies*.

"Drop it," I bark, catching her hand before it reconnects with the door.

She struggles to free herself, but I hold on tight. "Let go."

Part of me wants to throw her fragile body over my shoulder and lock her up in the car. One look in her clouded cognac eyes is enough to soften my stance. She's horrified. So much so, I too feel her fear in my bones. "We've been here for over half an hour, B." My voice is calmer than I am. "If she hasn't opened the door yet, she probably won't."

B's gaze drifts from me to the door and back. "You don't get it, do you?"

"Enlighten me then." I'm too cold to fight or argue. Let's hear her out and see what put the wrath of God in her.

She contemplates my offer. "M said she'd be

home." She tilts her chin at the Bishop house. "She'd never leave us out in the cold, Alex." Our eyes lock. "You met her, didn't you?" I nod. "Did she strike you as the kind of person who would risk her neighbors catching wind of the scene I've been making?"

"No," I admit, heavy hearted. Unlike Manda, Melinda cares a lot about other people's opinions. The two sisters are like yin and yang, black and white, fire and ice, Hitler and Gandhi. And while I wouldn't put it past Manda to let her best friend freeze to death, I highly doubt a chick who wears pearl necklaces and pumps at home would risk her neighbors calling the cops for a peace disturbance.

"I'm telling you something is wrong," B says, shoving her dislike for me aside. "Please, Alex. I'm begging you, if you ever cared about Amanda…do something."

If *I* cared about Manda? Never mind. I won't grace this comment with a reply. It would just end in another hunter-witch war. "What do you expect me to do?" I ask, rubbing my tired eyes. "Breaking and entering?"

She bats her thick lashes at me. I take that as a "yes."

Jesse's hand lands on my shoulder. "Maybe she's right, dude." He ogles the locked door. "I mean, what if the Malleus dicks got to them? Could you live knowing we didn't do shit?"

My little ass of a brother knows exactly how to get what he wants. Push the guilt button, add a little concern, and et voila Alex reaches for his lock-picking tools and breaks into the Bishop's house.

Takes me less than twenty-seconds to open the door B assaulted mercilessly. Someone oughta give

Melinda a lecture about alarm systems and safety locks.
Witch or not, she's a single mom. The world's full of
scum ready to take advantage of that.

"Whoa." Jesse's eyes almost pop. "What the
fuck?"

The neat hallway I remember is gone. Vases lay
shattered, flowers scattered across the hardwood floor,
picture frames everywhere but the wall. Either John
Wick was here, or someone broke in and ransacked the
place.

Queen B was right. Something *is* wrong.

"Melinda," B shouts, pushing past me.

"Wait." I catch her by her jacket, pulling her back.

"What the—"

"Whoever did this," I whisper. "Could still be
here." No way in hell I'll let her march into a death
trap. Just because the mamba annoys the shit outta me,
doesn't mean I want her dead. I owe her. She stuck with
me when most folks wrote me Christmas cards
addressed to hell.

"But—"

"Don't let her out of your sight," I order Jesse,
shoving her against his chest.

He throws both arms around her, securing her
fragile body. "She's not going anywhere."

I reach for my Beretta and head inside. For tactical
reasons—don't want to spook the mother—I keep the
lights out. Moonlight breaks through the large
windows, illuminating my path. Damn. What I saw in
the hallway is nothing compared to the living room.
Holy shit, it looks like a hurricane came by to say, "Hi."
The whole room is a hot mess—white feathers, torn
pillows, tossed drawers, broken chairs, and a sofa that

met Freddy fucking Krueger's claws.

I scan every corner, expecting someone to jump me. There's no one here, though.

Pushing through the swinging door, I move on to the kitchen. Gun pointed at the shadows, dancing over pieces of porcelain and crushed wood. Whoever did this gave vandalism a new name. Inching closer to the knocked over cupboard, I spot pieces of paper, flying around the room. At closer inspection, I realize they're recipes for spells and potions. Was someone looking for something magical?

The grimoire, the hunter inside yells.

Shit, this book in the wrong hands…Jesus, I don't even want to think about what could happen. I remember the "To Summon a Knight of Hell" spell, scribbled in it. God knows what else is in that book.

Rushing through the house, I search every room for Manda, Melinda, her son, the book, and the intruder. What I find is pure chaos, but not a single soul, or the grimoire.

Adrenalin flushes my system, keeping me on high alert. I'm aware how quickly the tables can turn. One minute, you point a gun at a pedophile. The next, you feel the barrel of a shotgun at the back of your head.

I don't lower my precious Beretta. Not even when I waltz into the bedroom of Melinda's son—Leandro. Compared to the rest of the Bishop residency, the room is pretty much unharmed. A rocking chair has been tipped over, but that's about all the damage I see.

I move closer to the cot, secretly praying I find the boy safe and sound. The bed is empty, except for a cute stuffed animal—a tiger cub.

I'm about to head back downstairs to Jesse and B,

when I catch a glimpse of crimson in my peripheral. My heart pounds harder than Joey Kramer plays his drums.

Please don't let it be blood... Please don't—

It's blood. A few drops on the blue sheets. More on the plush tiger.

Fuck.

"Alex?" B's voice carries up the stairs. "Alex, did you find them?"

I pick up the toy, slowly retreating from Leandro's room, and make my way down the stairs. "All clear," I choke out, unable to take my eyes off the bloody tiger.

Faster than a greyhound, B is inside, checking room after room, desperate to find her friends. I catch up with her in the kitchen. "They're not here," I say, blocking her path. "I checked the whole house. No one is here."

I expect something like "let me through, or I'll castrate you." Hell, a slap across the face would be more appreciated than what I get—tears. Buckets full of salty, desperate tears. "The Malleus Maleficarum Order," she sobs. "Do you think—?" B can't bring herself to finish the sentence and I get why. If they're the ones who did this, Manda's, Melinda's, and Leandro's survival chances are zero.

"No." Jesse wraps his arms around her, allowing her to cry into his shirt. "Manda is a fighter. They'd never be able to take her down."

God, I hope he's right.

He runs his fingers through her hair, pulling her even closer. "Besides, Bay would have called us." Jesse meets my gaze. "He likes Manda."

Yup, so much so I hate him for it. Jesse has a point

though. Bay would have done something to prevent Manda from getting hurt. But if the Malleus dicks aren't responsible for this, then who is? I know I said I'm done with the witch, but—I ogle the bloody toy—I'm beginning to wonder why she really ran. Was B right? Was Manda's disappearing act more than simple selfishness?

Bonnie wipes her face, trying to be strong. "That's Leandro's," she whispers, catching sight of the toy sitting in my arms. "He never sleeps without it." Meaning: Melinda wouldn't have left it here.

"B," I start, aware I have to tell her what I found in the boy's room.

She flinches at the sound of her name. "What is it?"

Fuck, I'd kinda prefer hell to this. "I…"

Shit. Shit. Shit. Shit.

"Alex," she barks. "What aren't you telling me?"

Man up. "There's blood in Leandro's bed and on his toy," I say quickly before I change my mind.

Jesse's eyes widen. "You sure?"

I nod.

B doesn't break down like I thought she would. Instead, her tortured eyes meet mine. "There's something about Leandro you need to know."

"Oh, lord. Please, don't tell me he's some kind of super-witch kid, or something." It's possible. Manda is one helluva witch, the boy looks exactly like her, and it's common hunter knowledge every witch generation gets stronger.

B averts her gaze. "Leandro is—" Her gaze darts to the window. The blood drains from her face. She's as pale as a sheet. "Oh. My. Gosh."

A shadowy figure rocking red, glowing eyes stares back at us. Is that—

A demon.

Chapter 4

Quicker than Wyatt Earp, I draw my Beretta, rushing into the full-blown snowstorm raging outside. The demon takes off, running through the slippery backyard toward the wooden fence separating the Bishop estate from their neighbors.

The bastard is fast.

I pick up speed, not sure what to do when I catch him. *If* I catch him. Quantico taught us never to go into battle without a plan. Experience tells a very different story. Dealing with the supernatural isn't an exact science. You can't always come up with a grand battle plan. Sometimes you've got a split second to deal with those mothers. And let's be real, our job is based on legends and myths—stake a vampire, use silver on wendigos, salt keeps evil at bay. Some of that shit is legit. The rest—like exorcising a demon with some Latin incantation—made up by dudes with pens and too much time on their hands. The ugly truth is demons are one of the few supernatural creatures that can't be killed. Bullets may hurt their vessels, same goes for any other weapon. Their demonic essence, however, just moves on to find its next host. Hunters had to learn that the hard way. So, yeah. I'm pursuing *Invincible* without a clue how to stop him. Any sane person would let the mother go. Me? I've never claimed to be sane.

Thick flakes, silver and dense, fall obliquely

against the lamp of the motion detector. The white swirls obscuring my sight. "Freeze," I scream, ignoring the sting of the icy snow on my heated face. Surprise, surprise, he doesn't. Hey, can't blame a man for trying.

The fence is close now. It forces the creature to slow down, giving me the chance to catch up. "I said, freeze." My voice is colder than the damn wind, lashing against my cheeks.

Glowing, garnet eyes dart from the fence to my gun and back. Demon-Boy weighs his options. He could climb the five foot ten wood, but not before I put a bullet in him. It's why he decides to stay and presumably fight.

"Where are they?" I ask, holding my gun as steady as the violent winds allow.

Dark, inhuman laughter ripples through the trees.

"Tell me where the Bishops are," I order him again.

"They"—Demon-Boy comes nearer—"are gone, hunter."

I raise my left hand, shielding my eyes from the snow. "What did you do to them?" Deep down I'm aware he won't give me the answers I want, the ones I *need*. I have to try though. It's all I can do.

Demon-Boy—a skinny, five foot seven, barely older than seventeen—crosses his arms above his chest. "Didn't they teach you shit in that fancy hunter school? Weapons"—he tilts his chin at my Beretta—"as useless as a lollypop, my friend."

"Is it?" I aim at his left leg and pull the trigger. The ear-splitting gunshot echoes through the quiet of the stormy snow night.

"Motherfucker." He winces, applying pressure on

the gaping hole in his shin.

I close the gap between us. "Tell me where Manda and her family are. Or so help me God I'll empty my magazine in you." He may not die, but it's gonna hurt like fuck.

Crimson pours out of his wound, coloring the white ground a nasty shade of dark red. "You think I'm scared of you?" He straightens, eyes blazing. "You're wrong."

What happens next is nothing more than a blurry chain of events. The demon lifts his hand, snaps his fingers, and my gun flies about two hundred feet backward. Words, in an alien language, are muttered. The veins in my temples expand, pressing against my skull with a force convincing me my head is about to explode.

Searing pain paralyzes me, knocking me down. My jeans are soaking wet from the snow or my boiling blood; I can't tell.

"Hunters," the possessed teenager grumbles. "What is it with you and your super annoying arrogance?"

I'd tell him it runs through our bloodstream, but I'm a little busy dying. No kidding. Whatever he did to me is slowly blowing out my lights. My lungs and my heart are collapsing under the pain. Looks like I am going to hell after all.

"*Sispann!*" Someone, I think it's B, yells.

In my peripheral vision, I catch a glimpse of the demon's frown. "Two is a party; four is a pain in the ass."

I spot Queen B's black, knee-high boots next to my hand. "*Sispann li, move lespri sou li.*"

Demon-Boy sighs. "Relax, mamba." He snaps his

fingers once more and just like that the pain subsides.

I can breathe.

Jumping to my feet, my gaze immediately lands on B. She holds her palm up, blood running down her wrist. She carved some creepy witch symbol into her palm. "You can command demons?" I ask, seriously startled. "Why didn't you say so?" I would have let her go after the creature. Okay, not really. But still, she should have said something about her very useful abilities.

She shrugs. "There are a lot of things I can do which you know nothing about." Take the smoky voice and the sexy smirk plastered across her face and it's easy to see why my little brother blushes like a fifth grader who just watched his first porn.

Once I digested her powers, I return my focus on what's really important. "Any chance you can force him to spill where Manda is?"

B, never taking her hand down, shakes her head. "I wish."

The demon ogles the fence. He's going to make a run for it, but B is aware of his plan. "*Mwen mande nou yo rete.*"

The demon freezes. His expression is the definition of anger and hate.

"What did you say to him?" Jesse inquires. He's just as curious as I am.

B doesn't answer. She's too focused on Demon-Boy. "*Deplase tounen nan kay la. Kounye a.*" I assume that means something like, "move your ass back to the house," because that's exactly where the demon heads.

B treads on the creature's heels. "Alex?"

"Huh?" I reply, picking up my gun from where the

bastard threw it earlier.

"There's a small black spell book in my bag," she says. "Go find it and follow the instructions on the first page to a tooth."

Jesse squints. "What are you up to?"

"We're going to trap this bitch," she replies, disappearing inside the vandalized Bishop house.

It's pretty damn obvious why Manda and B are BFFs. "She's fucking crazy."

"Guys," she barks from inside. "Hurry up, would ya? I'm not sure how much longer I can hold him."

Jesse and I look at each other, both fearing for the mamba's sanity. "It's not like we have a choice," my brother mumbles, not happy about the let's-trap-a-demon plan.

Someone once told me, you always have a choice. Right now, trusting B seems like the right one. "Let's go."

Chapter 5

Endless sex and girls is what I associate with small black books. Blame it on my little brother. He's owned one since junior year in high school, collecting numbers and names of every girl he's ever screwed. Not sure why. He makes them happy, walks away, and never looks back. Going through the trouble to take their names and numbers is sorta pointless in my opinion. But hey, what do I know? I don't own the man-whore title like he does.

Anyway, the black book I hold now has nothing to do with easy sex or fun. It's full of voodoo spells and incantations. Since B is a little busy commanding Demon-Boy, Jesse and I are tasked with the preparations of the "Trapping a Demon" ritual.

Step one: construct a massive pentagram with Eucalyptus leaves. *Check.*

Step two: place a chair in the midst of said pentagram and hang nine pieces of Devil's Shoestring—long, flexible twigs that look like rattan—over the chair. *Check.*

Step three: bless some ropes and tie the mother to the chair. *Working on it.*

"Okay," Jesse says, stirring the potion. "The water is boiling. Now what?"

I skim the entry again. "You need to add Devil's Dung to the water, stir some more, then soak the ropes in it." Witchcraft is a lot like cooking. Follow the recipe and you're good. At least I hope so. Because if we fail—and B can no longer keep the demon in check—it won't end pretty.

Jesse searches the herb cabinet. "There's no Devil's whatever."

"Devil's Dung," B says, forehead covered with sweat. "And, yes, there is. Melinda always keeps some Asafoetida powder in the house."

"Asa-what?" Jesse is at his wits' end. I don't blame him. You need a PhD to understand those names, let alone pronounce them.

B frowns. "Check the lower cabinet. Should be next to the Angelica Root which, by the way, you'll need, too."

Yup. Step four: burn some Angelica Root once the demon is secured.

He searches through the herb jars. "Got it," he proclaims, holding the thing up.

"Good," B murmurs, her body shaking violently. "Now, if you could soak those damn ropes before I faint, I'd greatly appreciate it."

My little brother rushes back to the stove—stirring, adding, soaking. He presents the dripping ropes to Queen B. "I think they're ready."

She ogles them suspiciously. "We'll see." The mamba doesn't have much confidence in our performance. I wouldn't either. We're hunters, not warlocks.

B flexes her fingers. *"Chita la sou chèz la."*

Reluctantly, Demon-Boy sits his ass down on the chair. He murders us with his glowing red eyes, and I have a feeling he'd call us every name in the book had

B not ordered him to keep his mouth shut earlier.

B looks at Jesse. "Tie him up."

She doesn't have to tell my brother twice. He's happy to put all those boy scout years to good use. Tying perfect two half hitch knots, he makes sure the demon can't get away. "What's next?"

I reach for my zippo, setting an Angelica root on fire. A woody, peppery scent wafts through what's left of the Bishop kitchen. Doesn't smell as unpleasant as I expected. "We're good."

B drops her hand. A sigh of relief escapes her when the demon remains calmly on the chair. "About time," she mutters, struggling to stand straight.

I give her a moment before I throw my million questions at her. "So, we trapped him. And now we do what?" According to B, she can't force him to tell us where Manda and the rest of the Bishops are. I don't see how any of this is going to help us figure out what the hell happened here.

B sways like a flag in the wind. My brother steadies her, his concern evident. "Why don't you take a seat?" He pulls out another chair, not really giving her a choice in the matter. "Can I get you anything?" he asks, once she's seated.

"Water," she chokes out, voice raw and husky.

I move to the tap, filling one of the glasses that survived the ordeal. "Here." I hand it to her. "Anything else?"

Brows furrowed, she stares at me. "Are you sick?" She doesn't trust me when I'm nice to her. Maybe I should keep up the asshole act.

"Drink up," I murmur, pointing to the cold water.

For once, she doesn't argue. The mamba gulps

down the whole thing at once.

Jesse hunkers down, wrapping a towel around her wounded palm. "Better?"

"Much." She gets on her feet. "Thanks."

Her gaze darts to Demon-Boy. "Alex?"

"Yes?"

B doesn't take her eyes off the creature. "Would you kindly pass me some vinegar, pepper, and garlic?"

"Why, you gonna make salad or something?" Stranger things have happened when witches are involved.

She laughs. "More like something."

Rummaging through the cupboards, I gather the stuff and display it on the kitchen counter. "That's all?"

She grabs an empty jar, emptying the whole vinegar bottle in it. "Yup." She adds the pepper and the garlic. "That should do."

Do what is the question.

She faces the red-eyed bitch. "*Ou ka pale*."

He cusses like a sailor. I assume she gave him permission to talk.

The atrocities leaving his mouth don't bother B. "You know what that is, right?" It's less of a question and more of a statement. Demon-Boy swallows hard. B takes that as a yes. "Good. Then you know what it'll do to you if I pour it on your ugly face."

The creature spits on the pentagram. "You're dead, mamba." He squints. "I'm gonna cut you head to toe, feeding your fucking insides to the hellhounds."

"Great," she cheers. "But first, you're going to tell us where Amanda and her family are. Or so help me Ayida, I'll throw that stuff in your face, watching it burn off your damn skin. Understood?"

I can't believe it. Fear creeps into Demon-Boy's blazing eyes. "You wouldn't."

"Try me," she shoots back, inching closer.

The creature realizes she's not fucking around. "You're barking up the wrong tree." His gaze drafts over the chaos. "I didn't do this."

"Right." I laugh. "And we're supposed to take your word for it because demons are known for their honesty?" *C'mon, mother. Give us some credit.*

Demon-Boy eyeballs me. "I don't care if you believe me or not. But *I*"—he tilts his chin at the shattered porcelain—"am not responsible for this." He casts B a sidelong glance. "And just for the record, I have no idea where the Bishops are."

Jesse grabs the jar from B. "Let's just melt the fucker."

He's seconds away from making good on his threat when Demon-Boy screams, "No. Don't. I'll tell you everything you want to know." Leave it to Queen B to put the fear of God in a demon with everyday household items. *Way to go, mamba!*

B's patience wears thinner and thinner. "Where's Amanda?"

"I don't know," he replies.

I get the feeling he's not selling bullshit.

Jesse isn't convinced. He pretends to throw the mixture.

"Wait," Demon-Boy begs. "I'm looking for her, too."

My interest is piqued. "Why?"

His gaze stays glued to the jar. "Because the world you know is about to go to shit and she's the key to—" He cuts himself off.

"The key to what?" I half scream.

He shakes his head, clearly debating whether to spill the beans or not. *Or not* is his preferred choice. "Look, I don't know where she is. When I got here, the place was a fucking mess. That's the truth and if you don't believe me go ahead and melt me. Still won't change a damn thing."

I want to know what the fuck he meant by *the world's about to go to shit*, but B is quicker. "What about Melinda and Leandro?"

The demon looks at me of all people. "Do I speak Mandarin? No one was here when I came by."

"Why did you *come by*?" Jesse inquires.

His lips are sealed.

"Have it your way." My little bro sprinkles some of the VPG (short for vinegar, pepper, garlic) mixture onto Demon-Boy's arm, burning off his skin.

He screams in agony. "So, let's try this again. Why are you here?"

Struggling with excruciating pain, the creature draws several deep breaths. "I was supposed to find the Bishop witches."

I move toward him. "Why?"

He says nothing.

I turn to Jesse. "Guess he wants some more."

My brother shrugs, ready to empty the jar on the demon's head. "His wish is my—"

"I can't tell you," he yells, yanking his head sideways.

B cocks a brow. "Why's that?"

"I have orders," he shoots back. "And if I fail—" He shakes his head. "Go on, pour it on my face. It'll be nothing compared to what'll happen if I return to hell as a snitch." Looking in his eyes, I realize how lucky I was not to be deported to the pit. Whatever awaits down there makes a demon act like a scared five-year-old.

Torturing him with VPG won't make him talk. We need to change tactics. Trying to think of something that will break him, I pace the kitchen when the bell rings.

Jesse stiffens. "Shit. That can't be good."

Someone ringing the bell in the middle of the night *never* is.

Whoever is outside bangs against the front door like a lunatic. I highly doubt he'll just go away. "Stay here with him," I order B. "You"—I nod at Jesse—"come with me."

Guns drawn, we move into the hallway. Jesse gazes out the small window, next to the front door. "Fuck," he hisses, shoving his gun back in the holster. "Cops."

Awesome. Someone must have called them after I shot Demon-Boy.

I, too, secure my gun under my jacket. "Do you have your badge?"

"Yeah, but—"

"Just follow my lead," I say, hoping the sight of FBI keeps them from checking our fugitive status and marching into the kitchen.

"Police," they call out. "Open the door."

Inhaling sharply, I follow the order. Two dudes— one rookie, one senior—glare at us. "Mr. Bishop?" The older one asks suspiciously.

I hold my badge up. "No, I'm Agent Remington."

Senior cop scans my badge thoroughly. "May I ask what the FBI is doing here?"

"We're checking on an old friend," Jesse says, quickly.

"The neighbors reported gun shots," Rookie explains. "We're here to check on the Bishops."

"That's commendable." Stroking their egos can't hurt. "But what they heard was my car backfiring." I tilt my head at my Mustang. "You know how it is with old beauties."

Rookie cop's eyes almost pop from his head. "Is that a '65?"

"Yup." I smile. "Original paint and all."

"She's beautiful," he says with an appreciation that makes me dislike him a little less.

"She is."

Senior cop doesn't care about the love of my life. "Can we talk to the Bishops?" He's all business and no fun. "You know how it is. Got to make sure they're okay."

Jesse throws him the famous Remington smile. "We understand, sir. But Melinda just put her baby to sleep. We wouldn't want to wake them, would we?"

Rookie shakes his head. "Of course not." He nudges his partner. "Right?"

Senior cop sighs. "I suppose not."

"Thanks for dropping by. We appreciate it," Jesse lies, slowly closing the door.

Rookie is halfway down the porch when Senior's gaze darts over my shoulder into the vandalized hallway. "What the hell?" he yells, pulling his gun.

So much for almost getting rid of them.

"Easy," I say, hands up. "It's not what you think."

He kicks the door open. "Really? Because right now I'm thinking you broke in here and shot someone."

I did break in. I also shot someone. I can hardly admit that.

He crosses the threshold, his partner now behind him. "Move back. Hands where I can see them."

"You're making a mistake," Jesse assures them as they make us walk toward the kitchen. "We're—"

"Shut up!" Senior cop isn't fucking around. He's going to pull the trigger, that's for sure. I recognize the look in his eyes. Have had it myself every time I sent some mother back to hell.

I'm trying to come up with a damn good excuse as to why we have a teenage boy with garnet eyes tied to a chair in the kitchen when B appears out of nowhere. "What's going on here?"

"Don't move," Rookie yells, trigger finger trembling.

Fuck, he's going to shoot her.

B's lips curl into a mesmerizing smile. "Why don't you lower those guns, guys?" Her voice is pure sex. I swear I've never heard anything like it.

Jesse obviously has. He winks at me, grinning like a bitch. "Watch and learn." Is that pride in his voice? Not sure if it's annoying as fuck or impressive.

B closes the gap between her and the cops. "I know you want to," she says, eyes white like snow.

What comes next is even creepier than B commanding a full-blooded demon. Both—Rookie and Senior—lower their guns.

"That's better, isn't it?"

In a trance-like state, they both nod.

"Now"—she runs her index finger over Senior's jawline—"it's been a long night and the two of you must be exhausted. Why don't you go back to your car,

42

radio in a false alarm, and grab some coffee at the diner across town?"

"It was a long night." Rookie sounds like a robot. "We should get some coffee."

Senior holsters his gun. "Yes, and radio in a false alarm."

"That a boy," B whispers in his ear. "Now, go and don't forget to make your wife happy when you get home."

Moments later, the door slams shut. The cops walk away as if nothing ever happened.

"Damn. That was…awesome." In a creepy, witch way. But still fucking awesome.

B turns, blood spilling from her nose. "I—"

Her knees give in. She's fainting.

Jesse barely catches her before she hits the floor. "B." Worried doesn't do his voice justice. "B, open your eyes."

"I'm okay," she whispers. "I just need a moment."

I'm glad she's talking. Hell, I truly am. She just saved our asses. "Let's take her to the kitchen and get her some water." I eye her pale face. "Maybe something to eat, as well."

Jesse swoops her up in his arms, carrying her through the swinging door.

His whole attention belongs to the mamba. He doesn't see what I see. "Fuck," I bark, gazing at the empty chair. Our only…witness? Suspect? Both. Gone.

"How the hell did he get out?"

Good question, brother.

B's chest rises and falls quickly. "The rope," she says. "You didn't stir long enough."

Is she for real? "It matters how long you stir?"

"Everything matters in the craft," she murmurs, resting her head against Jesse's chest.

I officially hate witchcraft.

Jesse places B on the counter, handing her soda and leftover chicken from the fridge. "So what's the plan?"

"We'll find Manda," I announce.

B drops the crispy meat. "What?"

"We have to find Manda," I repeat.

She doesn't trust my sudden change of mind. "But you said—"

"Look around," I say, pointing at the mess. "She's obviously in trouble." And lying, runaway witch or not, I owe her. She saved my little brother remember?

B sighs. "I thought she could rot in hell for all you care."

Jesse cups B's face. "He didn't mean it, B."

I'm all set to assure them I did when the mamba zooms in on me. "Okay, so how are we going to find her?"

I manage a half-hearted smile. "We're hunters, B. We make a living tracking down witches."

Jesse pulls out his phone. "I'll call JJ. See if she heard anything from Manda."

"Yup." I dial Bay. "I'm gonna check with Bay." In case the Malleus dicks have something to do with this, he's our best shot.

B picks up the chicken in one hand, pulls out her phone with the other. "I'll see if my mom can help."

Won't be long 'til we find Manda, her sister, and her nephew. I mean, how hard can it be for four hunters and two mambas to track down a witch family, right?

Chapter 6

The scent of coffee predominates the smell of bourbon, beer, and old peanuts. JJ is brewing the tenth pot. We're downing the shit as if it's water. Can you blame us? I can't remember the last time I got some shut eye. None of us can. B insisted we had to get out of Salem ASAP. According to the mamba, there was a possibility whatever mind-mojo she used on the cops could fade. Then they'd be back with backup and we'd spent God knows how long in a prison cell in Witch City. We can hardly put together a search and possible rescue mission from behind bars, can we? Anyway, after we spoke to JJ and Bay, we decided to regroup in Winter Harbor. That's where we are now. Inside JJ's dad's bar, figuring out how to find Manda, her sister, and her nephew. Dead or alive? Nobody knows.

Alive, something inside me roars. They have to be alive. No one kills Manda. I should know. I tried a few times, failing miserably. So, did Walter, Francoise, and Isobelle. The girl is like a cat. Has nine lives or something.

What about the boy, though? The blood on his sheets and plush tiger are bad signs. There were just a few drops of crimson, though. Not nearly enough to suggest death.

"There you go." JJ tops our mugs, flinging herself in the chair across from me.

B wraps her hands around the hot drink. "Thanks." I've never seen her like this. As if someone shattered her world and took away the glue to put the pieces back together.

"Nah, don't thank me," JJ says, forcing a half-hearted smile. "I hear my coffee tastes like crap."

We sip our drinks, silently. The air is thick. Overloaded with all sorts of nasty emotions—guilty being my poison. It crushes my heart to a point where it misses several beats. Despite everything Manda did for me—going against a bokor, saving my brother's life, taking a damn bullet, and walking away from her new life to get my ass out of hell—I prejudged her. I was so fucking hurt when she told me I was just another guy she screwed, I didn't even consider the possibility something was wrong. God, if it wasn't for B, I would have never driven to Salem to check on her. Funny, huh? I treated Manda like shit most of the time. Yet the chick I call selfish came running the second I needed help. When the tables turned, the great Alexander Remington safeguarded his heart rather than giving her the benefit of the doubt.

What a fine hero I am, huh? Manda is the second girl to vanish under my watch. The second girl I failed to protect out of selfish reasons. Natasha, my little sister, being the first.

****

I had one simple task. "Watch your sister 'til we get back from your grandmother's," my parents had said. Any other day, I would have been okay with that. Natasha was an easy-going kid. She sat in the garden for hours, talking to birds, spiders, and any other animal she encountered. But that Sunday afternoon I had plans.

Jeremy Kooks—my best friend back then—and the boys had invited me to a game of GTA, short for Grand Theft Auto. I can't tell you why I was so desperate to go. Maybe because Samantha Hanson, my major crush, was supposed to be there. Or maybe I was just a selfish brat. Either way, I went.

I'll never forget the look on Natasha's face when I walked away. Close to tears, she seized hold of my arm. "What if the witches come?"

I laughed. "Witches don't exist." They were a product of Mom and Dad's vivid imagination. A fantasy to keep the three of us in check. If only I knew how fucking wrong I was back then.

"Alex," she pleaded, giving me her best puppy gaze. "Please, don't leave me here. I can tag along. I promise I'll be quiet."

My heart ached for my little sister. But showing up at Jeremy's with my baby sister in tow? Hell, I'd become the running joke.

I got on my knees, hands on her shoulders. "You're brave, aren't you?" She nodded. "As brave as Natasha Romanoff?" It was a dirty move, considering Black Widow was Natasha's favorite comic heroine.

"Yes," she replied, spine straighter.

I smiled. "Do you think she'd be afraid if Hawkeye left her alone for a little while?"

"No," she murmured, gazing at the green grass.

"So, what do you say? Can I head to Jeremy's for a little while?"

She hesitated.

"Natasha?"

"Yes," she said, not particularly happy. "You can

go."

I didn't wait for her to change her mind. "Go inside and lock the door, will ya?" Then I sprinted down the street, not knowing those were the very last words I'd ever say to my little sister.

****

The double doors swing open, pulling me out of the past and back to the present.

Bay marches in, hands shoved in his pockets, gaze glued to his boots. Not a good sign.

"What did they say?" B is the first one to ask what we're all eager to know.

Bay pulls a chair, the wooden legs screeching over the sticky floor. "Legend didn't answer his phone," he explains, plummeting down. "I had to call an old pal of mine. He, too, works for the Malleus."

I have no patience today. "And?"

He exhales sharply. "They don't know where she is."

Which means they didn't ransack the Bishop mansion?

"I sense a but," Jesse says, shoulders tense.

His instincts are spot on. "Rumor has it there's a reward on Amanda's head." He draws a deep breath, meeting my gaze. "It says rather dead than alive."

B chokes back fresh tears. "Why?" She shakes her head, unable to comprehend the events unfolding in the past few hours. "She didn't do anything." Bonnie looks me in the eye. "You know she didn't."

I squeeze her hand, reaffirming her. She needs to know I believe her, that she isn't alone in this. Yeah, yeah, I know. I'm an asshole who claimed Manda could rot in hell a little while ago. But c'mon, cut me some slack, all right? I said those things before I understood my ex could be in real, life-threatening trouble.

Jesse pulls her against his side. "We'll find her, B."

We will. If it's the last thing I do.

Queen B pulls back. "How, Jess?" She rubs her tired eyes. "How are we supposed to find her when my mom can't?" Yup, here's another obstacle. Mrs. Lacroix—apparently, the most powerful mamba in Nola—crushed B's hopes to find Manda with a little help of magic. She's an untouchable. In other words, Amanda Bishop is immune to magic. Makes her ten times more powerful. And us? Ten times more desperate.

Bay and JJ avert their gazes.

"We're still hunters," I grumble, not sure whom I'm trying to convince we can pull this off.

Jesse nods. "Hunters who work for the government, B."

"Worked," she grumbles. "Past tense, remember?"

Jesse shoots her a mischievous smile. "Will be working again," he replies, pulling out his phone. "Future tense." The mamba is all set to argue, but Jesse disappears inside the storage room in no time. Ten bucks say, he's calling Carter.

"All right." Bay folds his hands on the table. "Let's go over this again, shall we?" Looks like he, too, is looking for the missing puzzle piece. "Amanda hijacked JJ's car, drove to Salem, and then?"

"Melinda called," B replies.

JJ tops our already empty mugs. "What exactly did she say? Anything could help. Even the smallest thing." Spoken like a true hunter. In our job, the most insignificant details—a flower, a chance encounter, an unsuspecting touch—can solve the case.

"Just that Manda left your car in her driveway and we can come pick it up," she says, voice cracking.

"Did she sound different?" Bay inquires.

B's gaze flicks to him. "Yeah." She furrows her brows. "She sounded like—" Her eyes widen.

"Like what, B?" I have a feeling she was hit by lightning.

The mamba shifts toward me. "She sounded like the day she called to say her grandmother came to see her, warning her about something awful about to happen to Manda."

"What?" I bark. That's the first time I hear of that. "Why didn't you tell us?"

She cocks a mad brow at me. "When, Alex? The day you barged into our apartment half dead? Or how about on our little road trip when we tried to keep your ass out of hell?"

Good point.

"About that," Bay says, zooming in on me. "Why aren't you in hell?" We were so busy talking about Manda's disappearance the whole Alex-is-still-alive topic took a back seat.

"I don't know." I ogle the booze behind the counter. Man, I could use some. "The clock struck midnight, the hellhound snarled. Then it vanished as if I didn't sell my damn soul."

JJ squints. "I've never heard of anyone who survived a deal, Alex."

Bay nods. "I've spent most of my life studying hellhounds. Once they track you down, they leave nothing but torn flesh and blood behind." Our eyes lock. "You should be dead, Remington."

"Tell me something I don't know." I signed the damn deal well aware how it would end. Sure, I'm a witch hunter and rarely came face to face with demons. Yet I grew up hearing all about dumbasses who traded their souls for fortune and fame. My grandma used to tell me stories about some dude in her mother's village in Germany. Yup, my mom's family is from Germany—descendants of the Arrows of Artemis, a hunter organization founded during the Trier Witch Trials. Legend has it they came together after the church killed innocent women, claiming they were witches when they really weren't. The Arrows, according to old stories, worked with a witch who hated her own kind so much, she gladly offered them up on a silver plate. Anyway, that dude from my great-grandmother's village worked for a rich farmer family. One sweet day, he decided working for them wasn't enough. He wanted to own the place, needed what they had—money and prestige. So he called upon a demon, offered his soul, and got everything he ever wanted in exchange. The farmer and his family died, leaving the whole estate to their trusted and beloved worker. Too bad a year later, the dude was found dead. He fell into the silo, breaking his treacherous neck. Karma, Manda would say. The price you pay for a deal with hell, I believe. So yeah. I know I should be dead. But I'm not and with Manda gone, I don't have time to worry about shit like that.

Bay stretches his neck, rolling his head from left to right. "All I'm saying is it's a pretty big coincidence."

"What is?" I bark, heat rising from my core.

"*You* not going to hell and *Amanda* vanishing," he replies, matter-of-factly.

I curl my fists, not liking where this is headed. "You got something to say, then say it." I'm not in the mood to beat around the bushes.

He sighs. "It's just weird."

Weird, huh? Bullshit. He has something else on his mind. We all know it. It's why JJ changes the topic before my guilt drives me to beat the living crap out of the Malleus dick, who digs my ex. "What about the demon?" She eyeballs B. "Do you buy his act of innocence?" She's talking about Demon-Boy and his it-wasn't-me speech.

Queen B blows out a frustrated breath. "I'm not Amanda. I can't sense lies the way she does. But"—she looks up—"yeah. I don't think he was responsible for whatever happened to them."

"Let me get this straight." JJ rubs her temples. "Manda took off, her sister called you, you guys drove up to Salem and found a vandalized home. Now, they're all missing, the Malleus dicks"—she faces Bay—"no offense."

"None taken," he assures her.

"Anyway, they put a reward on her head, some red-eyed sucker claimed hell is looking for Manda, and—"

"We have no fucking clue if any of them are still alive," B finishes for her.

"They are," I assure her. They have to be.

Bay folds his hands around the steaming mug. "I know it's a long shot," he says, voice low. "Especially after the shit Manda told me, but is there any chance they could be hiding out at their mother's?" What Manda told him, huh? Funny. We spent months together, on the road and in bed, yet she never even mentioned the woman. He's a damn stranger and she spilled her guts immediately? Obviously, she never trusted me. The only person I have to blame is myself.

"Manda hiding out at her mom's?" B laughs. "I can promise you, she'd rather go to hell and face Lucifer."

"She's right. Manda would never ask her mother for help." Don't blame her. I met Maria Bishop once. Yeah, I did. No, no one knows, not even my little brother. The thing is the woman is the devil incarnate when it comes to Manda. She hates her so dearly I wonder how witch-bitch survived her childhood.

"Still." JJ wanders off to put on a new pot of coffee. "Can't hurt to double check."

Bay agrees. "JJ and I can be there in a day or so."

"You and I?" JJ smirks. "When did that happen?"

Bay rolls his eyes. "Would you rather go by yourself?"

"No," B says. "Trust me, you need backup."

JJ makes a face. "Whatever." Teaming up with Bay doesn't sit well with her. Being a woman in a men's world took a toll on the feisty huntress. She constantly feels like she needs to prove herself to us. She really doesn't. The girl kicked my ass so bad I couldn't walk for days. She's a better hunter than most of her male counterparts.

"And what are we going to do?" I ask the mamba, hoping she's got a witchy plan up her sleeves.

And most certainly she does. "We're going to find Madame Josephine."

My brows fly up. "Madame who?"

Bonnie faces me. "She's the fortuneteller Manda went to see."

Wait. What? "Amanda Bishop went to see a fortuneteller?" I have a hard time believing that. I mean, why would super, smart-ass witch need a reading?

B swallows hard. "I kinda dragged her there. I thought Madam Josephine could help her find out why her abilities were fucked up."

"Her abilities were what?" Why the hell didn't I know about any of this?

B ignores my comment. "Madame Josephine sorta kicked her out."

"Why?" JJ asks.

"She said something about her being Elliot Ness and darkness claiming her," B replies, guilt washing over her face.

My heart stops beating. *Darkness claiming her?* I've heard this one before. It's why—

"Carter is on board," Jesse proclaims, stomping toward us, beaming with pride. "He's going to fix the bokor drama and have his agents looking for Manda, her sister, and the little boy." Jesse's gaze darts to me. "Oh, and he says he's glad your useless ass wasn't wanted in hell." Yup, sounds like the Carter I know.

"All right." Bay jumps up, almost knocking over the table. "What are we waiting for? Let's go find Manda and bring her back home."

I hate that guy. Mostly because unlike me, he doesn't mind showing his devotion to Manda.

"Go where?" Jesse is a little confused. He missed the whole Manda's mom, Madame Josephine conversation.

I reach for the keys, throwing them his way. "I'll tell you in the car."

Chapter 7

Amanda

Silence bites into my skin like a slow acting poison. Here in the darkness, surrounded by iron bars and magical runes, I search my soul for a glimmer of hope—anything that brings forth the fighter I grew up to be. Shame, my soul no longer answers to me. It belongs to hell and good old Dante was right. There's no such thing as hope in the pit.

Don't believe me? How about this then? The runes on the walls—ancient symbols, used by witches, and demons alike—are supposed to ward off magic, to keep the prisoner from using his or her abilities to break free. They don't work on untouchables like me, though. I feel my powers running through my system. They're stronger than ever. Auras once blurred like rainbows, up until a few hours ago, are now sharper than any HD screen. Visions come and go like express trains. Dark, twisted images of the world going up in flames and terrifying creatures wreaking havoc. I'm as charged up as a lightning storm since I signed that freakin' deal. Yet I don't use my magic to get out of here. Why would I? This—I look around, inhaling the scent of mold and sulfur—is the path I chose.

God, I am the prime example of stupid. I have betrayed everything I ever believed in—my family, my friends, *myself*. For what? To become a whore of Satan? *Way to go, Amanda.* Way to fucking go!

Tugging my knees under my chin, I tense against the shaking of my limbs. It's been only a few hours since my blood dripped onto the Knight of Hell's contract, making it go *puff* in flames. A few hours in which I've been taken to…actually, I have no idea where I am. The asshole blindfolded me. What I do know is I'm locked away in a dungeon like a caged animal.

What in God's name was I thinking?

Easy. I figured I'd agree to the Knight of Hell's terms and conditions, save Alex from the infernal regions, and make sure Leandro and anyone else I care about wouldn't be harmed by the Malleus Maleficarum Order. Too bad, I had no idea I'd become the Devil's new toy. I should have, though. C'mon, I'm a freakin' witch. How could I not be aware of what happens to our kind if we make deals with demons? To be fair, I'd never heard of any witch dumb enough to walk into hell or purgatory voluntarily. Books like *Faust* should have been a warning, I assume, but they're hardly bulletproof evidence.

Had I known, I'd—

You'd what? the censorious voice in my head barks. *You'd let Alex die? You'd endanger Leandro's life? You'd choose yourself over the people you love?*

Any sane person's answer would be "yes" to all of the above. Especially because I have no freakin' clue what the Knight of Hell has in store for me. What was it he said? "Don't worry. I already have the perfect job for you." Perfect in hell can mean just about anything. Hexing innocents, murdering babies—no atrocity is too shocking for those soulless creatures.

I should regret my decision, right? Yeah, I totally should. Only, I don't. Because here's the thing you need to know about Amanda Bishop. I have never been sane. I don't do the "greater good" shit. I'd rather save one sister—or in this case ex-lover—than ten strangers. I can't help it. It's who I am, who I've always been. All I care about is myself; that includes putting the people I love at the top of my I'd-do-anything-to-keep-them-alive list. So yeah, I'd sign that damn deal all over again. In a freakin' heartbeat.

There's something wrong with me, I get that. Ironically, Mother Dearest recognized it before I did. The vision she had of me as the queen of darkness, it's well on its way to coming true. I make a mental note to ask the next demon crossing my path where I can buy a post card. Mother Dearest will be delighted to hear she's been right about me all along.

Somewhere in the distance iron squeaks.

I hug my legs tighter, aware I'm due for a prison visit. Is it lunch time yet? I wouldn't know. The windowless box I'm trapped in is like a space-time continuum—an independent reality.

Heavy footsteps draw closer.

Chills run down my spine, raising awareness of the hellish creature approaching my cell. I close my eyes, counting the steps. *One, two, three, four—*

"On your feet," an unknown voice shouts.

I ignore the bastard.

Metal hits iron. The deafening sound roars through the dungeon, ready to wake the dead. "Hey," he barks. "Move your fucking ass, witch. The boss wants to see you."

Any other day, I'd tell him to go to hell. The saying loses its touch when you're already there. "Didn't your mother teach you how to say 'please'?" I grumble, slowly moving to the bars.

Murderous red eyes stare back at me. "No." The demon—a five foot ten, Bud Spencer lookalike—unlocks the cell, grabbing me by the hair. "She taught me how to treat whores like you," he whispers, dragging me up the stairs.

The rough bastard pushes me through an iron door. I lose my balance, falling headfirst. My palms deflect the impact, but my knees smash against the hard cement, spilling blood all over.

"Asshole," I mutter, inspecting my torn jeans. They were my favorite. Now, they're just another victim of my dumb choices.

In the corner of my eye, I spot his leg aiming for my stomach. I prepare for pain and some puking, but Knight of Hell is to my rescue. "Enough," he orders his minion.

Bud Spencer demon bows low. "Master."

The Knight of Hell cups my elbow, gently helping me up. "I'm sorry." He shoots his servant a killer look. "He was raised in hell."

I yank my arms out of his grip. "You don't say."

Amber eyes lock with mine. "How's my favorite witch adjusting to her new life?" he asks, smiling like a bitch.

I'd give my arms and legs to be able to cut that wicked grin off his handsome vessel's face. But I can't do shit. Not without sending Alex straight to hell. So I opt for a topic change. "Don't you guys have Ikea in hell?"

He furrows his brows. "I beg your pardon?"

"Ikea," I repeat. "This"—I point at the colorless walls in the windowless room—"could really use some Scandinavian charm." Truth be told even the mother of all furniture stores can't save this shithole.

"I'll consider it," the Knight of Hell assures me, sounding as if he actually means it. "But first we have work to do."

I cock a brow. "What, you need someone to babysit your minions?" I hope that's the kind of job he's talking about. All other options come with blood and death.

"Not exactly." He gestures for me to move through another iron door. "C'mon, love. I'll explain everything on the way." Everything could be anything.

God, I'm fucked.

Chapter 8

Not sure what's worse; sitting in a fancy, black Audi RS with a Knight of Hell driving me to my first hellish job, or listening to a demon yodel a Britney freakin' Spears song. Both, the prospect of what's to come and the singing Knight, give me a damn headache.

Resting my head against the hard leather seat, I focus on the scenery sailing past us. We're literally in the middle of nowhere. White fields and bleak trees. For all I know, we could be driving through the damn Alps. Though, I have a feeling we're still in the States. This Knight doesn't strike me as the road-trip-through-Austria type. Shame. Put him in "Lederhosen" and he'd fit in like a boss.

The pop princess' "Hit Me Baby One More Time" blends with another terrible pop song when the demon turns the volume down. "Your lack of conversation is slightly irritating, love."

I press my forehead against the cool window, gazing at the dense snowflakes falling from the dark sky. "What?" I sigh heavily. "Did you think we'd hit the road *Crossroad*-style, chirping Shania Twain?"

"Something like that," he says, not a trace of humor in his voice.

I cock a brow. "Thanks, but I'd rather spend the rest of my life in an Ikea free-zone." No kidding. Pop songs and demons? So much worse than a windowless dungeon in hell. Okay, I wasn't really in hell. Turns out the Douchebag of Hell held me captive in an abandoned, run down house, somewhere in the middle of nowhere. Classic.

Husky laughter roars through the heated car, bursting my remaining blood vessels. "Not a Britney fan?"

I say nothing. Anything I would say could be used against me in the court of hell. I hear it's ruled by injustice.

"Well." His all-too-familiar amber eyes gleam with excitement. "I have just the right song for us." He pushes some buttons on his phone, connecting it with the Bluetooth of his car radio. "You're going to love this one."

I can put a name on it after hearing the first note. "Bonnie and Clyde" by Beyoncé and Jay Z. One of B's all-time favorites. Don't ask me why, but my best, and only, friend has dreamed of a love like that of the famous gangster couple since we were kids. I tried to tell her they both died. She waved me off, flashed me a smile and said, "They rode together, they died together. Bad love for life." I blame her *Bad Boys* obsession for the misconstrued quote.

"See, I knew you'd like our song," he said, grinning self-righteously.

"Our song?" My head snaps his way. "We are so not going down the Bonnie and Clyde road. *Capiche*?" The only dude I'd ever die for is now enjoying his hell-free life, thinking he was just another good ride for me. Why? Because I told him so. One of the toughest lies I ever sold.

Mr. Knight of Hell faces me. "C'mon, love." He maneuvers the car over the slippery road without looking. "Think about all the damage we could do. An untouchable witch and a Knight of Hell. That's a match made in—"

"A place called Never Gonna Happen." He might own my soul, but I still have my dignity. Sorta.

He shrugs, nonchalantly. "We'll see."

All right, this is by *far* more than I can take. "Why don't you drop the bullshit and tell me where we're going, and what the fuck it is you want me to do?" I'd love to know—damn, I was gonna say, "for what sin I'll be burning in hell." Then I remembered I already am for past ones.

The demon frowns. "Can't we just enjoy each other's company for now?"

I'd rather be confined to a car with my mother than him. "Sure. Why don't you grab a bottle and we can play a round of Truth or Dare?"

"Seriously?"

Rolling my eyes, I face the window. "No."

"That's a damn shame," he replies, voice husky and low. "I happen to be the master of wicked dares."

Inhale, I send him back to hell.

Exhale, the deal would be void.

Inhale, I don't recall the contract saying anything about me not being allowed to exorcise the asshole.

Exhale, I can't unless he happens to spill his real name. "So." I shift in my seat, facing him. "Since you made me your bitch, you could at least have the decency to tell me your name."

One side of his mouth curls up. "Nice try." He pushes the gas pedal a little harder, angrier. "But I've been around for a very long time. Learned a thing or two about your kind over the centuries, and I'm afraid I have no intention of being exorcised." He looks down at his chest. "I sorta like this vessel." Who wouldn't like the body of a Greek god and the face of an Armani model?

I shrug. "It was worth a shot."

He studies me, long and hard. "Why do you despise me, Amanda?"

I squint. "Is that a rhetorical question?" He pretty much blackmailed me into selling my freakin' soul. Am I supposed to drop on my knees and thank him for an eternity spent as his whore?

The demon doesn't take his eyes off me. He's sorta driving blind. "I"—he draws a deep breath—"I understand this is awkward for you—"

"Awkward?" I laugh so hard my belly hurts. "Dude, awkward doesn't quite cut it. Try fucked up, diabolic, or wicked in the worst sense of the word."

He pulls the Audi to the side of the road, killing the engine. "This is no fun, Amanda."

Fun? What was he expecting? That I do a happy dance because I've been promoted from stab-worthy witch to slave of a freakin' Knight of Hell? "*Fun* wasn't part of our deal, was it?"

He runs his long fingers through his vessel's dark hair. "Maybe we got off on the wrong foot."

"Why?" I shoot back. "Because you forgot to mention the part of the deal where I'm forced to do your bidding no questions asked?"

"I'm not your enemy," he blurts out.

Did I mention my roaring migraine? It just crossed over to someone-cut-off-my-head-pretty-please.

"You're a fucking Knight of Hell, asshole."

His remarkable jawline tightens. A fraction of a second later, his face resembles granite. "I know what I am. Yet I saved your sweet ass over and over." I assume he's referring to the incident outside Rick's Cabaret in Nola. You know, the one where I almost got slaughtered in my underwear by a horde of crazy demons.

"I'll make sure I send you an Amazon gift card," I grumble, not in the mood to celebrate my self-proclaimed hero. Gee, what is it with me and dudes who think I need saving? I don't rock the damsel in distress look, do I?

His gaze skirts over my face, lingering on my lips. "I can see why the great Alexander Remington couldn't keep his hunter hands off you." He bites his lower lip. "You truly are one in a billion."

Up until this very moment, I've been mostly mad at myself. I signed the deal. I should have known the consequences. Bringing up Alex, however, turns the tables. All my bottled-up anger bursts out of me. "Don't you dare talk about him. Not after everything you did. You hear me?" I didn't even realize I'm yelling, but fuck I am. Hey, asshole of hell was the one who made me sign a deal that stated I'm never allowed to see Alex again. Now, he talks about him? Sorry, pal. I don't do hypocritical.

I'm ready for an argument that never comes. "As you wish, love." He taps his slender fingers against the steering wheel, gazing through the windshield. "What I said, however, stands true. I am not your enemy. I never have been."

I'm so over this conversation. "Dude." I shoot him

my bitch-I-kill-you look. "If this is going to be one of those frenemy speeches, you can shove it up your—"

"Amanda." His inhuman voice thunders through the car like a damn shockwave. "Would you listen to me for a second?"

"No."

Blazing amber eyes pierce through mine. Next thing I know, I'm burning inside out. The heat wave washes through my veins, shaking my very core. Pressure builds in my chest. I can't breathe. "What—"

"You might be an untouchable, Amanda." He balls his fist and my chest feels as if it's about to implode. "But your soul belongs to me, now." He shifts closer, his sulfur breath beating against my ear. "I can, literally, unleash hell upon you. Do you understand?"

Gasping for air, I nod.

"Good." He pulls back, slowly opening his hand. "Glad that's settled," he says, his iris shade changing back to a more natural amber.

I fill my lungs with much needed oxygen, rubbing my aching chest. "What the fuck, dude?" Yeah, not very smart after he…I don't know, strangled my soul?

He tilts his head, watching me like a hawk. I brace for more pain. The demon sighs instead. "Hurting you doesn't bring me pleasure. So I suggest you start being a bit more cooperative. For both our sakes."

Doesn't bring him pleasure, my ass.

Not up to another taste of the creature's hold on my soul, I change tactics. "Cooperative, huh? I hear it's a two-way road."

He raises a brow. "What do you want?"

Frustration seeps into my system. What I want he won't give me. Let's try something else, then. "Well, you won't tell me your name. So what am I supposed to call you? Master? Boss? Ass—" He casts me a warning glance and I swallow the "hole" part.

He thinks it over. "Why don't you call me Clyde?" He flashes me his brilliant teeth. "You know since 'Bonnie and Clyde' is our song?"

I want to spit in his damn face.

His grin widens. "But my king would also suffice."

"Will you tell me where we're going, *Clyde*?" No way I'll ever call the bastard *my king*.

"Washington D.C."

"The capital? Why?" Actually, I'm not sure I want an answer to that question.

He leans back, fiddling with his phone. "We have an appointment at 935 Pennsylvania Avenue."

Why does that address ring a bell? I could swear I've heard it before. *Pennsylvania Avenue…935 Pennsylvania Avenue…935*—fuck. I know why the address sounds so familiar. That's the J. Edgar Hoover building. The headquarters of the freakin' FBI.

"Are you all right?" He traces my stiff jawline. "You look a bit pale."

"W-why?"

He studies me. "Why do you look pale?"

Gee, I hate it when they play dumb. "Why are we headed to the FBI headquarters?" Whatever his reasons, they can't be good.

"You're going to get something from the PAU's secret collection for us," he explains, matter-of-factly.

I pray to every god there is I misunderstood him. "You want me to break into the headquarters of the fucking FBI?"

"Don't worry." He starts the engine. "It'll be fun. I

promise."

Our definition of fun? So not the same. "But what if they catch me?" Appealing to his rationality might be my only way out. I mean, a witch whore in federal prison can't do his bidding, right?

Clyde flashes me a half-grin. "You're a powerful witch. Now more than ever. I'm sure you know how to handle a few agents, don't you?" Translation: kill them and stop acting like a baby.

Horror claws my guts. "I…I can't…I won't."

"Oh yes," he shoots back. "For 'the one who shall not be named' "—he makes Alex sound like Lord Voldemort—"you can and you will." He meets my gaze. "Or would you rather I send my hellhound bitch after your lover?"

I'm fucked. Seriously, I am so fucked it makes the chick gangbanged by a hundred dudes look like a damn saint.

"That's what I thought," he mutters.

This needs to stop. *I* need to be stopped. Because Clyde is right about one thing: I'd do anything for Alex. Even if it means breaking into the damn headquarters of the FBI.

Clyde presses the play button on his phone. Another Britney song blares through the speakers, torturing my ears. Hell really does suck.

Chapter 9

Alex

"Dude." Jesse shakes me. "Wake up."

Blinking my heavy eyelids open, I feel like a damn baseball bat hit me in the head. "What's up?" I grumble; my mind still trapped inside the creepy dream I just had.

"I need a break." The shadows under my little brother's eyes speak louder than his words. "Can you drive?"

Someone snores like a sailor. I catch a glimpse of B in the rear-view mirror. She's tossing and turning. Looks like I'm not the only one having bad dreams.

I press my elbows into the seat, pushing myself up. Outside, I spot a guy with a flannel shirt. He gases up his white pickup, making googly eyes at some chick with a tight pencil skirt. "Where are we?" The yellow letters say Sunoco gas station, but I have no clue where it's located.

"Portsmouth," Jesse forces out, yawning like a damn lion.

"Let me stretch my legs," I say, yanking the door open. "Then, I'll take over."

He nods. "Thanks."

"It's all good." Secretly, I'm glad he woke me. That dream fucked with me. And not in a good way.

"Be right, back."

I head to the restrooms. I haven't opened the door yet when a breeze of urine and other unpleasant stuff crawls up my nostrils. My stomach demands I turn around and move back to the car, but I need to wash those dream images off.

I'm alone. No one takes a piss or bothers me.

Walking toward the sink, I focus on the quiet background music. Some pop song. I wouldn't bet my car on it, but I think it's Katy Perry singing something about a "Dark Horse."

Turning on the faucet, I splash some cold water in my face. It should wake me the fuck up. Except it doesn't. My brain refuses to come out of the REM-phase. It's still torturing me with memories turned nightmare.

I press my hands against the dirty sink, drawing a few, much needed, deep breaths. The radio moderator announces the next song. "It's been forty years since fate has taken those heroes from us. Let us sit back and remember the lost lives of America's number one southern rock band Lynyrd Skynyrd with one of their classics. Here's 'Simple Man' for you."

Seriously? From all their songs, he plays "Simple Man?" I gotta be the unluckiest son of a bitch in the whole music world.

The water is still running when the first guitar tunes send chills down my spine. I look up in the mirror. Instead of my reflection, though, I see the green flames blazing in her beautiful eyes. And just like that I'm thrown back into that fucking dream made of memories and fears alike.

****

The instant I laid eyes on Amanda Bishop—in a dark alley, pushed against a wall by a dude the size of Hercules—I knew I was in trouble. She was the girl my dad had warned me about—a beauty queen, from the horror movie scene. No kidding, if hell had a beauty contest, Amanda would have been crowned Miss Underworld. It wasn't the endless legs, the long blonde thatch, or the sparkling emerald eyes that would have won her the title. Oh, no. Amanda Bishop was the most selfish, reckless, and arrogant chick I'd ever met. She did what she wanted, when she wanted, never considering the consequences of her actions. Long story short: she was everything I didn't need in my already complicated hunter life. And yet despite all that, I couldn't keep my damn eyes off of her.

Jesse slammed a shot glass on the table, spilling the bourbon he'd ordered for us. "You gonna keep staring at her? Or are you finally going to man-up, bro?"

"I have no idea what you're talking about." I wasn't the one looking at her like he wanted to be the one for her. Couldn't say the same about every other guy in this rat-hole they called a bar. The moment Amanda had stepped onto the dance floor, moving her perfect body like a goddamn striper, every head—male and female—turned her way. Dudes watched her every move, dreaming about all the things they wanted to do to her. It made me sick. She, on the contrary, enjoyed every second of it, bathed in the attention of those horny mothers.

Jesse's eagle eyes remained on me. No one knew me as well as he did. Didn't surprise me when he called bullshit. "You do realize she's only up there"—he points to the dance floor—"to mess with you, right?"

"She can do whatever the hell she wants." I downed most of the bourbon. "I. Don't. Care." Only, I did care. The girl got under my skin like no one else. She had that certain something that could invoke a fatal mixture between attraction and loathing in me. Been like this since I'd saved her sorry ass from Hercules who tried to...rape? Kill? Or rape and kill her in that alley.

"If you say so." My li'l bro didn't buy my fuck-Amanda-Bishop attitude. "I guess you don't mind him then?" he said, a devilish grin spreading across his face.

I followed the direction in which he pointed. Amanda, or Manda—it pissed her off when I called her that, making it all the more fun—shook her hips to "Don't Cha" by the Pussycat Dolls. Judging by the show she put on, I'd say the girl missed her calling. She was better than any stripper I'd ever laid eyes on. I'd seen my fair share.

It wasn't her dancing skills that made my blood boil though. Hell, no. It was the low-life wannabe thug, who put his hands on her, sparking an ugly fire in the pit of my stomach. Unlike the rest of her male audience, he wasn't satisfied watching her. He wanted to be part of the fun. Correction. He wanted to have fun. With her. Right here in the middle of the fucking bar.

Jesse's hand landed on my shoulder. "What's the matter, bro?" Last time I saw him grin like that, he scored higher on the PAU Assessment Test than I did. I never heard the end of it. "Thought you didn't care about her that way."

"I don't." Considering her attitude, I should only

ever feel sorry for any dude dumb enough to fall for her crap. Manda was the devil in high heels and faux leather pants. I was a hunter who knew better than to be seduced by evil.

"Uh-huh. Sure," my annoying little brother said. "That's why you look like someone wrecked your precious Mustang, right?" I loved Jesse. God knew I did. Yet sometimes I wanted to slam his head against a fucking wall. Especially when he was right. I was pissed. Not because that asshole over there ground his willy against Manda's butt. I didn't give a fuck whom she screwed. What I did care about was the reality she was getting herself in trouble. Again. The dude didn't strike me as someone who liked to be teased. And we all knew that's what Miss Attitude did best. She promised you heaven and gave you fucking hell.

Not my problem, *I kept telling myself.* Let her play with fire. She'll be the one to live with the damn scars.

Done watching them, I got on my feet. "Refill?"

"Booze to help forget about boobs?" Jesse winked at me. "Bring it, bro."

It took me a while to get to the busy counter. "What can I do for you, hot-stuff?" the forty-something waitress greeted me. She could have been my mother. Didn't stop her from checking me out.

"A bottle of bourbon," I said, half facing the dance floor, half the counter.

Manda continued to dance. She rolled her hips, played with her hair, and smiled like the damn devil before he collects Jesus' soul. The girl, I had no doubt, was more than any guy ever bargained for—made of pure pleasure and stinging heartbreak. The asshole behind her had no idea what awaited him, but he pretty much knew what he wanted to do with her.

A nasty fire burned through my veins, waking the longing to wipe the floor with the dude's ugly visage. But when her emerald eyes met mine, I got the feeling that was exactly what she wanted. For me to lose my shit, so she could use it against me.

Sorry, baby. I don't play your games.

"Not sure who's luckier," the waitress said, the bourbon bottle pressed against her cleavage. "Her"— she arched a brow at Manda—"or you."

I played dumb. "Huh?"

She leaned over the bar. "C'mon, a blind man could see the way you two look at each other."

I swallowed the knot in my throat. "Like we want to kill each other?" No, that wasn't metaphorically speaking. I wanted to strangle the chick more times than I could count, since my annoying little brother offered her a ride. She took "stab-worthy" to a whole new level.

The waitress shrugged. "They call it 'little death' for a reason, hot-stuff."

Jesus, why did everyone think I was into her? Amanda Bishop wasn't my type. I liked nice girls. Not the ones who were so good at being perfectly bad. "I'm not—"

"Interested?"

I nodded like a dumbass.

"Is that why you'd love to shatter that bourbon bottle over the guy's head?" she asked, handing me the booze. "Or why she's stiffening every guy's penis just to get your attention?"

"She's just trying to piss me off." She lived and breathed screwing with my head.

She laughed out loud. "And why do you think she does that?"

Because she's Satan and I'm her favorite toy.

I shoved a twenty-dollar bill over the counter. "Thanks for the bourbon."

By the time I made it back to Jesse, the guy behind the turn tables decided it was time for slower tunes. Lynyrd Skynyrd's "Simple Man" blasted through the crowded bar. I didn't have the slightest interest watching Manda and that asshole do a slow dance. So I kept my back to them, and topped up our glasses.

I lifted the shot. "To—"

"Me?" I flinched at the sound of her voice. She stole my bourbon, downed it, and slammed the empty glass on the table. "How thoughtful of you, jerk-face. I really needed that."

Old me—pre-Manda me—would have walked away. New me—post-Manda me—took the damn bait. "Yeah. I can see how rubbing your ass against the douche's crotch made you thirsty." I sounded like jealous lover-boy on LSD.

Queen-bitch grinned from ear to ear. "Would you rather it be your crotch?"

I clenched my jaw. "You wish."

Manda's smile only widened. "Maybe I do." She played with a strand of her angelic hair. "Maybe I don't."

Our eyes locked in an epic stare-down. I had killed dozens of witches, been face to face with almost every supernatural scum there was, but nothing and no one could push my buttons the way she did. One smile, one word, one gesture was enough to transform me into the worst version of myself. And she liked to feed the beast inside me. Making me lose control brought her utter joy.

Jesse cleared his throat, muttered something under his breath, and headed to the counter.

"Baby?" Wannabe thug yelled. "You coming or what?"

Manda crossed her arms. "Are we done here?"

I couldn't believe she wanted to go back to the douchebag. "For a chick who claims to be all independent-feminist, you sure as hell got a thing for being treated like a piece of meat." Manda was the sorta woman who hated it if you paid for her drinks. She was also big on "I'll never marry some douchebag who thinks he can tell me how to live my life," and a fierce defender of "boys will be boys is just a lame excuse for I raised my son to be a dick." Why she allowed a dude to treat her like that asshole did, I couldn't possibly understand.

Defiance gleamed in her eyes. "Oh, that's rich." She raised her brows. "Comin' from a guy who hates my face but dreams of the color of my panties."

She spun on her heels, ready to continue her little game. But I'd had enough of being her pawn. Seizing her wrist, I pulled her back. "What is wrong with you, Amanda? Is this all just one big game for you?"

She flashed me a maddening grin. "Dunno what you're talking about."

As I said, one snarky reply was more than enough to free the beast I had caged so carefully. My brain stopped functioning, giving room to the most primeval urge—desire. And as I stood there, pushing her against the wall, I realized three things.

One: I hated her.

Two: I loved to hate her.

Three: I wanted her more than I ever wanted anything in my life.

It was insane, but I didn't give a fuck. I was tired of denying what we both knew was inevitable. "I said you could ride with us, but I won't put up with your shit any longer." I fisted my hand around her wavy thatch. "Why don't you do us both a favor and say what you really want?"

I closed my eyes, waiting for her retort. It never came.

Manda was gone. The bar empty.

What the fuck?

Panicked, I looked around. "Manda? Jesse?"

There was no one. Where the fuck did everyone go? They couldn't just vanish into thin air. Unless—

I reached for my Beretta. "Show yourself," I ordered, well aware only magic could make a full bar disappear.

Green flames danced over the counter. The scent of sulfur stung my nostrils. Then I heard her voice. "Relax, Alex."

"Manda?"

She moved out of a shadowy corner. Something about her was different. And it wasn't just the new scar on her chest. The spark in her eyes was missing. "Interesting choice," she said, scanning the bar.

"Don't come closer," I warned, gun pointed at her. For all I knew, she could have been a shapeshifter. Those creatures loved to mess with your head by posing as someone close to you.

A ghost of a smile played on her lips. "I'm not a shifter."

"How did you—"

"Look around you, Alex." She tilted her chin at the bar. But the bar didn't exist, only an ocean of green flames. "This isn't real."

I guess that explained why a white rabbit with red eyes hopped through blazing green fire. "Am I dreaming?" I asked, shoving the gun back in my holster.

"Sort of," she replied, leaning against the flames as if they were a solid wall.

When did she stop speaking in full, stab-worthy sentences? "Could you be a bit more specific?"

She moved toward me. "I sure could, but we don't have much time."

"Time for what?" She started to freak me out

Manda met my gaze. "I need you to listen to me real carefully."

"Manda, what's—"

"You're the only one who can stop this." The fire claimed her, pulling her away from me. "The only one who can stop me."

"Manda, wait!"

Too late. She was gone.

****

"You doing all right, pal?" a husky voice asks.

I shake the dream off and spin around. Flannel shirt dude stares at me, brows raised, arms crossed. "Yeah," I mutter, turning the water off.

He moves to the second sink, eyeballing me through the mirror. "You know what they say about fate giving you lemons, right?"

Did he just say fate giving you lemons? I thought life gave you lemons.

"Go get the tequila," he says before I can question his proverb skills. "And buckle up for a wild ride."

I gawk at the guy, not sure why chills run down my spine. Maybe it's the way he grins, like he knows something I don't. Or I'm just paranoid. Either way, his proximity gives me the creeps.

He taps his non-existing hat. "See you around, cowboy." Then he disappears inside one of the stalls and I move my ass back to the car.

Chapter 10

I have absolutely no fucking clue why everyone's in love with the Big Apple. Too many people. Too little space. No real community. To cap it all off, parking is a fucking nightmare. Only God knows how long I had to drive around the block 'til some dude gave up his spot in front of Mr. Wong's, a Chinese restaurant, the sorta gig Manda would go for—shabby, cozy, and exotic. The witch has a thing for foreign food. She dragged me into a Persian place once. I didn't hate the stuff she ordered, but I'm more of a good, old hamburgers and fries kinda guy. Short: American through and through.

"About time," B grumbles. "My grandpa would have gotten us here sooner. And he's blind." The mamba slept through most of the drive, woke up when we arrived in NYC, and has been a pain ever since. I get why she's on bitch crack. Manda's disappearance along with what we found in Salem and the reality Melinda and her son are gone, too, rang all her alarms bells. So she gets a pass. *For now.*

Jesse unbuckles his seatbelt, searching the area. "I don't see any fortunetellers." Yeah, unless Madame Josephine reads in the kitchen of Mr. Wong's, I don't see it either.

B jumps out of the car. "Hurry up, boys. This isn't a sightseeing tour."

Jesse gives me an apologetic look. "She's—"

79

"Intense," I murmur, swallowing what really lies on the tip of my tongue. Starts with a "b" and ends with an "h."

"Worried," he corrects. "Manda is like a sister to her."

She's not just worried—the mamba paces the pavement like a crack addict, looking for his next fix—she's close to losing her shit.

"I know she is," I say. "I am, too." Judging by his expression, he already figured that out on his own. Still, it feels good to actually say it. I've spent so much time pretending I don't give a shit about the witch, it's liberating to man-up.

"We'll find her," he assures me.

I yank the car door open. "We will." Come what may.

B shoots daggers at us. "What took you so long?" She doesn't wait for a reply, so I assume she felt compelled to make our life a little harder before she heads down the narrow alley, next to Mr. Wong's.

Night has already fallen. NYC is lit up like my mom's Christmas tree. Or maybe my mom's tree is inspired by the endless lights of the city. Either way it's a nice sight. Sorta comforting, considering the dark outlook of the past few days.

"B," Jesse barks. "Wait up."

The mamba ignores him, moving past several fire exit stairs. The farther we walk, the creepier it gets. Jesse and I are on high alert, expecting a gangbanger to mug us at any second. I wonder how that Madame Josephine chick stays in business. She probably needs to hand out bulletproof vests to her customers to get them here.

Chilling wind howls through the passage, beating against my skin like the whip of a dominatrix. I hug my leather jacket against my chest, spotting a blinking, neon green sign in the distance. Madame Josephine. Palmist, Tarot Reader, and Healer. That's code for witch.

B stops abruptly. She spins on her heels, facing us. Actually, she faces me. "Just so we're clear," she says, standing straighter than a candle. "I do the talking. You"—she casts me a killer look—"pretend you don't exist. Got it?"

I don't appreciate her telling me how to do my damn job. Unfortunately, I never get to share the intel because Jesse nudges me. Hard. "We understand."

B's gaze lingers on me.

"Fine." I wave my hands white-flag style. "You're in charge." As long as she gets what we need, I'm cool with staying in the background. If she doesn't…well, then I won't guarantee anything.

B doesn't trust me. I can tell by the wrinkles on her forehead and the "don't fuck with me, Alex" look plastered across her pretty face.

"He'll behave," Jesse promises her.

She turns to the iron door. "Yeah. Right."

The mamba has some unresolved issues with me. I sense the hostile vibes every now and then. She shoots them like a ninja throws his throwing-stars, in secrecy, whenever she thinks I'm not looking. At first, I figured it's because of Manda. You know the whole "sisters before misters" crap. But there's this nagging voice in the back of my head saying it's more than that. B blames me for something. I just don't know what. *Yet*.

"Josephine," she yells, slamming her tiny fists

against the hard surface. "Open up. It's me, Bonnie Lacroix."

Minutes go by. There's no sign of a fortuneteller or anyone else. Unless you count the rats squeaking in the sinister corners. I don't.

"Josephine." B sounds like a full-blooded siren. "Please. I need your help."

Jesse rests his hand on her shoulder. "Maybe we should—"

The door swings open. "Can I help you?" A twenty-something, very pretty—long black hair, nice body, Catherine Zeta Jones would envy her face— boohoo princess asks.

I guess this isn't Madame Josephine. How do I know? One look at B's aggravated face is more than enough. "Where's Josephine?" Wow. That was rude.

The girl narrows her eyes. "Who wants to know?"

B rolls her eyes. "Bonnie Lacroix from the New Orleans Lacroixs."

Boohoo Princess' demeanor changes instantly. "I'm sorry," she says, opening the door farther. "I didn't recognize you." B's family truly is royalty. Why else would the girl act as if she just came face to face with the Duchess of Cambridge?

B waves it off. "Just tell me where Josephine is. I need to talk to her. Now." The mamba left her manners somewhere in Salem, that's for sure.

Boohoo Princess raises her brows. "Josephine is...*was* in Cassadaga. She'll be back tomorrow morning." Cassadaga, huh? Also known as the Psychic Capital of the World, or like we hunters say the place where real witches hide amongst the fraud. It's a small community in Florida. Folks who live there do aura readings, tarot readings, crystal balls and whatever humbug brings their next paycheck.

B throws her hands in the air. "Fuck."

"Can I help you?" Boohoo Princess asks.

B cocks a brow, studying the poor chick. The mamba's gaze dissects her like a damn frog. "We'll be back tomorrow," she says before she marches back to the car.

Jesse chases after her.

I shove my hands in my pockets and sigh. "I'm sorry. She's—"

"Intense," Boohoo Princess offers.

I laugh. "Yeah." That's the second-best word to describe B, but the only one that isn't insulting.

"It's okay," the girl assures me, conjuring up a half-hearted smile.

"No, it's not." Boohoo Princess didn't deserve B's anger. She was just trying to help. "Anyway, thanks for your help."

She nods. "Sure."

I rush back when I hear B's voice. "No, you don't get it."

"Bonnie," Jesse roars. "You're overreacting."

I halt, peeking around the corner.

"Why?" She slams her hands on her hips. "Because he's your brother or because you don't want to hear the truth?"

My brother cups her elbow, pulling her closer. They exchange some hushed words. Dirty looks pave the gap between them. When I step out of the alley, they both shut up.

"What's going on?" I never saw them argue like that.

Jesse yanks the passenger door open, hops in, and slams it shut.

I eyeball the mamba. "What's going on?" I repeat.

The mamba smiles, bitterly. "Nothing." She reaches for the door handle. "Let's go."

I feel like I missed a whole episode of *Everyone Knows What's Next, Except Me*. "Go where?"

"We can crash at my place," she murmurs, shutting the door behind her.

Her place, huh? Awesome. Who wouldn't want to stay the night in the apartment he almost died in? The same apartment in which the girl I thought hated me cried for my lost soul.

****

Manda's hand laid on my chest. I hadn't been able to open my eyes, but I felt her the second she climbed into bed with me. The darkness that held me captive was no longer a cold bed of nails. With her there, I saw the shadows of the night. A glimmer of hope. Had I known that it took a deal with the devil and a near death experience to get her in my arms once again...I swear I would have called upon the demon sooner.

"What the fuck were you thinking?" she whispered.

Her tears broke and healed me at the same time. Part of me wanted nothing more than to wipe them away, to assure her it's going to be all right. But the sadist, hiding beneath the hero, enjoyed her tears. Tears she cried for me. *An ocean of salt that told me she did care, after all. I wanted to capture them in a jar, so I could take them to hell and remember why all the torture and pain was worth it.*

****

Yup. It was in that very apartment I understood Amanda Bishop was the only girl that could bring me back from the dead.

Chapter 11

I used to wonder why the mere thought of applying to university gave me insomnia. Back in the days before the PAU knocked on our door, Mom and Dad sat me down at the kitchen table, hell-bent to talk me into giving academic life a shot. "You can explore all your options," Dad said, grinning wickedly. Translated, it meant something like plenty of girls, son.

Mom tried a subtler approach. "Education is power, Alex. Think about it, you can be anything you want—a lawyer, a doctor…you don't have to follow in your grandpa's footsteps. The world is at your feet with the right degree. Don't waste your life chasing ghosts," were her exact words.

Neither the prospect of booze and boobs, nor money and power could change my mind. I was going to be the hunter I was born to be. The guy who would chase down the witch that took my little sister to put a damn bullet between her eyes.

And as I stand here in the overcrowded hallway of Green House, on a Friday night, I get why I'd rather spent my life on the road chasing ghosts than inside a library. Students are a breed of their own. Fun seeking Homo sapiens, breathing carelessness, while they have no clue what's happening outside their safeguarded university halls. Their worlds revolve around theories. The solutions to their problems is found in books. My world revolves around brutal realities. The solution is usually raw violence.

Jesse elbows me. "You good, man?"

The second B has signed us in as visitors and we shut the door of her apartment, keeping this alien world out, I will be. "Sure."

His gaze darts to his boots. "Good."

"Hey." I cross my arms. "What's with you and B?" They don't even look at each other anymore. The argument in front of Mr. Wong's seems responsible for the sudden "I ignore him, I ignore her, we both feel like crap" attitude.

My little brother won't look at me. "It's nothing."

That little nothing is somehow connected to me and I like to know shit when it concerns me. "I—"

Some douchebag bumps into me. Did no one ever tell him about the consequences of reading and walking?

"Watch it," I hiss, slightly annoyed.

You'd think as a future man in power, he'd have the decency to apologize, right? Way off the mark. He gawks at me, shakes his head, and moves on. Jackass.

I return my focus to Jesse and his bitch fight with the mamba. I want...no, I need to know what the deal is. Too bad, B marches out of the residence hall director's office before I get to interrogate him some more. "Let's go," she orders, pissed off like hell.

"Let me guess," I say, tilting my head at the office door. "They're not really up for visitors, are they?" University housing has strict rules. They don't just let anyone in. It's one of the reasons Jesse had to bring my half-dead ass in through the back door last time we were here. The other being the fact we were both wanted men—still are since Carter hasn't given us a green light yet—and drenched in blood. I highly doubt any sane person would have allowed us up to Manda and B's apartment, looking like victims of Michael fucking Myers.

She sighs. "Now, they are."

"You manipulated them?" Jesse asks, a bit nervous. "What if it fades?"

She doesn't grace him with a reply. Instead, she proceeds toward the stairs, shoulders and head hanging low.

A bunch of giggling chicks with belt-like skirts and extremely tight tops block the staircase. They eyeball Jesse and me like two pieces of yummy fresh meat. I swear if we looked at them that way, we'd be arrested for sexual harassment. So much for gender equality.

"Move," B barks.

The group pays no attention to the stewing mamba. They're too busy eating us alive. Kylie Jenner lookalike flashes Jesse a not so innocent smile. "How's it going, handsome?"

My brother wouldn't be the man-whore he is if he didn't wink at her. "It's going great." His voice drops ten octaves, making him sound like a male telephone sex-operator.

The group breaks into laughter.

And B? She's on the brink of slamming her fist into their Barbie faces. "Get the fuck out of my way, Romy." She knows Kylie Jenner wannabe by name. She also doesn't like her very much. Ten bucks says it's not just because the chick has her eyes set on my little brother.

Kylie-wannabe plays with a strand of her long,

dark hair. "C'mon, Bonnie. What about sharing is caring?" Her gaze darts from Jesse to me and back to B. "You can't possibly please them both."

Wow. Seriously, just wow.

B gets in her face. "Out. Of. My. Way."

Had she given me that killer-stare, I'd run for the hills. Romy, however, is too overloaded with hormones to care. "Fun killer."

B has had enough. She pushes past her, deliberately bumping into her.

"Apartment two B. Come find me if you want some real fun," Romy shouts after us.

"I don't get it," I murmur, still trying to wrap my head around the student species.

Jesse narrows his eyes. "Get what?"

I look down at the snickering chicks. They're undressing our butts. Superman would be jealous of their X-ray vision. "How did Manda do it, man? She doesn't fit." Between hipsters, privileged brats, and *Confessions of a Shopaholic* slash *American Pie* chicks, Amanda Bishop is *Pretty in Pink*—the outcast who happens to understand the definition of hardship without a damn dictionary.

Jesse's lips part, but the mamba with anger issues is quicker. "And why wouldn't she fit?" she asks, hands on her hips, eyes narrowed.

Something tells me the wrong answer will get me into real trouble. "She—"

"She what?" B barks, not waiting for a reply. "Is smarter than most folks, including you? Damn right."

Why does everyone—including Manda—assume I underestimate her intelligence? Jesus, I'm well aware the witch's mind is sharper than a katana. It can slice you in two with a single blow. I'll never forget the moment in Bakersfield, when she scientifically explained the ritual she was about to perform to find my missing brother. Manda sounded like Stephen Hawking, Freud, and Einstein all rolled into *Jennifer's Body*.

"As adjustable as a chameleon?" B continues her defense, lips curved into a half-smile. "You can bet your ass on it. Totally—"

"Stop." I hold my hand up. "All I'm saying is the girl isn't cut out for"—I scan the girls group down the stairs—"*this*."

B cocks a brow. "You don't know the first thing about her, Alex."

I know how much she loved to roam the country, seeing new places, meeting new people. Freedom is the one thing a girl like her wouldn't give up voluntarily. Not for *this*. So what made her change her mind? What turned a loose cannon like Manda, a girl who loved to live life on the edge, into a student? I just can't shake the feeling I'm missing a crucial piece of the jigsaw called Amanda Bishop.

"You coming or what?" B barks from the top of the staircase.

How the hell did she get there so quickly?

Jesse and I march up the final stairs, following Queen B aka Queen Bitch to her apartment.

The door hasn't shut behind us yet when B disappears inside the bathroom. The fraction of a second later, she turns the shower on, leaving Jesse and me all alone in the small common room, consisting of an open kitchen and a tiny living room.

"Hey." Jesse elbows me. "Didn't they mention a roommate?"

"Yeah." I squint. "Why?"

He points to the couch. "How did she not call the cops?" What used to be a cream couch looks like Dexter's new playground. Bloodstains cover the thing. My blood. "Looks like a prop from *Scream*."

I shrug. "Don't ask me, man." I gaze at the crimson spots on the couch that have no resemblance to corn syrup. "I'll never understand those kids."

My brother laughs. "Dude, you're barely older than they are."

"Age is just a number." It merely measures the years you've spent on this world, not the experiences you've had. And experiences are what make you, in Manda's words, an old soul.

Jesse rolls his eyes. "You sound like Grandpa."

"He was a wise man." Not kidding. Our grandpa, Mom's dad, was a genius. He invented shit in his garage. Granted, it wasn't the next iPhone, or Windows. Grandpa was a freelance hunter. He killed hundreds, if not thousands of witches, and when the time came to retire, he devoted the rest of his life to making other hunters' lives easier. Take my Beretta, for example. From the outside, it looks like any gun of the make and model, but inside it's warded with Celtic protection runes to keep the owner safe. So far, it's worked just fine. I mean I'm alive, aren't I?

"Whatever." Jesse moves to the coffee maker. "Want some?"

"Bring it on."

Three steaming cups sit on the coffee table when the mamba stomps out of the bathroom. She wears tight shorts, an oversized shirt, and her hair is wrapped in...I was gonna say towel, but from where I'm standing it looks like an old T-shirt. I highly doubt Mrs. Louis Vuitton bag slash Gucci boots can't afford a towel. Must be deliberate then.

Jesse points to the steaming liquid. "Coffee?"

I prepare for B to unleash the bitch. Instead, she plummets down on the armchair, grabs the mug, and looks completely at ease. "Thanks." Wow. Whatever is in the water, I need some of it, too.

Jesse and I pull up two chairs. "So what's the plan?" I ask, unable to shut my damn mind off.

B blows some air on her drink. "For now, we have to wait for Josephine to come back." She doesn't like it.

Neither do I. "Can I ask you something?"

She cocks a brow.

"Without starting a war?" I add, just in case the shower-effect wears off. She gestures for me to continue. "What's your theory?"

B squints. "My theory?"

"Yeah." I put my coffee down. "What do you think happened in that house, and why did Manda run?"

B's gaze darts to Jesse. He rocks an odd expression. A mix of worried and scared? Or maybe it's more "don't say anything" and "please, don't say anything"? I really can't be sure.

"Bonnie?" I meet her gaze. "What do you think happened to Manda?"

"I'm tired." She gets on her feet. "You guys can sleep in Manda's room, or on the couch. I really don't care."

What the hell is going on with her? One minute, she's a bitch. The next, she's bearable. Then, without any warning, she goes back to the Queen Bitch status? Her mood swings are worse than mine when Manda is around.

"Here." She throws a pillow, a blanket, and sheets our way. "That should do." A second later, she slams her door shut with a bang that has the ability to wake the walking dead.

My gaze shoots to Jesse. "What was that about?"

"She's tired," he says, spreading the sheets on the bloody couch.

I raise my brows. He's always been a rotten liar. Today, however, he'd get a Golden Raspberry for worst performance ever. "Dude." I grab him by the shoulder, spinning him around. "What aren't you two telling me?"

"I love you, big brother." A lopsided grin plays on his lips. "But some things are mine and mine only." I used those same words when he asked me why I sold my soul.

"Seriously?"

"I learned from the best." He looks me in the eye. "I learned from you."

Nicely played, Jesse. Shame I'd never, ever admit it. "Dude." I cross my arms. "What did I tell you about Mom's Whitney Houston LPs?" She's a huge fan. Her collection includes every album the queen of cheesy love songs ever made.

He throws the blanket on the couch. "To bring them to you once I'm done with them?"

"Jackass." I did no such thing. Songs like "I Will Always Love You" were never my kinda thing. Partly because I missed the guitar tunes. Mostly, because I never believed in the "forever" kind of love.

He flings himself onto the couch. "Goodnight, Alex."

Wait. If he takes the couch then— "Where the hell am I supposed to sleep?"

He lifts his head. "In a bed?"

"Quit being a smart ass." I'm not in the mood for his games.

He sighs. "Remember what Bonnie said about Manda's room?"

My gaze darts to the door I avoided since we walked in here. The door that separates reality from an ocean of painful memories. "You want me to sleep in Manda's bed?"

He smirks. "Gee, bro. You make it sound like it'd be the first time."

I don't like this cocky version of my brother. Don't like it at all. "You know," I say, facing the door I didn't want to open today. Possibly ever. "Hiding behind that attitude is only going to get you so far." I should know. I'm the master of pretentious jerkiness. "Don't make the same mistakes I did." One Remington brother fucked hard by karma is more than enough.

He doesn't say anything. He doesn't have to. Deep down, he knows I'm right.

I step into Manda's room. Her scent crawls into my nostrils. It's all over the place. Flowery, yet herb-like. Alluring, yet bitter. Just like her.

The bed is just like we left it. Messy, cozy, and drenched with sweat and tears. Hell, I can still see the imprints of our heads on the pillows. It feels like yesterday when I lay there, next to her. I remember thinking how dying in her arms would be worth going to the pit. She proved me right in that tiny apartment above JJ's bar. For the time being, Amanda Bishop dropped her guard. I know because a soft longing that she had never showed me before replaced all the hardness that formed her armor.

God, I miss her.

I miss her so much it fucking hurts, like it hurt every damn day after I pulled my gun on her.

I close my eyes, determined to lock those memories away. It wasn't the last time I felt her breath on my face, I assure myself. *Manda is okay. She's always okay.*

I rest my head on her pillow, drawing in her scent, begging every God I'd ever heard of to let her be *okay*. But that sick feeling in the pit of my stomach, the one I've battled since I spoke to Manda on the phone, grows like an inoperable ulcer.

Chapter 12

Amanda

A woman who called me Satan's bride, a woman who foresaw my future as the queen of darkness, raised me. Mother Dearest didn't keep my predicted fate under cloak-and-dagger. She shared her vision—the one she had while I grew in her womb—with anyone willing to listen. Other witches were afraid of me. They feared what I could...what I *would* become. They looked at seven-year-old Amanda Bishop, but didn't see a child desperate for her mother's love and approval. They caught sight of Amanda Bishop, the murderous witch, devoted to the dark side.

Present me.

The me I hate so much I'm unable to face its reflection.

The me with bloodstained clothes.

The me who used love as a scapegoat for evil.

The me who needs to be stopped before it's too fucking late.

"You did well," Clyde assures me, his voice nothing but a distant calling, echoing through the blackness of what used to be my soul.

I'm not sure what he expects. For me to smile and be proud of what I did? Does he want a "thank you" for his praise? Or should I empty my aching stomach in his freakin' face to show him how I really feel?

I'd opt for the latter. Except, it would require for me to shift in my seat. I can't do that. I'm paralyzed, my whole body frozen in a state of shock and disbelief. What I did—

God, I belong in hell.

I always did. Mother Dearest had been right all along. I was born to be evil. It explains how I could go through with Clyde's plan. How I—

My gaze darts to the scarlet stains covering most of my clothes. The stink of tinny metal crawls up my nose, invoking a gag reflex I can't control.

"Not in my car," Clyde barks, pulling onto the breakdown lane.

I yank the door open. Just in time. A fraction of a second later and the windshield of Clyde's precious Audi would be smeared with bile.

I don't bother holding my hair back. I'm drenched in the bodily fluids of strangers. What a hypocrite would I be if I minded my own goddamn vomit?

The Knight of Hell stands before me, watching me as I get rid of my last meal. "The first ones are the hardest," he says, pity in his amber eyes. "It'll get easier. I promise."

Fuck his promises.

Fuck easier.

Fuck him.

"Here"—he holds a bottle of water under my nose—"this will help."

I wipe some puke off my lips, the taste of acid still lingering in my mouth. I don't want to wash it down. I want to taste what I've become. What I am.

"Amanda." His voice is low and demanding.

"Drink the bloody water."

Climbing back inside the car, I slam the damn door in his face. He took my soul, my life. I'll be damned if he takes my last bit of free will.

The engine roars to life.

I scan the car, searching for a fixed point. Something to focus on. Something to keep my mind away from what happened in Washington D.C. Instead, I find the one thing reminding me of how evil I truly am. The book that cost several agents their lives—*The First Grimoire*.

Chapter 13

Alex

Sleep never came last night. The sandman had better places to be, less vicious dreams to feed. Frankly, I didn't need him to recall all the ugly things I said to Manda in the past. Didn't need a reminder of our last night together. The memories crashed over me like a fucking tsunami every time I closed my eyes. That wasn't even the worst part of my night. Creepy images haunted me—blood, more blood, death, darkness, and in the midst of it all Manda rocking flaming green eyes.

"Stop me, Alex. You have to stop me," Manda begged, her voice a constant feature in the back of my mind.

I tried to ignore it. Assured myself it was my guilty conscience plaguing me. But the more effort I put into shutting her out, the louder her pleas grew. "Stop me. Please. You're the only one who can."

It got to the point where I was absolutely certain about three things. One: I was losing my mind and I could do nothing about it. Two: I had to find her before it was too late—for what, I'm not sure yet. Three: Amanda Bishop was in trouble. The kind that made a girl afraid of nothing terrified of everything.

Now, in the wee hours of a hopefully better morning, I sit on the kitchen counter, waiting for my third pot of coffee, listening to my little brother's exhausted snores. He sleeps like a rock. Good for him.

B must have drifted off, too. She paced her room like a crazy person, last night. Shortly after three a.m., the commotion in B's room died down. I was tempted to check on her, see if she succumbed to weariness. After a quiet argument with myself, I decided against it. C'mon, it'd be kinda weird to waltz into the mamba's room to tuck her in, right?

With the sun slowly rising, casting a dim orange light onto the windowsill, I wait for the rest of the crew to wake from their slumber, so we can hit the road, paying the ominous Madame Josephine a visit. In the meantime, to battle the eerie silence cloaking the apartment, I check the news on my phone, hoping to find some sort of normalcy in an absurd situation.

The New York Times is my first stop. The headline of the first article reads *New York's Night of Terror*. Doesn't sound good. Skimming through it, I realize the headline doesn't do the shit justice. Apparently, some hardcore *The Purge* fans decided it was time to blur the boundaries between fiction and reality. They put on some fucked up clown masks, wreaking havoc all across the city. So far, the police confirmed ten casualties, over sixty-eight injured, and about two point one million bucks in property damage.

The world's going to shit.

I'm not joking. New York wasn't the only city hit by an unpreceded crime wave. CNN reports about similar incidents all across the country—Miami, Los Angeles, Martinsburg—no state was safe.

Even London had a rocky night, if one believes the videos of burning cars, and houses, on BBC's website.

Sorta feels like watching a damn end-of-days movie. You know the Arnold Schwarzenegger kind.

I'm about to move on to the *Washington Post* when my brother's sleepy voice wafts through the small apartment. "Have you even slept?"

"Sure." He's already worried about my not going to hell and Manda's vanishing act. I don't see any reason to add my lack of sleep to his list of sorrows.

"Uh-huh, right." He stumbles toward the coffee maker in need of black gold to cure him of fatigue.

He pours himself a cup. "Anything interesting?"

I press the lock button on my phone and sigh. "Other than the fact the world's about to go down in flames?" He nods. "Nope. Nothing." *The Purge* like riots aren't our gig. Why tell him about it?

We sip our steaming coffees in silence when B's door flings open. "Coffee," she grumbles, stomping into the kitchen.

Jesse hands her a cup, his gaze trained on the hollows beneath her cognac eyes. "You okay?" His voice is soft but demanding. I fear he might actually expect an honest reply. Something tells me he'd be more successful finding water in the desert.

"What time is it?" she asks, completely ignoring my brother's worries.

I glance at my phone. "Twenty past six."

She puts her cup down, rubbing the exhaustion off her face. Or she tries. "I'll hit the shower. Then we'll leave."

Jesse's gaze drifts over her unusually pale face. "Don't you think it's a little too early?" He tops up her cup. "Madame Josephine might not even be back yet."

B couldn't care less. "Give me twenty minutes."

The bathroom door slams shut behind her, leaving my little brother with an expression I know too damn well—hurt with a great amount of fret.

He glares at the full cup on the counter. "I just don't get this girl."

I pat his shoulder. "It's the curse."

"What curse?"

A smile pulls at the edges of my lips. "The 'man meets woman, likes woman, woman drives him insane' curse." I shrug. "You're not its first victim and will likely not be its last." I should know. Amanda Bishop took me to the madhouse, only to leave me in a straitjacket made of heartache and fear.

He cocks a brow. "I don't like—"

"Don't finish that sentence, little brother." I jump to my feet. "It's bad enough you're lying to me; don't lie to yourself."

He rolls his eyes in dramatic Jesse-style. "What happened to my brother, dude? The guy who hates chick-flick moments and thinks Dr. Phil is a charlatan?"

What I want to say is he understands that real hell is a state of mind in which you're bound to regret your failures over and over. What I do say is, "Shut up and drink your damn coffee."

Like clockwork, B marches out of the bathroom. Dressed like the showstopper of Prada—tight jeans, a rose-colored silk blouse, and ankle boots with killer heels—she moves toward us. All signs of debility hidden beneath carefully applied, natural makeup, emphasizing her stunning almond-shaped eyes. It's amazing what a girl can do in twenty minutes given hot water, some makeup, and decent clothes.

"Ready?" She certainly is.

I head to Manda's room. "Let me get the keys." I left them on her nightstand last night, when I engaged in the illusion to catch some sleep.

"Hurry," she orders, accompanied by a queen-like hand gesture.

The very instant I reach for the doorknob sharp pain hits my head. I inhale, hoping it'll fade. It gets worse instead. Feels like someone driving a sword right through my damn brain.

"Alex." In my peripheral, I spot Jesse running across the living room.

Hands pressed against each side of my head, I drop to my knees. The pain knocks the air out of my lungs. Soon, I find myself breathless on the floor.

"Alex." This time it's B's voice screaming my name in terror. "Alex, what is it?"

Jesse lingers over me, his shape blurring. "Dude…talk to me."

I blink. Again. Again. And again.

"Do something," he barks at B.

"What am I supposed to do? I don't even know what's wrong with him."

Their voices are farther and farther away. The darkness slowly taking my vision, closer than ever.

What the fuck is happening to me?

Green flames blaze in the distance, penetrating the blackness.

Green is good, I tell myself. *Green is hope.*

Except, it's neither good, nor hope. Green is—

****

Amanda's eyes burn brighter than a damn wildfire. I've never seen anything like it. "I knew you'd hear me," she whispers, sitting cross-legged on the cold cement floor. "You always have." The utter sadness radiating from her whole being drives a stick through my heart.

"Manda, what—"

"Don't," she warns, holding her palm up. "Don't come any closer."

What the hell is she thinking? That I just stand here like a damn statue?

Sorry, baby, ain't gonna happen.

"Alex," she pleads. "Please, for once…" She trails off, aware it's pointless.

I hunker down in front of her. My fingers itching to touch her marvelous face. A face that killed and revived me several times, one that haunted my dreams long before we met. Yup, that's right. I, Alexander Ethan Remington, dreamed of Manda long before I found her in that alley. She snuck into my world shortly after Natasha disappeared, comforting me. "Manda"—I lift her chin—"what's going on?"

She looks over my shoulder, refusing to meet my gaze. "You have to stop me." Those words had tortured me all night. "Please, Alex. You're the only one who can."

Cupping her face, I ignore her weird request. There are more important things to talk about. "Where are you?"

She says nothing.

I scan the surroundings. Brick walls covered with old runes, warding off magic. Some of them I've seen before. Hunters use them to protect themselves from hexes. Behind her, pushed against a damp wall, is a cot with a single pillow but no blanket. I don't spot any windows. And just when I thought things couldn't possibly get worse, I catch a glimpse of the iron bars, holding her prisoner in this godforsaken dungeon.

"Amanda." My pulse thunders. "Tell me where we are."

Our eyes lock. "Promise me," she says. "Promise you'll do whatever it takes to stop me."

I can't take it anymore. The events of the previous days tighten their grip around my throat—the love we shared at JJ's, the pain when she was gone the next morning, the fear of last night when I heard her calling, the desperation of seeing her locked away behind iron bars. "Drop the bullshit and tell me where the fuck you are, so I can come and get you."

"It's too late."

"What the hell are you talking about?"

Her gaze darts to a tattered book in the midst of what appears to be an altar. The edges are degraded. A symbol I've never seen before stamped into its center. "There's no redemption for what I did. But there's still time to stop me."

I stare at the aged book. Its blackened pages bear writing in an alien language.

That sick mother of a feeling chews at my gut. I refuse to acknowledge it. "Whatever you did," I say, voice low. "We can fix it. Just tell me where you are."

"I can't." Manda shakes her head, tears dwelling in her fiery emerald eyes. "I won't."

Anger strikes like a damn rattlesnake. "What do you mean, you won't? You brought me here for a reason, didn't you?"

"I did."

"Then tell me how I can find you."

"I can't."

Patience is for the strong, not the ones on the brink of maximum fear. "Amanda," I yell. "Stop playing games. This isn't funny."

Bitter laughter crawls up her throat. "No, Alex. No, it's not." She sighs. "That's why I need you to promise me that when the time comes you won't hesitate. Finish what you started the day you learned what I was."

Realization hits like lightning. "Are you asking me to kill you?"

She musters a smile. "I'm asking you to save me."

I want to rattle the madness out of her when a heavy door creaks. Instinctively, I get on my feet, ready to fight whatever is coming our way.

"Shit." Manda is next to me in a heartbeat. "He's coming." Fear clouds the flames, burning in her eyes. "You gotta go. Now."

"I'm not going anywhere," I assure her, standing my ground.

"Stubborn as always," she whispers, slamming both her palms against my chest.

The impact knocks me down. Darkness—the one that brought me here—swallows me.

I'm floating.

"Take care of our s—"

****

"Alex!" B's palm connects with my jaw. "Wake the fuck up!"

My head spins like a tumble dryer. Slowly, I manage to open my eyes. The light streaming through the windows pierces through my already scrambled brain.

"Dude." Jesse helps me up. "What happened?" The blood has drained from his face, leaving nothing but a ghostly shell.

"Manda," I choke out, mouth dry.

Hope sparks in B's eyes. "You saw her? Is she okay? Where is she? What did she—"

"She's in trouble," I cut her off, before she gives in to the illusion my little magical excursion is the answer to her prayers.

Horror claws into her expression, hardening her face. "What kind of trouble?"

The kind that makes her long for a bullet in her brain. I can hardly say that, can I? "We"—I struggle to my feet—"need to find her. Now." Preferably before she continues down suicide lane.

"Wait," Jesse insists as I try to get the keys from Manda's room. "I'll get them. You should…" He studies me. "I don't know…have some water, maybe?"

Water is the last thing on my mind. Manda is locked away in some magical dungeon, with a creepy old book, and begged me to kill her. It doesn't get much worse than that. And then there's the last thing she said, before B slapped me. "Take care of our s—"

Our S…? What the fuck does that even mean? What or who is S? And why does she beg me to take care of…it? Him?

I ogle the mamba. If anyone knows what Manda was trying to say, it'd be her. I'm all set to ask her when Carter's name flickers across the screen of my phone.

Maybe he found her, the last glimmer of hope says. But the cramping of my stomach speaks another language. One I'm not sure I want translated.

"Alex," he practically yells into the speaker. "Alex, can you hear me?"

"Yes," I choke out. "What's up?" I don't want an answer to that question. I have to hear it regardless.

"Where are you?" Carter is completely out of breath.

"New York."

"Stay there," he orders. "I'm on my way."

Carter leaving the safety of his office? This is apocalyptic bad. "Dude, what's going on?"

"It's Amanda." He pauses. "She…she…"

"She what?"

"You have to see for yourself," he says, fear dominating his voice. "I'll catch the next plane. Just stay where you are. I'm coming."

He cuts the line before I can say a damn word.

"What's going on?" Jesse asks, the keys to the Mustang dangling from his index finger.

"I don't know." But whatever it is put the fear of God into the leader of the Paranormal Analysis Unit of the FBI. A man who interrogated witches, demons, and monsters for the past six years of his life.

Jesse narrows his eyes. "Well, who was it?"

"Carter."

My brother frowns. "And what did he say?"

"That he's on his way."

"To New York?" A deaf man could hear the surprise in Jesse's high-pitched tone. Like me, my brother knows all about Carter's field phobia. We were both present in Bridgewater when a full-blooded succubus attempted to suck the life out of our boss. We barely managed to get him out of there alive. "Did he say why?"

"Something about Manda," I choke out, unable to face the mamba.

Chapter 14

Amanda

Standing on the other side of the bars, carrying a tray loaded with food, Clyde watches me, assesses me. His stone-like expression never wavers. His eyes remain on me and me only.

Clyde's aura is dark pink, indicating deceit and weariness. Yes, demons have auras, which means they have souls. And no, it's not plain black.

He knows.

Or at the very least, he suspects. Clyde's a Knight of Hell. A killer trained in the art of cabal and lies. Creatures like him spot the faintest signs of dishonesty.

Aware every misstep could give away what I did, I keep my gaze glued to the aged tome, a collection of spells and rituals written in an otherworldly language I didn't know I could speak. To my surprise, I do—speak alien that is. The grimoire, more dangerous than any nuke, rests on the altar Clyde's minion built. Its power electrifies the air.

Show no fear, a quiet voice urges me. It's the voice of the witch that died the second she signed that godforsaken deal with her blood. The only reminder of who Amanda Bishop used to be—fearless, selfish, alive.

He's going to kill him along with everyone you love

if he finds out you summoned him. The terms and conditions of our agreement specifically forbid me from ever seeing Alexander Remington again. I gambled with his very soul when I brought him to my new home—a dungeon made to imprison the worst kinds of evil. I had no choice, though. There's only one way to stop this madness; it starts with me and ends with death by the hands of—

Don't think of him!

Liquefying amber eyes lance through me. He uses his magic, trying to read me like I read so many people before. He can't get through my armor. His anger and anxiousness give him away.

You can do this. For Alex. For Leandro. For the people who care about me, regardless of my many flaws—my friends.

I breathe my fears out, draw the will to fight in. He can have my soul, my life, my everything. But he can't have my heart. It belongs to someone else. Someone who occupied it long before we even met. A knight in shining armor, who galloped into my life on his black steel horse—the hunter I went to hell for.

Play the game, Amanda. Just make sure you don't lose.

"You could earn some decent money," I say, attempting to sound cool rather than broken.

He remains quiet.

"I'm sure some folks would pay to see a freak show like me." They pay for zoos and haunted attractions. Why not for a supernatural prison cell hosting an evil witch?

The sound of Clyde's silence—an absence of breath and humanity—drives me toward my breaking point. If he finds out what I did, everything was for nothing. Those agents and all the other people died for nothing more than my failure. Alex will go to hell. And God knows what Clyde has in store for the others.

I can't let that happen.

"There's this dude on *Destination America*," I continue my charade. "Name's Nick Groff. Maybe you should give him a call. I bet he could set you up with the right people to promote what you've got here." The ghost hunter digs paranormal lockdowns. Something tells me an evil, untouchable witch, imprisoned by a Knight of Hell would be a dream come true for him.

I can't tell if Nick Groff provoked Clyde to unlock the cell, or if he's simply tired of my lame jokes. Either way, he comes at me.

"I hope you like burritos," he says, putting the tray onto the small table next to my un-comfy cot.

"I'm a vegetarian," I groan.

The ghost of a smile tugs at his lips. "Black bean and vegetables."

The reality a demon knows what I like sends shivers down my spine. "Uhm, thanks?"

Spine straight, he nods once.

Needing to escape his demanding stare, I pick up my drained body and move toward the delicious-smelling food. My bones have the consistency of mashed potatoes. Summoning Alex on top of the ritual Clyde forced me to do last night weakened me. In all my years as a witch, I never used or rather abused magic the way I did within the past few days.

Clyde takes a seat on the cot. "I'm glad you're doing better, love."

I shove some beans in my dry mouth, aware he's

still playing the game. We both know I'm not better. I'm just trying to hide what I did seconds before he came down in my dungeon.

"Have you slept?" he inquires, softly.

I swallow a piece of burrito. "A bit."

He cocks a brow. "Tell me the truth, Amanda."

"Why?" I ask, bile rising up my gullet. It's a familiar taste. Been puking my guts out all night.

He narrows his eyes at me. "What do you mean, why?"

"Why do you care?" I shove the tray away, sick of the smell. "I'm your whore, remember?" A slave bound to do his gruesome bidding. "What's it to you how I'm holding up?"

He scrubs a tired hand over his too-pretty face. Clyde's vessels—he changes them almost daily—are exquisite. This one belongs to a dude who rocks Italian handsomeness—black hair, sun-kissed skin, lashes any woman would kill for, and the bluest eyes I've ever seen. "You think I'm a monster, don't you?"

After last night, I think he's something far worse than a monster. A soulless, pain-inflicting thing with absolutely no moral compass. Amanda Bishop times a hundred.

"It brings me no joy to lock you away," he says when I don't reply. "But some of my people think you'd betray us, given the opportunity."

"Betray you?" I laugh. "Why would I do that? The life of every person I ever cared for depends on me honoring our deal. I'm not selfless enough to let them die for the greater good." And that is nothing but the truth. Last night, I did the wrong thing for the right reason. I hate myself for it. Yet I'd do it again. In a damn heartbeat.

He studies me closely. "You fascinate me, love."

"I beg your pardon?"

"I have been around for a *very* long time," he says, gaze darting to the rune of Isa, covering most of the ceiling. The straight line reinforces the power of all the other runes. "Came across thousands of witches, but none were quite like you."

"You mean they weren't dumb enough to sell their freakin' souls to you?" The edge in my voice is sharper than B's tongue.

Clyde smirks. "None of them were as bold and fearless as you are, love." His eyes pierce mine. "You live life regardless of consequences and opinions. You breathe freedom and embrace danger." He pauses. "The making of a true queen." To some, such a statement might be alluring. Charming even. Not to me.

Heat rises from my core. "I'm no queen." I'm a damn killer.

Clyde reaches for my hand, squeezing it gently. "Why do you fight it?" He's referring to the power coursing through my veins. A limitless potential that woke the moment I laid hands on the *First Grimoire*. "You're stronger than ever. Don't you appreciate the new you?"

The killer me? I yank my hand back. "No." I don't appreciate it at all. I'd rather be powerless than a power-slave.

He laughs. "See, that's what I'm talking about, brutally honest even in the face of hell."

I have been accused of a lot of things, but brutal honesty is a cherry popper. "I'm a lying, scamming witch who never cared about anyone but myself.

Honesty doesn't fit in my world."

Clyde folds his hands in his lap. "Are you sure?"

"Yes."

He tilts his head to the side, grinning wickedly. "I assume dishonesty no longer bothers you then?"

Tugging my knees under my chin, I cock a brow. "You say that as if it ever did."

"And it didn't?" he shoots back.

"No."

His grin widens. "I see."

He tries to bait me. Yeah, wrong girl, pal. I hate mind games as much as I loathe the Knight of Hell. It's why I refrain from engaging in the topic further.

Silence stretches between us, the only noise the squeaking of my new roomies—a bunch of rats. Hey, compared to Chelsea aka the Nun they're not so bad to hang with. At least, they don't try to preach to me moral values.

My ankh-shaped birthmark on my back burns like hell. Has been since I performed the ritual last night.

"What is it?" Clyde sounds way too concerned for my taste. Seriously, if I didn't know better, I'd say he actually cares about my well-being. Ridiculous. He's the master, I'm the slave. Worry doesn't fit in the combo.

Digging my nails into the mark, I scratch as hard as I can.

He's behind me in the blink of an eye. "Let me see."

"No." I pull my shirt down, denying the demon access to my skin. "It's nothing."

Knights of Hell, like hunters, don't take "no" for an answer. He slaps my hand away, shoving my shirt upward.

His sharp exhale, followed by eerie quietness unnerves me.

"What is it?" I ask, gazing over my shoulder.

Clyde looks away.

"What do you see?" I press for an answer. "Tell me."

The click of the camera shutter resonates through the dungeon. Did he snap a pic of my birthmark?

"Here," he says, holding his phone under my nose.

Yup, he took a pic. And I don't like what I see on the screen. The veins surrounding my ankh-shaped birthmark are black. I look like Carrie on the night of her prom right before she slaughtered a whole school. The black pest spreads across my body like a freakin' virus—the deadly kind. "What the—"

The warning on the very first page of the grimoire flashes across my mind. "Great power comes at a great price," it read. "Be certain you're willing to pay it." Those were the nicest words in the whole book. Whoever wrote it, a witch so ruthless she'd make the devil fear for his throne, drifted into madness soon after writing those lines.

"Don't worry." He rests his chin on my shoulder, breathing sulfur on my neck. "You'll be okay. I promise, love."

"Okay?" I gawk at the pic. "That doesn't look *o-kay* to me." Gosh, why am I even scared? I literally just begged Alex to put a bullet in my brain. It's the only way to stop the impending end without breaching my deal with Clyde. Nowhere in my contract did he mention Alex would die if he killed me. It's my loophole. Besides, I don't fear death. Never have.

Then why are you shaking?

"You're the witch," he whispers, tracing his index finger over my blackened veins. "Tell me if I'm lying." His voice is steady, his breath even and there aren't any dishonest vibes coming from him—he's telling the truth.

"Tell me what's happening to me," I half plead, half scream.

"Darkness claims you," he says, pulling me against his chest. "Soon, you will be the queen you're fated to be."

Soon, I'll be dead. Just like you.

After a while, he rises to his feet. "Are you ready for part two?" he asks, gaze darting to the open page of the tome.

Am I ready to tip the scales in favor of evil?

No.

Do I have a choice?

You always have a choice. Even if it's a rotten one.

If I was braver, stronger, better, I'd tell the bastard to shove the grimoire up his ass and do the next ritual—the second of six—himself. I'm neither of the above. "Yes," I choke out. "I am."

Chapter 15

Alex

Icy wind howls through the alley, piling up fresh snow in drifts. It started a little over an hour ago, but there's already a thick white blanket on the ground. The radio gave a blizzard warning earlier. Not exactly a surprise. It's way below freezing, the air is moist, and the white crystals fall mercilessly. Great ingredients for a mother of a snowstorm.

"What's taking you so long?" B snarls, protecting her eyes with her arms.

Jesse scrubs his pick back and forth in the key hole, waiting for the crucial click. "Almost there."

She hugs her black coat against her chest, probably trying to lock out the cold. "You said that five minutes ago." She's right. My brother did say the exact same thing five minutes ago. But picking a lock isn't as easy as it looks on screen. You need to apply the right amount of pressure on the tension wrench and have the finesse to set all the pins.

Still, this isn't Jesse's first break-in. The door to Madame Josephine's—the one we've been canvasing for over four hours—should long be open. Hell, the witch herself should have swung it open for us. But neither she, nor Boohoo Princess answered B's desperate, bordering on mad, banging.

That doesn't give us a free breaking-and-entering card, I know. It's just, Bonnie was very convincing when she insisted something must be wrong. "You don't understand," she said, standing taller than the skyscraper behind us. "They'd never intentionally piss off a Lacroix." Neither would I. So I sorta believed her.

B taps her foot to an unsteady rhythm. She's on the brink of a nervous breakdown, has been since I told her about Manda's prison cell and her suicidal tendencies. What can I say? The mamba knows exactly how to get what she wants. In this case, she didn't rest until I told her what I saw.

My little brother doesn't appreciate the sound of impatience. He peeks over his shoulder, drilling holes in B's head.

"What about you?" she grumbles, paying no attention to Jesse's ill-mannered look. "You doing okay?" Had she not spit venom at me for the past two weeks, I'd say she's concerned. But hey, this is queen B we're talking about. The chick hates my face.

Leaning against the brick wall, I manage a half-hearted smile. "Peachy." That's a flat-out lie. My brain is pudding, my chest weighed down by a ton of stones, and a black hole devouring my gut. Seeing Manda behind bars, broken beyond my darkest imagination, fucked me up good.

She squints. "Sure? 'Cause you look like shit."

"I'm okay." She casts me a doubtful glance. "Really. I am." Except for the fact, Carter is on his way, bearing more bad news concerning Manda.

Jesse throws his fist in the air like a boss. "Yes!"

"About time," B grumbles.

He pushes the door open. B is all set to march in,

but he wraps his arms around her waist, pulling her back. "What are you—"

"Do you have a gun?" he whispers in her ear, lips dangerously close to her neck.

She stills in his arms. "N-no."

"Then you'll stay behind us."

B's cheeks flush a bright pink. I get the feeling it's not from the cold. Quite the contrary. "Let go," she mumbles, her shield of defiance crumbling.

"Will you stay behind us?" he asks, voice low.

A pretentious eye roll later, she nods.

"Promise me," he insists, still holding onto her.

"Okay." Her angry breath clouds the air. "I promise."

Pushing myself off the wall, I draw my Beretta, and build the advance party.

The dim lit hallway smells like roses and incense. Candles in all sorts of colors burn on antique drawers. Walls, on each side, are painted ruby, decorated with golden ornaments.

"Someone's a little paranoid," Jesse whispers, pointing at the colored glass shards hanging from the ceiling. An old Romani custom to keep evil at bay.

"A little?" Judging by the amount of glass swinging above our heads, I'd say Madame Josephine tried to lock out the devil himself.

Like promised, B stays in the back. "The curtain," she says, pointing to the black velvet hanging from the ceiling.

I scan the hallway one last time in case we missed something. We didn't. Then, slowly and deliberately, I draw the heavy fabric aside.

A sour stink crawls up my nostrils. Rotten meat,

drenched in vinegar.

B holds her hand in front of mouth and nose. "What's that smell?"

Jesse and I look at each other, both aware the mamba won't like the answer.

"Stay with her," I order, advancing into the square room.

B—always a handful—catches a glimpse over my brother's shoulder. "Josephine?"

Across from me at a round ebony table sits an elderly woman. Long gray hair cascades down her shoulders covering her face. "Ma'am?"

She sits there like a damn statue.

I move past suitcases scattered across the floor. Crystals, candles, herbs—all sorts of witch stuff. Shouldn't surprise me. According to Boohoo Princess, Madame Josephine was scheduled to return from Cassadaga. Yet something strikes me as odd. I just can't put my finger on what it is.

"Ma'am?" The foul smell of rancid eggs and spoiled meat is omnipresent. "Is everything all right?"

"Alex." B tries to get past the wall that's my brother. "What's going on?"

I reach for the woman's shoulder.

Cold as ice.

I'm aware what that means even before her head snaps back, bringing forth a scene straight out of an Alfred Hitchcock movie. Her eyes—or what used to be her eyes—are hollow sockets. Bloody, dried tears smeared across her pale cheeks.

"Shit." Jesse's face hardens. "Is she—"

"Dead," I assure him. Has been for a while, judging by the rigor mortis.

B pushes my brother, escaping restraint.

"Oh. My. God." The color drains from her face the second she spots the gruesome scene. "H-her…her eyes," she stammers. "Where are her eyes?"

I search the room for Madame Josephine's eyeballs. They sit on top of a massive berg-crystal in the center of the table—watching, evaluating, being uncannily empty.

Sadistic bastard.

Sarcastic, too.

C'mon, the irony isn't lost on me. A fortuneteller's eyes, decorating the very tool they use to catch a glimpse of the future? You gotta be a real sick piece of shit to pull something like that.

An angered customer maybe?

Did Madame Josephine's predictions get her killed? Maybe someone didn't like what the future has in store for him? It's possible. Most folks have issues accepting the truth, the reason Manda used to lie to them. And that one time she didn't—to the guy who later tried to rape her, the guy I saved her from—she almost got killed.

Maybe he figured the Roma witch scammed him?

People have the impression the whole crystal-ball thing is nothing but a hoax. A fair attraction, pulling money out of people's pockets. I did, too. Then I came across Elsa Hartford. Sixteen-year-old Elsa worked a fair in Kansas City while Jesse and I were investigating the suspicious deaths of four teenagers her age. All kids were fine one day. Coughed blood and dropped dead the next. The PAU got involved due to the hex-bags— small cursed bags, mostly filled with bones, herbs, and a personal item of the target—a parent found in the youngest victim's bedroom. Though Jesse and I had only worked one case before, Carter decided to give us the job. We were the closest agents to the crime scene, having just solved another case in Wichita. Anyway, imagine what we thought when we heard stories of a girl who foresaw all four deaths? Yup. Jackpot. We went straight to the fair, stormed into Elsa's tent, guns drawn, ready to kill. Little Elsa didn't even blink. She just sat there in front of her crystal, and assured us she'd expected us. The girl didn't give off any witch vibes. Only after she told us where we'd find the real culprit—a teacher slash witch at the local high school who was fed up with those brats, her words, not mine— that we learned little Elsa was only a quarter witch. Her great-grandmother had the curse. Elsa only inherited her ability to see what hadn't happened yet. The girl didn't just help us end the killing spree of said teacher, she also foresaw Manda. Told me about this girl I'd meet on a Sunday in an alley behind a pool hall. "You might think you saved her, but it's really her who's saving you," she said, before Jesse and I hit the road again.

"Alex," Jesse chokes out. "You have to see this."

I move toward him. He hovers over one of the open suitcases, face slightly green. "What's—"

Jesus Christ is that...an arm? I hunker down, shoving a red blouse aside. Yup. That's definitely an arm. Female. Red nail polish. Two rings on each finger.

B presses her palm over her mouth, muffling a high-pitched scream. "That's the girl from yesterday."

Boohoo Princess. At least, part of her.

Angry customer, my ass. Either the two women had an encounter with the next Ted Bundy, or slaughtered by something strong enough to rip a body apart, yet with enough tact to remove the older woman's eyeballs with surgical precision.

Something inhuman.

The ragged edges of the flesh supports my suspicion. This arm wasn't cut off. Rather ripped from the shoulder like a lion tears apart its prey.

Jesse wraps his arms around B, desperate to give her some sort of consolation, a bit of security in a damn slaughterhouse. "C'mon," he says, softly. "Let's get you out of here."

For the very first time since Manda vanished, B doesn't protest. Lips sealed, hands trembling, she allows my little brother to take her away from the most vicious side of death—murder.

I stay back, walking about the crime scene, hoping to find a clue as to what the fuck went down in here.

The positioning of Madame Josephine's body—on display for anyone who enters to see—tells me whoever did this wanted to make a point.

She's his artwork.

A piece of his soul he needed us to see.

What are you trying to say, you sick mother?

My gaze darts to her eyeballs. She was clairvoyant, caught a glimpse of what's yet to come. My gut says she saw something she shouldn't have.

That's not all. I feel it in my bones.

I'm missing something.

What?

The dead woman's fists are balled. Upon closer inspection, I spot a piece of paper. I have to break her fingers to get it out of her death grip.

Heart racing, palms sweating, I unfold the note.

Words scribbled onto it in an unsteady hand. I have a hard time deciphering them. But I think they say something like, "On the first day, she saved his soul. On the sixth day, she'll climb the throne. The prophecy is—" The note ends with no further clues as to what the hell any of this means.

Heavy footsteps resonate down the hallway. "Alex?"

I shove the paper in my pocket, hiding it from my brother's sight. Don't ask me why. I just don't want him to see it.

"Did you find anything?" he asks, moving closer.

The weightless paper burns a hole in my pocket. "No." I clear my throat. "Not yet."

For a second there, his eyes gleam with skepticism. He quickly discards his doubts. "Let's take a look around before the cops show."

"Where's B?" The mamba appeared shaken to the very core. Leaving her without supervision is a bit reckless.

He scrubs his fingers through his untamable hair. "She's waiting in the car." His voice alone tells me she isn't holding up very well.

Neither am I, by the way.

Jesse searches through the suitcases when the note, in my pocket, drains me of all energy. "Hey." He looks up. "I'm gonna check on Bonnie, okay?"

"Be right there."

"Take your time." I sure need some to wrap my head around the fact our only hope to find Manda is dead.

Chapter 16

That damn note means nothing. *On the first day, she saved his soul?* C'mon, that's a coincidence. *She* isn't Manda. *His* isn't my soul. Sure, it's weird I didn't go to hell, but Manda said it herself. There's no way out of a deal with hell. She couldn't have—

"You might think you saved her, but it's really her who's saving you," little Elsa's voice thunders through my mind.

Bullshit. Manda isn't stupid enough to try something so reckless. She'd never risk her own life just so I wouldn't go to hell, right?

Wrong. She took a damn bullet for me. And there's the fact she said she'd fight Lucifer himself for my soul. Did she…could she—

No. Manda's disappearance has nothing to do with my not going to hell. It can't. Please, God…tell me she didn't—

"Alex?" Jesse cuts through my thoughts. "Do you agree?"

"Agree with what?" I have no clue what he's talking about.

Eyes narrowed, he casts me a worried look. "JJ and Bay," he adds.

"What about them?" My body might have been here at Green House, but my mind was somewhere else completely.

Frustration seeps into my little brother's expression. "Have you even listened to what I said?"

No. "Sorry, I'm…tired." Universal excuse. Works every time.

B puts her coffee mug down. She's still shaken from the gruesome scene we found earlier. Removed eyeballs and ripped off arms are pretty hard to swallow. Even for agents who've worked this job for years. "Your brother wants to send them to Cassadaga." She shrugs a lazy shoulder. "I told him it was a stupid idea. He won't listen to me."

"Why?" Jesse mutters. "They're already on their way to Manda's mother. They texted earlier saying they'd be there in a little less than an hour. What's the harm in sending them to Cassadaga?"

"They're wasting their time." Manda isn't hiding at her mother's place. She's locked away in a supernatural prison cell. Something tells me Melinda and her son aren't in Florida either.

Jesse frowns. "At Manda's mom's or in Cassadaga?"

Probably both. "At Manda's mom's." I always knew Amanda Bishop would never voluntarily seek out her mother. The woman is…there are no words to describe Maria Bishop. But if this was a fairytale, she'd play the role of Snow White's evil stepmother. You know the one who asked the hunter to take her child to the woods to rip her heart out.

****

The night started like any other since I'd aimed the muzzle of my Berretta at Manda's head. I'd waited for my brother to sleep, grabbed my car keys, and hit the road. Driving around aimlessly, looking for a shithole where I could drink my sorrows away became my nightly goal. Bars, clubs—anything serving booze was good enough for me.

That night, I ended up in a cheap "even the devil wouldn't drink here" strip club. I didn't give a rat's ass about the coke lines they sniffed at the table behind me, or the fucked-up truckers drooling over the naked bodies of worn-out dancers. I was a man on a mission. The Drink Amanda Bishop out of My System mission.

Forgetting the witch who played me was impossible. I tried and failed. But I quickly learned enough bourbon could ease the pain of her betrayal, stitch up the hole she left in my chest. Even if just for a little while.

Aerosmith's "Cryin'" blasted through the speakers. The song resonated with my soul. So much so, I couldn't help but wonder if Steven Tyler had been in love with Amanda Bishop, too.

The night moved on, but I remained stuck in time, reliving the moment I learned the truth about the girl I saved in a dark alley, over and over. God, I will never forget how I'd opened that letter, addressed to me and me only. The pictures inside had been gruesome—a body shredded to pieces—what was worse though was the note attached to it. Amanda Caroline Bishop, *it* read. Descendant of Bridget Bishop, the first witch to die during the Salem Witch Trials. I'm sure you recognize her victim. You broke his nose.

At first, I thought it was a vicious joke. Someone— maybe Jesse—trying to mess with me. Manda wasn't a witch. Jesse and I sensed these creatures effortlessly. A tingle on the back of our necks gave their true identities away. The tingle I felt when Manda was around was nowhere near my neck. It was a flutter in my stomach, making me hot and cold at the same time.

I'd made some calls just to be sure my hunter senses weren't clouded by her pretty face. What I'd found out blew up my whole fucking world. "It's true," Carter had said. "Amanda Bishop is the great-great-great-great-granddaughter of Bridget Bishop. I'm going to e-mail you a pic of her driver's license."

In retrospect, I wished I hadn't opened that goddamn e-mail. I wished it hadn't been Manda's sparkling emerald eyes gazing back at me. I wished—

Wishes were nothing but hopeless prayers. And I was over them. Like I was over the witch who lied to me whenever she opened her alluring mouth.

I had five...okay, more like fifteen shots, flirted with one of the strippers who didn't rock Manda's endless legs, her wavy blonde thatch, or her smart-ass attitude, and started to feel all around less fucked up when a woman with long, ginger hair appeared next to me.

"Alexander Remington?" Her voice was like honey, sweet and captivating.

I didn't feel like company. Yet I couldn't take my eyes off the forty-something woman. She looked uncannily familiar. I was almost certain we met before. "Who's asking?" I sounded like a drunk shithead. I was a drunk shithead.

Ankles crossed, she leaned against the sticky counter. Her silk blouse, the pearl earrings, and the glamourous watch around her wrist didn't belong in a place like this. She'd be lucky if she got out of here without being mugged—or worse—by one of the assholes at the coke table. "We need to talk," she said, casually.

The nagging suspicion she deliberately dodged the Who Are You question chewed at me. "Sorry," I muttered, gaze locked on my empty short glass. "Not in the talking mood."

A sigh of disapproval roared out of her. "I can certainly see why my daughter is so infatuated with you."

I looked up. "Come again?"

She lifted her chin with confidence, reminding me of the one person I was dying to forget. "My name is Maria Bishop," she announced, matter-of-factly. "And we need to talk about Amanda."

Three things happened at the same time. One: the sensation washing down my spine when she appeared made sense. Because if she was Amanda's mother, she was also a witch. Two: I came to the conclusion I was a rotten hunter when wasted. Three: I almost fell off the barstool. I mean what in the name of God was Manda's mother doing here? Did Amanda send her? Was this an I'm-going-to-kill-you-for-threatening-my-little-girl visit?

"Alexander?" My name rolled off her tongue like acid. "I've come a long way to have this talk with you. The least you could do is have the courtesy to listen."

"What do you want?" I hissed, overwhelmed by the reality that I sat face to face with Maria Bishop—Amanda's mother—the woman I thought was dead because her daughter never once spoke about her.

Maria scanned the strip club. "Let's go somewhere more private."

I was drunk, not stupid. Walking out of here with a Bishop witch was suicidal, and I wasn't ready to die just yet. "No thanks."

I fished a fifty-dollar bill out of my pocket and slammed it onto the counter, all set to run for the hills.

I made it to the exit when she caught up with me. "You're a hunter." She seized hold of my jacket. "An Arrow of Artemis. You have an obligation to humanity. Are you really the kind of man to run in the face of the impending apocalypse?"

The impending apocalypse? Now I know where Manda gets her melodramatic streak. *"I have no idea what you're talking about, lady."*

She frowned. "Please"—she tilted her chin at an empty table, next to the exit—"hear me out? You own it to yourself and your legacy."

To this very day, I'm not sure why I agreed to listen to her. Maybe curiosity forced my feet toward the table. Or maybe the hollowness in my heart sat my ass down. Either way, I should have walked out of that damn strip club and never looked back.

But I didn't.

"You might find it odd I'm here," she started.

"Odd?" I laughed. "Doesn't quite cut it, lady."

She dragged out a sharp exhale. "I need your help, Alexander."

I knew I shouldn't have had that last drink. It made me hear things. Weird, creepy, impossible things. *"I beg your pardon?"* Maria Bishop couldn't have possibly asked me for help. She's a witch. They didn't go around asking hunters for favors.

Her teal blue eyes stayed on me. "I wish there was an easy way to say this…" She shook her head. "There really isn't."

My stomach twisted. I had no idea what she

wanted. Yet I couldn't shake the dreadful feeling any second the world would blow up right under my feet. "No offense," *I muttered, trying to sound less petrified than I was.* "But could you stop speaking in riddles and tell me what you want from me?" Before I send you to purgatory, *rested on the tip of my tongue. But that was still Manda's mother sitting across from me. The mother of the girl I'd spent the last three months with, the one that had stolen my heart only to throw it into blazing flames of lies and deceit.*

She met my gaze. "I need you to kill my daughter," *she blurted out, as if she had asked me to do some grocery shopping for her.*

I laughed so hard my stomach started aching. No way in hell Maria Bishop just seriously asked me to kill her child. No mother—not even a witch—would ask a hunter to murder her daughter. That was just insane.

Then I looked into her cold eyes and understood Maria Bishop was beyond serious. "Let me tell you about Amanda's fate," *she went on.* "I assure you when I'm done, you will see why she needs to die."

Frozen, I sat there and listened to the tale of a mother who had asked me to put a bullet in her daughter's brain. She painted a picture of doom and darkness, of a world in which the witch I let live would move on to become the queen of darkness. "She's going to raise hell, Alexander. You have to stop her."

"No."

She squinted. "No?"

I shook my head. "I'm not going to be your executioner."

Her eyes widened. "You don't understand, she—"

"Oh, I understand." *I looked the woman over,*

131

poison in my veins. "I understand you are throwing your own flesh and blood to the wolves. I understand you're ready to send Manda to purgatory for no other reason than a stupid vision you had when she wasn't even born."

Maria Bishop's face turned to granite. "You understand nothing. Amanda will bring upon the apocalypse and if you don't stop her, the blood of her countless victims will be on your hands, too."

I was ready to get up and leave. I needed to know just one thing first. "Why me? Why don't you do it yourself?" I had the nagging suspicion she wouldn't mind driving a knife through Manda's heart.

"She trusts you."

My brows flew up. "Seriously?" Manda was a witch, a damn smart one. She trusted no one. Least of all me—a hunter who had a gun to her head.

"She loves you."

Whoa, the woman was madder than I thought. Amanda Bishop only loved herself. Me? I was just a game for her. The let's-see-if-I-can-seduce-a-hunter game. She exceled at it.

I rose from the chair. "You're a damn witch. I'm sure you can think of a few ways to get rid of her." What the hell? Did I just encourage her to kill Manda herself?

"Magic can't touch her," she yelled after me.

I stopped dead in my tracks.

"She's an untouchable," Maria added, desperation in her voice.

I wanted to know what an untouchable was, but I could no longer listen to the abomination who dared to call herself a mother. So I stomped out of the strip club and started down the rabbit hole that would eventually lead me to hell.

****

"Alex?" B's nails dig into my shoulders. "What the hell is wrong with you?"

"I—" *Just remembered the night I first met Maria Bishop?* Nope. I'm not going to open that can of worms. It would lead to questions I couldn't answer. Like why did you really sell your soul?

Luckily, B has more pressing matters. "Tell him. Tell him how dangerous it is to send Bay and JJ to Cassadaga. The witches there don't take hunters lightly."

"She's right," I say, banishing the painful memories.

Jesse jumps up. "But—"

"But so is he," I assure Bonnie. "Maybe someone in Cassadaga knows why our only lead to Manda is dead." Or what the note is all about. "We have to try, B."

She crosses her arms. "What if they get killed?"

"They won't." JJ is one of the best hunters in the States. She can handle everything. I should know; she kicked my ass several times.

"Whatever," B grumbles. "Just don't say I didn't warn ya."

Jesse grins victoriously. "I'm gonna call them."

He moves toward the kitchen when someone unlocks the apartment door.

B is on her feet in a nanosecond. "Amanda?" Her face falls. Clearly, it's not Manda, trying to get in. "What the hell are you doing here?" she barks.

"I live here," the girl retorts.

133

The ominous roommate, I assume. The girl is the last person I'd expected to share an apartment with Amanda and Bonnie. She wears a long, black, turtleneck dress, and a massive gold cross dangles from her neck. She looks like a preacher's daughter compared to the two witches.

B slams her hands on her hips. "I thought you moved in with Jules?"

The chick pushes past B. "And I thought you and your killer friend were on the run."

"How dare you—"

"Oh, my goodness," the roommate shrieks as she spots my brother and me. "Two, Bonnie? Really? Isn't it bad enough you turned our apartment into a brothel? Do you have to add swinger club to the description?"

B is about two seconds away from killing her. I gotta stop her before she, too, ends up in a prison cell. "We're FBI," I say, showing her my badge. "Mrs. Lacroix is helping us with a case."

The Nun, as B calls her, cocks a brow. "Are you here for her whore of a friend?"

Whoa, did she just call Manda a whore? Maybe I should let the mamba kill her. "We can't talk about the case," I force out, my voice sharp and merciless. "But we'd certainly appreciate some privacy."

The Nun's gaze darts from me to Jesse, and back. "I wasn't going to stay near the best friend of a murderer, anyway." That said she marches to her room and disappears inside.

"She's—"

"The nightmare of my existence." B pauses. "But there's something different about her."

"What?" I inquire.

The mamba gawks at the Nun's door. "I'm not sure yet."

Chapter 17

Carter texted a little less than an hour ago. His plane—a private FBI jet—landed at JFK despite the heavy snowstorm tying up most of the air traffic. Perks of working for the government. They play by their own set of rules.

We're about to meet at a small coffee shop near Green House. Bonnie recommended it. We'd all rather stay at her apartment, but her odd roommate is still hiding out in her room. We can hardly talk about Manda in her proximity. The Nun is convinced Manda murdered that Jules chick—a friend of the Nun. Apparently, they got into it because of Pony-Boy—the douchebag Amanda dated while at NYU. The mamba summarized the whole drama for us. Turns out, B set Manda up for a date with Pony-Boy; his real name is DeLuca. Just for the record, I don't give a fuck about the asshole's name. Anyway, Manda resisted. B persisted. They hooked up and had somewhat of a casual sexual relationship. I asked the mamba to skip the details. Just the thought of Manda with someone else kills me. I really don't need graphic images to spend the rest of my life wishing I could decapitate the bastard for touching her. Long story short, we had to find another location to meet Carter.

"It's freezing," B complains as we head down Seventh Street into the heart of East Village—a hot spot for funky restaurants as well as old-school record stores.

Jesse inches closer, shielding her fragile body from the snow masses blowing at us. Damn, I think I was teleported into one of those cheesy high school flicks. Any second he's going to offer her his—

"Want my jacket?"

She casts him a sidelong glance. "And you're going to walk in your shirt? Brilliant idea, Little Remington."

"Don't call me that," he grumbles.

A smile tugs at her lips. "Why not?"

"Just don't." The only person who gets away with calling him Little Remington is Manda. She nicknamed him the night I saved her, right after Jesse invited her to join us for a drink.

The mamba cocks a brow, assessing my brother's frowny face. "I sense an inferiority complex."

"Yeah?" Jesse sighs. "And I sense bullshit."

I'm not in the mood for drama. "Did you hear back from Bay and JJ?" When Jesse called them, they'd just crossed the state line into Florida. He advised them to head to Cassadaga first. Solving the Madame Josephine mystery is a top priority. Her murder is somehow connected to Manda. We all know it. I mean, c'mon, it can't be a coincidence she was offed when we were looking for her, right?

He checks his phone. "Nothing yet."

Fuck.

Patience, Remington. Rome wasn't built in a day.

Maybe so. Yet I can't get over this emptiness in the pit of my stomach, continuously whispering time is of the essence.

"Et voilà." B proudly presents the coffee shop of her choice. From the outside, it looks like a small antique shop—round, old-fashioned tables, old trunks in the shop window, and plenty of other useless junk.

I push the door open, rushing into the cozy warmth. Snow crystals fall from my jacket, melting before they hit the hardwood floor. I scan the square room. An original Italian coffee machine sits behind a small counter. The barista, most likely one of the less fortunate students at NYU, steams milk for his only customer. The man, in his late fifties, constantly glances at his watch. He's definitely a takeaway kinda guy.

B is next to me. "Perfect, huh?"

"Yeah," I admit. "Nice and quiet." A great location to talk supernatural.

"Be right there," the barista assures us, looking over the silvery metal of the coffee machine. B gives him a polite smile, nods, and moves us to the table farthest away from the counter.

"So," she starts once we're seated. "Your boss, is he the witch hating kind?"

"Carter?" Jesse laughs. "Nah, he's the goofy, nerdy kind." Yup. Carter loves *Star Wars*—almost all of his sentences start with a reference to the cult classic—talks way too much, and has absolutely no filter. Basically, he's a sixteen-year-old in the body of a twenty-eight-year-old.

B's brows fly up. "Is that a 'yes' or a 'no'?" The mamba sounds a bit scared. Maybe she fears Carter travels with green wood.

"Don't worry." I lean back in my chair. "Carter is cool." Unlike old Alex, he distinguishes between good and evil witches. Back when Jesse and I started at the PAU, I had issues with his attitude. Old Alex believed witches were universally evil—creatures stealing little sisters couldn't be anything but. After several heated discussions, I asked him why he thought some witches were good. He told me a story about his grandmother who was hexed by a striga and saved by a white witch. Prime example of irony.

She taps her slender fingers against the table. "If you say so."

"Relax." Jesse squeezes her shoulder. "He's not going to hurt you."

She shrugs his hand away. "I didn't say he would."

No, you just thought it. But hey, I get it. She has to keep face.

"Welcome to little Naples," the barista greets us. "What can I get for you?"

We order three Americanos and two cookies for B. Then he ambles back to the counter, and gets started on our drinks.

The small bell above the door rings. The first thing I spot is the *Marvel's Avengers* laptop case tucked under Carter's arm. Several agents tried to tell him it's not very FBI to walk around with comic figures. He couldn't care less.

B's gaze drifts over our boss. He wears a standard FBI suit, a long black trench coat, and white Chucks. "Nerd, huh?" Something tells me she doesn't quite agree with Jesse's assessment.

Jesse grins. "You'll love him."

"Alex." Carter waves at us. Why, I'm not quite sure. It's not like you could overlook a dude like him. He's tall, slender but well-built, wears horn-rimmed glasses, has an edgy rather than baby-face, and is loved by the ladies. Well, until he talks about his *Star Wars* figures, which cost him more than a new Porsche.

He stomps toward us, shaking fresh snowflakes out of his light brown man bun. Oh, yeah, I never mentioned that, did I? Carter loves his hair. In fact, we believe he has a slight obsession with his long thatch. The only time I ever saw him lose his shit—apart from the succubus dilemma—was when Jesse playfully threatened to cut his bun off.

"Man"—he throws his arms around me—"I can't believe you found a way out of hell."

I'm about to clarify I did no such thing. Hell decided it didn't want me at the end of the day. But what's the point?

"You look like crap," Jesse says when Carter lets go of me. It might be rude, but it's the truth. He's paler than usual. Dark shadows linger beneath his eyes. His bun is what chicks call "messy perfection," and his beard hasn't been groomed in days. Did I mention Carter's hairy obsession extends to his face?

Carter pulls out the chair next to B. "You would, too," he says, plummeting down, "had you walked into a damn massacre last night."

"Massacre?" B's curiosity is obviously stronger than her fear of our boss.

Carter drinks her in. He's not the drooling kind. Beauty like B's, however, is hard to ignore. The instant Jesse casts him his best killer look he swallows his appreciation and smiles. "You must be Bonnie?" She nods. "From the New Orleans Lacroixs?"

Her spine turns to steel. "I am."

Carter extends his hand, a boyish grin tugging at

his lips. "Well, it's nice to meet you, Bonnie Marie Lacroix."

A real smile touches her cognac eyes. "Call me B."

Seriously? Up until a few seconds ago, she was petrified he might burn her at the stake. Now, he gets to call her by her nickname? I'm more and more convinced she doesn't have a hunter problem per se. More like an Alexander Remington issue instead.

I frown, frustrated by life itself. "Carter?"

He looks at me. "Huh?" He's so easily distracted. I wonder how he managed to get his PhD. Yup, it's *Dr. Landon Carter.* He's the youngest Harvard metaphysics PhD alumnus.

"The massacre?" I jog his memory. "You were saying?"

His smile fades into oblivion. "What I'm about to tell you isn't pretty." As if the dread in his voice hasn't told me already. "Promise me," he urges, his light blue eyes piercing mine. "Promise you'll keep it together."

I had the sneaking suspicion whatever made Carter leave the safety of his office would shatter my world into pieces. As he sits there, pleading with me to keep calm, I understand it won't just shatter it. It'll irrevocably alter it.

"Alexander?" Last time he called me by my full name, he was on the brink of death. "Promise me. Please?"

"Just spill it, dude." Making promises I'm not sure I can keep isn't my style. And beating around the bushes only agitates me. All things considered, it might not be such a great idea to fuck with me moments before he delivers a sucker punch.

A long stretch of silence poisons the air. At every

inhale, my lungs burn with...fear? Despair? Hopelessness? Jesus, I wish I could ignore the dreadful feeling in the pit of my stomach, the one that's been torturing me since Manda vanished. But I'm neither dumb nor naïve. It's time I faced reality. However cruel it may be.

"Do you guys remember the WW-mission?" he says, glaring at the napkin holder.

Jesse furrows his brows. "Kinda hard to forget, don't you think?" It's not every day the PAU sends you to Wewelsburg Castle, Germany to catalog the occult book collection of the notorious Nazi bastard Himmler.

"I told you the mission was about Himmler's whole collection, but—"

"Three Americanos." The barista puts the cups on the table. "And two cookies."

"Thanks," B says on behalf of all of us.

"Sure." He faces Carter. "What can I get for you, sir?"

Carter eyeballs our steaming coffees. "The same."

The barista nods. "Coming right up."

"Where was I?" Carter continues after he gets his coffee and the barista is out of hearing range. As I said, he's easily distracted.

"You told us the mission was about Himmler's whole collection," I jog his memory.

"Right." He shifts uncomfortably. "Well, I lied."

"Why?" Jesse asks. Carter never lied to us. He's always been an open book. So what was it about that mission that changed his honest nature?

He won't look at any of us. "Director's orders."

Surprise, surprise. The government has secrets.

"We were looking for a specific book," he goes on,

adding a ton of sugar to his Americano.

He sent twenty agents halfway around the globe for one lousy book? We had to go over the German's heads to get our hands on Himmler's collection. They had no clue we were there, acquiring—or rather stealing—books from the Black Sun room. The secret chamber, hidden behind the walls of the old castle, was an almost exact replica of King Arthur's infamous round table. Only Himmler had a black sun wheel carved into the stone table—pretty sure King Arthur didn't have one of those.

I narrow my eyes at him. "Must be one helluva book."

"It is." There's no hesitation on his part.

B cocks a brow. "And why's that?"

Our boss sighs heavily. "Because it's the *First Grimoire*."

The color drains from B's face. "T-The *First G-Grimoire*?" she stammers. "That's impossible. It's been lost for over two thousand years."

"It *was* lost," Carter corrects. "But the Germans found it when they invaded Egypt in 1941. The mission was called Sonnenblume."

B leans over the table. "That means Sunflower, right?"

Carter's appreciation of the mamba grows steadily. "Correct. Himmler convinced Hitler the ancient tome could help him build a new world order. He promised him the world would return to its former glory, blossoming like a sunflower. Ergo, Hitler named the mission Sonnenblume."

"Thanks for the history lesson," I grumble, slightly annoyed we're so far off topic. "But can we get back to the part where you tell us what this book has to do with Manda?" He clearly stated this was about her, didn't he?

"The *First Grimoire*," Carter says, hiding his trembling hands beneath the table. "Is the most powerful grimoire that ever existed. According to old legends, it was written by the First Witch."

"The First Witch?" Jesse sounds as clueless as I feel. Our mom used to tell us all sorts of stories. She'd sit Jesse, Natasha, and me down before bedtime, disguising old legends as fairytales. She never mentioned the First Witch.

Carter peeks over his shoulder. "We don't know much about her," he says, when he's sure no one is nearby. "There are a gazillion myths circulating around her. Some say she was half human, half demon. Others claim she was part goddess. The only two things everyone agrees on is she was the most powerful witch that ever walked the earth, and she went completely insane."

B nods. "From what I heard, she was betrayed by her one, true love. My mom said the pain froze her heart and drove her to darkness."

Yup, love can do that. Drive you insane, I mean. "All right, so a powerful witch went ballistic and wrote a book. I still—"

"A book?" B's eyes widen; her breathing becomes ragged. "You have no idea, Alex."

"She's right," Carter adds. "The *First Grimoire* in the hands of the wrong people? Worse than Hitler armed with nukes." An implication like that sounds beyond crazy.

"Are you saying the spell book of some lovesick

witch can end the damn world?" My belly cramps. That's never a good sign.

"If there's any truth to the things my mom told me about it"—B massages her temples, her eyes growing wearier by the second—"then yes. That book has the capacity to start the damn apocalypse."

Jesse's jaw drops. "For real?"

"Yes," Carter replies. "For reals."

"One story says the First Witch made a deal with hell. She would do their bidding in exchange for more power and access to the oldest secrets," B explains. "Hell agreed. And she quickly became their best asset, a fearless solider. Unfortunately, they didn't reckon what revenge could do. While the witch worked for them, she used the forgotten knowledge to find a way to punish her traitorous lover."

"But soon that wasn't enough for her," Carter continues the tale. "She looked at mankind and saw nothing but heartache and pain. That's when she decided to end it all. Legend has it, she was about to bring hell on earth."

"Hell on earth? Literally?" I sure hope that's a metaphor for something.

Carter shrugs. "We don't know."

Jesse scrubs his fingers through his hair. "You didn't read it?"

B props her elbows onto the table. "The *First Grimoire* was written in hell's language. Neither witches nor humans can read it."

"She's right," Carter says. "We had our best men trying to translate it. But it was impossible. They couldn't decipher it."

All right, Carter lied to us and sent us on an

unauthorized mission to Germany to get the grimoire of a revenge-seeking, mankind-hating witch. A book no one can use because it's written in hellish. That part I understand. "I still fail to see how any of this is connected to Manda."

"The book was stolen last night." Carter's shoulders sink. "They marched into the J. Edgar Hoover building, killed at least fifty-six agents, and broke into the high-security facility below ground."

"They?" The instant the word comes out I regret I asked.

Carter opens his laptop bag, pulling out his MacBook. "Here"—he shoves it my way—"see for yourself."

The screen flickers to life. The video playing belongs to a night vision camera right outside the main entrance. Two dead agents lie beside the revolving door. They wear their faces on their backs. Literally. Their heads turned 180-degrees.

"Shit," B hisses behind me. "That must have hurt." Like Carter, the girl has absolutely no filter.

Paying no attention to her and my little brother—both look over my shoulders—I keep my gaze glued to the screen. The timestamp below reads eleven twenty-two p.m. when a woman with long blonde hair marches out of the building. A large book tucked under her arm. She sorta looks like—

She turns to the camera.

"Manda?" I bark.

I was about to say that's impossible, but Carter zooms in on her. Flaming green eyes gaze back at me. They are unmistakably hers.

Carter squeezes my shoulder. "I'm sorry, Alex. I

wish things were different."

I jerk my head his way. "What are you saying?"

"The director saw the video." He pauses. "Manda is on the *Hunter's Most Wanted* list. Every single agent and freelance hunter is out looking for her. And if they find her, they will…" He trails off.

"Kill her," I finish for him.

He nods.

The next few minutes are a blur. Someone screams. Someone whispers. Someone paces. And I? I get up and walk the fuck away.

Chapter 18

I footslog through the blistering cold. Aimless. Clueless. Hopeless. I used to preach to Jesse that running is not an option. That someday, somewhere, shit comes back to bite you in the ass. Now, look at me. Marching through the snow, not the slightest idea where I'm headed, all because I couldn't man up and face the reality Carter presented.

I'm a fucking hypocrite.

But my mind is blank. I need time to think, to—fuck. Can I believe what I saw? Was it real or just a twisted fantasy? Did Amanda Bishop, the girl that would have died to save the kids of strangers, stomp into the J. Edgar Hoover building? Did she slaughter those agents? Did she steal a book with the power to end the world?

On the first day, she saved his soul. On the sixth day, she'll climb the throne. I can't forget that damn note.

The night is black, my soul dead. There's no use holding the contradicting voices in my head back. They speak louder than any AC/DC song ever could. *She's gone dark.* No, she hasn't. *She murdered federal agents.* She wouldn't. *She walked out of there with the* First Grimoire. There has to be an explanation for it. *Maybe Maria Bishop had been right all along. Maybe Manda was born evil. Maybe she is the bringer of the damn apocalypse.* Bullshit. I fixed fate. *Did you? Then why are you still alive when you should be in hell?* I...I don't know.

All I know is I want to forget. I *need* to forget.

A couple of feet ahead, I spot a sports bar—Dorian Gray Grill. I don't care for burgers, or shit. Booze is what I want.

"What can I get you, handsome?" a middle aged, pixie-haired waitress asks.

I climb onto the barstool. "Bourbon. Bottle."

She studies me. "Tough day?"

Tough year. I shrug.

She gets the I'm-not-in-the-mood-for-a-bartender-therapy hint and moves behind the bar to get what I so desperately crave. He's called Jim, surname Beam.

The bottle is empty. There's nothing left but me, myself, and a future reeking of darkness and pain. Drunk or sober, witch or no witch, evil or good—I love her. I, Alexander Ethan Remington, am in love with Amanda Bishop. A witch destined for darkness. A witch that might have killed over fifty people to steal a damn book.

You think that's bad? Here's what's worse; I don't care about those agents, the *First Grimoire*, or the pending apocalypse. All I want is Manda to be safe.

I can't explain why her life is more important to me than that of every other human being on this planet. I don't understand why all I'm worried about is her. But even when we're apart, I feel her pull. She's a magnet, attracting and repelling me at the same time. The reason I tried to push her away. Why I turned into a fucking asshole every time she was around. Don't just assume for a second I'm not aware of how awful I treated her.

The things I said to her—though she took a bullet for me and my brother—were wrong and shameful. The hurt in her eyes when I told her I only ever felt sorry for any guy dumb enough to fall for her? I saw it. Felt it. As if I had committed hara-kiri, stabbing a damn samurai sword through my own beating and bleeding heart. I deserved the pain, though. I mean who the fuck brings up the mommy issues of the girl he loves when he's aware her mom is out there looking for a way to put her in the grave?

An asshole, that's who.

A fucking coward who didn't know how to survive her proximity any other way. You see, Amanda Bishop was never just a forbidden drug, getting me high. She was…still *is* the girl I was…I *am* ready to live for. Yeah, I was supposed to say the girl I'd die for. Every damn love song ever written is about some dude who's ready to bite the dust for his girl. But here's the thing, I'd die for a fucking stranger. Almost did. Several times. Sorta comes with the job description of a hunter. PAU looks for Heroes Ready To Die For Others— that's me, Alex Remington. Except, I'm not a hero. I wouldn't take a bullet for selfless reasons. I'm the guy who isn't afraid of death because deep down he's aware he doesn't deserve to live. Natasha did. My little sister was sweet and caring. She had her full life ahead of her. Me and my selfishness are the reasons she never gets to grow old. Had I watched her, like my mom asked me to, she'd still be here. Instead, I chose a fucking PlayStation game over her. So yeah, dying is easy. Living for someone, knowing you'll have to carry all that guilt for another fifty or sixty years? That's petrifying, at best. Impossible, at worst. Yet despite everything, I saw a future when I gazed at Manda—our future.

None of that matters anymore, Remington.

Nope, it doesn't. After what went down last night in Washington, Manda tops the *Hunter's Most Wanted.* Freelancers, PAU agents—they're all out looking for the witch who presumably killed over five dozen of their own. Guilty or not, they will hunt her down, and kill her.

I slam the short glass on the table. *Over my dead body,* a roar echoes through my burned soul. I will not stand by and watch her die. I will find a way to fix this. Whatever the fuck it takes, I am going to make sure Manda is okay.

Oh, Remington, you said that before, remember?

How could I forget? It's how I acquired a first-class ticket to hell.

****

I lay in my motel room, eyeballing the Jim Beam bottle on the table. Whiskey in the morning. Tequila in the afternoon. Bourbon at night. Repeat. Sticking to this daily routine helped me through the past two weeks. The booze erased the images Maria Bishop had planted in my head in that rat-hole of a strip club. When I drank, I didn't think of Manda as the queen of darkness and bringer of doom. I only thought about getting my next fix so I wouldn't see her mesmerizing emerald gaze every time I closed my eyes.

Things changed last night. I'd woken to twenty-two missed calls from JJ. The huntress—one of the few humans who could actually kick my ass—and I had a casual Friends With Benefits *thing going in the past. For the time being, we had screwed each other's emptiness away. Good sex had always been the best way to forget how fucked up one's life truly was. But even back then, she never called me twenty-two times.*

Hazy and still wasted, I'd keyed in her number. She'd picked up on the first ring. "Alex," *she'd barked.* "Where the fuck have you been?"

Sleeping the bourbon out of my system. "What's up? Where's the fire?" *I'd assumed she needed help with a case. Never in a million years had I been prepared for what she had to say.*

"Have you heard from any of your grandpa's old hunter-pals, yet?"

"No. Should I have heard from them?"

"Shit. So you don't know, do you?"

My mouth tasted like a damn bar after weeks of neglecting to wipe the booze of the counter. I had no patience for rhetorical questions. "JJ, what the fuck is going on?"

"Is it true you dated a witch?" *JJ had never beaten around the bushes. Why would she start now?*

"Alex," *she yelled when I kept quiet.* "Did you date Amanda Bishop?"

I could have lied. "Yes. So?"

"Do you love her?"

Odd questions had always been her specialty. "No."

"So you do."

"I—"

"Then you should know her mother was here yesterday."

Wait. What? *"You spoke to Maria Bishop?"*

"She asked me to kill her daughter."

Yeah, I wasn't the only hunter Maria Bishop had

approached. According to JJ, the woman had been a busy bee, moving up the east coast, begging every damn hunter crossing her path to off Manda. She shared her horror tales, convincing them her daughter had to die, or all was lost. The icing on the bloody cake? The damn bitch made sure everyone knew about Manda and me. She had told them I refused to kill Manda, because I was truly, madly, deeply in love with her daughter.

And as if that hadn't been bad enough, I'd gotten hundreds of texts in the past few hours. All from hunters. All asking the same damn thing: Is it true, you're in love with a witch?

The only person who wasn't aware of what was happening was my little brother. And I was going to make sure it stayed that way.

"Sure you don't want to come?" he asked, strolling out of the bathroom, all dressed up in his FBI attire.

I shoved the pillow under my head and nodded. "You've got this." He wasn't going to hunt the vamp we've been tracking for days. He was just going to talk to some witnesses. Jesse could handle that. And more.

"All right." He grabbed the car keys. "See you, later."

"See ya."

"And Alex," he said, hand on the doorknob. "Try not to drink yourself into the grave, okay?"

My gaze darted to my best friend—bourbon. While he'd helped me through the past weeks, I had a nagging feeling he couldn't solve my current state of misery. "Get out of here."

He sighed heavily. There was something bothering him. But he knew me too well to get on my bad side on days like these. "Take care."

My thoughts revolved around hunters, witches, and death when someone knocked on my door.

I got up, certain Jesse had forgotten his keys. Again. But it wasn't my brother glaring back at me when I swung the door open. It was a tall dude dressed like James Bond with better shoes. Seriously, the leather sparkled.

"Can I help you?" I grumbled, on the brink of slamming the door in his face.

His lips twitched into a half-smile. "Alexander Remington?"

"Who wants to know?"

"I'm Legend," he said. "And we need to talk about Amanda."

Legend? As in the fearless and ruthless leader of the Malleus Maleficarum Order—a society dedicated to rid the world of demons? *I had heard stories about him and his companions. They were living legends in every sense of the word.*

I stood there, dumbstruck. What the hell was the super-hunter doing here? And had he really said we needed to talk about Manda, or was I imagining things?

"Can I come in?" He pushed past me, not interested in my answer.

I didn't appreciate the dude's attitude. "What do you want?" The edge in my voice clearly defined my emotions.

"Maria Bishop said you refuse to believe her?"

If I heard that name one more time, I was going to find her and kill her myself. Manda's mother or not, the woman was a piece of work I couldn't handle.

"Maybe you're more inclined to believe your ancestors." He pulled an ancient tome out of his bag.

I gazed at the blackened monstrosity, unsure what to make of it. The pages were tattered, the writing illegible.

Maybe you're more inclined to believe your ancestors, *he'd said. Probably because the book was written in old German. Despite my heritage—my mom's family had moved to the States from the land of Oktoberfest and beer—I'd never learned the language. I only recognized it because my grandpa had old hunting books in German.*

Legend rolled his sleeves up, exposing his arm-full of symbolic tatts—old, protective runes, Buddhist mantras, Hindu prayers, the Muslim symbol for Allah. The guy was a walking and talking manifestation of religion in all its forms.

"Let me help you." He hovered over the ancient tome and read, "And with the help of the First Knight, the queen of darkness shall rise. Born of the ashes of the oldest magic, blessed with second sight and endless power, the untouchable brings forth hell. For she is the key. She is the beginning and the end. Woe to you, Prince of the Dark. She will be what makes you afraid of the dark."

I had no clue what any of that meant. Frankly, I didn't want to know Legend's theory either. Something told me I wouldn't like it.

I was right. "I'm aware you have feelings for Amanda Bishop." He took a deep breath, masking the pity in his cold blue eyes. "But she needs to be stopped."

My voice slowly returned. "What makes you so sure this is about her?" It could be about any witch fated to be the new ruler of hell.

Legend came prepared for that question. He pulled a stack of photos out, scattering them across the table. "Look at them," he urged. "You know him, don't you?"

I recognized the photo he pointed at immediately. It was sent to me, anonymously, with a note stating Amanda Bishop was a witch. Yup, Legend had a photo of the dead mother who tried to assault Manda in that alley. "So?"

"All of these men are dead because they fucked with your witch one way or another," he blurted out.

I narrowed my eyes. "What are you saying?" Of course, I knew what he hinted at. That Manda killed them. That she was a killer that needed stopped. But I had to hear him say it.

"See that symbol?" He pointed at the chest of the alley asshole. A sigil—the personalized mark of a demon—had been carved into it. "Every single victim has the same mark. It's the mark of a Knight of Hell."

I burst into laughter. Not because any of this was funny, but what Legend suggested was even crazier than Manda being a heartless killer. "You think Amanda Bishop works for a demon?"

He shook his head, slow and deliberate. "No."

He confused the fuck out of me.

"I'm saying the Knight of Hell goes beyond and above to protect your witch," he continued his cryptic speech. "Why do you think he does that?"

I grew tired of the asshole. "Enlighten me," I barked, arms crossed.

"Amanda Bishop is the key to unlocking hell," he said. "And this Knight of Hell will do anything to draw her to the dark side."

Fear chewed at my gut. "Did you watch too much

Star Wars *as a kid?" I tried to sound cool and funny; he didn't need to know how petrified I truly was.*

He drew a deep breath, meeting my gaze. "Unlike Maria"—they obviously knew each other well enough for first name basis—"I'm not here to ask for your help, Remington."

Had I mentioned how badly I wanted to smash the dude's face? "Then why are you here?"

He gathered the photos and the book, shoving them in his bag. "This is a courtesy visit," he announced after a short pause. "We're both hunters. You deserve to know that all of my men are out looking for Amanda. They have strict orders to kill her."

My heart failed me. The tales told about the Malleus hunters were gruesome. They had never shown mercy, and once they set their eyes on a target, they finished the job. In short, Amanda was a dead woman walking.

I wanted to throw the bastard out and call her. Someone needed to warn her. Handling a bunch of freelance hunters was one thing. Being on the kill list of the Malleus Order something completely else. There was just one problem. Legend's visit wasn't just to inform me. The guy was smart. He'd calculated the odds and assumed I'd get in touch with Manda. Then he'd only have to track my call, or follow me and bada bing, bada boom Manda would be six feet under pushing daisies.

Nope. I wasn't going to play his game. Manda was intelligence walking. She had never used her real name when checking into motels, only paid cash, and hadn't left a paper trail so far. I had always kept tabs on her— even when I tried to forget her existence. So it's safe to say it's easier to spot Elvis' ghost than Manda. Meaning, they wouldn't find her unless I helped them, or she wanted to be found.

"Thanks for the heads up," I said, holding the door for him. "And good luck with your hunt."

He left without another word.

I swore an oath, right then and there. I would not stand by and watch Manda die. I would find a way to fix this. Whatever the fuck it took, I was going to make sure Manda would be okay.

****

"Classy." Jesse yanks the short glass out of my hand. "Real classy, bro."

My gaze darts from him to Carter. The two have me surrounded. Carter raises his brows. "You're getting shit-faced while your girlfriend is out there wreaking havoc?"

I smirk. "What do you want me to do? Call the witchbusters?" It's either sarcasm or a mental breakdown. I don't think Carter and Jesse could handle the latter. Not when I have a gun in my holster.

"Shut up," Jesse hisses. Last time he wore that particular expression in tenth grade, he'd beaten up Tom Stratford for being an asshole to his girlfriend Kimberly. The girl wasn't the brightest bulb and Tommy-boy loved to embarrass her. By the time my little brother was pulled off Tom, Tommy-boy lost most of his front teeth. Guess the joke was on him. Yup, high school never forgets when a senior gets his face smashed by a fifteen-year-old.

I keep my gaze on the counter. "How did you even find me?"

Jesse pulls a barstool out. "Your phone has GPS,

remember?"

How the hell could I forget little brother is watching me? I scan the bar for the mamba. "Where's B?"

Jesse averts his gaze.

Uh-oh, I sense trouble.

"She wanted to be alone," Carter answers.

"Like me?" I shoot back.

Carter sighs. "All right, Remington, spill it."

"Spill what?"

He nods at Jesse, signaling it's his turn to break down my walls. "Carter thinks you're hiding something."

I eyeball my boss. "Does he, now?"

"C'mon, Remington." He inches closer, lowering his voice. "Do you think I won my PhD in the lottery?"

God, he's killing my last nerve. "Will you leave me the fuck alone if I say 'yes'?"

"I saw the look in your eyes when you watched the video," he goes on, constantly scanning the bar for spies. "You weren't surprised. You were scared. And when I told you about the prospect of Amanda raising hell, you didn't even blink. Why's that?"

I try to play it down. "I'm unshockable."

"That's not even a word," Carter counters.

"Dude." Jesse's hand lands on my shoulder. "Carter has a point. I know you better than I know myself. Your reaction was definitely odd. So how about you drop the bullshit and tell us what the fuck is going on?"

Whatever deal I made with the demon is void. I'm not in hell and—whatever. The point is why am I sticking to the terms and conditions of a deal that no longer exists? I meet my brother's gaze. He was turned into a zombie, trying to save my soul. At the very least, he deserves the truth. "You want to know why I sold my soul, Jess?"

He furrows his brows. "Yeah, but—"

"For—"

Two phones cut me off. Jesse's rings; mine buzzes.

A text from B. "There's something I have to tell you about Amanda and Leandro," she wrote. "Meet me at my apartment in twenty."

I don't have time to question her weird message. Mostly, because my brother screams into the speaker of his phone. "Are you sure? They're all...*dead*?"

All heads turn our way. Jesse couldn't care less. He paces up and down, up and down—kinda like Road Runner on steroids.

"Shit," Jesse barks, once he's off the phone.

"What's up?" I ask.

"They're all dead," my little brother murmurs, eyes wide.

"Who's dead?" Carter inquires.

"The witches," Jesse says.

I understand jack. "Which witches?"

He sighs. "JJ called. Cassadaga is a ghost town. Literally." He swallows hard. "The whole community was slaughtered, Alex."

What? "How's that even possible?"

He shoves a text from JJ under my nose. It's a pic of several corpses. Behind them, on a wall, is a note written in blood. It reads, *On the first day, she saved his soul. On the sixth day, she'll climb the throne. The prophecy comes true when the moon*—it ends right there. Awesome. Just awesome.

Carter's lips part. But whatever he's got to say dies along with the lights, and all electric equipment. Folks groan. Some, including us, move outside.

NYU is dark. There's a damn power outage across the city.

What the fuck is happening?

Chapter 19

Amanda

The *First Grimoire* is lit up. Letters glow like molten lava. Blood—my blood—courses over the blackened pages of the oldest and most powerful spell book ever written.

"Finish the spell," one of Clyde's minions—a faceless creature with hollow eyes, and no nose—barks.

Knees weak, palms sweaty, I face Clyde. He sits across from me, completing the circle his five faceless minions formed around the makeshift altar. He shows no remorse, no mercy. And I know...I just know it's pointless to argue.

"Do it," faceless creature one barks. "Do it now!"

Icy shivers run down my spine. I have already unleashed darkness. The moment I finish the spell, the instant I chant the last line, the eternal balance between good and evil will tip. Only God knows how many innocent people will lose their lives due to what I'm about to do.

Can you really live with that, Amanda?

Now I have a conscience? Where were you when I barged into the headquarters of the FBI, huh? Or when I caused riots all over the damn country?

Fuck. I close my eyes. Alex's remarkable face blazes behind my eyelids. If I don't follow through with this, he's going to rot in hell.

Yeah, but what happens if you do go through with it?

The world is based on the Yin and Yang principle—light and darkness weigh each other out. A tip of the scale in favor of evil could have unforeseeable consequences. And I'm not just talking about more wars, mayhem, or demons and other evil creatures flooding the world. I'm talking about upsetting Mother Nature which, if you look at history, never ends well.

"Amanda." Clyde's smoky voice roars through the dungeon. "I understand you're scared, but it must be done."

Heat flushes my veins. "Why?" I narrow my eyes at the Knight of Hell. "Why do you crave destruction, Clyde? Don't you understand this book will be the end of all things?" I eyeball his minions. "Including hell?"

He blows out a pained breath. "Destruction is an ugly word, love. I'd like to think of it as a new beginning." He smiles. "A new world order."

He's insane. The Knight of Hell has lost his damn mind. "A new beginning?" I slam my hands on my hips, before I jump over the altar to cut the stupid grin off his face. "How is opening the gates to hell a new beginning?"

"We'll be free," he replies, matter-of-factly. "Free to go wherever we please, to do whatever we want. To be with—" He stops himself.

He truly is delusional. "Have you read the *First Grimoire*?" I don't think he has. Or else he'd know what happens when I do the last of the six rituals. "There'll be no freedom for you and your kind, only death and—"

"Enough." Clyde's voice shakes the walls of my prison. "You will do as I say, or our deal is void and your lover boy will go to hell."

I love Alex. Gosh, I wish I didn't, but he's the only man I ever pictured a tomorrow with. But this…it's no longer about the lives of a few in exchange for his. It's Alex or the whole fucking world.

Clyde is done being patient. "Amanda, finish the bloody ritual."

I'm sorry, Alex. I'd die for him. Fuck, I would have gone to purgatory for the hunter who hates my guts. But I won't do that. "No."

Whispers roar through the dungeon. The five faceless demons are frozen.

Clyde slowly rises to his feet. "Come again?"

Balling my fists, I dig my nails into my palms. Warm crimson traces down my wrist. "I won't do it."

He laughs. "Oh, yes. Yes, you will." The bastard is so sure of himself, he doesn't even blink.

He forgot whom he's dealing with. Broken or not, I still invented this game. No one will beat me at it. "I said, no, Clyde." The jugular vein in my neck pulsates. "If you want to end the damn world, you better do it yourself. I'm done being your bitch."

I halfway expect him to snap his finger and kill Alex and me right away. When his expression softens instead, I'm even more worried. "Tell me, love. Is it really wrong for me to aspire freedom? You, of all people, should understand how it feels to be locked away in a dark place, knowing everyone else can roam around freely and carelessly." He's in front of me, squeezing my hand. "Can't you see we're not that different? You broke out of your prison. All I want is to get out of mine."

"How do you even know all of that?" Last time I checked, I didn't advertise the reality my mother locked me away in the attic, or how I swore to myself no one would ever cage me up again when I grew up.

His liquefying amber eyes pierce mine. "I know *everything* about you, Amanda Bishop." He inches closer, his sulfur breath beating against my cheek. "Help me," he pleads. "And I will honor our deal. Alexander Remington can go on living his life. He'll grow old and gray with a pretty girl, raising his own family. Isn't that what you always wanted for him?"

Sure. There's just a tiny problem. If I do as Clyde asks, there won't be a future for Alex. There won't be a future for anyone. "No," I say, standing my ground. "I won't become the destroyer of the freakin' world. Take my contract and set it on fire, send Alex to hell, and ship me to purgatory. I. Don't. Care."

He sighs heavily. "You leave me no choice." He nods at faceless demon number two. "Show her," Clyde demands.

The creature floats toward me; his hooves never touch the ground. An iPad rests in his massive palm. "Press play," he orders.

I hesitate. Judging by the nasty, dark red surrounding the minion's whole being, I'd say I won't like what I'll see. The thing is I don't have much of a choice. My thumb connects with the display.

I hear crying. A child sobs uncontrollably. Someone—a woman—screams, "Don't make him watch, I beg of you."

It takes a second, but I quickly realize I'm well acquainted with that voice. "Melinda?"

The camera swings to the left, exposing a scene right out of a *Saw* flick. Melinda is chained to a rusty hook in the ceiling. She's naked except for a steel head-cage sitting on her shoulders. Her body is covered with cuts and bruises, and she's forced to stand on the tips of her toes, or else the chains around her neck will suffocate her.

Pressure builds in my chest. I'm going to kill the bastard. I swear, I'll—

The cameraman turns the focus on a playpen and my heart stops beating altogether.

Clyde grins. "I told you I've been around for a very long time, love." He traces a finger over Leandro's red face. "Did you really think I hadn't considered resistance from you?"

I'm drowning in Leandro's tears. His bloodshot shamrock eyes crush my lungs. Breathing is no longer an option. Clyde has Melinda and Leandro. My sister and my little boy are prisoners of a freakin' Knight of Hell.

What have I done? Striking a deal with hell was supposed to keep the people I care about safe. Clyde swore he'd protect Melinda and Leandro from the Malleus Maleficarum Order gunning for me and therefore my family. But what was it Grams used to say? *It's all about the wording, Manda.* How freakin' right she was. Because Clyde never once said he'd keep my family safe from himself.

Clyde snaps his fingers. Minion number two floats back, taking his place in the circle. "So." The bastard lifts my chin. "What do you say, love? Shall we finish the ritual?"

They say you always have a choice—get up or stay

down, live or die, love or hate, destroy the world or watch your family die. I'd gladly accept eternity in purgatory. But I wouldn't trade the life of my little boy for the world. Literally.

"I knew you'd come around," Clyde says as I reach for the bone of a saint sitting next to the evil tome.

Don't do it! Once the gate is open, all will be lost. You can't save them. They'll perish regardless. Maybe so. But I have to try.

Once the circle is complete, I lift the bone above my head. "*Tsud ot nrut llahs yloh sgniht lla.*" I pierce the ulna into the blazing book and watch as it turns to ashes and dust before my eyes.

Clyde and his minions clap and cheer.

Mother Nature responds, too. Her wrath moves the ground. Her scream sounds like extended thunder, but the vibrations come from below.

Walls crack, pieces of ceiling come down, and the lights of the seven black candles flicker rapidly before they finally go out.

Clyde's hands are on either side of my shoulders. "You did it, love."

Yeah, I have become death.

"We can't lose the crescent moon." He glares at his watch. "The third ritual must be done, now."

"I've read the book," I grumble. The second and third ritual are connected. One tips the scale, the other summons Clyde's legion. The bastards will bring chaos and murder once they escape hell.

"Would you like a moment before we continue?" He almost sounds worried.

A moment to think about what I just did? Who I've become? "Nah, thanks. Let's get this over with."

Chapter 20

Alex

The City of Dreams is reduced to rubble. Carter, Jesse, and I stood outside Dorian Gray's gazing at New York's dark skyline, when a petrifying rumble from deep within the belly of the earth struck fear in every living and breathing creature.

At first, I couldn't figure out what the terrifying noise was. Someone, I believe an elderly man, screamed, "We're under attack!" He waved his hands frantically. "Everybody get off the streets!"

Images of falling twin towers and folks leaping to their death flickered across my mind. Terror seemed a valid explanation for a city wrapped in darkness, a city hit by the snarl of a beast. Then the ground beneath our feet shook. Cars tossed about. The earth cracked right in the middle of the street. The building across from us collapses like a Lego brick tower. A dust avalanche came down. Screams echoed through the night. People ran like headless chickens—into the buildings, away from the buildings—looking for safety when there was none.

I turned and watched concrete rain down on the folks in the sports bar—the same bar I just had a few drinks in. Until the day I die, I will never forget the look on the waitress' face when a heavy chunk of ceiling crashed onto her head, splitting it in two.

"Run," Carter yelled. "We gotta get away from the buildings."

Jesse and I looked at each other, both sharing the same thought. *Where do you run when the whole city comes down?*

Carter seized hold of us, dragging us into the center of the street. "Stay away from walls and exits, you hear me?"

I'm not sure how long we stood there, but it was long enough to catch a glimpse of death and destruction, endless fear and desperation.

After the big one ended, we tried to help the ones that weren't lucky enough to have a Carter by their side. The three of us pulled folks out from underneath concrete, secured a family trapped in a thrown over car, and tried to keep our own fears in check.

Soon, though, we'd be tossed into a pit of despair. A fire truck got to us. "The quake shook the whole world," the chief said, after Carter showed him his badge. "London, Berlin, Moscow, Canberra—every country has been hit."

"That's impossible," Carter said. "Seismic activity is usually confined to one area."

"Don't tell me, son," the chief replied, gazing at the ashes of what used to be East Village. "Tell Mother Nature."

Our boss didn't feel like a chat with nature. Instead, he organized a satellite phone and called his boss, Agent Jack Melbourne, Director of the PAU. He confirmed what the chief had said. A magnitude nine earthquake had hit the world. The energy—an energy unlike any ever detected—according to specialists released from the inner core rather than the lithosphere. We all knew a quake like that couldn't be natural and if it wasn't natural it was most likely supernatural.

Melbourne sent a helicopter for Carter. He needed him back at headquarters to go over the data and coordinate the next steps. Jesse and I were offered a place, too. But we declined for the same reason. B was still in Green House. We had no idea if she was alive or dead. Neither my brother nor I would leave without checking on her.

So, that's where we're headed now. To Green House, praying the mamba made it out of there in one piece.

"Hurry up," Jesse barks, jumping over debris. I understand his fear better than I care to admit. Even though B hates my face, and despite her annoying attitude, I grew to like her. Besides, after everything that happened today—Manda possibly stealing an end-of-world-grimoire, a power outage, and a world under quake attack—I'm not sure I could handle a dead mamba on top of it.

Green House still stands. A good sign.

Without a second thought, we move inside. Miraculously, the building is mostly unharmed. Except for a few pieces of cement that came down from the ceiling and a couple of unhinged doors, the student accommodation looks like heaven compared to the hell we just escaped.

The hallways are deserted. Books and papers scattered over the floor. I step on abandoned horn-rimmed glasses. It appears most students left their apartments when the earth roared to life. Grave mistake. The streets outside are death zones. Bodies strewn all across the ground. Houses reduced to ashes.

Jesse reaches the apartment first. He doesn't bother knocking. He kicks the damn door down. "B?" He searches the place. "B, where are you?"

Faint sobs float through the common room. "Hey." I seize hold of my brother's jacket. "Do you hear that?"

We try to locate the source. "There"—he points to the room of the roommate—"see the light?"

"C'mon," I say, wasting no time.

The Nun rocks in a corner. Knees tucked under her chin, she holds her phone in a death grip.

"You okay?" I ask, extending my hand.

Eyes glazed over with horror, she manages a nod.

"C'mon"—I pull her up—"let's get you out of here."

Jesse is between us in a heartbeat. "Have you seen B?"

"S-she…" Her voice trails off.

"Where is she?" My brother urges. "Tell me!"

"Basement. They all went to the basement."

Why would B go to the b—?

"What are you waiting for?" Jesse barks, dragging me toward the hallway. "Let's go find her."

"Wait," Chelsea half-screams, half-pleads. "Can I…can I come?"

Annoying or not, we can hardly leave her here. "Come on."

Green House is a damn labyrinth and if it wasn't for the Nun, we probably never would have found the damn basement.

It's dark and shabby down here. The scent of mold wafts through the air. Our only light source is the flashlights on our phones. The farther we head into the blackness, the harder I'm hit by an odd sensation—something isn't right. B is too smart to run through the whole building to hide out in a death trap. Let's face it; the reality Green House is still standing is sheer luck. Had it collapsed like so many other houses, the basement would be the last place anyone wanted to be.

We walk past the bike storage. Chelsea is behind us, shaking with fear. "Are you sure B went to the basement?" I ask, unable to shake the nagging feeling we shouldn't be down here.

"Yes," she said. "A few of the guys came for her. I heard them talk about the basement."

Jesse thinks I didn't see him flinch when she mentioned guys. I did.

"B?" he yells. "B, are you down here?"

She doesn't reply. No one does.

Jesse's calling grows more frantic by the second. "B, for fuck's sake! Answer me!"

Water drips from the ceiling. The quake must have burst a pipe. The sound immediately takes me back to the basement of pedophile Walter's lake house. I'll never forget what went down there. I almost had to decide between my little brother and Manda—an impossible choice. Not to mention the sight of kids, confined to dog kennels, abused on a daily basis by Walter and his bokor friend Francoise. As I stood there gazing into horrified eyes of innocent children, I couldn't help but think of Natasha. What if the witch that took her didn't just kill her? What if she was tormented like the kids in Walter's kennels? A fate worse than death. The prospect of my little sister enduring such things turned my stomach upside down. For the first time since she'd vanished off the face of the earth, I prayed she was dead rather than tortured alive.

"Alex." Jesse nudges me. "Do you smell that?"

The hair on my neck stands on end. Something stinks. Literally. It smells like rotten eggs. "Sulfur."

Adrenalin pumps through my system. Instinctively, I reach for my gun. Jesse does, too.

Alert, we move through the last door on the corridor. A bunch of cartoons lie around. Killer heels peek out from underneath. "Bonnie?"

Jesse runs toward the boxes, kicking them aside. "Shit. It's her," he says. "She's bleeding."

I'm all set to attend to them, but I never get a chance.

A snap echoes off the walls. Jesse drops like a sack of hot potatoes.

I spin around. "What the—"

A familiar face looks back at me. "Hello, hunter." Demon-Boy smiles. "Nice to see you again."

Then something wooden aims for my head. It looks like—

Fuck!

A baseball bat.

Chapter 21

Somewhere in the distance water drips onto metal. The only other noise, a remorseless high-pitched ringing assaults my scrambled brain. I will my eyelids open. They don't comply. Darkness swallows me like a hungry T-Rex.

What the hell happened?

I don't remember shit. My memories are obscured by a misty veil of pain and cluelessness.

The harder I try to recall how I got here—wherever here is—the worse my head hurts. It's comparable to someone using my left temple as a voodoo doll. Last time I felt so fucking awful, I woke in a motel room wearing nothing but boxers and Manda's bra. I've never been into crossdressing and didn't have the slightest idea how I ended up in Amanda's lingerie. Luckily or shamefully—depending on how you look at it—my little brother brought me up to speed. He shoved a video under my nose. Turned out, I was so wasted I voluntarily put on the witch's bra to imitate Taylor Swift. My performance of "I Knew You Were Trouble" was epic, or so Manda said. Like now, I couldn't remember the actual deed. All I knew was I should have never had that last drink.

Did I gulp down gallons of bourbon again?

I taste blood, not booze.

But if it wasn't bourbon that did this, then what

did?

"Alex, open your eyes."

Manda? Is that her? How did she—

"Jerk-face," she barks. "Open your freakin' eyes. Now!"

Yup. It's her, all right. No one else gives me orders. They treasure their lives.

"C'mon." Soft fingers trace my aching jawline. "You gotta pull it together, hunter-heroic. They need you."

They? Who are they? Need me for what? Fuck, what the hell is she talking about?

She cups my face. Her warmth spreads through my body like a wildfire. "Alex, please. You gotta trust me. Jesse and B need you. Just…open your eyes."

Jesse…B…Jesse…B… Their names play in my head like a broken record. Shattered memories flash across my mind's eye.

Dripping water.

Boxes.

High heels.

Jesse dropping to the ground.

Then—

Wood.

Wood and pain.

Was I…was I hit on the head?

"Alex," Manda yells. "Why do you have to be such a stubborn jerk? For once…just for once listen to me and wake the fuck up!"

I want to scold the witch for shouting at me while I'm rocking a Terminator-fist-fight headache. I can't move my damn lips, though. Every time I try, it feels as if someone is giving me a shave with tweezers.

Seriously, what the actual fuck is going on?

I focus on my eyelids. It takes all my energy to open them. Seeing through two thin slits, I scan the murkiness for Manda. My vision is too damn blurred to make out shit.

Warm liquid curves down my temple, spilling into my left eye. The scent of rusty iron stings my nostrils— blood. My blood. I attempt to wipe it off my face. Only, I can't move my hands either. Metal bites into my wrists, burning off skin and exposing flesh. Shackles. My hands are cuffed behind my back.

Shit. This is bad. You're-going-to-end-up-dead bad.

I gotta get the hell outta here and find my brother and B. The hunter instinct kicks in. Pushing the heels of my shoes into the ground, I want to lift myself up, but fail miserably. Partly, because I'm dizzy as hell and totally off balance. Mostly, because my damn ankles are in shackles as well.

"Manda?" I choke out, mouth dry. "Help me."

She doesn't.

Sadistic thoughts crawl out of the depth of my soul. *Did she—could she—what if—* I can't bring myself to finish them. Manda would never intentionally hurt me. Besides, why would she plead for me to open my eyes if she had anything to do with this? It doesn't make any sense.

I put a lid on the I-doubt-Manda cup when I hear footsteps. Someone's coming. Someone who stinks like rotten eggs. A demon. Or two, judging by the different set of steps.

A bucket of ice water lands in my face. The cold ripples through my skin, causing violent shudders.

My eyes pop open. A figure approaches me, remaining in the safety of the shadows. "About time, sleeping beauty." The woman's voice rings several bells. "I was *that* close to kissing you awake." Whoever the woman is, it's not Manda. Of that I'm one hundred percent certain.

My heart races like a mother. Struggling to free my wrists, I fight the metal. My only achievement? I tear my skin some more. *The cuffs are too tight*, the hunter suggests. *Only three ways to get out of them. One: cut off a thumb.* Not going to happen. *Two: pick the damn lock.* How? I ain't got no tools. *Three: the key.* I don't think the chick—probably a demon—is going to hand it over without a fight, one I can't possibly win when I'm cuffed.

"Don't bother, hunter." She laughs, wickedly. "You aren't my first rodeo."

I'm dying to tell the bitch to go back to hell. But remember the shave with the damn tweezers every time I attempt to open my mouth? Well, that might be due to the duct tape, covering my lips.

"Believe it or not," she says, her face obscured by darkness. "I am truly sorry we must meet like this. But desperate times...yada, yada, yada. You get the point, don't you?"

I, too, am sorry we have to meet like this. I'd rather be able to stand on my own damn feet to put a damn bullet in her brain.

"You and your brother are quite the legends where I'm from," she continues. "Would have loved to see if the rumors about the mighty Remington brothers are true. But what is it you humans always say?" She pauses, tapping her foot against the concrete. "You don't always get what you want, do you?"

What I want to say is, I'm gonna send you back to hell, bitch. What comes out of my mouth is, "M mm m m m m m, m."

"What was that?" Her nasty laughter echoes off the damp walls. "Sorry, I didn't get you."

Fuck you! "M m!"

"Oh, you enjoy my company?" She sounds so damn innocent I want to puke. "You're so adorable. A real sweetheart."

"M m m m m m." Translation: I'll rip your fucking head off.

"Love your enthusiasm, Alexander. I'm absolutely certain we're going to have a fabulous time together." She turns away. "In the meantime, make yourself at home."

The bitch and her silent companion walk away.

The instant I hear a heavy iron door slam shut, I try to free myself again. The problem remains the same; without a bobby pin, or a nail I can't pick the damn lock.

I think of my mom. What is it she used to say? *There's always a way out, Alex. Sometimes you just have to think harder, be smarter.* In this case, I'm afraid, I'd have to be Harry Houdini.

C'mon, Remington. Think!

I scan my surroundings. Old pipes climb up the walls, covering most of the ceiling. I search for rusty nails or anything that could help me escape. But nothing appears. The chick was right. I am not her first hostage. Most likely won't be her last either.

I have no clue how much time slips through the hourglass, how long I sit in the dark, desperate to find a way out of this mess. Slowly, though, I begin to lose my fucking mind. My brain conjures up a million horrifying scenarios—Jesse and B hurt, Jesse and B being tortured, Jesse and B dead. The fear of what the bitch did to them, what she might still do to them, drives me insane.

God, what the hell did we get ourselves into? Who is the bitch? And what does she want from me? She took me hostage. I'm fairly certain she could have killed me, too. Why didn't she? I've been doing this job for so long, how did I end up captured and cuffed in the first place? Questions over questions. Damn shame I ain't got a single answer.

My head feels as if Tico Torres—Bon Jovi's drummer—uses it for a rehearsal. The pounding in my left temple, along with the blood rush in my ears makes me dizzy as fuck.

Resting against the cold, damp wall, I try my level best to get a grip on the pain. What a pity I haven't mastered the Shaolin-I-can-send-my-mind-to-Hawaii thing yet.

Remember, Remington. You gotta remember how you got here.

Dripping water, boxes, high heels, Jesse dropping to the ground, wood, and pain—the images pop back in my head.

Think, Remington. What happened before that? Where were you?

"New York," I whisper. I was in New York, drowning my sorrows in bourbon at some sports bar. Jesse and Carter showed. I was close to telling them the truth about the deal I'd made, but the power went out. Then, the earth shook.

Yes, I remember now. There was an earthquake. People got hurt, even killed. Carter went back to Washington, and Jesse and I searched for B. We found Chelsea, the roommate, instead. She led us to the basement, claiming B was hiding there.

Then what happened?

We called for the mamba. She didn't answer. In the far back of the basement, Jesse spotted her heels peeking out from underneath boxes. I heard a snap. My brother dropped to the ground. I spun. That's when I saw him—Demon-Boy. The guy who broke into the Bishop residence. The demon B was able to command. The demon that escaped because my brother didn't stir the potion for his shackles long enough. He hit me on the head with a damn baseball bat.

The heavy iron door creaks.

Next thing I know Demon-Boy smiles at me. "I hope you have a pleasant stay," he says, throwing a body at my feet.

I gawk at the bruised body, hot and cold at the same time. *Bonnie!* "Mm!" Fuck, she's barely breathing.

I fight the metal around my wrists and ankles. "M m m!" *Let me go!*

"Relax." Demon-Boy grins. "She's fine. For now."

Fine? She looks like she had a fistfight with Rocky after she was hit by a damn truck. That's as far from fine as one can be.

Glowing amber eyes step out of the shadows and into the dim light. They burn through the darkness like a fucking torch. "I think it's time we have a little chat," the Nun, aka Demon Bitch says.

Damn, I knew that voice rang a bell.

Chapter 22

The possessed Nun rips the tape off my mouth. "Sorry, what did you say?"

"I'm going to kill you, bitch!" The instant I get out of these cuffs, I'll send her sorry-ass back to hell. Never mind I have no fucking clue how.

Arms crossed, she grins like the Cheshire cat. "You truly are a sweetheart, Alexander."

"What the hell do you want?" In all the years on the job, I came across demons twice. When I sold my soul and in Rick's Cabaret while we were trying to save it. Now, all of a sudden, these bitches are everywhere. Call me crazy, but the whole thing stinks.

The Nun raises her brows, staring at me in awe. "You have no idea, do you?"

B convulses on the ground, her chest rising and falling quickly. She's hyperventilating to cope with the pain. She needs a doctor like yesterday.

"You're right." I straighten as much as the cuffs around my wrists and ankles allow. "I have no clue why a demon wears the meat suit of a preacher's daughter." Some would say it's poetic justice or shit.

The Nun's smile never wavers. "Let's just say believers tend to say 'yes' when approached by an angel, and asked for a vessel."

"Angel?" I laugh. "Hardly."

"Fallen or not, I *am* still an angel." She shrugs.

"Anyway, I haven't gone through all this trouble to talk rules of possession with you."

"Let me guess," I spit back, lips twitching into a half-smile. "You needed someone to end your miserable existence?" Yeah, yeah. It's dumb to be rude to a demon who could wipe me out with a snap of her fingers. But I've done dumber things and am still breathing.

The Nun hunkers down. "I know you spoke to the witch, hunter."

I squint. "The Enchantress? Esmeralda? Willow Rosenberg? Which witch?"

She rolls her eyes. "The one you were willing to die for—Amanda Bishop."

"You're wrong." Not about the dying part. "I haven't seen or heard from her in days."

She bursts into cruel laughter. "And you want me to believe that?" She shakes her head. "A connection like yours goes beyond rules of heaven and hell. I have a hard time believing she didn't visit you in your dreams."

How the hell does she know about my dreams?

The Nun traces her blazing hot fingers down my cheek. "You're going to tell me where she and the boy are"—she sighs—"or your little brother is going to learn the hard way how wretched my kind truly is."

"You're nuts." Connection or not, I have no clue where Manda is. Or else I'd be there, breaking her out of that damn dungeon.

Her lips curve up. "No, *you* are if you don't tell me what I want to know." Her amber eyes lock with mine. "Where are the boy and Amanda?"

"What boy?" I assume she's referring to Leandro,

but I can't be certain. I mean, why does a demon care about a little witch child?

She cocks a brow. "Don't play dumb. You know as well as I do I'm talking about Leandro Alexander Bishop."

Wait. What? Did she just say Leandro Alexander Bishop? Impossible. Why would Melinda name her boy like me? That's—

"Tell her," Demon-Boy demands, kicking me.

"Okay." My spine turns to steel. "I don't know where hellish bitches like you get their intel from, but in case you haven't heard we, too, are looking for Manda and her family." *And even if I knew where they are, you'd be the last I'd tell.*

She sighs like a full-blooded drama queen. "Wrong answer, Alexander."

"It's the only one I have," I bark, not liking the way B moans every time she moves.

The possessed Nun gets on her feet. "Don't lie to me," she thunders, her voice cracking the wall behind me. "Hell doesn't appreciate bullshit."

A demon accuses me of lying and demands honesty? That's paradox, at best. Totally fucked up, at worst. "Believe me, or don't." I gaze into her glowing eyes. "Doesn't change a damn thing."

She spins. "Well, then…let's see if your brother is smarter than you, shall we?"

My heart goes into overdrive. "Leave him alone," I yell after her and Demon-Boy.

She keeps moving, completely unimpressed.

"Hey! I swear if you so much as touch a hair on his head, I'll—"

The iron door slams shut. They're gone.

"Fuck! Fuck! Fuck! Fuck!" I need to get us out of here before we all die.

My gaze darts to B. Unlike me, she isn't cuffed. Guess they figured the mamba is in no shape to escape.

I gently push her with my feet. "Bonnie?"

Nothing.

"B, open your eyes. Please," I beg her.

Nope. No reaction.

"Hey!" I nudge her again. "You—"

A blood-curdling scream freezes my soul.

Jesse!

"Bonnie!" I push her harder. "Open your fucking eyes."

She's out cold.

Somewhere, outside, my little brother screams as if someone skins him alive. Here I am, trapped and cuffed. He keeps crying out in pain and there's absolutely *nothing* I can do to help him. I am failing him like I failed Natasha. Like I failed Manda.

Chapter 23

I have no idea how long I was forced to listen to my brother's screams. Minutes? Hours? A fucking lifetime is what it felt like. His yelps stabbed through my heart like the barbed stinger of a stingray. Hell, I would have sold my soul all over to trade places with him. Then the screams stopped and I could no longer suppress the fear of losing another sibling to the supernatural.

They didn't kill him, I keep telling myself. The possessed Nun is too damn smart. She's gotta know dead men don't tell tales, and dead brothers are rotten bargaining chips.

A faint gasp floats through the dark room. "Bonnie?" Her eyelids flutter. "B, can you hear me?"

"Alex?" she chokes out, voice barely a whisper. "Is…that…you?"

"Yes, it's me." I shift as close as the shackles let me. "Are you okay?" She's not. But I wouldn't mind if she lied.

She drags her battered body closer. "What"—her face is a mask of pain and terror—"happened?" She breathes like a ninety-year-old chain-smoker.

"Don't move." The last thing I need is for her to pass out again. Or worse, drown in her own damn blood.

B wouldn't be Manda's BFF if she listened to me.

Stubbornness must be a witch trait. "I'm okay," she assures me, digging her sharp, fake nails into my leg.

She has a dislocated jaw and sounds like Donald Duck. "Easy," I warn, bending my knee to help her straighten.

She gathers enough will power to crawl up. "What happened?" she asks again, leaning against my shoulder.

I wish I knew. One minute, Carter blames the death of over five dozen agents on Manda. The next, an earthquake hits the world and B's possessed roommate walks us right into a trap, capturing two trained hunters and a damn powerful mamba.

B looks around. "Jesse…where is Jesse?"

Averting my gaze, I glare at the old pipes on the ceiling.

"Alex," she urges. "Is he…is he—"

"No." He can't be. "He's okay." Or so I'm begging every damn god there ever was.

Demon-Boy and Chelsea walk up to us. The bitch flashes B her brilliant teeth. "Welcome in the land of the living, doll."

"Fuck you," the mamba spits back.

Demon-Boy kicks B in the shin. "Show some respect."

The mamba doesn't flinch. "Respectfully, fuck you then." She has more balls than most hunters I know.

Demon-Boy is all set to assault her some more, but the Nun holds him back. "Enough. We're on a clock. Pleasure has to wait." She zooms in on me. "You see, your brother is just as stupid as you are. He'd rather die than betray your witch girlfriend."

B's eyes widen. "What did you do to him? I swear,

I'll—"

"Relax." The Nun waves her comment off. "He's alive. For how long, very much depends on your answers."

"What do you want?" B asks, as calmly as possible.

Demon-Boy crosses his arms. "Tell us where the witch and the boy are and we can all be on our merry way."

I face the Nun. "I told you, we have no idea where Manda is."

"And we told you, we don't believe you," Demon-Boy shoots back.

I've had enough of their games. "Go to hell!"

Demon-Boy smirks. "At least try to be original, Remington."

My gaze drifts over his vessel. "Says the demon who possessed Justin fucking Bieber?"

He lunges forward, but the Nun seizes hold of his pink Lacoste shirt. One look from her is enough to freeze him. "So"—she faces me—"why don't we have a civilized conversation before we slaughter all of you?"

"Civilized?" B laughs. Or tries to. Dislocated jaw and all, remember? "You don't even know how to spell that, bitch."

A lopsided grin plays on the Nun's lips. "Maybe you should reconsider your attitude toward me, little mamba. I am, after all, the only one who can stop the apocalypse your witch friend started."

I laugh. Manda can be blamed for a lot of things, but the goddamn apocalypse? That's reaching. Sure, Carter mentioned the *First Grimoire* has the power to bring the end, but Manda would never do that. The end of the world means the end of Amanda Bishop—she'd have to be suicidal to go through with that. Except, last time I saw her, in that dungeon, she was hell-bent on convincing me to off her, wasn't she?

Chelsea squats down. "You think this is some kind of joke, hunter?" Damn, the demon sounds pissed. "Your beloved witch already broke the first three locks of the gate to hell. If she breaks the remaining three, the world will end and you pitiful humans will be the first to perish. So let's try this again. Where is Amanda Bishop and her son?"

"Her what?" Did she just say Manda's son? Bullshit.

Chelsea sighs. "Her son, Alexander. Where is he?"

"Leandro isn't her son," I correct her. "He's her nephew." Why would hell get such a crucial detail wrong? They seem to know everything else. Why confuse that? Manda doesn't have kids. She would have told me.

Like she told you she's a witch? That's hardly the same. Lying about her witch heritage, I get. The truth could have gotten her killed. But why would she have lied about her son? She must have known I'd *never* hurt a child—witch or not. Besides Leandro is what? Eighteen months old? I suck at math, but I'm pretty sure Manda and I were still together when the little man was created.

Leandro isn't her son. The demon is lying. *Or is she?*

****

My ex-witch-girlfriend sat over her family's damn grimoire, searching for a way to keep my soul out of hell, Judge Judy *stated her opinion on cheating asshole boyfriends, and I stood by the fireplace staring at the picture of Manda's nephew. The boy looked so familiar it gave me chills. "Your sister has a son?" I asked, taking the photo from its rightful place—the center of attention.*

Manda kept her gaze glued to the pages of the book. Her rosy cheeks paler than usual. I blamed lack of Red Bull for it.

Had she not heard me? I snapped my fingers in her face. "Earth to Manda?"

She balled her fists and drew a deep breath. "Yeah."

My gaze drifted back to the little boy's smile. There was something incredibly peaceful in looking at him. Almost as if his sweet face were the answer to all the problems in the world. "What's his name?" I didn't know why I cared, but I did.

Manda's face turned to granite. "Leandro," she replied, voice hard.

Leandro, huh? "Nice name." It sounded like a warrior. "How come we haven't met him yet?" How come I give a shit? I'd never been a kid person. They're loud and nosy, irresponsible and uncontrollable. Sorta like Manda.

She flipped a few pages. "He's with one of Melinda's friends." Her short answers irritated me. It wasn't like her.

I pulled up a chair and plummeted down, not ready to let the topic go. Partly, because I wanted to know what was going on in that head of hers. Mostly because that little boy had enchanted me. "Is he a warlock?"

She sighed heavily. "He's what we call a

hereditary."

I laughed so hard the pain in my chest almost killed me. "Sounds like some kind of aristocrat." Fitting. The boy had the name of a warrior and the looks of a king.

"Simply means he descends from witches," she muttered, eyes on the book.

She didn't like my questions. I didn't like her odd reaction. "What about his dad? Is your sister married?"

The remaining color drained from her face. She wasn't that pale when she'd died on a morgue table in Los Angeles after Isobelle—one of Walter and Francoise's victims—killed her. "Was married," she said, fingers clenched around the edge of the table. "She's a widow."

Shit, was that why Manda acted all bitchy-witchy? Because Leandro's dad was gone and she still mourned him? "I'm sorry. I didn't mean to—"

"Don't be." A ghost of a smile appeared on her lips. "My sister has crappy taste in men." Nope. She did not mourn the guy; I didn't get it. If she wasn't sad about the boy's fatherless fate, then why the fuck did she act like that?

I studied her, searching for any hints. The girl was a professional liar and master of deflection. Short: unreadable. But the longer I stared at her, the more I realized the similarities between her and Leandro. "You know, he looks one helluva lot like you. Same eyes. Identical smile." Leandro was the spitting image of his aunt. So much so, anyone could mistake him for her—

****

The Nun's high-pitched laughter echoes off the walls. "Nephew?" She shakes her head. "Is that what you think the boy is? The witch's nephew?"

Does hell have an asylum for mad demons? If so, she should be in there wearing a damn strait jacket.

"Oh, lord." She rests a hand on her belly, trying to calm down. "You really don't know anything, do you?"

She's a demon. Creatures like her are made of lies. I shouldn't care about what she says, shouldn't engage. Damn shame, I can't help myself. "Why don't you enlighten me then?"

B looks up at me. "Alex, you—"

"Leandro is the son of Amanda Bishop and"— meeting my gaze, the demon pauses for dramatic effect—"*you*, Alexander."

It's my turn to laugh. C'mon, she thinks he's *my* kid? I guess I was wrong about the Nun. She's not mad, she's simply crazy. No fucking way Leandro is my son. Manda and I always took care. We never—

Okay, just once, in the heat of the moment, we were carless enough to forget about protection. But it was just once. What are the chances I got her pregnant?

"Hey!" Demon-Boy kicks me. "Still with us?"

"I—" I what? Jesus, my fucking mind is gone.

"Face it," Demon-Boy says. "You're a daddy, Remington." He grins. "A rotten one, at that."

"He's not my son," I yell, my stomach cramping like a mother. Maybe Leandro is Manda's. But not mine. Never mine. I don't have a kid. I *can't* have a kid. Not with the life I live. Not with the hunter curse I'd pass on. And sure as fuck not with a witch. Because that would make Leandro what? A witch-hunter? How fucking ironic would that be?

I face B. "Tell them," I order. "Tell them they're wrong. Leandro isn't my son."

The mamba averts her gaze. "I...I—"

The Nun sighs. "Maybe you're more inclined to believe the witch?" She pulls a letter out of her pocket. "He"—she tilts her chin at Demon-Boy—"found this when he searched the Bishop residence. We thought it might come in handy one day."

My name is written on the envelope. I recognize Manda's handwriting immediately.

"Would you like to read it, or should I?" the Nun asks.

I say nothing.

"Fine," she snarls, pulling the letter out. "I'll do the honors." She clears her throat, making a big fucking deal out of it. "Dear Jerk—"

"Stop." It sounds less like an order and more like a damn plea. "Just stop."

The Nun cocks a brow. "All right." She puts the letter in my lap. "You have ten minutes. Make them count."

They walk out, leaving me with words that will change everything.

Dear Jerk-Face,

Have you ever written a damn letter? I haven't. Gee, I never even wrote a freakin' X-Mas card. Not that anyone would be keen to get one from me, but what I'm trying to say is spilling your guts on a piece of paper is hard. So much so, I'm on the brink of throwing the freakin' pen away to drown in a bottle of bourbon.

But what I'm about to tell you is too damn important and I'm aware I've already kept this secret for too long. A secret I was never going to share with you. But life doesn't play by the rules, does it? And "never" is a term the universe can't comprehend. The prime example? Well, I never wanted to fall for a hunter. Yet I did.

My heart slams against my ribcage like a beast trying to escape its cage. That last line? It killed and revived me at the same time. *I never wanted to fall for a hunter. Yet I did.* Amanda Bishop openly admitted to falling in love with me. God, whatever she's gotten herself into is worse than I fathomed. Because let's face it; Amanda would rather bite her tongue off than admit she has any kind of feelings for me.

Yeah, yeah, yeah, the letter continues. *I know what's going through that stubborn head of yours. "Shit, she's lost her mind. She must have or she'd never tell me she fell for me." (Don't be so surprised. I know you inside out, jerk-face.)*

I promise you, though, I'm sane. As sane as a girl like me can be.

I am in love with you. Have been since you stalked into that alley like Captain freakin' America. What can I say? Even wicked witches like me fall for good guys like you. Your aura? Damn, it was the purest I ever caught a glimpse of—golden perfection. Your breathtaking, malachite eyes, the ripped jeans, and all around bad-ass look didn't hurt either.

I should have walked away. It would have been the right thing to do. Instead, I jumped into your car, knowing where the road would lead—heartbreak and pain.

There were days when I wanted to regret my choice. But I couldn't. For Leandro's sake.

The instant I spot his name, my heart races like a

mother.

B's hand lands on my knee. "You okay?"

I look at her. Really look at her. She knows. She always knew.

Part of me wants to yell at the mamba. I crave to shake the truth out of her so I won't have to finish this stupid letter, sparing my heart the pain that's about to come. But this isn't B's story to tell. It's Manda's and I owe it to her to hear her out.

I know what you're thinking, Manda wrote. *What's Leandro got to do with any of this, right? I promise I'll get to that. First, however, I need to get a few things off my chest.*

Seriously, Manda*?*

I am sorry, Alex. (Yes, I said I'm sorry. No, I didn't fall on my head. And no, don't get used to it, because it's the first and the last time you'll ever get an apology from me.)

You deserve one, though. I was a selfish bitch for thinking we could have a future. I mean, a witch and a hunter? How fucking stupid is that? It's just my heart didn't give a fuck about our fated enemy status. It wanted you for who you were rather than what you were.

You weren't the only one, Manda. I had my moments, too. Moments where I believed in *us*, in what we could be. Those feelings didn't just go away when I learned the truth about her. Her being a witch didn't stop me from dreaming about a world in which we both belonged, regardless of what we were.

I blink over and over hoping to keep the salty liquid from rolling down my cheeks. When I'm certain I can keep myself in check, I read on. *I was foolish,*

Alex. Naïve enough to engage in that sweet illusion of us. We never had a future, though. I'm not cut out for a love like yours. You're righteous, caring, and good. Me? I'm the bitter chick everyone has a theory about. Some say I got like this because Mom never loved me, and Dad always got wasted. They believe I came into this world never having a real shot at becoming something other than the source of all evil.

Guess what? They're wrong. My parents aren't the reason I shy away from human affection. Back in the day, when I still believed in love, I packed my bags and stood in our driveway, waiting for a knight in shining armor to take me away from all the pain and misery. Every damn Sunday, I expected him. The knight never came. The hurt never went away. When I grew older, I understood there was only one person who cared enough about me, to get me out of this godforsaken town. That person was me, Alex. I had to step up and become my own hero. So I packed my bags one last time and walked away, never looking back. But everything comes with a price tag. The armor I put on suffocated the girl I used to be. And then...

Then I met you, Jerk-Face.

Fuck. I draw several deep breaths before I'm able to go on.

Did you know it was Sunday when you barged into my life? You stomped into that freakin' alley like a damn knight, determined to save the damsel in distress I no longer was. I knew right then and there it's you I'd been waiting for all my life. It's why I couldn't walk away, why I didn't.

Hell, I wanted to drop that damn armor so badly, Alex. But reaching out for your love was like a journey

I just didn't have a map for. And so I continued down the only path I ever knew—the one where Amanda took care of Amanda.

Bonnie squeezes my arm. Ugly tears prick at the corners of my eyes. Why did she never tell me any of this? I would have…man, I don't know what I'd have done, but it'd have surely involved kissing.

So, now you know, Alex. I have loved you long before I met you, and I will continue to love you until the day the universe ceases to exist, and we all return to ashes. It's why I can't lose you, jerk-face. Not to heaven, and especially not to hell. Neither can Leandro.

Yup, we're finally back to Leandro. I freakin' hope you're still awake because damn this letter is one helluva cheesy chick flick moment. If you are, then here's what this is really about. When I walked out of your life that fateful night you learned what I was, I took a part of you with me. Nope. This isn't a metaphor and damn I should get to the point because I'm talking rubbish just to avoid the truth.

Anyway, here it goes. I was pregnant with your son when I left you.

My son…my son…my…son! The demon told the truth. Leandro Alexander Remington is *mine*. I am a…father? All of a sudden, I feel like a damn actor, supposed to portray emotions I can't even comprehend.

My gaze darts to B. "Did you know?"

She nods.

Of course, she did. She's her best friend for fuck's sake. I should probably be mad she didn't mention it was my son who's missing. I'm just too damn numb to feel anger or anything other than a complete state of shock. I held a gun to the head of a pregnant woman.

Worse, I threatened to kill the mother of my unborn child. If I want to hate anyone, it should be myself.

For a while, I just sit there, falling into an abyss. Then I gather my last courage and gaze at the blurring letters. *You have every right to hate me, Alex. Keeping your son from you is unforgivable, but there's something you need to understand. I didn't mean to hurt you. And not once did I believe you'd hurt him, even after you had a gun to my head. Let's be real for a sec, though. What was I gonna do? Pick up the phone and say, "Oh, hey, jerk-face. I just call to say your first born is going to be half witch?"*

Yeah, no. I couldn't do that to you. You deserved a perfect life. Being the father of a half-breed doesn't exactly qualify for that, does it?

And Leandro? He wasn't going to grow up and feel unwanted. He was going to be loved and cherished every second of his life. Neither of us could give him that. I was a freakin' tarot reader with no roof above my head. You were a hunter, killing his kind. So I asked my sister to take care of him. She might despise me, but she would die for Leandro. The second she laid eyes on him, I saw pure love in her eyes. In Melinda, he had a mother who could put his needs before her own, who would love and protect him always and forever.

Me? I stayed far, far away from him. I'd screwed up enough lives. Hell, I'd rather die than screw up his. But I missed him, Alex. Every day it got worse. It felt as if a part of my heart were ripped out. That's when I decided to change my life, to become the mother he deserved. I applied to NYU, the same summer.

Why am I telling you all this now? Well, let's just say the prospect of you going to hell gave me perspective. You see, Alexander Remington aka jerk-face, aka the father of my son doesn't belong in hell.

I do.

By the time, you're reading this I won't be around anymore. For once in my fucked up life, I decided to be someone else's hero—Leandro's. I'll never be worthy of his love, Alex. But you are. You can be a father he looks up to. A father who protects him, no matter what.

Please, please, please don't hate me for trading places with you. I was always fated to go to hell. You? You are destined for greatness, jerk-face.

Wait, what? She…traded places with me? *On the first day, she saved his soul. She,* that's really Manda. *His* soul, that's mine?

So I'm begging you, the letter goes on. *Be the man I know you are, the father I foresaw in all my visions. Love our son for the both of us. Don't despise him for what he is; love him for who he is—a part of you. I promise you, Leandro is the best thing I've ever done in my life.*

Love,

Manda

P.S: I do have a bucket list and being stuck in a closet with you was on it.

P.P.S: Don't you dare raise my boy as a Zeppelin fan. Show him some real music, will ya?

Somewhere in the distance, the heavy iron door creaks. The Nun, Demon-Boy, and some other chick I haven't seen before stroll toward us, dragging my unconscious brother along. "Ready to talk?" the Nun asks, smiling like the devil himself.

Chapter 24

I'm accustomed to nightmares. They've haunted me since the cradle. Mostly, witches. Occasionally, vamps and other supernatural scum. Then, after Natasha was taken, the nightly images turned into a slasher flick. I've been tortured by the same vicious dream over and over. My little sister—not so little anymore—standing in front of an altar, white dress and all, with a dude who rips her heart out the second she says, "Yes."

So yeah. I'm used to horror. But nothing, and I mean absolutely nothing, compares to sitting in the dark, shackled, and beaten at your own game, gazing into the eyes of a demon who just told me I have a son.

"Alexander," the Nun hisses. "I don't like to repeat myself."

Demon-Boy—he has rotten football taste (who the fuck wears a Browns cap voluntarily?)—shows off his bleached teeth. "Give the hunter a break. He just learned he fathered an abomination." He bursts into cruel laughter. "I bet he regrets those five seconds of condom-free bliss, already."

Something inside me snaps. "Say that again," I demand, voice low and edgy.

He crosses his arms above his pink Lacoste shirt. "Which part?" He thoroughly enjoys this. "The one where you regret fucking a witch whore, or the whole your-son-is-a-natural-abomination business?"

The other chick—a pearl necklace wearing, "Hit Me Baby One More Time" Britney wannabee, rocking ugly pink nail polish—rolls her eyes at Demon-Boy. "Stop taunting him, G."

He cocks a brow at her. "Hey, I'm merely stating facts. It's not my fault he couldn't keep his manhood in his pants." Demon-Boy looks me in the eye. "You could have summoned me, you know? I'd gladly offered my fertilization skills. Anything to make sure that *thing* wouldn't have been born."

That thing? Did he just refer to a child—*my* child—as a damn thing? What the fuck is wrong with that asshole? He makes Leandro sound like some kind of monster.

Pink Nail Polish slams her hands on her hips. "Once a prick, always—"

In the blink of an eye, he's in her face. "What was that, sis?"

The Nun has had it. "Enough."

Demon-Boy meets her gaze. "But—"

"Remember what happens when I have to repeat myself?" The Nun smiles, but her eyes burn with wrath.

Demon-Boy gets the message. "I'm sorry," he apologizes, bowing low. "Won't happen again."

"No," the Nun says, with a confidence rattling my bones. "It won't."

The bitch hauls Jesse toward us, dropping his beaten body in B's lap. Utter fear glazes over the mamba's cognac eyes. "What did you do to him?"

The Nun winks at her. "Nothing we didn't do to you, doll."

"Bitch," B barks.

The Nun frowns. "Tell me something I don't know yet." She zooms in on me. "Like where your girlfriend and your son are."

Let me get this straight; she tossed a letter at my feet, stating Manda traded her soul for mine and Leandro is my son. Now, she truly thinks I'd hand him over? She's neither mad nor crazy. The chick's from planet insane-beyond-comprehensible. Half-witch or not, I'd die first before I gave her his location. Not that I have a damn clue where he is, but still.

"Alexander?" She taps her foot impatiently.

"I'm curious," I say, breathing fire and smoke. "What the fuck makes you think I'd tell you shit, now that I know he's my flesh and blood?"

The Nun hunkers down, folding her manicured hands in her lap. "Well, let's just say I had a hunch you might want to save your little boy's life."

B stiffens. "What are you talking about?"

"The prophecy," she replies, matter-of-factly.

The pic JJ sent Jesse flickers across my mind. *The prophecy comes true when the moon—*

"What prophecy?" I ask, not sure why I'm talking to a bunch of demons who tortured B and Jesse and called my son a natural abomination.

Demon-Boy, aka G, sighs. "You guys really don't know shit, do you?"

"What prophecy?" I repeat, harsher.

The Nun furrows her brows. "I'm sure you've all heard about the *First Grimoire*?"

"The one even your boss fears?" B replies coolly, trying to coax a reaction from the demons. "Legend has it Satan himself hid it."

"And sometimes," Pink Nail Polish says. "Legend

gets it right."

Wait, did she just insinuate that Lucifer is scared of a damn book? I'd laugh my ass off, but my facial muscles are frozen.

"*The First Grimoire,*" the Nun continues, "belonged to the most powerful witch of all times."

"Bellatrix Lestrange?" Hey, even Voldemort looks like a puppy compared to her.

"No," the Nun grumbles. "It was written by the First Witch, Lilith's daughter."

Jesse is the history slash mythology geek, but Lilith is a name even I've heard before. According to the Bible, she was Adam's first wife. The chick refused to be his sub, was banished to the desert, and—"Wait, didn't Lilith eat all her children?"

B opened her mouth to answer, but Pink Nail Polish beats her to it. "Don't believe everything the Bible says, hunter."

B casts her a killer look. "I have a feeling your vessel doesn't agree. Jules adores the Bible."

"So Lilith wasn't a child-devouring demon?" I bring the topic back on track.

The Nun looks me straight in the eye. "Lilith, was...*is* something far worse, Alexander."

Worse than a child eating demon? I had no clue anything like that existed.

"Anyway," the Nun goes on. "There's no time for a history lesson. You see"—she shifts closer—"your girlfriend and my brother will use the *First Grimoire* to open the gate to hell. And if they succeed, we're forced to fight the final battle, which will inevitably end all life on this planet."

She lost me. "One: why would Manda help your

brother? Two: what does Leandro have to do with any of this? Three: why the fuck should I believe anything you say? You're a demon. Shouldn't you be thrilled about open hell gates?"

"Long ago," she starts, "the boss came across a prophecy about an untouchable witch that will raise hell."

I've heard this one before. "Get to the fucking point."

Demon-Boy frowns. "She, who bears the mark of the gate-keeper, is the alpha and the omega. The key to life itself."

"And you think Manda is that witch?"

The Nun shakes her head. "I *know* she is."

"How?" B asks.

Demon-Boy rolls his eyes. "Hello? The ankh-shaped birthmark on her back?"

"That's how you recognize the keeper of hell's gate," Pink Nail Polish aka Jules adds, studying her claws. "The ankh represents the key to life."

This gets madder by the second. "First, you're saying Manda is the bringer of the apocalypse and now she's the key to life itself?" Do they even listen to themselves? "That's insane."

"Is it?" the Nun shoots back. "Think about it, hunter. The one who holds the key to the gates of hell is the one who holds fate of all life in her hands. Because, let me assure you, once the lines between hell and earth blur, the final battle must be fought. None of us"—she tilts her chin at her demon pals—"want that."

"Except your brother?" Isn't that what she just said? That her brother is helping Manda raise hell?

"My brother's lost his mind," she defends him. "He

thinks we can win. That we can restore the world to its former glory and be freed of our prison."

B studies her closely. "But you don't?"

"Neither heaven nor hell can win this war." The Nun's eyes grow distant. "We'll all perish, and your kind"—she points at me—"will be the first ones to die." Man, I wish I could say she's full of bullshit, but that hollow look in her eyes tells me she's anything but.

"Let's say you're right. Why would Manda help your mad brother?" The witch I know would never consort with demons.

"Would? She already performed two of the six rituals. Hello? Riots? Earthquake? You think that's a coincidence?" Pink Nail Polish's eyes darken. She sorta looks like she wants to bite my head off.

Wish I could say she's lying, but I read all about the *Purge*-like riots, and had a front row seat to the quake.

The Nun nods. "And to answer your question, because she couldn't let the love of her life go to hell, moron."

I think of her letter. *Don't hate me for trading places with you...*

"When she traded her soul for yours," Demon-Boy says. "She became the whore of the First Knight of Hell, Lucifer's left hand."

"Now, she's bound to do his bidding, or you will go to hell," the Nun goes on.

"So why doesn't Lucifer stop your brother?" B asks.

The Nun averts her gaze. "The boss is currently unavailable."

"Unavailable?" B laughs. "Why, is there a how-tostarve-more-kids-and-start-more-wars conference in town?"

"No." The Nun cocks a brow. "He's got some family business to attend to."

The devil has a family? Jesus, my fucking head is close to exploding. Amanda Bishop gave up her soul to save me from hell, because she thought I was a better parent. Now, she's the slave of some demon, wreaking havoc and bringing about the end. And Lucifer is having a family meeting? Sorry, but that's just too damn much.

Pink Nail Polish lips curve into a lopsided grin. "All of this is pretty much your fault, you know?"

B straightens. "What the hell are you talking about? Why is any of this Alex's fault?"

The Nun gets on her feet. "When you sold your soul out of righteous reasons, you broke the first of the seven seals."

"Seven seals?" Why does that ring a bell again?

" 'And I saw when the Lamb opened one of the seals,' " Demon-Boy quotes. " 'And I heard, as it were the noise of thunder, one of the four beasts saying, Come and see. And I saw, and behold a white horse: and he that sat on him had a bow; and a crown was given unto him: and he went forth conquering, and to conquer.' "

"Isn't that from the—"

"Revelation," Jesse croaks, finally coming to.

"What's that got to do with Alex?" B is as confused as I am.

"As previously mentioned, the Bible didn't get it all right. I would go into detail, but we are running out of time here," the Nun murmurs. "The point is you're the rider of the white horse, a son of the Arrows of Artemis. And when you sold your soul out of love, you broke the first seal, hence paving the path for my brother's end game."

Demon-Boy casts me a killer-look. "Seriously, Remington? How dumb are you? Selling your soul to save the witch?" He shakes his head. "She never needed saving, dumbass."

"Wait," my brother interrupts. "You did what?"

Pink Nail Polish grins. "He sold his soul to make sure Amanda Bishop wouldn't become the queen of darkness."

B glares at me. "Is that true?"

"Alex," Jesse yells. "Answer the fucking question."

"Yeah, Alex." Demon-Boy smirks. "Tell them. Tell them what went down in that bar. How you craved death after Amanda's mother asked you to kill her daughter, after the Malleus leader told you he'd kill her if he found her."

"Maria Bishop, as in Amanda's mother, came to you?" B barks.

"She begged me to kill Manda," I admit.

Jesse squints. "And the Malleus dicks?"

"Legend came by the night you interrogated the vamp suspect. Told me his men were out looking for Manda." I draw a deep breath. "He, too, was approached by Manda's mom. Unlike me, he gladly accepted her kill-my-daughter offer."

My brother's face speaks murder and mayhem. "Then what happened?"

I might as well tell them the whole story.

****

Legend had left. But what he and Maria Bishop put

in my head remained, sucking the damn life out of me. I needed to get out of this motel room before Jesse returned.

As drunk as I was, I grabbed my car keys and drove. I drove into the sunset, and back into the night. I drove until I couldn't drive anymore.

Then I pulled into the parking lot of a biker bar that would make a great setting for a new Tarantino flick, and drank some more.

Maria Bishop is a liar, I kept telling myself as I sat there, downing shot after shot. No way in heaven or hell, Amanda—the girl I'd spent the last few months with—was the future queen of darkness and bringer of doom. Sure, she was a witch. And yes, I always believed witches universally evil, but I had never gotten to know one as intimately as Manda. She was without a doubt selfish, reckless, stab-worthy, and a major pain in the ass. Yet she was also the girl who gave her last twenty bucks to a homeless guy when she thought no one was looking. The chick that picked the spot next to the old lady in Starbucks just so she wouldn't have to sit alone. Amanda Bishop went the extra-mile to convince everyone how badass evil she was. But I saw her. The real her. She loved cuddling, adored animals, and had never been anything but kind to people on the uglier side of life. None of that sounded like attributes the future ruler of hell would have.

What about Legend, though? *Why would he work with Maria Bishop? He's known for walking a straight, white line. He'd never help a witch unless he truly believed the lives of millions depended on it.*

Still, Manda isn't evil. *She walked the edge, but never crossed the line.*

But if she's good then why didn't she tell you she's a witch? *A dark twisted voice taunted me.* She played you. And you know what they say. Fool me once, shame on you. Fool me twice, shame on...*me.*

The cramping in my chest took my breath away. God, I hated myself for doubting Manda. I knew her, inside out. How dare I trust the word of two strangers over my own gut? What if they were right, though? What if Manda had played me? What if what we had was nothing but a game for her? What if she had manipulated me? She was a witch, after all.

I downed another shot and waved the bartender over for a refill. He cast me a haven't-you-had-enough look. I ignored him and pointed to my needy glass. "More."

He rolled his eyes, slammed the bourbon bottle on the counter, and headed to his next customer.

The bar filled up quickly. Drunk lowlifes lingered in the dark corners, waiting for anyone dumb enough to pick a fight. I knew the look in their eyes all too well. It said, life fucked me hard let me return the favor and fuck you even harder. They needed an outlet for their aggressions. I needed pain to reassure myself I was still breathing.

Swaying like a damn flag, I approached the three bikers by the door. At least, I assumed they were bikers. Maybe they just had a thing for leather jackets and bandanas—in places like these, you never knew.

These ones, however, weren't book covers I misjudged. The instant I bumped into the tallest of the group, he caught me by the throat. "Watch where you're going, motherfucker."

He presented me with a great possibility to start a

fight. "Shit." I grinned from ear to ear. "Who told you?"

Eyes narrowed, he tightened his grip on my throat. "Told me what?"

"That I screwed your mother?"

His fist landed in my left eye before I could even blink. "Wanna say that again?"

The pain roaring through my head was delicious. It silenced the voices in my head, and filled the hollow in my chest. I wanted more. Needed more. "You deaf or something? I said, who told you I screwed your mother, bitch?"

A flash of crazy mixed with a hint of killer sparked in his creepy dark eyes. "You think you're tough, huh?" He dragged me out of the bar. "Let me show you what we do with college boys like you."

I laughed. I was a lot of things. College boy wasn't one of them. "Gag them, flog them, apply nipple clamps?" I crossed the line between madness and suicidal in a matter of seconds.

His fist came up. "You stupid—"

"What? Wrong order?" I added fuel to the fire. "You apply nipple clamps first because you want to hear them college boys scream?" I winked at him with my good eye. The one that wasn't swelling up like a damn party balloon. "Get off on it, do we?"

And just like that, I freed the starving killer inside him, the one I spotted long before I deliberately bumped into him. He shoved me against the wall and assaulted my face.

Every hit I took was an explosion of pleasure. The throbbing in my temples, the ache in my jaw—I embraced it.

By the time, he started kicking me in the gut, the pain slowly transformed into nothingness. It got harder to enjoy the sweet hurt as the world around me was wrapped into a veil of misty darkness.

He's gonna kill you, Remington.

Yup. And it was too damn late to stop him. I was done. Every bone in my body ached. My ribs were probably cracked and I could no longer fight back. I wasn't sure I wanted to either.

"You stupid motherfucker," he yelled. "You have a death wish or something?"

It hit me then and there. I did have a death wish. Why else would I have gotten into a fight with Hercules the biker?

Manda's face flickered across my mind. I could never hurt her. Queen of darkness or not, killing her was not an option. I'd rather die than pull that damn trigger.

"You"—in the corner of my eye I spotted his boot aiming for my head—"stupid—"

The hit never came.

"Whatever happened to good old manners?" a voice echoed off the brick walls. A fraction of a second later, I heard a snap and Hercules the biker dropped to the ground next to me.

My nose was broken. I couldn't smell shit, but I tasted blood and sulfur on the tip of my tongue.

The hair on the back of my neck rose as fine leather shoes moved closer. I wanted to look up. Fuck me, I couldn't even lift my head. "Alexander Remington," the dark voice said. "Clearly not your brightest moment."

I wanted to tell the creature—a demon for all I

tasted—to go fuck himself, but my jaw was dislocated, my mouth full of crimson.

"Let me help you." I heard another snap. The past few minutes rewound like a damn movie. First, the nothingness was gone. Then the sweet pain of fists and hurt washed over me. When it subsided, my body was good as new, my soul as broken as ever.

Driven by instinct, I jumped up and reached for my Beretta. "Who the fuck are you?"

Amber eyes looked back at me. " 'What is in a name? That we—' "

"Cut the crap," I ordered, gun pointed at his head.

"Hunters." The demon, who looked like a damn hipster—skinny jeans, angled fringe, tight white shirt—frowned. "Such ungrateful creatures."

Hercules the biker lay next to my feet. He didn't bleed and from where I stood it seemed as if his chest rose and fell evenly. "What did you do to him?"

Hipster-demon grinned. "Don't worry. He's just taking a little nap."

I didn't know if I believed him, but I had other problems than Hercules' well-being. "You've got about two seconds to tell me what you want," I warned. I couldn't kill Manda, but offing a demon? I had no issues with that. Even when I knew a bullet couldn't send the bastard back to hell. Killing demons wasn't as simple as murdering witches. But hey, my choices were pretty limited.

He pulled a pack of smokes out of his jeans. "Want one?"

Surprisingly, I'd given an arm for a deep inhale. Though I'd never smoked a day in my life. "Talk!"

He smiled. "Don't rush me, Alex." He lit the thing

up and took a long, deep drag. "So," he went on. "Word on the street is you're having trouble with a witch."

"They have gossip phones on the highway to hell, nowadays?" I shot back.

The demon shrugged. "We even have iPads and Macs. You'd be surprised how tech savvy our boss is." A boyish smirk played on his lips. "He just loves Twitter."

The devil tweets, huh? Shocker.

"Anyway," he said. "That's not why I'm here."

"Yeah?"

He smiled. "I have a proposition for you."

"Shove it up your demon ass, pal." I'd never do business with demons or any other supernatural scum for that matter.

His amber eyes roamed my face. "Fine." He spun around. "If you're not interested in saving your little witch and the whole planet." He sighed. "I have other places to be."

Let him go. Just let him go!

"Wait." What the fuck was wrong with me? He was a demon for heaven's sake. *"What proposition?"*

He faced me with a sickening grin. "You want to save your little witch, don't you?"

Can someone be saved from what seems to be her fate? *"So?"*

"I can help you." He drew closer. "I can make sure the vision her mother had won't come true."

Demon's lie, *my inner hunter screamed. "How?"*

He looked me in the eye. "I assume you know by now that your precious little girlfriend will become a dark queen?"

Did I? All I had was the word of Manda's mother and some ancient prophecy foreshadowing Manda's fate.

"I don't like change," he went on. "And I absolutely abhor answering to a woman who could wipe me out with the power of her thoughts while being so painfully immune to my magic." *He was scared of Manda.* "So I'm offering you a one-time deal. I make sure she won't go dark—"

"Why?"

"I just told you," he replied. "I'm not into feminism. Plus, the boss would be eternally grateful for saving his throne." *I always figured even the devil would bow down before Manda.*

"And what is it you want in return for your service?" *I couldn't believe I considered his offer. Hunters—drunk or not, suicidal, or not—know better than that.*

"What demons always want..." He shrugged one shoulder. "Your soul."

I laughed so hard, my guts cramped. "You're insane." *He was more than that; he was fucking delusional. I'd never in a million years make a deal with hell.* Never.

"Am I?" he questioned. "Let's see. It's either this." *Like a flash of lightning he stood in front of me, pressing his index finger between my eyebrows. Vicious pain stabbed through my head, my heart, my soul. It was pure torture. Only lasted a few seconds though. Then the pain gave away to images of Manda walking toward iron gates. Green flames lit up everything around her. Screams echoed through the smoke. Hands stretched through the ashes. She walked over corpses with a damn smile plastered across her face. And the world, the world we knew, it no longer existed. It was an extension of the pit. A dark hole without any sense of hope or love. "This." Another image popped up. Amanda on her knees. I had my gun pressed against her forehead and pulled the damn trigger, scattering her brain tissue all over the ground. "Or this." I saw Manda, old and gray, on a porch watching her grandchildren plant some herbs in the garden.*

I stepped back, unable to process what just happened.

"So what's it going to be, hunter?" He tilted his head to the side. "Door number one, two, or three?"

"Fuck you."

He rolled his eyes. "Tick tock...tick—"

****

All demon, witch, and hunter eyes are on me. They share the what-the-fuck-is-wrong-with-you look.

"Back up," Jesse says, lifting himself up against the wall. "You made a deal with a demon to keep Manda from becoming a dark queen and now that very deal is what's forcing her to go dark?"

My heart skips a few beats. "I—" *Never saw it like that? Didn't know she cared enough about me to trade places with me? Was a stupid asshole for doubting her?*

"Why the fuck didn't you talk to me, Alex?" Jesse isn't just pissed. He's raving mad and on the brink of sending me to hell himself.

"It was part of the deal," Chelsea says. "My brother made sure Alex couldn't tell anyone about Amanda, or the deal would have been void."

Yup. She's on point. "It's why I begged you not to tell Manda. It's why I refused to ask her for help."

Jesse's eyes widen with realization. "Man, and all this time I thought you truly believed she didn't care about what would happen to you."

"I still don't get it," B grumbles. "If you weren't supposed to tell Manda, then—"

"We are thousands of years old," the Nun cuts her off. "And my brother has been planning this for a very long time. You"—she looks at me—"were a pawn in his game, Alexander. And let me assure you, he plays chess like nobody's business."

"Think about it," Demon-Boy goes on. "The vision Amanda's mother had of her ruling the underworld, the mysterious death of the guy who attacked her in that alley, you selling your soul to the First Knight to save her, even Francoise enslaving your little brother—it all led up to this."

Pink Nail Polish blows out a frustrated breath. "It all led up to her trading places with you, therefore being forced to do the First Knight's bidding."

B gets it. "He planted the vision?" The Nun nods. "You're saying he made her mother believe she was evil, so she'd become evil?"

"That's sick," Jesse hisses.

"Or"—the Nun straightens—"ingenious. I mean, once he killed the guy in the alley and planted enough evidence that would lead you to Amanda's witch-secret, he knew you'd never be able to trust her again. So he approached you and offered you the one thing he was certain you would do anything for—Amanda's life."

Pink Nail Polish nods. "Yup, and then he made sure the bokor enslaved your brother, knowing there's only one person you'd ask for help. Amanda."

I'm still stuck at the she-turned-dark-because-of-you part. "Are you saying all of this is happening because I didn't trust her?"

The Nun's harsh eyes soften. "Yes, Alexander. That's exactly what we're saying."

"It's called a self-fulfilling prophecy," Pink Nail Polish explains. "You were so scared she would go dark, you made her go dark."

Have you ever been blown up? No? Good. Because after your soul shatters into pieces and unspeakable pain digs into your heart, you're left with nothing but a burned-out shell.

"What about Leandro?" At least B's still able to speak. "What's his role in all of that?"

The Nun faces the mamba. "Knowing my brother, I assume he'll use him as a bargaining chip." Her gaze darts to me. "The witch would have gone to purgatory for you, Alexander. But as much as she loves you, and as selfish as she might be, she wouldn't end the world for you. The boy? That's a whole other story."

A story about a mother who would do just about anything to keep her child safe—even if it brought upon the apocalypse.

"If we find the boy," Demon Boy says. "We might be able to stop her."

"That is if the other hunters don't find him before us," Pink Nail Polish adds.

"What's that supposed to mean?" I ask, heart thundering in my ears.

The Nun squints. "I'm surprised your Malleus friend didn't tell you. There's a bounty on your son's head. Every Malleus member is looking for him. It's why my brother hid him and the witch's sister."

I have a son. I'm the reason Manda is some

demon's bitch. And the Malleus Maleficarum Order is trying to kill my son. I swear if this day gets any worse, I'll voluntarily go to hell.

Jesse stares me down. "Your son?"

"Long story," B says.

"I have time," he assures her.

"No, you don't." The Nun sighs. "None of us do."

"Wait." B's brows fly up. "If Leandro was hidden by your asshole brother then why do you think we know where he is?" That girl's mind works despite a dislocated jaw.

The Nun gawks at me. "We know Amanda contacted you. She must have told you something."

"Yeah, she begged me to put a bullet in her brain."

"Liar," Demon-Boy yells.

Jesse narrows his eyes. "Rich, coming from a demon."

"Enough." The Nun pulls a knife out of her pocket and presses it against my brother's throat. "Either you tell us what we want to know, or you all die. Choice is yours."

"We don't know where she is," I repeat with enough force to pull Pink Nail Polish's gaze off her nails.

The Nun sighs. "Well, then we don't have any use for you."

She slices Jesse's skin.

"Stop," B yells.

"Give me one good reason."

"I'll help you find Amanda, b—"

"Bonnie," Jesse shouts. "What are you—"

"But," she goes on, "on my terms."

I shoot daggers at her. "What the fuck are you

doing?"

She ignores me. Focusing solely on her possessed roommate. "Do we have a deal?"

The demon grins like the Cheshire cat. "Lay out your terms, doll."

Chapter 25

Amanda

I should focus on getting Leandro and Melinda away from Clyde's men. I should plan an escape for them, a rescue mission. Instead, I press my forehead against the cool window of Clyde's Audi, trying to silence the voice coming from that damn *First Grimoire*.

Yeah, the book speaks. It calls out to me from the backseat. "You can't trust men," it says over and over. "They make you then they break you. They don't deserve to breathe. They need to perish. All of them."

I'm a feminist at heart. This, however, isn't feminism. It's pure and utter hate, directed at one gender only. And while I had my heart broken before, I fail to understand how bitter one must be to fall into the abyss of such hostility.

"How are you, love?" Clyde keeps asking me every five minutes. I blame the black veins spreading from my hands toward my heart. "Do you need a break?"

A break from life itself would be much appreciated. A break from driving to the location of the next ritual? Not so much. What's the point? It's not like I can escape its performance.

"Amanda," he whispers. "Talk to me." He bats his thick black lashes, courtesy of his newest vessel—a five foot ten, future rock star—at me. "Please?" The creature is a walking and talking contradiction. One minute, he's full of wrath and loathing. The next, he acts like the mother I never had. You know, one who actually cares about my well-being.

"I'm fine," I hiss, unable to keep the loathing I feel for this creature under the blankets. What did he expect? That I'd roll out the red carpet, and drop on my knees to worship him after he showed me that video of Melinda and Leandro? Yeah, not going to happen, pal.

His gaze remains on me. Luckily, he keeps his damn mouth shut.

We drive for hours without exchanging any more words. That doesn't mean silence rules the fancy car. Quite the contrary. The voice of the book grows louder and louder. At first, the book keeps on repeating its men-hating mantra. But as time passes, it starts to speak to me directly. "Why do you resist me?"

Because you're a mad bitch who wants to destroy the damn world? A world in which the people I care about live.

"You're weak, Amanda." It laughs like a damn hyena. "Look at you. A mighty witch, born of the strongest blood and all you care about is saving a man who despises your very existence."

Shut up!

"I was in love once, too."

No fucks are given.

"He was beautiful. Strong and kind, sweet but protective—the perfect man," she continues. "We were going to give ourselves to each other, tying the everlasting red knot that would bind our lives together forever."

Let me guess, he stood you up because he realized what a crazy bitch you were?

"No." The voice thunders through my brain. "He promised me to stay with me for all eternity. Then he found out who I was, the daughter of the Queen of Night, the creature who broke every law between heaven and hell."

Sob story. Yay!

"Be quiet!" it yells, bursting my damn eardrum. "You don't know what it feels like to be left for your blood. I wasn't my mother. I despised her just as dearly as he did. And yet he gave me no chance. Instead, he went on to live happily ever after with someone else."

All right, I get it. It sucks what he did to you. But just because one dude is a freakin' asshole doesn't mean all of them are.

"See," it says, cheerfully. "That's where you're wrong. They use you, abuse you, then leave you."

Have you ever considered therapy? I bet Dr. Phil would love to work your men-hater case.

"How many times did your great hunter threaten to kill you, Amanda?"

None of your damn business.

"He pointed his gun at your head when you were carrying his child," it goes on. "Tell me, is a man like him worth your love? He used you to save his brother, then abused you when he no longer needed you." It pauses. "He never loved you. And he will never be able to love your son."

Shut up!

"It's true," it says. "You know it is. Why else would you have kept that boy a secret for so long?"

I throw my hands over my ears. "Shut the fuck

up!"

Clyde's disturbed gaze darts to me. "I didn't say anything, love."

"I...I—" I shake my damn head, trying to rattle the madness out of me.

"Are you sure you don't need a break?" he asks, crossing the state line into Idaho.

"Just drive," I bark, fire coursing through my blackened veins.

Chapter 26

Alex

When it comes to women, my brother has an exclusive taste. Bonnie Lacroix isn't just a pretty face with the body of a Victoria's Secret model and the brains of Stephen Hawking. The mamba is one helluva negotiator, too. The terms she threw at the Nun? They were meticulously worded and thought through 'til the very end. I sincerely wish she'd been by my side when I struck my deal. I have a feeling we wouldn't be in this mess had she been.

The Nun gazes at the blazing contract. "Who taught you how to deal with hell?" Yup, I'm not the only one impressed by B's skills.

She shrugs. "You learn a thing or two when demons can ride you anytime they please."

A thing or two, huh? She's big on modesty. B got Jesse and herself healed, made sure the demons wouldn't harm Leandro in any way, and convinced the Nun to free me from my shackles. In return, she swore to find Manda and promised neither Jesse nor I would attempt anything stupid. You know, like shooting at demons with bullets that can't kill them.

There's only one term the demon refused to agree upon—keeping Manda safe. Not from a lack of trying on the mamba's part, that I can assure you. She did her best, came up with plenty of arguments to talk the Nun into it. But one argument trumped all the others. The Nun pointed out that when it came down to rescuing Manda or the whole of creation, she'd opt for the latter. Of course, a demon doesn't give a shit about the greater good. What she does care about, however, is the survival of her own kind. To secure it, she would gladly sacrifice Manda. I guess it's a good thing I didn't sign the deal. Because there's no way in heaven or hell, I'll let them hurt Manda.

The Nun's gaze drifts over the mandala B draws onto the cement floor of the NYU basement. Yeah, looks like we never left the building. The demons simply locked us in the boiler room. "And you're absolutely certain this will work?" she asks, less than convinced.

B casts her a murderous look. "Will your lackey get me the ingredients?"

"Don't talk about my brother like that," Pink Nail Polish warns.

B rolls her eyes. "Can't believe I'm saying this, but I'm beginning to miss old Jules." Oh, yeah. I almost forgot. Between dealing with the Nun and getting us out of the boiler room, B mentioned Pink Nail Polish's real name is Jules. Apparently, she and the Nun—both members of the religious fanatic league—are BFFs. B said their mission was to make her and Manda's lives hell. Ironic, considering they're now possessed by demons.

"He'll get what you need," the Nun assures B, stepping between the two girls.

B conjures up a half-hearted smile. "Then, yes. I'm sure it'll work."

Jesse drops his hands in his lap. "What the hell does she think she's doing?" he murmurs, next to me. "She's a goddamn voodoo priestess. She should know better than to deal with hell." He's pissed and worried. Never a great combination when it comes to a Remington.

"She'll be okay," I assure him. B's as tough as they come. She can handle the demons.

Jesse casts me a sidelong glance. "And what about Manda, Alex?" His nose twitches. "Is she going to be okay, too? Because last time I checked, those mothers didn't guarantee her free passage."

"I'm not going to let anything happen to her," I swear.

He laughs dryly. "Like you didn't already."

Damn! A fucking stab in the heart is what that was. Can't blame him, though. I am responsible for Manda's misery. I have no one but myself and my lack of faith in her to blame for the shit that's going down.

Jesse sighs heavily. "I'm sorry, man. I—"

"Don't be." I glare at the gray floor. "You have every right to be pissed at me."

"I do." He pats my shoulder. "But I also know you have a lot going on and none of this can be easy on you." He's referring to Leandro. B filled him in after she got him healed and before she signed the deal.

"I'm okay."

He shifts closer. "C'mon, man. Whom are you trying to bullshit? This has got to fuck with your mind. Knowing you have a s—" He cuts himself off.

"A son?" I finish what he clearly can't.

"Yeah."

Choking back the lump in my throat, I stare at the

colorless walls. "I just…I can't believe she didn't tell me, Jess. I had a right to know." Sure, her letter gave me reasons as to why she kept Leandro from me, but I can't shake the feeling her fear—I couldn't love him due to his witch blood—played a major role in her decision. "Did she really think I'm that kinda guy?" I ask more myself than anyone else. "A guy who would leave his own child?"

Jesse props his elbows on his knees. "Did you ever tell her how you feel about her?"

"What's that got to do with keeping my son a secret?" Plenty of parents are separated. Doesn't mean they can't be there for their kids.

"Dude," he says, pressing his thumbs against his eyebrows. "Are you serious right now? You threatened to kill her"—he meets my gaze—"how many times?"

"If I wanted her dead, she'd be dead." It's true. I never hesitated before a kill. The second I aimed my Beretta at her, and gazed into those sad emerald eyes, I knew I'd rather shoot myself than her. How could she ever think I'd pull that fucking trigger?

Jesse leans in. "You know it, and I know it." He draws a deep breath. "Manda didn't."

"She's an aura-reading-future-seeing witch," I justify myself. "How could she have not seen what she meant to me?"

Jesse arches a brow. "Even witches as powerful as Manda can be tormented by fear."

He's right. None of this is Manda's fault. I was the one who pushed her away, the one whose actions forced her to keep our son a secret, the asshole who's responsible for her going dark. "I fucked up, Jess."

"Yeah. Yeah, you did." He averts his gaze. "But

you're not the only one," he says, eyeballing B.

"What do you mean?"

He blows out a frustrated breath. "Wanna know why she won't even look at me anymore?"

Ever since the fight they had outside Mr. Wong's, I've been dying to know what went down between my brother and the mamba. "Shoot."

"Bonnie knew, Alex."

I narrow my eyes. "Knew what?"

"When we drove to Salem, and you fell asleep, she told me Manda summoned a demon above JJ's bar hours before she vanished." He frowns. "B suspected Manda did something stupid, like trading places with you. She said it was the only explanation to why hell didn't claim your soul."

My eyes went wide. "Wait. What?" Amanda summoned a demon in JJ's bar? Why? And B suspected Manda traded her soul for mine but she kept her mouth shut about it? That's gotta be a mistake. "Why didn't she tell me?"

He gawks at the wall, his shoes, the floor— anything to keep his eyes off me. "Because I told her not to."

"You did what?" I bark.

Shame colors his face cherry red. "I was so happy you didn't die, Alex...I just couldn't risk losing you. I knew you'd walk right into hell for Manda." He meets my gaze. "And I was right, wasn't I?"

"That's your defense?" I ball my fists. "You wanted to protect me by keeping the truth from me?"

"Look, it was just a theory," he says, desperately trying to ease his guilty conscience. "We didn't have any hard evidence." He pauses. "I should have told you."

"Yes, you should have."

"I'm sorry, brother. I truly am."

He betrayed my trust and lied to me. But didn't I do the same to him? Closing my eyes, I take several deep breaths, swallowing all the senseless anger that won't change a damn thing about our current situation. "So am I, Jess." *So am I.*

"Man," he says, eyes lit up. "I can't believe I'm an uncle. How fucking cool is that?" Wow, where did that sudden change of mood and topic come from? "I'm so going to take him to a Lakers game," he continues, grinning from ear to ear. "Do you think they have jerseys in his size?"

"Probably," I mutter, startled about his sudden outburst of happiness in a more than murky situation.

"Good. Oh"—he shoots me a warning glance— "and just for the record, I'm the one who gets to teach him how to treat women. One Remington pointing a gun at a woman is more than enough."

Jesse's excitement about a future with Leandro is somewhat contagious. The pictures he paints are a bright canvas of happiness—basketball games, Disney World—shit families do. Except, without Manda we won't be a family.

"Promise me something?" I whisper.

"Sure." No hesitation, never hesitation. "What's up?"

I inch closer, making sure the Nun and Pink Nail Polish can't hear me. "We won't let Manda die, right?"

"I…"

"Promise me," I beg. "Please."

He looks me in the eye. "I promise."

That's all I needed to hear.

Silence stretches between us. We both focus on B. The mamba eagerly prepares her location spell. A spell that won't work on Manda because she's an untouchable, but it will most certainly work on the First Knight who forces her to end the damn world. At least, that's what B said when she told the Nun about her plan to track her brother rather than Manda.

B places a silver bowl in the center of her mandala when the iron door swings open and Demon-Boy barges in. He throws a paper bag at B. "Your stuff," he grumbles, face pale.

B eyeballs him suspiciously. "Uhm, thanks?"

Demon-Boy doesn't care for the mamba's gratitude. He bows to the Nun. "Can I speak to you?" She nods. "Privately."

They retreat to a dark corner. When they come back just a few moments later, they share the same the-shit-is-on look.

"What is it?" B is the first one to ask.

The Nun rubs a hand over her tired face. "We have to hurry."

I jump up. "Why?"

The Nun nods at Demon Boy. "Tell them what you told us."

"The First Knight's army has been freed." He swallows. Hard. "The city is crawling with demons. And…" He trails off.

"What?" Jesse barks.

"If CNN is to be believed," Pink Nail Polish says, "New York isn't the only playground of the First Knight's legion. They're wreaking havoc all over the country."

Fists clenched, teeth gritted, I get ready for the worst. "How bad is it?"

The Nun's chest inflates. "Are you ready for the location spell?" she asks B.

The mamba nods. "As ready as I can be."

"Then I suggest you go to work. Before there's no world left to save."

That bad, huh? Well, this shit just keeps getting better.

"On it," B assures her.

Chapter 27

Amanda

Clyde and I proceed toward the three-story mansion, reeking of money and wealth. Silvery moonlight illuminates the natural gray stone foundation. It looks idyllic, the perfect place to raise a family. But I know best how deceiving looks can be. Glimmer and gold on the surface doesn't mean there can't be brimstone and ice beneath.

I feel the Knight of Hell's eyes on me. "What?" I bark, tightening my grip on the grimoire.

"Feeling better, love?"

I still hear the damn voice, and we're about to perform the fourth ritual, breaking the fourth lock on the gate. Oh, and then there's the fact my son and sister are hostages of freakin' demons, all while I'm struggling to keep the wrath blazing inside me under control. "Peachy."

The ebony door swings open. One of Clyde's faceless minions waits for us on the other side. "Master," he bows low. "Everything is ready."

Old Amanda would flinch. Especially because I'm fully aware what "ready" means. New Amanda, the one who's close to losing her mind, doesn't feel a thing. All right, maybe a tiny stab in the chest, but it's as painful as a prick with a needle—not at all.

Clyde gestures for me to move inside. "Ladies first."

I bump into him. Hard. Why? Because I can. What can he do? Send me to hell or purgatory? I fucking dare him.

Soaring ceilings, the best hardwood floor money can buy, and fancy designer furniture. They are...*were* rich.

"This way." Faceless minion walks us into the living room.

A black velvet cloth with Clyde's sigil sewn into it lies on the floor. Seven black candles circle it. I move over, putting the book down.

"Help us," someone croaks. "Please."

I look up. Two massive, inverted, wooden crosses dangle from the ceiling. A man is nailed to the first one. His blood drops onto the floor, coloring the white marble dark sangria. He's dead. I guess I should care, huh? Well, I don't.

Crucified to the second inverted cross is a woman, Mother Dearest's age. Her long blonde hair touches the ground, her pale blue eyes glare at me, petrified. Unlike her husband, she's still alive despite a slit throat. Not for long, though.

"Help me," she repeats, blood dripping from her mouth.

Feel something, my brain screams. *Horror, fear, disgust—anything is better than nothing at all.* The thing is; I'm numb. I see her, can read her terrified aura, and am aware the woman is taking her last breaths. But...I just don't care.

Clyde puts two fingers under my chin, inspecting my neck. "Would you like to sit down first?" Judging

232

by the ring of his voice, I'd say the black poison has spread farther.

"No." I pull back, heading to the grimoire that calls out for me.

My gaze darts to the pictures on the wall. Circling a Last Supper painting are images of a happy family of three. Father, who's dead, mother, who will be any second, and a fifteen- or sixteen-year-old daughter. No clue where she is. Maybe they offed her first? The ritual only requires two god-fearing, human sacrifices.

"Bring me the chalice," I order.

Faceless minion, the one who opened the door for us, frowns. "Watch your tone, witch."

"You let him talk to you like that?" the book asks. "No wonder they treat you like their whore."

She's absolutely right. Who is he to talk to me like that? My skin is on fire; scorching heat wraps around me. Like a robot, I stand up. "Hey."

Faceless creature looks over its shoulder. "What now?"

I tilt my head to the side, smiling. "Next time you talk to me like that"—I slowly lift my hands—"you won't be so lucky."

The creature levitates above the floor. "What…what are you doing?"

"Teaching you a lesson on how to treat women," I reply, before I snap my fingers and faceless minion flies against the wall. The impact cracks the plaster and possibly his head.

"Amanda." Clyde's voice is like thunder. "What are you doing?"

I shoot him one look and he shuts his damn mouth. "Get me the fucking chalice. Now."

"Well done," the book praises me. "Very well done, Amanda."

By the time Faceless minion comes to, I'm all set to unlock lock number four. The silver chalice—it belonged to none other than the First Witch herself—sits in my lap. It's filled with the blood of Mr. and Mrs. Crucified. Oh, did I mention she bit the dust a few minutes ago? I breathed a sigh of relief when her annoying pleas faded into oblivion.

"Love." Clyde feels up my back. "Maybe you should take it slow. The power of the books is co—"

"Start the chant," I say, daring him to disobey.

Real shame, he doesn't. "You heard her," he addresses his minions. "Form the circle and start the chant."

Monotone voices float through the bloody living room. Power electrifies the air. I touch the book, soaking up its energy, bathing in it for a little while before I join the chant. "*Sreveileb fo doolb eht uoy evig dna nerdlihc yht ecifircas I. Lleh fo swal eht yebosid I. Nevaeh fo swal eht yebosid I.*"

Once I repeat the incantation three times, I lift the silver chalice and gulp down its bloody content. My mouth tastes like rusty iron and rotten meat. I fail to see why vamps dig that shit.

"Delicious, isn't it?" the book says. Or maybe I do. Who knows?

I set the cup down, ready to read the last line, to break the fourth lock, but Clyde's scream stops me. "No!"

I frown. "What is it?"

"Your mamba friend," he replies, the color draining off his face. "She's doing a locator spell."

I shrug. "Let her." They won't get here in time to stop me.

"No." He shakes his head. "It's too risky."

Risky? As if B could stop me. As if anyone could.

"Finish the ritual," he demands. "I'll take care of your friend."

A faint voice in the back of my mind pleads with me to stop Clyde. It tells me to give a fuck about my best friend.

I can't be bothered. "Keep on chanting," I order Clyde's minions, as amber mist leaves his vessel.

Chapter 28

Alex

"*Mwen mande nou yo montre m 'ki kote ou ye a, premye knight nan lanfè.*" Crimson slithers down B's finger, landing on the map Demon-Boy got her earlier. "*Mwen mande nou yo montre m 'ki kote ou ye a, premye knight nan lanfè,*" the mamba repeats, eyes closed, spine straight.

The flames of the purple candles rise high to the ceiling. Icy wind sweeps through the heated boiler room.

"*Mwen mande nou yo montre m 'ki kote ou ye a, premye knight nan lanfè,*" she chants one last time.

Her blood courses over the map. All of us—the demons, Jesse and I—follow the crimson-line from New York to Ohio, Wisconsin, Minnesota, North Dakota, Montana, until it eventually stops somewhere in Idaho.

I stretch my neck, trying to get a better look.

The Nun gazes over B's shoulder. "Bayview," she reads.

Bayview, Idaho? "What's a Knight of Hell doing in that godforsaken place?" We passed through that town once. There's nothing but a few houses and the lake up there.

A husky voice echoes through the dark. "I don't

think that's any of your business, Alexander."

The Nun's eyes widen to a point where I'm afraid they might pop out. "Shit." Yup. That's pretty much the last thing you want to hear from a demon.

B spins. Only it's not B anymore. Amber eyes stare back at us. I'd recognize those eyes anytime, anywhere. What can I say? You don't forget the demon you sold your damn soul to.

A nasty grin is plastered across his—or should I say B's—face. "Hello, my love." He bows to the Nun. "It's been a while."

Pink Nail Polish and Demon-Boy jump in front of the Nun, shielding their boss. "Don't talk to her, traitor."

"G." The First Knight smiles at Demon-Boy. "Still haven't learned your lesson, have you?"

"Shut up," Demon-Boy barks, hiding his trembling hands behind his back. He's scared of the First Knight. Yet he stands his ground. Sorta impressive. If he wasn't a damn demon, that is.

The Knight of Hell strokes his chin. "I admire your love for your boss. I truly do. But"—he snaps his fingers—"little demon bitches keep it zipped when the grown-ups are talking." We watch in utter horror as Demon-Boy's lips are sewn together by an invisible hand.

Pink Nail Polish lunges forward, aiming for B's throat. Jesse is quicker. He deflects her attack with a single blow to her chest.

"What the fuck are you doing?" she yells at him, struggling to regain her balance. Her eyes are literally on fire, burning the brightest garnet I've ever seen.

"I won't let you hurt her," Jesse shoots back,

drawing to his full height. "You wanna fight him; wait 'til the bastard wears his own suit."

Pink Nail Polish narrows her eyes. Her posture screams I-will-rip-your-damn-head-off-hunter. The Nun interferes before she gets the chance to follow through. "He's right." Her gaze darts to B, currently possessed by the First Knight. "We still need the mamba."

"Need her for what?" The First Knight's deafening laughter roars through the gloomy boiler room. "We both know you can't stop me. I've always been stronger than you." He shrugs a shoulder. "Now that I have an untouchable by my side, I'm invincible. By the way"—he winks at me—"thanks for that, Alexander. Couldn't have done it without you."

Heat rises from my core. "You played me," I say, inching closer.

"I'm a demon," he replies nonchalantly. "What did you expect?"

What did I expect? Surely not for him to enslave the mother of my child. And certainly not abducting my son to use him as a damn bargaining chip.

"Where's Manda?" Jesse asks. "What did you do to her?"

"She's a little busy, right now." He shows off B's brilliant teeth. "But I'll tell her you said 'hi.' Though I'm fairly certain she won't care."

She won't care? He doesn't know the first thing about her. I'd tell him, but we have more pressing matters that need to be addressed. "Where is Leandro?"

The First Knight cocks a brow. "Someone told you you're a daddy, huh?" He eyeballs the Nun. "I should have known you can't keep a secret, love."

"Tell me," I yell.

"Suddenly you care?" He moves toward me, eyes narrowed to two thin slits. "Where were you when he was born, hunter? Did you know Amanda almost died giving birth to *your* son? No?" He pauses. "Well, how could you? You left her, pregnant, with no money, and no place to go." He shakes his head. "I don't think you have the right to act all protective super dad, now."

What the fuck? Manda almost died giving birth? That's bull—the nasty horizontal scar at her pubic hairline flashes across my eyes. The one I spotted in Bakersfield when I tried to talk her into having sex with me for old times' sake. I always knew I'd seen one like it before. My mom had the same, after Natasha was brought into this world with an emergency C-section.

"That's right, Alexander." He gets in my face, his sulfur breath beating against my cheek. "If it wasn't for the mamba's brother, your beloved witch would be long gone." His lips twitch upward. "And it'd be your fault."

The worst part is the bastard is right. It *is* my fault. All of it.

"You know," he says, voice cold and hard. "I never understood how a woman like Amanda could love a pitiful creature like you. But"—he pulls his shoulder to his ear—"I am grateful she did. Because without you, I would have never gotten her soul."

Pure and unfiltered madness corrupts my system. "I'm going to kill you," I promise him, closing the little gap between us. "I don't know how or when, but I will. This I swear to you."

He bursts into laughter. "Oh, goodness. Aren't you tired of making promises you can't keep?" He meets my gaze. "You can't stop me." He eyeballs the other demons. "No one can. Not with Amanda Bishop by my side."

The Nun steps between us before my balled fist lands in B's face. "Please...I beg of you. Stop this madness before it's too late."

He pulls his brows to his hairline. "Why would I do such a stupid thing, love?" He scans her face. "We always dreamed of this. Walking the world freely, getting rid of those"—he shoots Jesse and me a killer look—"monkeys. Why don't you stop fighting me and join me instead? Together we're unstoppable."

The Nun shakes her head with a desperation that's almost human. "You say freedom, but at what cost? You, of all knights, should know best what happens when the gates are open. The battle—"

"Will be fought," he cuts her off. "And once we win, we'll reclaim what was taken from us."

The Nun steps closer. "We won't win," she barks. "No one will. Lucifer—"

"Lucifer is gone, remember?" His lips curve into a wicked grin. "Hell needs a new leader."

"And you think you're the man for the job," Jesse teases, laughing. "Sorry, pal. You ain't got the King of Hell look going for ya."

"Careful," the First Knight hisses. "Only takes a second to send your precious little mamba to purgatory." And as if that weren't enough, he glides his hand down B's chest, pinching her nipples. "Would be a damn shame to off such a nice piece of ass, don't you think?"

Jesse is seconds away from finishing what Pink Nail Polish started. Luckily, I manage to get a grip on his shirt. "You're just going to hurt Bonnie."

My little brother's muscles relax a bit, giving me

time to return my focus to the First Knight. "So what brings you here? Surely, Mr. Invincible-Unstoppable isn't afraid we might come find you to send your sorry ass back to hell, right?"

"Afraid?" His gaze darts from me to my brother and the demons. "Of a bunch of demons, a mamba, and two hunters? I don't think so. Not when I have the most powerful untouchable by my side."

The First Knight's gaze locks on the Nun. "You've always been my favorite, Berith. It's why I have a proposal for you and your legion."

The Nun aka Berith—I have a feeling he slipped her name on purpose, hoping we used it to exorcise her back to hell—cocks a brow. "I'm not interested."

"Hear me out," he demands, taking both her hands in his. "Help me unlock the gate and we can rule hell together. It'll be you and I…like old times, remember?"

The Nun's eyes grow distant.

"C'mon, Berith." He smiles at her. "Why be a princess when you can be a queen?"

She's a princess of hell? Damn.

"Let's conquer this world together," he continues.

A dry laugh escapes the Nun's mouth. "I'm impressed. Did you rehearse this crap, or are you so desperate to buy your witch some time you actually came up with this bullshit as you went?"

"I take that as a no." His amber eyes catch fire. "Very well then. I shall see you at your funeral, Berith." A fraction of a second later, B's eyes clear up and she drops to the floor. Her head barely misses the boiler.

"B?" Jesse is next to her in a heartbeat. "Hey"—he slaps her gently—"you with me?"

"Hit me again," she mutters. "And I'll make you do

the Macarena." At least one of us hasn't lost her humor yet.

"Mm…mmm!" Demon-Boy waves his hands, desperately seeking attention.

Pink Nail Polish has him covered. "You'll be good as new." She puts her palms on his mouth, chanting some spell that reverses the First Knight's magic.

"He's fucking crazy," Demon-Boy yells the instant the thread is gone.

The Nun stares at the spot where the lunatic demon just stood. "We have to stop him."

I can't believe I find myself agreeing with a princess of fucking hell. But she's right. This crazy mother needs stopped before…well, before the world ends by Manda's hands. "Any idea how?"

Demon-Boy casts me a sidelong glance. "You sound as if we're playing for the same team."

"Don't we?" Jesse shoots back. "I mean, we all want that crazy demon back in the pit, right?"

Pink Nail Polish sighs. "Maybe so. But we're demons and you guys are…" She trails off. "Anyway, why should we trust you?"

Seriously? "Because we're the good guys, remember?"

"Whatever that means," the Nun grumbles.

I approach her. "It means we don't stab people in the back."

Demon-Boy faces the Nun. "We can't trust them. They're—"

"The only ones who can stop Amanda," B says, surprising us all.

The Nun frowns. "You can't. No one can. The power of the *First Grimoire* will corrupt her. And by the time she's given in to it, she won't be the same."

"She won't hurt us," I say, feeling the truth of those words rattling through my marrow. Manda took a bullet for Jesse and me, walked away from her new life the moment she learned about my deal, and traded her soul so I wouldn't go to hell—she'd *never* harm us.

The Nun gazes at the map, considering her options. You don't have to be a mind-reader to understand she ain't got many left. "Well then." She meets my gaze. "Go to Bayview, try your luck. We"—she eyeballs her demon pals—"will gather some reinforcements in case you fail."

"Which you will," Demon-Boy adds, grinning like a mother.

Not if we have some help. "Where's my phone?" I ask, not finding it in my pocket.

Pink Nail Polish pulls it out of her jacket. "Sorry." She shrugs. "Couldn't have you call for backup, could we?"

"Just give me my damn phone," I mutter, snatching it from her hand.

Jesse squints. "What are you doing?"

"Calling for backup," I reply, dialing JJ's number.

Chapter 29

I begin to realize why demons are so damn hard to hunt. Those mothers are a resourceful bunch, having everything at arm's reach. A private jet? Just a call away. Getting permission to take off despite the reality all other planes are grounded due to the earthquake? No problem. Organizing a brand new, silver Mercedes G65 AMG? It waited for us, fueled and ready to go, at Spokane International Airport. So yeah. Thanks to the Nun aka Berith, aka Princess of Hell, we made it to Idaho in a little less than six hours. Without her demonic assistance, it would have taken us at least forty.

"We're almost there," Jesse says.

According to the fancy German GPS system, we're just six miles outside Bayview. Our calculated estimated arrival is less than twelve minutes. "Question is what we're going to do once when we get there?" It's not like the locator spell gave us an exact location of the knight. All we have is Bayview, Idaho. And while this isn't New York, we still don't have time to search the whole damn town. Especially since the demon has a six-hour head start. He could be halfway across the country by now.

Jesse eyeballs B in the rearview mirror. He looks like he's waiting for her to tell us what to do, but the mamba stares ahead, unresponsive and slightly out of it.

She's been like that since we walked out of Green House. I can't say I blame her. It's not every day the Big Apple is reduced to ashes and dust. The images of hurt folks, tossed cars, and collapsed houses—they'll haunt you for the rest of your life.

My phone buzzes. "It's JJ."

"What did she say?" Jesse inquires.

"On our way," I read. "Will be there early tomorrow morning." Good. When I called her and gave her a quick summary of what happened, she immediately agreed to meet us in Bayview. So did Bay, by the way. I might not like that dude—for obvious, Manda-digging reasons—but he's reliable and loyal.

"We need all the help we can get," Jesse murmurs, eyes distant.

Another period of silence stretches between us. I'm done replaying the conversation with the First Knight. I've been tortured by it for the past six hours. It didn't get me anywhere. Okay, it sorta led me into a spiral of self-pity and hopelessness, but that's hardly helpful.

I switch the radio on. Music always had a calming effect on me. Sometimes, however, the wrong song comes on and fucks with my mind some more. Kinda like now. When God decides to torture me with "Cat's in the Cradle" by Harry Chapin. C'mon, from the millions of songs out there I get the one that's about a father who neglects his son?

The damn lyrics cut through my marrow. It's as if the big man up there, on his golden throne, needs to remind me how badly I fucked up. Trust me, he doesn't. I'm aware of what a bastard I was. I have a son I never met. A son I never got to hug. A son who'd be raised thinking his father had died. Manda was wrong.

She's not the one who doesn't deserve to call herself a parent. I am.

He's too young to blame you, a faint voice whispers in the back of my mind.

Maybe, but I blame myself enough for both of us. Let's face it; while I was busy treating Manda like garbage and playing the hero for strangers, my own flesh and blood was exposed to all kinds of dangers. Now he's in the claws of demons, and every Malleus hunter is out there looking for him.

Why didn't Bay say anything? His old pals probably figured where his loyalty truly lay. Bay could have handed Manda over on a silver plate back in Winter Harbor. Instead, he kept his mouth shut, lying to his fellow order members.

I wonder if those Malleus assholes know who Leandro truly is. Half witch, half hunter, something tells me they don't like that combination.

Demon-Boy flashes across my mind. "*He's an abomination,*" the asshole said, fear dominating his voice.

I still want to smash the bastard's head for calling my son an abomination. But like it or not, I get why that little boy makes a grown demon pale. Amanda is the most powerful witch I've ever encountered. It's why I turned to her when Jesse was MIA in Bakersfield. I knew if anyone could find him, it would be her. All right, I also missed her and sorta wanted to see how she's doing, but that's a story for another time. Anyway, with her abilities—reading people like damn books, seeing past, future and present with just a single touch—and her sharp mind, she's a force to be reckoned. If her child only inherited some of her gifts, hunters would regard it as a danger. Leandro, however, isn't just her son. He's mine, too—a descendant of the Arrows of Artemis, the most feared hunters in the world. Add all those ingredients and you have a recipe for a power vacuum. So yeah, only God knows what he's truly capable of.

Power doesn't make him evil, I assure myself. Leandro is just a child. He deserves a chance to prove himself, regardless of who his parents are. And if he's just a bit like his mother, he'll never be a danger to others.

Unless they're bullies, torture animals, or—

Stop. I won't go down this road again. It turned Manda into the slave of some demon. I'll be damned if the same happens to Leandro. What he is doesn't matter. Who he is, is what counts. For now, he's just a little boy. Nothing more, nothing less.

B's hand lands on my shoulder. "Stop the car," she orders, out of the blue.

I maneuver the Mercedes to the side of the road. "What's up?"

She gets out of the car. Both, Jesse and I, follow her. "B," Jesse shouts. "Where are you going?"

Like a robot, the mamba crosses the road. She halts in front of a ponderosa pine. There, hidden beneath a branch, is a street sign. It reads, Cape Horn Road.

"He was here," she whispers, eyes glued to the sign.

"The First Knight?" I gotta be sure.

She nods. "I feel his essence." She looks me in the eye. "The stink of him is still fresh."

Nothing good can ever come out of a road that has the word "horn" in it. It's basically destined for evilness. "All right." I reach for my useless Beretta. "Let's go."

"Yup." Jesse has his Glock out in under a second. "Let's rock n' roll."

B moves toward a small bridge. "Hey." Jesse pulls her back. "Where do you think you're going?"

She cocks a brow, and I catch a glimpse of the old, defiant, don't-fuck-with-me B. "Wherever this path leads me," she shoots back.

Jesse shakes his head. "No way." He circles her wrist, hauling her toward the car. "You're gonna stay right here."

"No," she says, digging her heels into the ground, refusing to move. "I won't."

"B—"

"Don't make me use magic on you," she cuts him off, face like stone.

"You—"

"Last time I checked," she says. "I was the only one who could command a demon. So"—she slams her hands on her hips—"unless you're a voodoo priest and forgot to tell me, I am your best shot at getting out alive."

What she said is logical. Jesse, however, doesn't do rational when it comes to the mamba with the cognac eyes. The one that teased him in a damn strip club, just to walk away and leave him dry and high. "B—"

I get between them. "That's enough."

"Tell her to get her ass back in the car," Jesse barks.

"Tell him to stop treating me like a damn child," she shoots back.

I've had a rotten day. The last thing I need is a

bitch fight. I face my brother. "She's coming."

B grins. "Ha!"

"But"—I cast her a sidelong glance—"you'll stay behind us and do exactly as we say. Got it?"

It's Jesse's turn to gloat.

I head toward the small bridge before another fight ensues.

"Shit," Jesse hisses, somewhere behind me.

I spin, half expecting to find the mamba at his throat. But like Jesse, B's frozen. "What's—" *Fuck.* Beneath the bridge is a landscaped creek with a waterfall. That's not why we're rooted to the spot with dropped jaws, though.

"Is that…is that…" B can't say it.

So Jesse does it for her. "Blood."

Yeah, the water isn't casual blue, it's not even a dirty brown. It resembles a pool of red wine. I'm no end-of-days specialist, but water turned to blood? Can't be a good sign, can it?

"Alex." B is next to me. "We better hurry." One look into her eyes and I can tell this whole water-to-blood thing is worse than I thought.

I nod, forcing my feet into action.

The closer we get to the gray-stone mansion, the weirder I feel. My stomach cramps, my eyes water, and my chest is heavy yet empty.

I ogle the name below the bell. It reads Blair.

"Door's open," Jesse whispers, kicking the massive wood.

On high alert, I move in first. The weight of my Beretta is nothing compared to the pressure building in my chest. B's right. Something stinks.

The hallway is open with high ceilings, and plenty

of fancy furniture. The walls on each side are covered with crosses and religious paintings. Some I recognize from research. Yes, hunters don't just kill. No, I don't like that part of the job. Jesse does. Anyway, there's Mother Mary with baby Jesus, the lamb in heaven, and several of the Savior himself—half of the churches in Texas aren't as well equipped.

"Alex." Jesse nudges me. "Listen."

I stop dead in my tracks. Somewhere, not too far from where we stand, music plays. It's just a faint noise, at first. The farther we walk, the louder it grows. Soon, I find myself humming to the tunes of "Stairway to Heaven" by Led Zeppelin.

Shivers course down my spine. And I know…I just know I won't like what I'll find behind that wooden door to my right.

Face your demons, Remington.

I draw a deep breath, steady my Beretta, and push inside.

"Fuck!" is the only damn word that comes mind, but could never do the *Kill Bill* battlefield justice. There's blood everywhere—the walls, the ivory sofa, the marble floor, all across the fireplace.

"Jesus," Jesse hisses.

And B? Remember the elevator scene in *The Shining*? The look on Wendy Torrance's face when she encountered a wall of blood oozing from the elevator shaft? It's pretty much the same expression B rocks—terrified, tortured, damaged. It doesn't surprise me. I bet the mamba doesn't get to see crucified folks very often. Yeah, that's right. Dangling from the ceiling are two inverted crosses. Nailed to the first one is a dude; his head barely attached to his spine. On the second, secured with long rusty nails driven through hands and feet, is a woman. Her throat is slit, but at least her head doesn't look like it'll fall off any second.

I'm ready to haul B's pale ass out when an all too familiar sound echoes through the living room—the removal of a safety click.

Chapter 30

"Drop your guns," some dude screams. "Drop them *now*."

I lower my Beretta, and turn slowly.

"Don't move!" he warns, voice trembling.

"Help me out, man. How can we drop our guns when we're not supposed to move?" Hey, I'm not trying to be an asshole here, but we can't possibly do both.

The dude groans. "Put them down. *Slow-ly*."

Jesse and I follow the directions.

"Good," he says. "Now, kick them away."

We do as we're told.

"Show me your hands," he continues.

We lift them above our heads. All of us, except B. The mamba can barely lift her jaw from the ground, let alone her hands. She just stands there, staring at the corpses hanging on the crosses.

"You too," he yells at her.

"Listen," Jesse starts. "This isn't what it looks like." He reaches for his badge. "We're—"

"I said don't move!"

"We're FBI," I blurt out, quickly. "I'm going to get my badge, okay?"

"Don't even think about it," he barks.

Heavy footsteps echo through the living room. A dark-haired, twenty-something deputy stands in front of me. He holds his gun with one hand. Rookie mistake. I could disarm him in the blink of an eye. He'd never knew what hit him.

"Where's your badge?" he asks, giving me a once over. Yeah, ripped jeans and leather jacket doesn't look very federal agent. I get it.

"Left, inner pocket," I say, sounding calmer than I actually am. We have enough on our plate. A meet and greet with local law enforcement is the last thing we need.

The deputy wrinkles his hooked nose. My guess, he had it fractured once or twice. He's either into boxing, or bullied relentlessly as a kid. "Don't try anything stupid," he warns us.

"We won't," I assure him.

He draws a deep breath and finally gathers enough courage to get my badge out of my pocket. "Agent"— he looks from the badge to me—"Remington?"

I flash him a fake smile. "That's me."

He lowers his gun just slightly. Then faces Jesse. "And who are you?"

"May I?" my brother asks, pointing at his back pocket.

The deputy with the hooked nose nods. A second later, he has Jesse's badge under his nose. "Agent"—he pulls his brows up—"Remington?" We get that a lot. The are-you-fucking-with-me-or-are-you-related look.

"We're brothers," I explain, knowing he'll ask anyhow.

The deputy's gaze darts to B. "And who is she?"

A mamba who could talk you into wearing lingerie while doing the damn Macarena. "A consultant."

"I see." He sighs. "And may I ask what you're

doing"—his gaze darts to the corpses—"here with two crucified bodies?"

Oh, you know. We're tracking the First Knight of Hell and a super witch who happens to be the mother of my missing child. Yeah, and they're about to end the damn world.

I have a feeling the truth wouldn't go very well with Deputy—I glare at the name tag on his uniform—Ford. "We're working a case." I tilt my chin at Jesse and B. "The..." Shit, what was the name on the doorbell? Black? No. Bourne? No. Ah, yes. "The Blairs were witnesses. The front door was ajar, so we checked it out. And found"—I tilt my chin at the horrific scene—"*this.*"

Pretty lame excuse, but Ford holsters his gun. Guess he bought it. "What the hell happened here?"

"Someone nailed the Blairs to crosses," my brother states the obvious.

Ford squints. "That I can see. But why?"

Because they performed a ritual from the *First Grimoire*? "We don't know."

Jesse straightens. "What are *you* doing here?" He can't hide the suspicious undertone. Hey, I don't blame him. We got abducted by college girls. Granted, they were possessed college girls, but nevertheless there's a lesson somewhere there. One that taught my brother not to trust anyone when dealing with demons.

Deputy Ford eyeballs the corpses. The color drains from the poor dude's face. I guess he doesn't come across shit like this very often. "We"—he wipes some sweat off his forehead, focusing on Jesse—"got a call from the Blair's neighbors. They reported a 415 a few hours ago. A 415 is—"

"Disturbance," Jesse mutters, proving what a smart-ass he is. "And what took you so long to answer it?"

Ford's jawline hardens. "All units had been dispatched to the lake."

All units? Did I miss the president's announcement to go swimming in Bayview? "Why? What happened at the lake?"

Ford glares at his shoes. "The water…it…well…"

B's head snaps in Ford's direction. "What about the water?" I'm glad to hear she's still able to talk. I kinda feared she might have lost her voice after walking into this hell.

The deputy frowns. "We got calls from all over the county reporting bloody water."

Awesome. So the landscaped creek isn't the only water-to-blood attraction in Bayview. Shit just keeps getting better.

"When did the water turn to blood?" B inquires.

Ford narrows his eyes at her. "It's not real blood. It can't be."

"When?" B barks, fists balled.

Deputy Ford pulls a Clint Eastwood—crossing his arms, acting all cool and shit. Too bad, he can't cover up the slightly greenish tone of his skin. "The first call came in about the same time we got the 415 from the Blairs' neighbors."

B stalks toward me. "We have to find them, Alex."

"Find who?" Ford inquires.

B ignores him, focusing solemnly on me. "I'm serious." She looks to the inverted crosses. "This is as bad as it gets. Human sacrifices, one of the seven plagues…" She takes a deep breath. "I'm telling you,

255

we have to find them. *Now*."

Ford steps between us. "Human sacrifices? Are you saying this is the work of Satanists?"

The deputy clearly watches too many bad movies. Contrary to widespread beliefs, normal Satanists don't sacrifice humans. According to their bible—a piece of brainwash par excellence—they follow the golden rule of "I do what I want, when I want, but harm no others." Kind of like Manda.

When Ford catches my amused expression, he explains his conclusion. "I read this article once. An interview of some lady who works for the Institute of the Research of Organized and Ritual Violence. She said ritualistic killings happen more often than serial killings. And they're always accompanied by mutilation and symbols." He points to the crosses dangling from the ceiling. "Inverted crosses are as Satanist as it gets, right?"

I'm not sure what to say to be honest. Thankfully, I have my little brother. "We can't talk about our case, but we can tell you we're hunting some extremely dangerous individuals."

It's not what the deputy wanted, but better than nothing. "And you think these individuals are in Bayview?"

"They were," I say.

"They might still be," B adds, giving me the impression it's more than just a hunch.

He reaches for his radio. "I'm going to call for back—"

"No!" I stop him.

He casts me a WTF look. "But you said—"

"I know what we said," I go on. "But those people

can't know we're here. They have connections to the local police. It's why our boss sent us without notifying the sheriff." Damn, I've spent too much time around Manda. Lying has become too damn easy for me.

"A-are you for real?"

"Wouldn't lie about it," I promise him.

"Is there anything I can do?" he asks, paler than a ghost.

Jesse approaches him. "Actually, there is."

"Anything," he assures my little brother.

"Check with your colleagues. See if anything suspicious happened."

He cocks a brow. "Like?"

"Fireballs dropping from the sky, folks killing each other—anything that's not normal around here," B explains.

He smiles, until he realizes no one smiles back. "You're serious?"

"Do I look like I'm joking?" B hisses, hands on her hips.

Ford swallows hard. "I'll be right back." He grabs his radio and moves out of the bloody living room.

I pick up my Beretta. "I'm going to check out the rest of the house." If we're lucky, they left some clues as to where they're headed.

"We'll take the basement," he says, hauling B along. She doesn't put up a fight or protest. Probably because she'd rather be anywhere than in a living room with two dead folks, hanging head down on crosses.

"Be careful," I say, heading upstairs.

The second floor of the Blair mansion is equally impressive. The ceilings are high, the walls painted a nice shade of beige, and the furniture made of solid ebony. I guess it's the perfect home to raise a bunch of kids and grow old in. Then again, what do I know of growing old and kids? My life expectancy doesn't exceed thirty and if it wasn't for the demons I would have no idea I have a son.

Moving down the long hallway armed with my Beretta, I catch a glimpse of the Blairs' love for Jesus. No kidding. There's not a single wall not plastered with the Savior's face. Being watched by God's son creeps me out. It's like his eyes are everywhere.

The first door on the left leads me right into the master bedroom, sending me *Back to the Future*. The Blairs' bedroom is one big, high-tech gadget— electronic shutters, a Dolby Surround system most folks don't have in their living rooms, a spacey-looking radio alarm with iPhone docking station—it's every nerd's paradise.

I proceed to the bathroom. It features LEDs in the step-in shower, a water-resistant speaker for music, an automatic toilet lid, and...wait for it...a fucking towel warmer. Who the hell needs heated towels for Christ's sake? Sometimes, I think the more money folks have the weirder they are.

Chills run down my spine as I move toward the large window front. They're locked from the inside. And when I say locked, I mean locked with a key. Seems like the Blairs took safety real serious. Not that it did them any good—they were murdered nevertheless—but at least they tried.

The ever-growing black hole in my belly expands continuously. Something is incredibly wrong. I examine the carpet closer. There are no traces of sulfur, no scent of rotten eggs. Quite the opposite. It smells like roses and lemon in here.

I keep searching, but find no hint of any supernatural activity. What I do find are more religious paintings of Mother Mary and infant Jesus as well as two Bibles on each nightstand. Call me crazy, but I don't believe it's a coincidence they sacrificed the Blairs. Those people gave god-fearing a new meaning. I'd bet my life that's why the First Knight picked them.

Frustrated, I search the other rooms. Mr. Blair's large office, stacked with all sorts of religious books, is right next to the master bedroom. Turns out the man was the local pastor; at least that's what the paperwork on his desk suggests. It certainly explains the paintings and the arsenal of Bibles I found.

I head to several guestrooms, equally as well equipped as the master bedroom. Whoever said high-tech and religion doesn't go together never met the Blairs.

After coming up empty handed, I move on to the last room on the floor, finding myself in the midst of teen idols, creeping down at me from pinkish walls. I'm not nearly *Entertainment Weekly* enough to recognize them all, but I do know the blue-eyed bloodsucker every teenage girl seems to be crazy about. Damn, what was his name again? Damon something, I think. Anyway, I don't get the hype about this dude. He's a ruthless vamp who digs his little brother's girlfriend. How is that worship worthy?

Anyway, I come to the conclusion the Blairs must have had a teenage daughter. I don't think grown-ups would plaster their walls with Selena Gomez and Taylor Swift. And dudes? They'd go for cars or pin-up girls. Like Jesse and I did.

On a white dressing table in the corner, I spot perfumes, makeup, lipsticks, hairbrushes, curlers, a hair straightener—the Blair kid could host one of those damn beauty pageants.

Soaking it all in, I come to the conclusion my little sister, Natasha, would have loved this room. She'd be seventeen now. My gaze darts to the bloodsucker. Something tells me he'd smile down from her wall, too. Natasha had always been a hopeless-cases magnet. The girl believed she could reform the bad boy of her class with cookies and sandwiches. The weird part? She succeeded. Phoenix Ashton was as rotten as a first grader could be. The boy constantly got into trouble for fighting and being a mean-ass in general. I warned Natasha to stay away from him, told her guys like Phoenix were no good. But my little sister didn't give two shits about her big brother's opinion. She simply turned to me and said, "Stop judging him, Alex. You have people who love you. Phoenix doesn't." I call that moment: life lessons from a first grader.

I still hated the idea of them together, but I knew better than to argue with a Remington girl. Natasha had made it her life's mission to save the brat and I knew nothing could change her mind. I gotta admit, she did a bang of a job, too. The more time she spent with Phoenix, the better he got. Until—

I shake the memories off. This isn't the time nor the place to open that can of worms. To take my mind off Natasha, I go through the kid's desk. A college application for the University of Idaho is scattered all over it. It's filled out and ready to send off. I find more application forms in her drawer, hidden beneath lots of loose papers. Stanford, Harvard, NYU—I get the kid wanted nothing more than to see Idaho in her rearview mirror. Her parents weren't on board. Or why else would she have hidden the forms?

Flinging myself in the desk chair, I lean back and ogle the pink dream. The room is neat and clean just like the rest of the house. Yet something in here is odd. There are no bibles, crosses, or religious paintings for starters. And the longer I drink it all in the higher the hair on the back of my neck stands. That tingling feeling creeps into my system, the one that says, *look closer, Alex.*

I check the windows for sulfur. There's none. Then, I move to the bed. An iPod lies on a purple pillow. Don't ask why, but I pick it up and check out the playlists. Adele, Ed Sheeran, Taylor Swift—typical sucky teenage pop. By the time I get to the recently played songs, I'm certain the girl suffered from severe heartache. She listened to "Someone like you" by Adele on repeat. How fucking depressing is that?

I almost put the iPod back when I spot a playlist called "Freedom." Excitement rushes through my veins. The hunter in me senses something. I scroll through the songs. Imagine my surprise when I find Zeppelin's "Stairway to Heaven"—the same song that played when we got here.

What the hell is going on here?

"There ain't no such thing as a coincidence, jerk-face," the witch's words echo through my subconscious.

But if this isn't a coincidence then what the hell is it? Better question: where the fuck is the kid? She wasn't crucified like her parents and I have a hard time believing the knight spared her. So where is she and how is she connected to all of this?

I open the girl's nightstand. Inside a pair of socks, I discover birth control pills, along with pics of a pretty, brown-haired girl about sixteen—I assume that's Mrs. Blair junior—and some blond dude, sticking his tongue down her throat. They were taken in a photo booth. I start to think blondie is the reason for the girl's Adele obsession.

Rummaging through the drawer, I find—

Holy Mother of Christ. Is that—

Shit. It's a pink fucking vibrator.

How old is this girl again?

I glare at the photo. She's Natasha's age.

Oh, hell to the no. I'm not going down this road. I will not think of my sister in connection with a damn vibrator. Never.

"Alex?" Jesse yells from down the stairs.

Thank God. I slam the drawer shut. "Coming."

"Alex." B's halfway up the stairs, face pale.

My heart races like a mother. "What's up?"

"We gotta go," she says, seizing hold of my jacket and dragging me down the remaining stairs.

"Go where?" I ask, trying not to break my damn neck.

Jesse and Deputy Ford wait on us by the front door. "We have a situation." Jesse sounds like the world's already going up in flames.

I narrow my eyes at them. "What situation?"

"A hostage situation," Ford replies, voice edgy.

I'm about to question how a hostage situation is connected to us when B slams her hands against my back, shoving me outside. "We need to go."

Chapter 31

"A woman and several men hold hostages at the Light Haus B&B," Ford explained when I refused to go anywhere unless they told me what the hell was going on. "All units have been dispatched."

B thinks the woman is Manda. Me? I'm not so sure. Why would the First Knight draw so much attention? Why hold hostages? Why didn't they pack their bags and leave? They knew we were coming.

"Fucking awesome," Jesse murmurs, pulling the car to the side.

Looking up, I spot the reason for his discontent. "You've gotta be kidding me." The place is crawling with reporters. Media vans from six different stations, including CNN, block the driveway of the B&B.

We get out of the car. Deputy Ford is right behind us, slamming his car door shut. "Jesus," he says, eyeballing the vultures also known as journalists.

"How the hell did they get here so fast?" Bayview is in the middle of nowhere for Christ's sake.

Ford wipes his sweaty forehead. It's December, but the weather is as fucked up as the world. Eighty-four degrees and rising. "They're probably here for the bloody-lake story." The deputy sighs. "Looks like they're more interested in hostages, though."

Thanks, Randy. You just made our already fucked up lives a whole lot harder. There's a reason the PAU stays away from high-profile cases. Imagine the riots and chaos arising should people learn the truth about the existence of the supernatural. They'd build zombie bunkers, at best. Reestablish the Salem Witch Trials, at worst. But when the world's about to go up in flames, risking exposure seems a little less than a black stain on a white sheet.

Deputy Ford straightens his uniform. "I'm going to find the sheriff and let him know you're here."

"Don't tell him about the Blairs just yet," I remind him. "We still don't know who we can trust."

Ford hates the fact I'm accusing his boss and colleagues of corruption; I can tell by the wrinkles on his forehead. Yet he doesn't argue with me. Instead, he heads toward the yellow crime tape separating the cops from the media.

Jesse flexes his muscles. "I guess we'll just have to deal with them, huh?"

"Or"—B's lips curve into a wicked half-smile—"I could send them all to Hawaii."

I squint. "You can do that?"

She shrugs.

"No." Jesse faces her. "You can't manipulate them all. Remember what happened when you talked the two cops in Salem into leaving? Your nose bled and you blacked out."

Okay, so we can't send them to Hawaii. "How about we arrest them?" Don't get me wrong. I'm a fierce defender of the first amendment. Yet I hate reporters. They're obtrusive little mothers. All they care about is the next big headline. Never mind who gets hurt in the process.

Jesse sighs. "We still live in a democracy, dude."

I'm damn glad we do, but I still think they should grow a conscience.

"Agents!" Deputy Ford waves us over.

"Ready?" my little brother asks.

Would it make a difference if I said no?

The sun beats down on us. Sweat rolls down my spine, gluing the fabric of my sweater to my skin. It really shouldn't be this hot in December. I'd blame global warming, but I have a feeling the real culprit is the First Knight and his apocalyptic horror show.

B catches me battling with the sleeves of my sweater. "You okay?"

"It's too damn hot." I'd give my poker wins for a sleeveless shirt.

Jesse pinches his brows together. "It's warm and all." He pauses, ogling my face. "But dude, your skin's redder than the tomatoes Grandma used to grow. Did you catch anything?"

I don't feel sick per se. Just a little weird. Remember the hole in my belly? Well, it just expanded to the size of North America. And my heart? It's about to jump out of my chest.

"Alex?" B elbows me. "Are you sure—"

"I'm okay." I think I am.

We march toward Ford. A shitload of deputies are with him, trying to keep the reporters at bay.

Pushing through the vultures, someone seizes hold of my sweater. "Agent Remington?"

Startled, I spin.

Oh, Fuck!

"Remember me?" Shirley Partridge lookalike asks, shoving a mic in my face. "We met in—"

"Kansas City." She covered the story about the

four teenagers whacked by their witchy teacher. I'd never forget a pit bull like her. She made our life living hell by asking all the right questions. No matter how hard Jesse and I tried, we couldn't get her to believe the killings were the work of a madman.

Shirley Partridge lookalike cups her cameraman's elbow, spinning him around, forcing the poor bastard to film us. "Can you tell us anything about the hostages? Do you know who's responsible for this? Is the bloody lake connected?"

Could she talk any faster?

"Can you give our viewers anything?" she presses as more reporters circle us, aiming their cameras at us.

Not nearly dumb enough to engage in a conversation with her, I keep moving. Journalists might not have an ounce of decency, but they sure as hell don't lack a brain. The slightest slip and it's bye-bye PAU, hello SupernaturalLeaks.

She treads on Jesse's heels. "Don't you think the public has a right to know what's happening? Especially after the super-quake and the riots that broke out across the country?"

My brother—always the lady's man—musters up one of his panty-wetting smiles. "Your hair looks gorgeous."

She so didn't expect that. The compliment, along with Jesse's charm, catch her completely off guard. "Well, thank you." Her voice is softer, her cheeks flushed. "That's very nice of you to say."

Jesse winks at her. "Beauty such as yours must be acknowledged."

If looks could kill, B would have offed Shirley.

But Jesse's plan works. The vulture is busy

gloating and we escape. By the time she remembers why she's here, we already made it to the yellow crime tape.

"Let them through," Ford orders his colleagues.

A beer-belly-rocking deputy holds the tape up for us.

We slip through, heading straight toward Ford. "What do we know?" Jesse inquires.

Ford takes his hat off. "Sheriff Vincent is inside. He's one of the hostages. They"—he points to a dozen cops—"tried to go in, but…" He trails off.

"What?" Patience isn't B's strong suit.

Ford sighs. "See for yourselves."

He leads us closer to the B&B. Then, he stops abruptly. "Wait."

"For what?" I ask.

He picks up a rock, throwing it against an invisible electric shield. Sparks fly as the stone connects with the power source. By the time it lands on the ground, it's reduced to ashes.

"A protective shield." B shoots daggers at me. "I told you she's here."

Ford inches closer. "Who is she? And what the hell is that? My men are growing increasingly twitchy. They've never seen anything like it."

I'm a PAU hunter and I've never seen anything like it.

"It's a force field," B explains. "No one gets in unless—"

Hope sparks in his eyes. "Unless what?"

B turns to Jesse and me. "I might be able to get you past the shield, but you'd be on your own." She eyeballs the invisible wall. "And I'm not sure I can get you out."

If Manda is in there, I'm going. "What do you need?"

"A quiet place"—she looks over her shoulder at the vultures—"away from all the cameras, and some booze."

My gaze darts to Ford. "You heard her."

He scans the area. "There's a fishing cottage by the lake on the opposite site of the house. Will that do?"

B nods. "What about the booze?"

"I've got a bottle of bourbon in the car." Bought it before we went to Anna's, and after Manda walked away. I figured I might as well be drunk when I'm dragged to hell.

"Let's go to work," she says, spinning on her heels.

****

It was harder than expected to get rid of Ford. The deputy wanted in on the action. Though he had no clue what was about to go down in the shabby fishing cottage located behind Light Haus B&B. Luckily, we had B. She used her special gifts to convince him he's needed up front to make sure his colleagues wouldn't walk in on us.

"All right." The mamba throws the chalk on a small table. She drew one of those famous voodoo mandalas on the ground. "I'm good to go."

Jesse rests his hands on her shoulders. "Are you sure you can do it?" B told us she'd have to invoke a couple of Loas to get us through the protective shield. And even then, she wasn't one hundred percent sure it'd work.

"As long as the First Knight created the barrier, we're good." In other words, if it's Manda's magic keeping us out, we're screwed. She's an untouchable. Meaning, B can invoke the whole of Olympus and they couldn't help us through the invisible wall.

I move to the door. Jesse follows me, but I stop him. "Whoa, where are you going?"

He smirks. "Are you fucking with me?"

"You're not coming," I say, not the slightest trace of humor in my voice.

"What do you mean I'm not coming?"

"I'm going in alone," I clarify.

"Are you crazy?" he barks, murder on his face.

Maybe, but if the mamba is right this could be a one-way trip. No way in hell, I'm taking my little brother with me. We have no idea what's waiting inside. The First Knight didn't strike me as the kinda demon traveling on his own. God knows how many of his kind are on the other side of the barrier waiting to kill us. "Someone needs to take care of B," I say, hoping his feelings for the mamba can nip an unwanted argument in the bud.

The mamba cocks a brow. "Don't you dare use me to justify your suicidal plan." She slams her hands on her hips. "I'm pretty sure I can take care of myself, Alex."

"She's right," Jesse hisses. "And I'm not going to sit back and watch you walk into a demon trap by yourself."

Why does he have to be so damn stubborn? Oh, right. He's a Remington. "You don't get it," I say, running my fingers through my hair. "What if B can't get me out, Jess? Someone needs to keep the cops and media under control."

"No." He crosses his arms. "Not happening. I'm

coming. Period."

"Jess," I roar, on the brink of tying him to the old rocking chair in the corner.

He shakes his head. "You're crazy if you think I'll let you walk in there by yourself. The demon is going to slaughter you."

"Manda won't let him." She sold her soul for me. Never in a million years would she stand by and watch the First Knight murder me.

B frowns. "Alex, you—"

"Enough." I hold my hand up, silencing her. "I'm going. And I'm going alone. This is my responsibility. I fucked up. I'll fix it."

Jesse realizes there's no point arguing with me. I made up my mind. I won't change it. "Fine. I'll wait here, but if you're not out in twenty minutes, I'm coming after you and I don't give a shit about what you say. Got it?"

I'm not thrilled at the prospect, but I don't think I can negotiate better terms. "Deal."

B is on her knees. "Go," she says, nodding at the door. "He'll text you when the shield is down."

"Sounds like a plan." The kind that'll get me buried six feet under.

"Alex." Jesse stops me.

"Huh?"

A long period of silence stretches between us. "If you die, I'm selling your car."

"Then I'll haunt your ass."

"And I'll call the *Ghostbusters*," he replies, flashing me a wicked smile.

Chapter 32

The closer I get to the shield the higher the hair on the back of my neck stands. The energy radiating from that thing is inhuman, in every sense of the word. I hope…no, I pray B can take it down. If—and that's still a big *if* for me—Manda is in there, I need to get her away from that demonic bastard. It might seal my fate and I'll be deported straight to hell, but that's a small price to pay for the lives of Leandro, Manda, and the rest of the human race.

An icy breeze beats against my hot cheeks. Trees rattle behind me. Terror creeps down my spine. I've been a hunter for too long to be oblivious to the side-effects of magic. The mamba must have started the ritual.

Heart kicking into high gear, I scan my surroundings. Not a single soul at the back entrance of the B&B. Good. I don't think B could manipulate a whole nation if the reporters caught wind of what we're up to.

Minutes slip through the hourglass. The wind whips violently. Until—

The trees circling the Light Haus B&B stand still.

I smell bourbon and cigars.

A fraction of a second later, an otherworldly voice wafts through the air. "Come with me," she says.

My hunter-bells ring. That can only mean one

thing: something supernatural is with me.

"Alexander," the voice, distant like wind chimes, sings. "Follow me."

I stay rooted to the spot. Sorry, I don't trust invisible creatures.

"I am here to guide you," the woman assures me.

In that very moment, my phone buzzes. "All clear," Jesse wrote. "B says you can trust her."

Her? As in the voice, or the mamba?

"Hurry," she says. "We can't keep it open for long."

A leap of faith is required. For the sake of Manda and Leandro, I'm jumping. Or should I say I'm walking? Yup. Toward the protective shield which turned a damn stone into ash.

"Pass through," the woman mutters. "Now."

I hesitate and I'm not quite sure why. Death has been my constant companion since I got the job at the PAU. C'mon, I voluntarily walk into witch dens, encounter all sorts of creatures that can rip my heart out without breaking a sweat and never dodged a bullet. But that was before I learned I have a son. If things go south, Leandro will be an orphan. Sure, he'll still have Melinda, Manda's sister, and I'd bet my life Jesse would be there for him, too, yet I'd never get to meet him. God, things were so much easier when it was just me and Jesse.

"You must go!" A pair of hot hands are on my back, pushing me. Hard. It happens so fast, I can't do anything about it.

Luckily, I make it to the other side in one piece. "Thanks," I grumble. "Whoever you are."

"You're welcome," the woman whispers, her voice

only a distant howl.

I draw a deep breath, eyeballing Light Haus. Without the cops and media vans, it appears so normal. Looks can be deceiving. I learned that when we found a bunch of kids in dog kennels in the basement of an idyllic lake house.

"All right, Remington." I reach for my Beretta. "You've got this."

The veranda door is open. I approach it, my stomach heavier than that of the dead wolf in *Little Red Riding Hood*.

It's a trap, the hunter within screams. I'm inclined to believe my gut, but it doesn't change a damn thing. I need to get to Manda, come what may.

I move inside, gun drawn, finger on the trigger. What I find is—

God, I'm not sure there are words to describe what I see with my own eyes. The sunroom of the B&B resembles a damn slaughterhouse. Body parts are scattered all over the hardwood floor. A left arm secured on a piece of rope hangs on the ceiling fan. Judging by the red nail polish, I'd say female. Right beneath it sits a head on a wooden chair. Long, brown hair glued to the bloody face. If I had to take a wild guess, I'd say the head belongs to the arm.

To my left, I find the corpse of a heavy weight man. Contrary to the unknown woman, he's still in one piece. But there's one thing they have in common— they're both very much dead. A piece of his skull is missing.

There are two more victims—both of them my age, both of them killed with a damn steak knife. How I know? It's still sticking in their fucking hearts.

I really wish I could give my brain some time to process that shit, but I have the nagging feeling I'm already late to the party.

Careful not to make any noise, I tiptoe into the hallway. There's nothing but the main entrance and the staircase on the left. One floor at a time is what they teach you at Quantico. So I head toward the large, double swinging doors on my right.

Voices float into the hallway. "Please, let us go," a woman begs.

"Don't bother," a husky, male voice, grumbles. "Those freaks will never let us out of here alive."

"Freak?" The sound is otherworldly. Sorta like nails on a chalkboard, only ten times creepier. "Whom are you calling a freak, monkey?"

"I don't understand," the woman cries. "Why would you do that? Why kill all those people?"

Slow and on high alert, I open the swinging door just enough for me to peek inside. Across the room, I spot the sheriff. Yeah, his uniform sorta gives him away. Poor bastard is cuffed to a chair. Below him, carved into the hardwood floor is a sigil, hunters call them demonic nametags, and an Enochian key aka angelic nametag. Sigils are used to summon a demon, Enochian keys to summon an angel.

"Please." The thirty-something woman is tied to a radiator. "I have a daughter."

Black, six-inch, stiletto heels move into my view frame. Tight, black leather pants hug those endless legs in all the right places. "Tell her to shut up!"

The sound of her voice startles me. I step back, knocking right into one of those damn dressers.

Shit!

Flaming green eyes catch me off guard. Full lips, colored dark, matte red, curve into a wicked half-smile. "No need to hide." She moves toward the ajar door. "Come on in, Alex."

Steadying my Beretta, I push the swinging door open.

The First Knight lounges in an armchair by a coffee table. A steaming cup of tea and an ancient-looking tome sit beside him. Around him, forming a half-circle, are five faceless creatures, uglier than Voldemort himself. No kidding. Their eyes are hollow sockets, they lack a nose but rock two major holes, and don't even get me started on those yellow, razor-sharp teeth.

"Hello, Alexander." The bastard knight lifts his cup, saluting me.

I aim my gun at him, but keep my eyes on Manda. "Let's go."

She crosses her slender arms above her illegally perfect hips. "Go where, Alex?"

"Manda, I know what you did." She doesn't need to do the asshole's bidding to save me from hell. "I read your letter. And I get it. I do. But—"

"You don't get shit, Alex." She tilts her head to the side, exposing black lines. Wait, did she get a tattoo? If so, she went all the way and covered her whole damn body with ink. Arms, cleavage, neck, even part of her face up to her cheeks is laced with those damn black lines. Inching closer, I realize those aren't tatts. They're her damn veins.

Black. Fucking. Veins.

She winks at me. "Do you like what you see?"

"Manda, please…"

She pulls an athame out of the back of her pants, tapping the sharp blade against her temple. "Manda is dead," she says, voice cold and distant. "She died for an asshole who treated her like a piece of garbage."

"What the fuck are you talking about?"

She looks at the First Knight, grinning like the Cheshire Cat. "He wants to know what I'm talking about."

The First Knight eyeballs the terrified woman. "Why don't you show him?"

"It'd be my genuine pleasure." She walks up to the poor chick, pressing the damn blade against her throat.

"She's insane." The chick's vocal chords are strained. "Just shoot her. Please, just—"

I swore I'd never point my gun at Manda again, but she doesn't give me much of a choice. Not when the chick she threatens begs for my help, reminding me she has a two-year-old daughter at home. "Put the athame down, Manda."

She throws her wavy thatch over one shoulder and applies more pressure. The blade slices through the woman's neck, spilling fresh blood.

"Amanda," I yell. "Put that fucking thing down."

"Or what?" she says, batting her thick black lashes. "Are you going to shoot me?" Manic laughter assaults my ears. "Haven't we been through this already?"

"*You have to stop me*," her pleas come back to haunt me. "*Don't hesitate, Alex.*"

I can't and I'm done acting as if I could. "I'm not going to hurt you." I holster my gun. "Please, Manda, just—"

"What are you doing?" the sheriff yells. "Kill them, you idiot."

Manda's eyes catch fire. Literally. They burn like a fucking wildfire. "Quiet." Her voice thunders through my brain. "All of you."

My jaw clenches. I try to speak, but can't even move my damn mouth.

A hand lands on my shoulder. "Isn't she just amazing?" the bastard aka First Knight whispers.

I'm torn between slamming the asshole into the fucking wall, and cutting his smug smile out of his stupid face. Unfortunately, I can't do neither. Why? I'm pretty much rooted to the spot.

Manda steps back from the chick, shoving the blade into her waistband. Her lips curl into one of those aggravating smiles. You know, the one that makes me want to kill and kiss her at the same time. "Will you behave?"

Who is she? My mother?

Our eyes lock, her icy stare eliciting a shiver. "I think you will."

The feeling returns to my limbs. I can move my damn mouth again. "Manda, listen to me," I beg. "I know you sold your soul for me, but you don't have to do the asshole's bidding. Just walk away with me. Please?"

"It's a little late for that," the First Knight says. "Amanda is no longer under your spell, hunter. She caught a glimpse of darkness and it's so much sweeter than what you have to offer."

I ignore him, focusing on her and her only. "What, now he talks for you?" Bitter laughter crawls up my throat. "Wow. What happened to the girl that made her own decisions? The one who'd rather die than be somebody's bitch?"

"I told you she died."

I search for emotions, any emotion. There are none. The fire, the passion, the resistance, the fight—it's gone. *Puff*! Vanished. Whoever stands catty-corner from me isn't the girl I used to know. She's someone…something else.

Bastard knight wraps his disgusting hands around Manda's waist and lowers his chin onto her shoulder. He's so damn close, his lips touch the skin on her neck. "We're running out of time, love."

Man, I think I'm going to empty my stomach in his face.

Manda moves away from him and toward me. "Do you know why you're here?"

Because B did a locator spell and got me through the shield? "Enlighten me."

"Because I wanted to see you," she says, matter-of-factly.

Hope sparks in my heart. She wanted to see me. Maybe old Manda is still somewhere in there. "Well, I'm here."

"Yes, you are." She traces a finger down my cheek. Her touch is cold, yet like coming home after a long, exhausting hunt. I close my eyes, leaning into her. "And just like I thought," she says, withdrawing her hand. "I feel nothing."

My jaw drops. "Manda—"

"You're nothing to me, Alexander. Absolutely nothing." She laughs like a hyena. "I'm finally free. Your opinion means nothing to me. Living up to your expectations is just a distant memory of a past life."

My heart misses several beats. "You don't mean that," I say, not sure to whom. Her or me?

"Oh, yes." She cups my cheeks. "Yes, I do."

My gaze lands on the ancient tome on the coffee table. What was it Berith aka the Nun said? The book will corrupt her. Yup. That's what this is. Manda is under the influence of that damn book. Or else she'd never say shit like that. "This isn't you talking."

"Always looking for the good in me, huh?" She rolls her eyes. "Didn't anyone tell you? I was born to be evil."

"Stop that shit," I yell, at the brink of insanity. "You're not evil. This"—I look around—"all of this is my fault. I should have never doubted you."

"But you did," she says. "And now it's too late."

Manda spins on her killer heels, heading straight for the grimoire. Whatever she's up to it can't be good.

Stop her. You gotta stop her before it really is too late.

"What about Leandro? Is he nothing to you, too?"

Her shoulders tense.

"You have every right to hate me," I go on. "Trust me; I hate myself for what I did to you. But Leandro? You swore he'd grow up loved and cherished. And now you want to help that bastard kill him?"

She faces me, her eyes an ocean of blazing green flames. "Shut up."

I am getting to her. "That asshole"—I point at the damn knight—"abducted your son, Manda, and you're helping him?"

She lifts her hands. The room fills with electric energy. "I said shut up, Alex."

"No." I shake my head. "You were ready to give up your whole life for that boy. Don't you dare tell me you don't feel anything for him. That book might have you under its spell, but I know you, Manda. I know you better than you know yourself. And I'm telling you, you care about Leandro. Remember his smile? Are you sure you never want to see it again? Are you sure you want to leave him like your father left you? Treat him like your mother treated you?"

"Enough." Her voice rattles the damn walls. "You know nothing about me. Absolutely nothing."

You're wrong, Manda. And I'm gonna prove it to you.

Chapter 33

Amanda

Malachite eyes pierce mine. Once upon a time, I drowned in those eyes. They were everything I ever wanted, everything I could never have. Now that they look at me the way I always dreamed of—lovingly, longingly—they mean nothing anymore. I feel *nothing*.

Except for the power of the book.

Alex comes closer. "You're right, Manda. I don't know the girl standing before me. But the girl I fell in love with, the one who swore to fight the devil himself over my soul? I know all about her." He reaches for my hand. "She's still in there somewhere. And trust me when I say, she's one helluva lot stronger than some stupid book."

I step back, dull pain roaring through my chest. Looks like I do feel something after all. A shockwave from a different life. I remember saying I'd fight Lucifer over his soul back at Green House, shortly after I learned the truth about the deal he'd struck. I meant it, too. There was a time I would have died for him. But—

"He betrayed you," the book whispers.

Did he? Alex is a straight shooter. He learned I was a witch and pulled his gun on me. It's not like he set up a trap, or sent his hunter pals after me.

Alex cups my face. "Manda, please. I'm begging

you. Don't let my mistakes ruin your life." He pauses, looking me straight in the eye. "Your son needs you. *We* need you."

My son. Leandro. He was everything to me.

"This"—Alex tilts his chin at the sheriff—"isn't you, Manda."

Then why is part of me thrilled to break the fifth lock? "I…I—"

Alex grabs me by the elbow and spins me around. "Look around you, Manda. Just take a damn look."

The middle-aged, salt and pepper dude secretly tries to get out of his cuffs. Across from me is the sobbing chick. Knees tucked under her chin, she cries for the life she's about to lose.

I did this.

I barged in here with Clyde's minions, watched silently as they slaughtered four people and ordered them to tie those two up so we could use them as vessels. I didn't care about the screams of the deceased, had no regard for the lives of the living. A huge—very huge—part of me still doesn't mind the slaughter. But the look in Alex's eyes brings back memories of a girl that would care, a girl that sold her soul expecting to go to purgatory just so Alex would be okay.

Clyde watches me with eagle eyes. His minions shield him, observing my every move. The color of their auras tell me they want to interfere. The reason they don't? I could off the Voldemort fan club with the snap of my finger.

"Just come with me," Alex begs. "We'll figure this out. *Together.*"

"Together?" The book laughs. "Are you really falling for this? He's lying, Amanda. The second you give in, he'll kill you."

I drink in his light blue aura. He's not lying. He's never been so freakin' honest with me. "You don't know him."

Alex squints, assuming I speak to him. "Who?" He eyeballs Clyde. "The demon bastard?"

"Watch it," Clyde hisses.

"We can handle him," Alex says, ignoring him completely.

My gaze darts to the book. There's a spell in there. It's strong enough to kill a Knight of Hell and an angel. We were about to use it to break the fifth lock. But I'm not so sure I want to—

"You stupid child," the book barks. "He'd say anything to stop you. Don't you see? He doesn't care about you, or your son. All he cares about is saving the world."

Distant memories flash through my mind. Alex calling me names. Alex threatening to blow my brains out. Alex sitting beside me, begging me to open my eyes when I was shot. Alex consoling me after another one of Melinda's you-are-the-black-sheep-of-the-family speeches. He didn't always treat me right, but when I needed him he was there.

"You think he loves you, don't you? Then why don't you ask him about his business with your mother?" the book suggests. "Go ahead, Amanda. Ask him."

My gaze darts from the book to Alex. "You know my mother?" I barely recognize my own voice.

He looks up, sighing heavily. "Yes." His aura remains blue. He's telling the truth.

I don't understand. "How?"

"She came to me," he replies, his face a mask of regret and pain. "A few weeks after I learned the truth about you."

"Why?"

"Because"—his gaze drops to his boots—"she wanted me to kill you."

Heat rises in my loins. "And you didn't tell me?"

"I…I'm sorry." He caresses my cheek. "I—"

I slap his hand away. "You lied to me," I yell, voice like rolling thunder.

The book laughs. "Yes, he did."

Alexander Remington met my freakin' mother. She asked him to whack me and he did…absolutely nothing? Never even warned me.

Why are you so shocked? Since the day we met, the hunter treated me as if I were the reason for all the things that are wrong with this world. He disrespected me, called me names, and used me whenever he was in need of a bad girl to satisfy his senses.

Alex closes the gap between us. "I was a jerk, okay?" He scrubs his fingers through his messy, uncombed hair. "And I know I should have told you, but the things she said…" Trailing off, he shakes his head.

Energy buzzes through my hands. "What, Alex? What did she say? That I'll become the queen of darkness? That I'll end the fucking world?" I throw my head back and laugh. "Looks like she was spot on, huh?"

"No!" he half-shouts, half-pleads. "You're not evil."

"Sure I am." I tilt my chin at the sheriff. "Look around you. I did all this." I grin. "I walked into the FBI headquarters and watched over five dozen agents die. I turned the streets into war zones, and shook the earth."

He swallows. Hard. "You had no choice, Manda."

I laugh. "You always have a choice, remember?"

"No." He crosses his arms. "That bastard"—he eyeballs Clyde—"tricked us both. This isn't your fault. It's mine. I should have trusted you to make the right choices. But I was afraid. Afraid to lose you, Manda. Whatever you did it's not on you. It's on me."

"See," the book whispers. "By saving you, he's simply easing his guilty conscience."

"Yes, he is," I snarl. "And he calls me selfish?"

Alex narrows his eyes. "Manda, who the hell are you talking to?"

I lift my hands, a smile tugging at the edges of my lips.

"Manda, what are you doing?"

"Teaching you how to fly."

"Don't," he pleads. "Don't do it."

I snap my fingers. "Too late."

Alex smashes into the wall. Plaster crumbles. The skin above his left eyebrow tears, spilling fresh blood. By the time he drops to the floor, he's out cold.

Barbaric laughter crawls up my throat. He came to save me, thinking I'm some stupid damsel in distress, waiting for a white knight to lead me out of the darkness. Newsflash: I don't need saving. Not anymore.

"That's right," the book assures me. "You're better off on your own."

I fended for myself for as long as I can remember. Who is he to come barging back in my life pretending he gives a fuck or two about me?

Clyde breathes a sigh of relief.

"Tie him up," I order his minions, the hollow in my chest growing at a rapid pace. "Make sure you're thorough. I won't tolerate failure." The fifth ritual is too important to have Alex or anyone else screw it up.

Two Voldemort lookalikes seize hold of his arms, dragging his unconscious body over the floor to the radiator. Under my scrutiny, they cuff him with the sheriff's spare shackles.

Clyde appears next to me. "We've got everything ready, love."

My gaze darts to him. "What are you waiting for then? Summon them."

He flinches. "Watch your tone, Amanda."

I'm in his face. "Or what? Are you going to torture my soul?" I wink at him. "Go ahead and try. We'll see how that goes." The power buzzing through me numbs any pain Clyde could inflict on me.

Clyde cusses under his breath. Then he and his minions grab the woman they spared, the one we still need as a vessel, and tie her up on a chair next to the sheriff. Once they secured her, they step outside the circle and I secure it with the juniper mixture.

"Are you sure this will hold them?" Clyde asks, pointing at the herbs.

I cock a brow. "Are you sure you can summon them?"

He doesn't reply. Why would he? We both know he can.

They form a half-circle around the hostages. "What are you doing?" The woman cries. "Please, let us go."

"Don't bother," the sheriff barks. "They won't let us go." He eyeballs me. "Will you?"

"No. Not really." I shrug, lazily. "But if it makes

you feel any better, we greatly appreciate your sacrifice."

"Go to hell," he spits at me.

I laugh. "Nah, I'd rather bring hell to me."

Clyde slices his palm. Charcoal blood slides down his wrist, dripping onto the sigil and the Enochian key he drew earlier. *"Eerf uoy tes em ot emoc eeht nommus I em ot emoc, retsis, rehtorb."*

The foundation of the B&B rumbles, announcing the arrival of an upper-class demon, a Knight of Hell, and a cherub, one of the most powerful angels.

"Eerf uoy tes em ot emoc eeht nommus I em ot emoc, hsilleh retsis, ylnevaeh rehtorb," he repeats, his eyes burning like molten lava.

Glass shatters. Pictures fall. Furniture is tossed around.

He murmurs the incantation one last time. The ground stops shaking and an eerie silence settles upon us.

The woman's head jerks from side to side like a yoyo. She digs her nails into the chair, stiffening like a surfboard. The same goes for the sheriff. The vessels attempt to reject their possessors. Without much luck, I'd like to add. Knights of Hell and high-ranking angels don't necessarily need an invitation. They're powerful enough to possess anyone at any time. Unless, you wear a pentagram. Or better, get a permanent one with ink.

"Brother," the woman says, blinking her glowing amber eyes open. "What are we—" She attempts to get up. "What is this? Untie me. Now."

Clyde sighs. "Sorry, sis. Can't do."

"It's true then?" Possessed sheriff asks, eyes glittering like diamonds tossed in the ocean. "You are betraying your own kind with"—he shoots me a killer look—"*the* witch?"

Clyde moves to the edge of the juniper line. "I'm not betraying my kind," he justifies his treachery. "I'm freeing us. All of us."

The female knight bursts into laughter. "You clearly lost your damn mind, Beelzebub."

Clyde's jawline hardens. He's less than happy his lovely sister spilled his name.

"If you go through with this, we'll have to fight—"

"The last battle," he cuts her off, slightly annoyed. "Yeah, yeah, yeah. I heard that one before, sis. And I'm telling you what I told Berith, we will kick those"—he casts the angel a disgusted look—"bastards in the nuts, reclaiming what they've taken from us."

That's where he's wrong. The book doesn't want demons to rule the world. Neither does it root for angels. It wants the world gone, diminished to ashes and dust. I could tell him, but I sorta like the idea of destroying this shithole, including all its—my gaze lands on Alex—treacherous inhabitants.

Angel sheriff's eyes catch fire. Blue flames gaze back at us. In the blink of an eye, he gets rid of his shackles. "Stop this madness," he thunders, approaching us with a flaming sword. "Or—" He reaches for Clyde aka Beelzebub's throat, but the devil's claw I added to the juniper line sears his skin.

"Did you really think it'd be that easy?" Clyde smirks. "I am the First Knight, after all. You can't stop me. No one can."

"You're wrong," female knight blurts out.

"Am I?" Clyde teases her.

"Yes, brother." She zooms in on me. "There's

someone stronger than you. We both know she could kill you without breaking a sweat."

"She won't," Clyde argues, confident. "I have something she cares about."

The sheriff narrows his eyes. "Are you really that blind? Look at her," he urges. "She doesn't care about anything anymore."

Clyde has had enough. "Kill them," he orders me.

"My pleasure," I say, happy to send these bitches to purgatory or wherever else angels go when they push daisies.

I grab the *First Grimoire*. It opens the page of the ritual by itself. Sweet, huh?

"What do you need us to do?" Clyde asks, ready to assist.

I flash him a smile. "Just stay out of my way." The first four rituals might have required some help. Now that I'm pulsating with energy, I can do it all by myself. Besides, it's an easy one. All it requires is for me to read a line. Boom, the lock is cracked; demon and angel are dead.

Clyde squeezes my shoulder. "Amanda, your face…it's—"

"Beautiful?" I shrug. "Tell me something I don't know yet."

"No." He turns me to the broken mirror, near Alex. "Your veins are—"

"Black as my soul," I say, not impressed by my reflection. The black pest is all over me. But I already knew that. I felt the rush of power, spreading from my heart to my head.

"Maybe—"

"Step away," I warn him.

He eyeballs Alex. He's still unconscious. But I hear the Knight's thoughts. "She loved him. She didn't hesitate throwing him against a wall."

"That's right." I'm in his face. "I didn't. Imagine what I'll do to you."

The female knight bursts into laughter. "You created a monster, brother. One you cannot control."

"Shut up," he yells at her.

"She's right though," the angel says. "You found your master, demon. And she will be the end of you."

"The spell," the book reminds me. "It's time, Amanda."

Yes, it is. *"Rewop rieht em tnarg won, ssenkrad uoy evig I, thgil uoy evig I."*

Both angel and demon stare at me, eyes wide open. Next thing I know, light streams out of the angel's eyes just as darkness pours out of the demon's.

The angel drops his blade moments before the vessels go up in flames. I reach for the sword, handing it to Clyde. "Let's hit it." I turn to the door. "Hellam Township is a two-day drive and the full moon won't wait for us."

I stop next to Alex. There's a pretty bad hole at the back of his head. He's going to bleed out. Maybe I should end his suffering. Kill him right here, right now.

"No," the book insists. "Death is too easy. Let him watch the world burn."

Whatever.

Chapter 34

Alex

An annoying as fuck beeping echoes through my scrambled brain, and my ears ring like a mother. Last time I felt so miserable, I struggled to survive a hellhound attack.

"Are you sure Amanda did this to him?" a familiar voice pushes through the ringing and beeping.

After a short pause, B says, "We weren't inside. But..."

"He kept saying her name when we found him," Jesse adds.

When they found me? Does that mean I'm not in the B&B anymore? Then where am I?

"Sorry," another well-known voice mutters. "I just don't believe Amanda could have done this to him. She loves that asshole."

"Hey," Jesse barks. "That's my brother you're talking about."

"Yeah," the male voice shoots back. "I know."

"You're a prick, Bay."

Bay, huh? Yup, explains why his voice reminded me of hemorrhoids. On the bright side, it means the other familiar voice belongs to JJ. They were headed our way together.

"Guys," B barks. "Break it up, all right?"

"I just said what everyone else is thinking," Bay replies, matter-of-factly. "When it comes to Amanda, Alex actcd like an ass." Can't argue with that.

I try to open my eyes before the two strangle each other. Too fucking bad my eyelids are heavier than the rock securing Jesus's grave.

"Mr. Remington?"

Yes?

"Doc," Jesse says. "Any idea when my brother's going to wake up?"

Dude, I am awake. Sorta.

"Can we speak in private?" The doc sounds as serious as the one in Bakersfield who told us Manda might not survive the gunshot wound Walter inflicted.

"We're his family," JJ interferes. "Whatever you have to say, you can say it in front of us."

"She's right," Jesse adds.

Someone, I assume the doc, sighs heavily. "Your brother suffered major trauma to his head causing brain swelling. We administered some drugs to help relieve the swelling, but we had to put him in an artificial coma."

An artificial coma? How's that even possible? I can hear what they're saying, goddammit. It does explain why I can't open my eyes, though.

"What does that mean?" B sounds worried. I'm pretty sure that's a failure in my perception caused by the drugs they gave me. The mamba can't stand me. I don't think she gives a fuck if I ever wake up again.

"It means we have to wait and see." The doc sighs again. "If the swelling goes down, we can slowly wake him up. Until then, we'll keep him as comfortable as possible."

"In other words, you're pumping him full of pain meds hoping his brain returns to a normal size?" JJ earns a gold star for bitchiness.

"Yes," the doc replies. "You could say that."

Wait. What? No! I gotta get the hell out of here and find Manda. I recall her saying something about Hellam Township, a two-hour drive, and the full moon.

*On the first day, she saved his soul. On the sixth day, she'll climb the throne. The prophecy comes true when the moon—*is full, I guess. We have to find her before it's too late. Before she unleashes hell on earth.

"And there's nothing else you can do for him?" Jesse is beaten up.

"I'm afraid there isn't."

My little brother won't take no for an answer. "But—"

"Thanks, Doc," B cuts him off. "We understand."

"What the hell?" Jesse barks.

"There's only so much *Western* medicine can do, Jess." The way she emphasizes Western, tells me she has something voodoo up her sleeves. "Trust me," she pleads. "You know you can."

"Fine. We'll wait."

"I'll check in later," the doc says.

A door slams shut.

"Okay, whatcha got, B?" JJ sounds curious as hell.

"I'm gonna write down a list of things I need," she explains. "Get me the stuff and I'll try to get someone who can help Alex."

"Whatever you need," Jesse assures her.

I'm not a fan of witchcraft, but if it can get me out of this delirium I'm game. It's two minutes to midnight. Not just for the world, for Manda too.

****

I'm not sure how much time passes. One minute, I feel like I'm floating. As if I'm outside my body roaming the world. I walk bare foot through sand dunes, stick my toes in warm salt water, and gaze at the blue sky. Then I'm back at the hospital, listening to my worried friends. Jesse isn't sure B's plan—whatever it is—is so great. JJ thinks he's overreacting. And Bay, believe it or not, agrees with my brother. Me? I just want to be able to open my damn eyes.

I think I'm taking a sunbath somewhere in the Indian Ocean, when pressure builds in my chest. It hurts like a bitch. Comparable to an elephant napping on top of me.

Distant voices break through the clear, cobalt sky.

Whispers.

Groans.

Chants.

A dark cloud obscures the blazing fireball above. Palms leveled by heavy winds. My chest is lighter, but my head pounds like a damn drum.

The voices grow louder, closer. I can't make out what they're saying.

The winds rouse the sands. Soon, I'm in the midst of a sandstorm and the sun is completely swallowed by the dark cloud.

"Alexander?" None of my friends calls me that. "Open your eyes, hunter." The tone is sharp and unforgiving.

Chills ripple through me, the warmth of the Indian Ocean long forgotten. But no matter how hard I try, my eyelids won't move. I'm a prisoner of my own mind.

"It's not working," Jesse hisses.

A tongue clicks. "Give it some time," B says, her voice like a bucket full of ice. "His brain was damaged good."

A finger is between my eyebrows. The touch is cold and unpleasant, but it does something to me. I start to feel my limbs again.

"C'mon, hunter."

Ants crawl all over me.

"Yes, good."

My eyelids twitch.

The pressure between my eyes grows stronger, forcing the blackness into oblivion.

My eyes pop open. The fluorescent light blinds me. I blink over and over. Then, after an eternity of blurriness, I spot them—eyes the color of snow. "Welcome back."

Instinct kicks in. I sit straighter than a damn candle. "B?"

She smiles. "Not quite, but a close call."

I'm not into puzzles right now. "Who…"

"Berith," she replies.

The Princess of Hell? She healed Jesse and B after she tortured them. It was part of the deal the mamba struck with her. The demon would heal them, swear not to harm Leandro, and in exchange, B would find Manda. Question is why would she heal *me*? Did B strike another deal with her? Did Jesse?

Scanning the sterile room, I find my little brother next to the demon. He looks pale and tired, but his palms aren't bleeding. Good. You need to sign hellish contracts with crimson. In a chair, by my bed, sits JJ. Spine straight, she squeezes my hand. Bay, the Malleus hunter, is next to her. A half-smile on his lips, he nods once.

"What…the…" My brain has the consistency of pudding, making it hard to form coherent sentences. "Hell?"

Berith, aka the Nun, aka Princess of Hell inches closer. "I'm sure you've got questions, hunter. But so do I."

I reach for a glass of water, but JJ is quicker. "There you go."

"Thanks," I croak, mouth dry.

Gulping down the whole glass, I face the demon. "What do you want to know?"

"You saw Amanda, didn't you?"

I nod.

"She's infected, I assume?"

If by infected she means Manda has lost her damn mind and rocks a body full of black veins then, "Yes."

Her shoulders droop; hope escaping like hot air. "How bad is it?"

Everyone stares at me, expecting the worst, praying for the best.

"It's bad." So much so, she almost killed me. What am I saying? She left me there to die. She wanted me gone. That much I remember. But there's something else I recall. "It's not too late."

Berith squints. "The injuries she inflicted on you say differently."

"No." I prop my elbows into the mattress, pushing myself farther up. "There's still part of old Manda inside her." I pause, her emerald eyes flashing across my mind. "I almost got through to her. But somehow, someone told her about my encounter with her mother. Then…" I trail off. They already know what happened next.

Jesse's jawline hardens. "Alex, I get you want to save her. Trust me, I'm aware what she means to you…to *us*, but—"

"No!" I bark, strength returning to my voice. "She's not lost, okay?"

"She isn't," JJ says, probably to make me feel better. "Amanda is strong. She can fight this."

Berith rubs her chin. "Did she act weird?"

I almost laugh. "Apart from the fact she had the sheriff and a woman cuffed and almost killed me?"

"They needed them as vessels to break the fifth lock," Berith explains. "Now we have a dead Knight of Hell and a dead cherub on our hands." She draws a deep breath. "I understand you want to save her, but she's—"

"Going to be okay." I have to believe that. Or else I might die from desperation. "I can fix this. I swear I can get through to her."

Bay rubs his temples. "Hate to say it, Remington, but after what she"—he tilts his chin at the princess— "told us, there's no way you can fix this on your own." A dry laugh escapes his mouth. "Man, I'm not sure an army could stop the world's end."

"Maybe not *one* army," Berith says.

I ogle her. "What are you saying?"

Her gaze darts from my brother to me. "I'm saying this is an all-hands-on-deck situation."

JJ frowns. "Elaborate."

She studies us. "The way I see it we all want the same, don't we?"

"So?" Bay grumbles.

"Let's combine forces," she suggests.

Bay laughs.

Jesse's jaw drops.

JJ gives me the what-the-hell look.

Me? I think this might actually be the answer to my prayers. A Princess of Hell commands a legion. Together, we might stand a chance. "Hunters and demons working side by side?"

"If you have a better idea, I'm all ears." Working with hunters can't be her first choice. But the demon seems to be running out of options.

"You can't be serious," Bay barks. "Hunters will never, ever go for this."

"You better convince them." Berith flashes me a half-smile. "Because my demons found your son."

I'm on my feet in a heartbeat. "Where is he?"

"Alex," JJ hisses.

I ignore her, getting in Berith's face. "Where is Leandro?"

"Alex!" JJ is killing my last nerve.

"What?"

She points to my arm. "You're bleeding."

Yup, I am. Looks like I pulled the IV when I jumped out of bed. "I don't care." I just want to know where my son is.

Berith scans my face. "I'll tell you where he is." I literally hear the "but" coming. "But first I need to know if you guys are in."

I don't hesitate. "I am."

"Alex," Bay starts. "The others—"

I shoot him a killer look. "You think they'd rather watch the world go down in flames?"

"No," he replies. "But—"

"No buts. We're in," I reassure the demon. "But

there have to be some rules."

She smirks. "Lay them out."

It's simple. We kill no demons; they kill no hunters. No one and I mean absolutely no one, touches a hair on Leandro's scalp. And Manda is my responsibility. I screwed up her life; I'm the one who fixes it. Oh, yeah, there's the all-rules-apply-after-the-fight-too term. You know, just in case we make it out alive and Berith here thinks she can whack us.

There's a spark of respect in her eyes. "You're a quick study, hunter."

I think of B. "Had a great teacher."

"All right." Jesse steps between us. "I hate to break the news, but we don't even know where Manda is."

"Hellam Township," Berith and I say in unison.

"In sync with a demon," Bay grumbles. "How very Justin Timberlake of you, Remington."

Jesse pays no attention to him. "How can you be sure?"

"I overheard them talking about it," I admit.

He eyeballs Berith, waiting for her to answer.

She rolls her eyes. "What kind of hunters are you?"

JJ cocks a brow. "The kind that sends bitches like you to purgatory, darling."

She waves a non-existing white flag. "Relax, sweetheart." She draws a deep breath. "Hellam Township is where the main gate to hell is located."

The gate to hell is in Pennsylvania? Damn, I always figured the way Donovan McNabb played was inhuman.

Chapter 35

What's normal? For some, it's being greeted by your Martha Stewart-like wife and the scent of fresh-made lasagna. For me, it's walking into a shabby motel room, smelling like old socks and mold. Pretty much like the Modernaire Motel in York, where we'll rendezvous with Berith. The Princess of Hell allowed us to use her private jet again. It took us to Lancaster Airport where Demon-Boy and Pink Nail Polish waited on us with two cars—a pink Mini Couper, and a Bumblebee Camaro.

Jesse, B, and I were lucky enough to catch a ride with Demon-Boy. He drove like a lunatic. Once or twice, I pictured us kissing a damn tree. Jesse and JJ? Well, let's just say they're still a few miles away. Pink Nail Polish, opposed to her brother, drives like a snail.

I haven't thrown my duffle bag onto the bed yet when B's phone buzzes. "Mom," she half-yells into the speaker, throwing her curls over one shoulder. "Tell me they agreed." She pauses, her face unreadable. "So what does that mean?" The mamba's face lights up. "Awesome. I'll see you tomorrow then."

She shoves her phone in her pocket, facing me with a massive grin. "They'll be here early tomorrow morning."

I breathe a sigh of relief. "Good. We can use all the help we can get."

"Dude," Jesse grumbles. "Who are you?"

I'm the guy who needs to make sure his family gets out of this in one piece. And if it requires working with demons and witches then so be it.

Demon-Boy draws a deep, unhappy breath. Probably because *they* are B's two older brothers, and her mom. Rumor has it; she's the high-priestess of the New Orleans coven. Or in Demon-Boy's words, she's the mother of all mambas. When the demon heard B had invited them to join the end-of-days party, he lost it. "Are you fucking kidding me?" he barked. "I'm not going anywhere near your damn family." He already struggled with the fact Jesse and I had called Carter and Amelia, asking them to gather as many hunters as possible to meet us in Hellam Township. Adding B's family was just too much for the skinny demon.

B just laughed. "Scared they'll sent your sorry ass back to hell?"

Demon-Boy shut his mouth and kept driving.

The door flings open. Pink Nail Polish and the rest of the gang finally made it to the motel. The demon's gaze darts to her brother. "I got a call from the boss. We need to go."

"A call?" Bay grumbles. "I didn't see you on your phone."

B blows out a frustrated breath. "Because demons don't need Apple to communicate." She casts the hellish siblings a dark glance. "Isn't that right?"

Pink Nail Polish, aka Jules, aka former classmate of Manda, shrugs. "Looks like we're just cooler." B's about to argue with her, but the chick's already hauling her brother to the exit. "We'll be back in a few. And"— she peeks over her shoulder—"don't do anything stupid. Remember, we're the only ones who know where your little boy is."

"How could I forget?" Berith refused to share Leandro's location in the hospital. She didn't trust me to stick to our agreement once I had his location. Sorta hurts when a demon accuses you of treachery.

She studies me. "Just needed to make sure you know what happens if you fuck with us." That said, she's ready to hit the road to take care of whatever it is they have to take care of. I'm pretty sure it involves murder and mayhem, daily demon madness.

"Hey." B stops them. "You better come back and tell us where Leandro and Melinda are. Or—"

Demon-Boy is in her face. "Or what?"

"Or"—the mamba flashes him a scary smile—"I'll introduce you to my brothers."

Demon-Boy's eyes widen. It takes a second for him to regain control. "Maybe I should kill you right now."

Jesse is between them in a heartbeat. "Get the fuck out of here."

"C'mon, G." Pink Nail Polish drags the aggravated demon toward the door. "You know the boss hates it when we're late."

The moment they leave, Jesse sees his chance to let me know what he truly thinks of all this. "Dude." He scrubs his fingers through his hair. "I know you think this is the right thing to do, that you can save Leandro and Manda with the help of those bitches, but"—he sighs, heavily—"what happened to sticking to the golden Alexander-Remington rule?"

The never-consort-with-witches-and-demons rule? "I'm out of options, Jess."

"They're demons," he barks.

B wrinkles her forehead. "Demons, huh?" She slams her hands on both hips. "You were okay with a *demon* healing your brother, weren't you?"

"That's something entirely else," Jesse says, eyes clouded with...pain? Regret? Fear? A little bit of everything.

Wrong answer dude. B is boiling. No kidding. Her face is redder than a glass of Merlot. "I see." She throws him a disgusted look. "It's okay to work with hell as long as it benefits your brother. But when it comes to Amanda, the rules change, right? Why, Jess? Because she's a witch? Her life isn't as worthy as that of your jerk brother, is that it?"

Jesse shakes his head. "I never said that."

"You didn't have to," B shoots back. "Your actions speak louder than words, *hunter*."

He narrows his eyes at her. "So we're back to the hunter thing, huh?"

JJ hauls Bay to the door. "I think we'll crash in our room." In other words, they're exiting the war zone.

Damn, I wish I could tag along. But those two might kill each other without a buffer. "Guys." I hold my palms up. "Just—"

"Stay out of this, Alex." Whoa, it's official. My little brother has turned into a full-blown bitch. He returns his focus on B. "I'm not the bad guy here. I want Manda and Leandro to be okay, but—"

"Not as badly as your brother." B laughs. "I know, *hunter*. You made that perfectly clear when I shared my suspicions with you and you demanded not to mention it to your brother. I don't forget when someone threatens me, you know?"

"Threatened you?" Sorry, I don't want to get involved in their shit. It's just I have a hard time believing Jesse would do that.

"What?" Dark laughter escapes the mamba's mouth. "He didn't tell you how he threatened to send hunters after my family?"

"You did what?" I yell, unable to comprehend Jesse would do such a thing. He might not admit it, but a blind man could see he's head over heels in love with B. No way he'd threaten her family.

His gaze drops. "I was afraid, B. Afraid to lose my brother to hell. You, of all people, should get that."

Wait a minute. Was that an admission of guilt?

Bitter laughter crawls up the mamba's throat. "Should I, now?"

"Yes," he says, shoulders dropped, head hanging low. "You know how it feels to lose a sibling. I already lost a sister; I couldn't lose my brother, too." He exhales, sharply. "That's why I said all those things to you. I was scared you were right about Manda trading places with Alex. I just knew Alex would never accept that and I thought—"

"You thought I would find a demon who would trade again?" The second I say those words, I'm hit by a pang in the chest. Jesse had mentioned B's suspicions. He apologized for not telling me the truth, but now I understand he was ready to sacrifice Manda's life for mine.

He nods, never looking me in the eye.

"What the fuck is wrong with you, Jess?" He's the good Remington. The one who has compassion, a damn heart. "You love Manda. Why would you—"

"I don't know, okay?" He throws his hands in the

air. "I don't know what was going on with me. I thought of those past few months, the constant fear of watching you being dragged to hell, and I just…I snapped."

I get it. He didn't want to lose me. "But threatening B's family?" I can't believe he went that low.

"I didn't mean it," he assures me.

"Sure, you did," B hisses, before spinning on her heels.

She slams the bathroom door so hard, I'm afraid it might come off its hinges. The shower comes on. I get the feeling B is trying to wash off the hurt my brother caused her.

Jesse stares at the door. I've never seen him so low, so ashamed of himself. "I fucked up, huh?"

He lied to me, threatened B's family, and would have happily let Manda rot in hell. "You think?"

"I'm sorry," he says over and over.

Sorry, doesn't always make shit right. "I need some air."

****

"B!" Jesse bangs against the bathroom door. "Did you drown in the shower?" She's been in there for over two hours. He's running out of patience.

"Relax, dude. You screaming at her won't make her come out faster." A little birdy called intuition tells me it has the opposite effect. B's deliberately trying to piss Jesse off.

"But she's been in there forever," he justifies his worries.

Pressing the heels of my palms against my aching temples, I focus on my breathing. Inhale, exhale. Inhale, exhale. The shit usually helps me deal with aggressions. Not today, though. I walked around aimlessly for over an hour, trying to put myself in Jesse's position. I get why he was afraid. What I don't get is how he was so quick to give up on Manda, the girl he calls a sister. Anyway, being mad at him ain't helping us. I'll deal with his lies when this is over. "Just leave her be, all right." There's an edge in my voice I can't cover up.

"Whatever," he grumbles.

Silence stretches between us. It's a haunting sound, especially because it makes the voices in my head so much louder. *She almost killed you. Did you see the look in her eyes before she slammed you against the wall? Do you really think Berith will tell you where Leandro is? Are you sure you can stop Manda without hurting her?*

The dungeon flashes across my mind. Manda summoned me there when she was still herself. She knew what was about to happen to her. The reason she practically begged me to end her life before it's too late. After everything I've said and done, she thought I could kill her. God, I'm such a bastard. How awful did I treat her to give her—a witch who can read people like a damn book—the impression I wouldn't think twice?

Before the nasty voices in my head answer that, B marches out of the bathroom. She pays no attention to Jesse. Instead, she sits on the bed next to me.

"You okay?" I can't believe I actually care.

She shrugs. "Sure. Why wouldn't I be?"

My gaze darts to Jesse. He stands by the window, drowning in his own guilt.

"Have you heard from Berith?" she asks, changing the focus of our conversation to more pressing matters.

I grab my phone and show her the text I got earlier. "Tell them we'll met at the Redrock Café, seven a.m. Sharp," B reads.

"I already texted Carter and Amelia," I explain. "They'll tell the others."

B bites her lower lip, occasionally shooting Jesse a killer look. "My mom and my brothers should be here around six a.m." She stares at the windows. "I'll tell them to come here, first." She pauses. "If that's okay?"

"Sure." It'll give us time to prepare them for what's to come. Can't be pleasant for them to walk into a café full of hunters and demons. A little heads-up seems appropriate.

Jesse flings himself onto the free bed. "What about Leandro?" He sounds all business, but his voice trembles. "Did the demon say anything about his location?"

I wish Berith would drop from her high horse. I'm the hunter, she's the demon. And why would I abandon the mission, anyway? It'd be Manda's certain death. "Only that I should pick someone I trust for his rescue."

Jesse squints. "Wait, so we aren't going to get him out together?"

Yeah, I don't like that part of the plan either. "No." I steady my breath. "The demon thinks it's better we do it simultaneously. That way the First Knight can't interfere."

B lies back, gazing at the ceiling. "So whom did you pick?"

"Come again?"

She props on her elbows. "Whom do you trust enough to get Leandro back?" She smirks. "And before you say me, I should probably let you know my abilities are required on the battlefield."

Damn! I *was* going to pick her. Looks like I have to go with the next best option. "JJ and Bay."

"What?" Jesse jumps up. "You're trusting that Malleus dick with my nephew?" He's disappointed and hurt I didn't pick him. I'd feel the same if the roles were reversed. But this isn't just about what he did. Jesse is one of the best hunters I ever had the honor to work with. I need a man like him beside me.

"Like it or not," I say. "They both adore Amanda." Bay a bit too much, if you ask me. "I'm pretty damn sure they'll take good care of her son."

"Opposed to me?" he shoots back.

In a few hours, we'll host one of the most awkward meetings ever. I need to catch some sleep before that happens. "Let's hit the sack."

Jesse's eyes are full of pain. Any other day, I'd do my best to make it go away. This week has been rotten and I just can't deal with him right now. "Night," I say, rolling over.

Chapter 36

I tossed and turned all night, playing out a million horrific scenarios. They all ended in Manda and Leandro's death.

Crossing my arms behind my head, I gaze out the window. The sun slowly rises. Possibly for the very last time. If the First Knight succeeds, the world we know will no longer exist. All the scum locked up in hell will be freed; the final battle—whatever that is—initiated.

Weird. It kinda looks like any other sunrise to me. Maybe that's the point, though. You never know when it'll all be over. One second, the world revolves around the sun. The next, it ceases to exist. Life is unpredictable like that.

"Here." B shoves a steaming mug of coffee under my nose. "You look like you need it more than I do." I doubt that. She's been up all night, too.

"Thanks." Taking a few sips, I ogle the mamba. She's so fucking nice to me it's sorta scary. I am, after all, the Remington brother she can't stand. Hey, I'm not complaining. The last thing I need is her hating on me.

She plummets down next to me, watching my brother sleep. I recognize the look in her eyes. She still cares about him, despite the shit he's done. I used to think witches were the source of all evil, but they happen to be more forgiving than most humans.

"So," she says, eyeballing Demon-Boy. He walked

in here a little while ago. Without his other crewmembers. "You sure your boss is in?" She points at the guitar-shaped clock on the wall. "They've been gone for a while."

Demon-Boy leans against the wall. "They'll be here."

"If you say so," B grumbles, less than convinced.

"Hey." Demon-Boy smirks. "Don't bitch at me because you have trouble with your boyfriend."

Yeah, he shouldn't have said that. B is on her feet in a nanosecond. Her index finger comes up. "One: he's not my boyfriend." Her middle finger follows. "Two: mind your own damn business, asshole."

Demon-Boy lifts his hands. "Easy." He shoots her an annoying-as-hell grin. "I'm just saying I didn't screw you over." He tilts his chin at Jesse. "He did."

B moves to the door. "I'm going to check on Bay and JJ."

She's back in less than two minutes. "JJ is in the shower. They'll be here soon."

Sounds good. The shower part, I mean. I smell my shirt. It's disgusting. Happens when you don't change in two days.

Grabbing a towel, I move toward the bathroom when Demon-Boy shouts, "They're here." He paces the room like a maniac, searching for the quickest escape.

The commotion wakes Jesse. "What's going on?" His voice is sleepy and rough.

"They're here." Demon-Boy brings him up to date.

Jesse rubs his eyes. "Who's here?"

B's hand lands on my shoulder. "Do me a favor?"

"What's that?"

The ghost of a smile appears on her lips. "Try not

to be your usual jerkish self." She heads toward the door. "My family isn't big on hunters."

Jesse puts one and one together. "Shit." He's out of bed in no time. "Give me that," he barks, snatching the towel from my hand.

Next thing I know, the bathroom door slams shut.

Son of a bitch.

Demon-Boy hides in the corner farthest away from the door. "A word of advice?" he says, acting all Scooby-Doo. "Don't fuck with them."

"Wasn't planning to." The Lacroixs put the fear of God in a demon. Who am I to screw with them?

"Mom," B squeaks, jumping at a woman that can't possibly be her mother. She appears thirty max; her petite, curvy body is the definition of "wow," and her face…man, it's so perfect, Tyra Banks—a goddess in my book—can't compare to her.

The woman—still can't believe it's Mrs. Lacroix—kisses B's cheek. "I missed you too, honey bee."

I'm trying to wrap my head around the reality this *is* B's mom when Hulk—the dude's broad shoulders barely fit through the door—sweeps the mamba off her feet. "How many times have I told you to eat your spinach, sis?"

B's bitch face comes on. "I'll eat my spinach when you stop pumping weights to impress all those fake Hollywood chicks."

His eyes—they have the same cognac color as B's—light up. "Gosh, I fucking missed you," he says, hugging her so tight, he's practically suffocating her.

B hides a proud smile behind her famous bitch mask. "Of course, you did." She runs her knuckles over his short-cropped hair. "No one else gives you hell."

"Hey," he grumbles, pulling back. "You know I—"

"Hate it when I do that," she finishes for him. "That's the point."

Hulk frowns. "You're such a—"

"Goofball," a darker voice chips in.

Whoa. And here I thought Hulk was intimidating. Let me tell you, he's nothing compared to Goliath. B's other brother is at least two heads taller than I am. Built like a damn tank, he's ready to waltz down anyone dumb enough to stand in his way.

Goliath drops his bags, pulling B in a tight embrace. "Looking good, sis."

B throws her arms around Goliath's neck. "As charming as ever, Raphael."

"So." Hulk cracks his knuckles. "Where's the fucktard of a demon messing with my favorite Bishop witch?" he asks, immediately zooming in on Demon-Boy.

"N-not me," Demon-Boy assures him, hands up in defense. "I-I'm...team witch."

Hulk and Manda are close. A stab of jealousy pricks at my gut. They'd make a great couple. A witch and a brawny, way too handsome—Scott Eastwood with better skin color—voodoo priest. A match made in witch heaven.

B rolls her eyes. "Chill, Constantin." B faces her mom. "We're pretty sure it'll go down tonight." B already told them about the raising hell part. She points at me. "Alex heard them talking about the full moon."

"Makes sense," B's mom says, while her sons kill me with their eyes. "According to old legends, the gate was sealed during a winter solstice."

"A what?" Sorry, I don't speak witch just yet.

B is all set to translate, but Constantin aka Hulk has other plans. "Well, well. If it isn't Alexander 'the dickhead' Remington." He scans me head to toe. "Gotta say, I don't see it."

Defensive, I cross my arms. "See what?"

He approaches me, murder on his face. "How a girl like Amanda could fall for an asshole like you," he replies, matter-of-factly.

You have no idea how badly I want to aim my fist at his nose. Only reason I don't? The dude's not completely off the charts. Amanda does deserve better. Doesn't mean I'll admit that. "Guess I'm just awesome like that."

His steaming breath beats against my forehead. "Awesome?" He draws to his full height, not once taking his prying eyes off me. "You hear that, Mom? He thinks he's awesome. Ain't that sweet?"

Mrs. Lacroix straightens her cashmere coat. "This isn't the time, Constantin."

"I think it is," he shoots back. "He should know how awesome he was when he abandoned a pregnant girl, who had nowhere to go." Constantin closes the tiny gap between us. "Did you know she had to get food from a shelter while carrying your son, Mr. Awesomeness?"

Cold shivers curse down my spine. "I—"

"You what?" he barks, voice filled with disgust and hate. "You celebrated your awesomeness while she was in labor for over eighteen hours? Where were you when I held her hand during an emergency C-section my brother had to perform?" He spits on the floor. "You're right. All that awesomeness must be acknowledged, Alexander."

I've been shredded to pieces by a hellhound, assaulted by several deadly weapons, and thrown against a damn wall by the girl I love. No pain I suffered compares to the one Constantin just inflicted. My chest cramps. Hell, I can barely breathe. But I don't deserve better. I left Manda to fend for herself while she was pregnant with my child. I pointed my fucking gun at her head when his heart was already beating inside her. I can't even begin to imagine how terrified she must have been when she learned about Leandro. She had to go through all of it by herself because I was so damn *awesome.*

"What?" Constantin flashes me a wicked smile. "Ain't got nothing to say, Mr. Awesome?"

Old me would jump the dude. New me is tired of living a lie. "I'm sorry." The words are barely a whisper.

His eyes widen. "Come again?"

I swallow all the self-loathing crawling up my gullet. "I'm sorry," I repeat a little louder. "I'm sorry I wasn't there when she needed me. And I'm sorry I didn't get to see my boy's first breath, smile, or hear him say his first words. I wish I could go back and change it, but—"

"You can't," he barks.

I shake my head. "But I can make it right. I can and I will."

Goliath aka Raphael is next to his brother. One hand on his shoulder, he says, "He deserves a chance, Constantin."

Constantin frowns. "Why?" His gaze stays glued on me. "He's just like all the other hunters. Thinks he's better than us. That his mighty ancestors had a right to burn our families at the stakes for no fucking reason."

B's mom moves closer. "He's not responsible for the deeds of his ancestors. Just like you aren't accountable for that of yours." I like that woman already. "Besides, he'd die for his child."

I would? His angelic face flashes across my mind. Yeah, I would.

Raphael nods. "I know you can feel it, too, brother."

Constantin shoots me a killer look. "You hurt that boy or Amanda again," he says, breathing in my face. "And I will personally end your pathetic existence. Did I make myself clear?" Even if his fists weren't balled, I could tell he's not fucking around.

I study him long and hard. Anyone who's ready to protect Manda has my gratitude. "Wouldn't want it any other way." Truth be told, should I hurt her again, I'll swallow my own bullet.

"Great." B smiles approvingly. "Now that that's settled, can we focus on saving them?"

"Finally," Demon-Boy murmurs.

Constantin's unforgiving murderous gaze darts to the demon. "What's this scum doing here?"

Demon-Boy aka G shifts his weight from one foot to the other, growing increasingly twitchy. "I...I..."

Constantin is in his face. "You were about to move your bony ass out of here?" He laughs. "Good choice."

The demon's shoulders tense. "I-I'll get some soda," he stammers.

"Damn," I say, stunned by how quickly he's out of the room. "He—"

"Knows what's good for him," Constantin says.

B throws her arm around me. "Did I ever tell you

about my big brother's special gift?"

"As in seeing the future or compelling poor mothers?"

Raphael's lips curl into a half-smile. "More like being able to cast lower demons back to hell."

My eyes widen. "You can send these bitches back to hell? Just like that?"

Constantin's chest swells. "Unlike you, I truly am awesome." He ain't got no issue with confidence, that's for sure. But having the ability to send demons back to the pit is pretty fucking amazing. Kinda makes him my new hero.

Mrs. Lacroix moves to the table, swinging her hips like a stripper with the grace of a ballerina. Man, hate to say it but she's the reason the expression MILF exists. "Why don't you tell us what happened?" Her voice is soft and sweet. Yet I wouldn't want to cross her.

We gather around the table. B and I take turns filling them in on what went down before all hell broke loose.

Raphael folds his hands on the table. "Let me get this straight. You, a hunter, sold your soul to make sure Manda wouldn't become the queen of darkness. She, in return, sold hers to save you from hell. Now she's corrupted by the *First Grimoire* and helping the First Knight raise hell?"

Smooth summary. "Pretty much."

"Whoa." Constantin stares a hole in my head. "Rewind. You, Alexander 'fucktard' Remington, sold your soul for one of us? For Amanda?" He shakes his head as if he's trying to wake from a dream. "I...you...why?"

B smacks him.

"Hey, what was that for?"

Mrs. Lacroix is the one who answers. "Because you had to ask." She flashes me a brilliant smile. "It's obvious how much he loves Amanda."

It is?

Constantin's face turns to stone. "Enough to get her into this damn mess in the first place, I assume."

Ouch.

B is about to smack him again, but I catch her hand. "He's right." They all gawk at me. I don't care. They need to hear the truth as much as I need to get it out. "Everything I did since the second I learned Manda's secret was despicable. I treated her like shit. Over and over." I draw a deep breath, gathering as much courage as I can. "I was a coward. But I never wanted to see her hurt." I look at them. "You have to believe me."

"We do," Mrs. Lacroix assures me, taming her long curls with one hand. "We do believe you, Alex."

Raphael and B nod.

And Constantin? He shrugs, unimpressed.

"This is worse than we thought," Raphael murmurs.

"Yes." Mrs. Lacroix straightens her silk blouse. "But we all sensed the shift in balance."

Raphael sighs. "We need some assistance."

Mrs. Lacroix grins. "It's why I have Louisa and the others on stand-by." She draws a deep breath. "As soon as night falls, they'll initiate the ritual."

"What ritual?" Jesse asks, coming out of the bathroom.

Both Lacroix brothers shoot daggers at my little brother. Hey, I don't blame them. I'd do the same if B was my sister. "Jesse Remington?" Raphael breaks the silence.

Taken off guard, Jesse drinks in the brawny brothers. "Yeah." Swallowing his unease, he moves closer. "And you must be"—he faces Hulk—"Constantin and"—his gaze lands on Goliath—"Raphael?" They both nod. "Nice to meet you," he says, trying his famous Remington charm on them.

They're immune. Most likely because they rock a penis, not a vagina. "Wish I could say the same," Constantin grumbles.

B elbows him. Hard. "Shut up," she hisses, blushing like a teenager. I wonder what she told her siblings about Jess. Enough to heat her face.

Constantin's lips part, but his mother is faster. "Come sit with us," she invites Jesse.

My little brother hesitates. Then he shakes off whatever fears he has and joins us.

"So the ritual." I try to take the focus away from Jesse and B. This is awkward enough as it is. No need to make it worse. "You were saying?"

"Louisa and the rest of our coven will slow the First Knight down," Constantin explains, voice sour, eyes screaming "murder."

It's moments like these I wish I spoke witch. "How can they slow him down?"

"If they channel enough energy, they can weaken the demon," B explains.

Raphael cups his chin. "Yeah, but not for long. A Knight of Hell is stronger than ordinary demons. We have a five-minute window max."

"What about Manda?" There's gotta be something they can do to bring her old self back.

They all avert their gazes. "Amanda can't be touched by our magic," B's mom finally says. "Only she can break the curse of the *First Grimoire*."

"How?" I need to know.

"She has to fight the book's influence." B sighs. "And she can. We both know Amanda can do anything she sets her mind on. But…"

"She'll need a little reminder of her true self," Raphael adds. "That's where you come into the picture. You can bring her back. If you truly love her, Alex, you'll find a way to break through her fears."

No pressure there. But he's right. I got to her at the B&B. I knew it the instant her eyes turned emerald again. I can get through to her again. Only this time, there are no more secrets that can get in the way. "I'll fix her," I swear.

Mrs. Lacroix smiles. "We know you will."

"Speak for yourself," Constantin grumbles.

Ignoring his side-blow, I focus on Mrs. Lacroix. "There's something else."

Constantin cocks a brow. "Yeah? What's that?"

I head to the window, searching the parking lot for Demon-Boy. He's nowhere in sight. So I tell them what's been keeping me up all night. "From what I've heard, everyone—demons and hunters alike—want Leandro gone. They think he's an…an…"

"Abomination," B says, realizing I can't get the damn word out.

Chewing on my lower lip, I sigh. "Yeah, that."

Constantin cocks a brow. "Continue."

"I don't trust the demons to keep him safe," I admit.

"Understandable," Raphael says.

"Do you know where he is?" Mrs. Lacroix inquires.

"No." I dig my nails into my palms. "The demons do."

Constantin is on his feet in a heartbeat. "Where is that little scum? I'm gonna beat it out of him."

His mom seizes hold of his shirt, pulling his butt back down. "Not so fast."

He casts her a surprised glance. "Why? He knows where Leandro is."

"He also works for the Princess of Hell," B shoots back. "Your magic won't work on her. Besides, we need them if we want to stop the apocalypse, remember?"

Constantin isn't the kinda guy to take no for an answer. In another life, we might have actually become friends. "Fine." He crosses his arms above his brawny chest. "What's the plan then?"

The door swings open. For a second, we all freeze, thinking it might be Demon-Boy. Luckily, it's JJ and Bay. "What did we miss?" the huntress says, winking at the Lacroix brothers. One of which practically drools over her. That'd be Constantin.

Mrs. Lacroix's smile is devilish. "Divide and conquer."

"Come again?" Bay murmurs.

The mother of all mamba's rises to her feet. "That's how you beat the devil." She untangles her curls. "Should work with demons, too."

I was right. I *do* like that woman.

Chapter 37

It's ten to seven when Constantin pulls into the overcrowded parking lot of Hellam Township's Redrock Café. It's a notorious biker bar, owned by some of Berith's friends if we can believe Demon-Boy. He assured us we'd have the place to ourselves.

A bar full of hunters, demons, witches, and booze. What could possibly go wrong?

A lot, but I better not think this through. Instead, I ogle the cars. Carter's SUV sits next to Amelia's purple '59 Buick LeSabre. I spot a couple of other government SUVs. The tinted windows give them away. Several other cars line the front of the bar. The brand-new Mustang belongs to Kyle Torres. He was one of the hunters at Amelia's when the four of us—Jesse, B, Manda, and I—stayed there. "Can't believe she called him," I grumble.

Jesse gazes out of the window. "I don't think Torres is our biggest problem," he says, tilting his chin at the army green disaster—a Nissan Frontier.

"Fuck." I have nothing against the car per se. The "Still a Virgin? I Can Help" bumper sticker on its tail, however, is as tasteless as its owner, Peter Draco. The second hunter at Amelia's the night we stayed there. He's a freelancer who treats women like whores, kills everything crossing his path, including witch kids—he helped Legend off the Kansas coven—and is a misogynistic bigot. We worked *one* case together. A wendigo hunt. The victim, a nineteen-year-old transgender student, had been attacked by one on his way home from college. Unfortunately, he'd scratched his leg on a branch during the attack. Peter spotted the wound and pulled his gun on him. If it wasn't for Jesse and me, the kid would have swallowed Draco's bullet. We confronted Peter. He swore the kid's sexual orientation hadn't influenced his decision; he'd merely thought the kid had been infected by the wendigo. None of us—not even Peter's BFF Torres—bought his bullshit. Wanna know what's worse? A couple of days after we saved the kid, Torres set a trap for him and killed him nevertheless.

B's gaze darts from the car back to us. "Someone tell me why you look like Negan is waiting on us inside?"

Compared to Draco, the *The Walking Dead* villain is a saint. No fucking around. Draco is as rotten as freelancers get. I can't tell her that. Not just because Constantin casts me killer looks from the driver seat. Nope. B is already worried enough. I don't need to scare her with horror stories of the asshole Draco. So I just say, "Amelia brought backup."

"Is that a good or a bad thing?" She most likely senses my worries.

"We're about to find out," Jesse replies as Constantin maneuvers his Mercedes S-Class coupe into the narrow parking slot next to Demon-Boy's Camaro.

JJ, Bay, and the skinny demon are already waiting on us. Told you, the crazy mother drives like a lunatic.

Raphael and Mrs. Lacroix are the last ones to arrive. Like his brother, he drives a fancy German car.

And not just any one either. He's the proud owner of BMW X5M G-Power Typhoon—one of the most expensive BMWs ever built.

Guilt nags at me as I exit the Mercedes. Two voodoo priests, two mambas, and a skinny demon walk into a bar full of hunters. No, that's not the beginning of a joke. It's brutal reality. Our reality.

Demon-Boy grows increasingly twitchy. He scans the parking lot, probably calculating his chances of getting out of here alive. Oddly enough, I feel sorry for the poor mother. Berith and his sister are nowhere in sight. Can't be pleasant to walk into the lion's den without backup.

"Hey." I nudge him. "You okay, dude?"

"Yeah," he lies, acting all confident and shit. "Why wouldn't I be?"

I could think of a dozen reasons. A bar full of hunters hating his very existence is just one. "Are you sure the rest of your crew is coming?" They should have been here by now.

He peeks at his Mickey Mouse Swatch watch—a fashion relict of the 80s. "They'll be here any minute." I sure hope he's right. For all our sakes.

Constantin enjoys Demon-Boy's uneasiness. I can tell by the way he looks at him.

"All right, let's do this," I say to the odd group standing before me.

We head toward the entrance when Demon-Boy seizes hold of my jacket. "Hey."

I glare at his hand and he immediately drops it. "Did you change your mind?" I wouldn't blame him.

He shakes his head. "Just keep this one"—he points to Constantin—"away from me, okay?"

"He won't send you to hell." *Yet.*

"Yeah." He plays cool. "Just don't want the stink of voodoo-ass on me."

I laugh. "Right." That's the only reason he doesn't want to be anywhere near the dude who could send him straight back to hell.

I join the rest of the gang on the porch. "They have no idea we're coming, do they?" Raphael whispers.

"Nope," I answer honestly.

Constantin flashes me his brilliant teeth. "All the more fun."

"You and I," I say, "have a very different definition of fun."

The real-life exorcist just shrugs and moves on.

Considering the place is crawling with hunters, B's family is pretty chill. Jesse and Demon-Boy not so much. They're both worried. The demon for himself. Jesse for B.

Constantin halts in front of the door, shooting Bay and JJ a look. When they nod, signaling they know their parts, he pushes the double doors open.

We cross the threshold and every movement inside the bar stops. It's so damn silent you'd hear a needle drop.

Hello, awkward!

"Interesting," Constantin says, ogling the crowd.

Yeah, not the word I would have used to describe the bizarre scene. Scattered around the tables are Carter's men. Like every good PAU member, they wear cheap, black suits, white shirts, and black ties. Coffee mugs sit in front of them.

Lined up at the bar is the freelance faction, easily distinguishable by their flannel shirts, ripped jeans, and all around messy looks they rock. Instead of coffee, they downed a couple of beers. It's crazy. They're all hunters yet they couldn't be more different.

Scanning the murderous faces, I search for familiar ones. Amelia is at the bar. Hand on her gun, she studies B's brothers like a damn hawk.

A chair screeches over the floor. Seconds later, Carter moves toward us. His gaze barely graces mine before he averts it. Something's up. "I'm sorry," he mutters, once he's right across from me.

My stomach twists and turns.

Jesse cocks a brow. "What's up?"

Carter looks over his shoulder, tilting his chin to the back of the bar. "I had to tell them," he whispers. "I just had to."

By the time, I realize who *they* are I want to slam my fist in his face. How could he do this to us? How could he call the one person I begged him not to?

"Alex." B tries to loosen my grip on the collar of Carter's shirt. I didn't even realize I grabbed him. "Don't make this worse than it already is," she pleads.

I'm convinced worse is not an option. Legend, the leader of the Malleus Maleficarum Order is here. Carter, my friend, the guy who knows exactly what this douche and his men are capable of, invited him to the show. There's no way he'll let Manda walk out of this alive. And Leandro? He'll slaughter him like he did the kids of the Kansas coven. So yeah. It can't possibly get worse. Except maybe when I spot Carter's men—my colleagues—on their feet, reaching for their guns. I worked with some of those guys, would have died for them. Now, they're ready to take me down without fair warning? So much for the hunter code.

Jesse is behind me. His uneven breath beats against the nape of my neck. "Just relax," he whispers. "We're on a clock, dude. Let's not waste our time on"—he casts Carter a dark glance—"him."

Carter looks up. "Alex, this isn't just about you or Amanda," he argues, sounding all PAU boss. "This is about the survival of humanity. We need all the help we can get."

"Wanna know what I needed?" I inch closer. "For you to be my friend," I say quietly, before bringing some space between us.

Carter exhales sharply. "I *am* your friend."

"Yeah." I laugh. "With friends like you who the fuck needs enemies, right?"

"That's enough, Remington." Legend approaches me. Behind him, treading on his heels is Hillbilly Mountain Man. The dude's beard resembles the wilderness, growing in all directions aimlessly. His yellow rotten teeth probably never saw a damn toothbrush. "Daryl and I are here to help," the Malleus leader dick assures me. "Nothing more, nothing less."

Constantin raises his brows to his hairline. "Help, huh?"

"Yes." Legend looks me right in the eye. "The way I see it"—he scans the crowd—"you could use a hand or two."

"To murder innocent children?" Raphael asks, drawing to his full, scary height. "Like the ones in Kansas?"

Legend rolls the sleeves of his shirt up, showing off his tatts. "Correct me if I'm wrong, but there won't be any innocent children left if we don't stop Amanda Bishop and the First Knight."

"None of this is Amanda's fault." God, I have no clue why I just said that. It's not like I hoped he'd believe me. "That damn book has her under a spell or something."

"Dude's got some nerve." Draco, king of assholes, nips on a beer at the bar. "After everything, he's still defending his witch whore."

A rush of adrenalin accelerates my heartbeat. "Wanna say that again?" I bark, muscles stiff, eyes narrowed.

Draco puts his beer down, slowly turning to face me. A nasty, self-righteous grin plastered across his ugly visage. "I think you heard me, Remington."

In my peripheral vision, I catch a glimpse of Hillbilly Mountain Man aka Daryl. He, too, grins, clearly enjoying himself. I don't ask myself if I should kill them. All that bothers me is which one I off first.

Draco jumps from the barstool, moving nearer. "Do you think we're stupid, Remington? Do you honest to God believe we don't know whose fault all of this is?" He points at the crowd. Some, like Torres, nod. Others, like Amelia, avert their gazes. "You could have killed that witch." Disgusted, he shakes his head. "Hell, her own mother came to you, begging you to kill her. But you screwed the little whore some more, didn't you?"

Lunging forward, I aim my fist at his crooked nose. Crimson splatters. My elbow thirsts for more, delivering a precise uppercut to the bastard's left temple.

Draco's hip knocks into a table. The skin above his eyebrow is torn. "Witch-fucker," he yells, attempting to strike back.

I dodge his right hook, bringing my fist up to his chin. The impact sends him flying to the ground. I could stop. I should stop. I don't.

In a flash, I'm on top of him, assaulting his ugly face. The shit of the past few days bursts out of me. I'm a man out of control.

"Alex!" Jesse catches my arm before I land another hit, demolishing Draco's nose some more. "Stop."

It's too late to stop the beast. Now that it's unleashed, it demands blood. Draco's blood. "Let the fuck go," I yell, murder running through my system.

Someone, I think Constantin, chuckles.

"You're killing him," Jesse reasons with me.

"Let. Go," I warn, a deadly ring to my voice.

Somehow, Draco manages to crawl out from under me. "Yeah," he says, spitting fresh blood on the floor. "Let him go." He wipes crimson off his face. "Let him show everyone what a failure of a hunter he is. It's not like we didn't already know." He zooms in on the Lacroixs. "Look at him," he says to the crowd. "Even now he consorts with those abominations."

Constantin steps forward. "Careful, dickhead."

"Or what?" Torres barks, helping his beat-up friend to his feet.

Raphael, the calm and reasonable Lacroix brother, smiles. "Or we could show you what those abominations are capable of," he says, with a calmness that's both scary and downright impressive.

Draco sways toward me. Looks like he hasn't had enough. "You can hide behind your witch friends all you want, Remington. At the end of the day, you know damn well I'm right. This"—he tilts his chin at the other hunters—"is on you. Had you killed that whore when you had the chance, we wouldn't face the end of days."

Whore. There's that word again. It's my fucking kill switch, turning me into a machine. My fists come up. I'm seconds away from ending Draco for good. Too bad Legend steps between us. "Enough." He turns to Draco. "You don't know what would have happened had he killed her." Legend faces the bar full of hunters. "None of us does. And shoving the blame around isn't going to help anyone right now."

Everyone, including the witch faction, stares at the Malleus dick, who did a very undickish thing. Hell, even Demon-Boy peeks over Mrs. Lacroix's shoulder. He's been hiding behind the mother of all mambas since the second he saw Legend.

"All right." Legend scrubs his inked fingers through his hair. "Let's not waste any more time, okay? We've got a war ahead of us. A bloody one at that."

"He's right," Mrs. Lacroix agrees. "There's plenty of time to murder each other *after* we kept hell at bay."

Draco laughs. "I ain't taking orders from a—"

"Shut your cakehole, Draco." Amelia rises from her barstool, hand on her gun. "The woman has a point."

Draco gawks at Amelia. You could think the old woman is a damn alien or something. "But—"

"You know how much I hate to repeat myself, don't you?" She sounds like Berith, only scarier. Her face is like stone, but her trigger finger ready to do some damage.

Draco—he's always been petrified of Amelia—swallows. Hard.

A victorious smile spreads across the huntress'

face. "All right, Alex. Let's hear what you've got for us."

I'm in no position to fill everyone in. My thoughts revolve around broken bones, blood, and a very dead Draco. Jesse and B do the honors. To my surprise, the hunters listen to the mamba without cutting her off once. I attribute it to the fact most of them have penises and mamba or not, B is stunningly beautiful and incredibly smart.

Torres is the first to speak once B and Jesse shared all the intel we have on the impending apocalypse. "What you're saying is that Knight of Hell—"

"The First Knight," B corrects him.

Torres waves her off. "Anyway, the demon is using the witch to open the gate to hell to let out…what exactly?"

"Your worst nightmares," the Princess of Hell answers.

Chapter 38

All eyes are on Berith. The Princess of Hell, who still looks like a devoted Sunday school goer, leans against the doorframe, her amber eyes roaming the crowd. Pink Nail Polish is by her side. Unlike her boss, and much like her brother, she's a nervous wreck.

The bar is wrapped in utter and complete silence. Berith pushes herself off the wall. "Did you miss me?" she whispers in my ear, her cold breath electrocuting the hair on the back of my neck.

I ignore her flirtatious act and focus on what's really important. "Where's your backup?"

She smiles like the devil. Then turns to Pink Nail Polish. "Would you?"

The demon nods. Pushing the double doors open, she exposes a parking lot full of demons. Fuck. That's…a damn legion. Seriously, there are hundreds of red-eyed mothers staring back at us.

In the corner of my eye, I see hunters reaching for their guns, pointing them at the demon horde outside. *As if bullets can help them.*

For once, the Lacroixs and the hunters share a common enemy. The witches stand taller than a skyscraper, ready to jump those bitches.

In a dramatic motion, Berith rolls her eyes. "Would you all relax?" She sounds rather bored. "We all have the same goal," she assures the anxious crowd.

"I doubt that," Mrs. Lacroix hisses.

Amelia is by the mamba's side, nodding. "Me too."

Berith turns her attention to Legend. The Malleus leader and his Hillbilly Mountain Man are calmer than the other hunters. But I recognize the spark in their eyes. It's the same one I rocked every time I sent a witch to the wasteland. The Princess of Hell must see it, too. She just decides to ignore it. "You know you can't stop them alone." She gestures at her army. "But together, we stand a fighting chance."

Legend mulls it over. "A truce?"

"Only until this is over," she replies, making it clear she doesn't want permanent peace.

Daryl, the Mountain Man, nudges Legend. "You're not buying this, are you?"

The Malleus leader pays no attention to his protégé. "Make your case, demon. We're listening."

Who the fuck made him boss?

Berith addresses the crowd. "The First Knight wants to resume the finale battle. By breaking the last of the six locks, with the help of the witch, he will release every god, creature, and demon in hell, thereby forcing the creator's hand. If they succeed, if the last lock is broken, there is no turning back. We will fight and"—she looks around—"all of you, petty humans, will perish first."

Whispers roar through the crowd. Fear, terror, desperation—it stretches like wild fire, poisoning the already thick air.

Draco steps up. "And how do you suggest we stop his witch whore and her knight?"

I swear, by God, if he calls Manda that one more time, I will send him to hell. I have a feeling he'd be a great asset in the infernal regions.

Mrs. Lacroix draws a deep breath. "We"—she gestures at her kids—"will slow the knight down."

"And they"—Berith points at her demon legion—"will take care of his army."

Of course, he has an army, too. Life isn't fucked up enough already.

"What about Amanda?" Legend sighs. "She's an untouchable. Their"—he tilts his chin at the Lacroixs—"magic won't affect her."

"I'll take care of her," I say, quicker than a bolt of lightning.

Draco bursts into cruel laughter. "Hate to break it to you, pal, but screwing her ain't going to solve the problem."

I'm all set to punch the bastard again. Too damn bad Jesse is quicker. "You just don't know when to keep your fucking mouth shut, do you, Draco?"

Peter presses the heel of his palm against his swelling eye. "Son of a bitch," he cusses, under his breath. "You're just like—"

Berith snaps her fingers, sealing Draco's mouth shut. "You're giving me a headache," she justifies her use of demonic power on a hunter in a bar full of hunters.

No one—not even his BFF Torres—objects.

Ignoring his why-the-fuck-aren't-you-helping-me look, Amelia pushes past Draco. "All of this sounds good," she says, bringing the conversation back on track. "You just missed one crucial fact. It's a Knight of Hell we're talking about; even if the witches can weaken him, he can't be killed."

"Yes, he can." Daryl's chest swells with pride.

"Killing those mothers is our specialty, ma'am."

Legend nods. "We'll take care of him," he assures the huntress, more serious but not less confident than Mountain Man.

"And I'll help them," Berith adds.

"Well then." Amelia taps the heels of her red cowboy boots against the floor. "What are we waiting for?" She casts the other hunters a look. "Get ready. We're about to go to war."

The crowd breaks into smaller groups. Weapons gathered, guns loaded, and new friendships made. Every now and then, a dirty look shoots my way. I ignore them to the best of my abilities.

"Alexander?" Berith is beside me. "It's time."

My heart swells, aware she's about to give me Leandro's location. But when I catch sight of Draco, joy turns into anguish. "Not here."

She walks out of the bar. I'm right behind her. The army of demons stares at us. I don't give a rat's ass. "Did you choose your people?"

"Yes."

The princess smirks. "Well, I hope they deserve your trust."

JJ, Bay, and Constantin—a huntress, a Malleus member, and a voodoo priest—they couldn't be more different. Yet they have one thing in common. All of them care about Manda. They won't let anything happen to her son. "They do."

She waves two of her demons over. One, possessing a middle-aged woman. The other, a twenty-something dude with bad hair. "They'll accompany your friends." It's an order, not a request.

I don't trust them, but what choice do I have?

Besides, Constantin is there. He can send them back to hell if all levees break. "Fine."

She hands me a small piece of paper. On it, an address not very far from here. "They better hurry. My sources say the witch's sister is in pretty bad shape."

She's about to head back inside when I stop her. "Hey."

"Yes?"

I hate to ask demons favors, but beggars can't be choosers. "We could use a little distraction." I point at the bar. "You know, to get them out without anyone noticing."

"Don't worry." Berith's wicked grin says she has something up her sleeves. "I got you covered."

She marches back into the bar, clapping her hands. "Listen up everybody," she shouts over their heads. "Here's a little 'How to survive a demon' crash course for you. Knowing the First Knight, you'll need it."

The hunters are a bit reluctant. When Legend abandons his—judging by the looks on their faces—not so pleasant conversation with Bay to join the Princess of Hell, the others follow suit.

Berith teaches them counter attacks and mentions weaknesses. Legend adds a few tricks as well. Me? I nod at the trio about to save my son, signalizing it's time.

Slowly withdrawing from the crowd, we meet outside. "Is that it?" JJ asks as I hand her the address.

"Yeah, that's what the demon gave me," I assure her.

Constantin yanks the paper out of JJ's hand. He shuts his eyes, doing God knows what. "It's legit," he says, after just a few seconds.

I truly want to know how he can be so sure, but Bay's sullen expression draws my attention away from B's brother. An odd sensation courses down my spine. He spoke to Legend and now he looks like it's the end of the world. Well, it sorta is; the end of the world I mean. Still, I don't like it. "What did Legend want from you?" I figure it's best to address the issue head on.

Bay cocks a brow. "You mean apart from throwing me out of the order?"

"He did what?" JJ barks.

Bay rubs his bald scalp. "Yeah, well. He didn't appreciate that I kept Manda's whereabouts a secret."

Any other day, I'd feel for the hunter. It's his life and Legend just took it from him. I know how that feels, believe me. But this isn't any other day and the life of my son is, literally, in his hands. "I need to know," I say, closing the distance between us. "Will this affect your mission?"

He smiles. "You want to know if I would harm your little boy to get back on Legend's good side?"

"Yes."

"No, Alex." He looks me in the eye, proving his point. "I won't. I only ever joined them to find the killer of my father. They taught me everything I need to find him by myself."

I'm still not relieved, but I do believe him. "Good." I ball my fists. "Because if anything happens to Leandro, I will kill you."

Constantin squeezes my shoulder. "Don't worry, dickhead." He flashes me an innocent smile. "I got your boy covered. You better make sure you got my girl."

Your girl? "Amanda isn't—"

"Hey," one of the demons who will join the

mission barks. "Can we hit it? We ain't got all day."

"Let's go," Constantin says, heading to his car.

I watch as they drive away, hoping, praying, begging I made the right choice.

"Alex?" Carter peeks out of the door. "Can we talk?"

I cross my arms. "There's nothing to talk about." He betrayed me. It's that simple.

"Please," he begs. "Just hear me out."

He won't stop until he lays his heart out. I gesture for him to get it over with, so I can go back inside to join the others.

"I had to call them," he says, sounding as miserable as he looks. "The world's about to go up in flames. What did you expect me to do?"

I look him in the eye. "I expected you to trust me, Carter."

"I didn't have a choice, Alex. It's the fucking end of the world."

"You *always* have a choice, Carter." Manda taught me that.

Chapter 39

Three hours. Three fucking hours. Not a single text or call. The address Berith gave us is about twenty miles south of York. No way in hell it took them three hours to get there. Earlier, when I checked Google maps, I spotted the cottage almost immediately. It's a bit hidden in the woods, but findable. So where are they? Why don't they reply to my texts? Better question, why the fuck did I think it was a good idea to send them rather than going myself?

Fuck! I should be the one out there looking for Leandro. He's *my* son, *my* responsibility. So why am I sitting in a bar full of hunters and demons, watching them bitch at each other, while they get ready for a damn war instead?

Because it's safer for Leandro. My involvement in all of this made me the center of attention. Hunters would have asked questions had I vanished. And what would I have said? Sorry, guys, I gotta go get my half-hunter, half-witch son out of the First Knight's claws? I might as well stick a bull's eye on Leandro's forehead.

Draco walks past me, ogling my phone. I shove it in my back pocket, determined to keep it there for longer than two seconds. The mother is suspicious. Has been for a while. Even asked me about JJ. I made up some lame she's-off-to-buy-herbs-for-the-charms excuse he didn't buy.

Distraction is what I need. I could join the rest of them. Maybe help Mrs. Lacroix carve protective charms out of greenwood like Amelia does. Or spar with the demons like all the other hunters do. Unlike me, they get ready to fight and die. The die part sounds fucked up, huh? The thing is we all know some of us, possibly all of us, won't make it. You'd think there would be fear in the eyes of the hunters. Nope. There's a spark of determination instead. Becoming a hunter means choosing death. We were aware of that when we signed up for the job. Some rainy day the hunter will become the prey. Manda calls that shit karma. Take enough lives and one day, you'll pay with your own. But when you've lost someone at the hands of the supernatural—most of us have—you're more than willing to pay the price. It's why we look at death and see honor rather than fear. Taking your last breaths knowing you had purpose keeps us going. Well, it kept me going. My perception of death is no longer the same. It changed when Berith tossed Manda's letter at my feet. The prospect of dying comes with guilt and fear. C'mon, where's the honor in letting your son grow up without a father? Without someone to love and protect him, to teach him how to ride a goddamn bike? So yeah. Death, all of a sudden, seems like the coward's way out.

B slams a shot glass onto the sticky counter, pulling me out of my pity-party. "Bourbon?" I ask, ogling the amber liquid.

She climbs on the barstool and shrugs. "You looked like you could use some." Her voice lost the I-hate-Alex edge.

I fake a half-hearted smile. "Have you never heard

of the 'don't drink and hunt' rule?" Drunk hunters are
dead hunters. No kidding, all it takes is one moment of
weakness and you're gone.

B winks at me. "Since when do you give a crap
about rules?"

The girl has a point. I pretty much broke them all
when I fell in love with a witch, and sold my soul to a
demon. "Thanks," I say, gulping down the booze.

"Sure."

We sit quietly, listening to Berith and Legend.
They cleared out all furniture and gathered in the midst
of hunters and demons alike, giving them lectures on
how to kill the First Knight's army. Legend emphasizes
demons can't be killed by weapons. They are still
vulnerable, though. A bullet or a stab to the vessel's
heart or head will force their demonic essence to look
for a new host. The gate is in the middle of nowhere;
ergo they'll be gone for a while. Hopefully, long
enough for us to kill the mother who tricked Manda and
me into all of this.

Berith adds a little warning. "Don't ever take the
charms of the witches off," she says, voice low. "Not
only will they protect you from any magic, they'll make
sure you can't get demonized as well."

On the other side of the bar are Amelia, Raphael,
and Mrs. Lacroix. Together, they must have carved
dozens of charms already. To my surprise, Amelia
seems to get along just fine with B's mom. The two
almost look like old friends.

"Gives frenemies a whole new meaning," she says,
smiling at her mom and Amelia.

For once, demons, witches, and hunters are united
in a single goal, stopping the impending end. I savor the

moment, knowing nothing like this will ever happen again. "I wish Manda was here to see this."

B nods. "Me too." She reaches for an empty shot glass, across the counter, pouring us a drink. Her hand trembles like crazy. "So"—she downs the bourbon—"how are you holding up?"

Should I lie? Should I tell the truth? Should I keep my damn mouth shut? Several pained breaths later I decide she deserves honesty. "Not so good."

Sadness laces her pretty eyes. "Me neither." Of course, not. Manda is her best friend. When I first saw them together, I knew they'd do just about anything for each other. She'd never hurt her, even if the world was at stake.

B refills our glasses. "Can I give you some advice?"

"Ugh, sure?"

Her gaze darts to Jesse. He pretends to help Amelia, but the hollow, distant look in his eyes is a sign his mind is somewhere else. "Make your amends before we leave."

Bitter laughter crawls up my throat. "Why, because we all die?"

She pulls her left brow up, casting me a dark glance. "Because some of us might live, Alex."

"Maybe you should take your own advice?"

"Yeah." She jumps down. "In another life, maybe."

"Hey." I cup her elbow, pulling her back. "He hurt you. And trust me when I say, I get it if you can't forgive him, but…it's just not worth it, B."

She stares at me as if I just gave her some unsolvable jigsaw. "What?"

I shove my hands in my pockets. "All I'm saying is

don't be like me. Don't let something good pass by because you're scared." I wish someone had told me the same back when all I had to do was find Manda and apologize.

"I—"

"Bonnie," Mrs. Lacroix shouts. "We need you to bless the charms."

"Coming." She heads to her mom, but her eyes are on my little brother. Good. Maybe one Remington brother gets to make shit right before it's too late.

Chapter 40

Mrs. Lacroix, Raphael, and B gather around a table. A bottle of rum, a cigar, a knife, and a silver bowl filled with the charms lay across the makeshift altar. "Ready?" Mrs. Lacroix asks her kids.

Raphael flashes her a smile. "Sure." Unlike his sister, he doesn't seem to care about the nasty looks hunters and demons alike shoot them.

Mrs. Lacroix faces her daughter, most likely sensing her hesitance. "Bonnie?"

"Let's do this," B says, wiping her palms on her jeans. The mamba looks miserable. Her skin is pale, her eyes clouded.

Mrs. Lacroix addresses the crowd. "Lay your weapons down."

Draco's lips part. He surely has some nasty remark on the tip of his tongue, but one look from Berith and he keeps it zipped.

Amelia is the first one to surrender her guns. "C'mon, folks," she addresses the resistant crowd. "We ain't got all day."

One by one, hunters and demons bring their weapons—guns, knives, brass knuckles—*The Walking Dead* crew would kill for an arsenal like this. Legend and Berith surrender theirs last. "I hope this works," the Malleus dick murmurs.

Mrs. Lacroix meets his gaze. "It will." Confidence

sure as hell runs in the family.

Jesse, Amelia, and I are closest to the witches. Everyone else moves back, keeping a safe distance.

Raphael lights one black and one red candle. When the flames rise high, his mom leans back in her chair and starts the incantation. *"Papa Legba, louvri pòtay yo. Pitit ou chache èd-ou. Papa Legba, louvri pòtay yo. Pitit ou rete tann."*

B opens the rum bottle, pouring some of it into a steaming mug of black coffee. Together, they repeat the chant, each taking a sip of the punched drink.

Queen B lights the cigar next, passing it around like a good old joint. They all take a drag. *"Papa Legba, louvri pòtay yo. Pitit ou chache èd-ou. Papa Legba, louvri pòtay yo. Pitit ou rete tann."*

The flames of the candles dance a slow Tango, rising higher and higher. A deep, animalistic groan roars through the bar. Demons and hunters alike freeze as the terrifying sound echoes off the walls.

Mrs. Lacroix's head jerks up. White eyes stare back at us. "How can I assist?" The deep, inhuman voice doesn't belong to B's mom. It's that of the loa possessing her. The one they call Papa Legba.

Raphael bows low. "We seek Ogoun's help, Papa Legba."

The loa bursts into laughter. "And what makes you think I'd grant you that wish?" He gestures at the demons and hunters. "You're breaking the codex, son. Why do you believe I'd willingly do the same?"

Well, that's a bummer. I didn't expect obstacles just yet. Judging by Raphael's confused expression, neither did he. "But you don't under—"

The loa lifts his hand stopping Raphael. "You

consort with demons, son." His voice is deeper, colder than before. "Go ask Kalfu for help. I only assist pure souls."

"Kalfu assists no one," B shoots back. "You know that as well as we do."

The loa shrugs. "I don't see how any of this is my problem, child. You chose darkness over light. Now, you must live with the consequences of your actions."

B furrows her brows. "Do you have any idea what's been happening?" Her fists are balled, her face hard like granite. "The First Knight is—"

"Trying to open the gate to hell," he says, bored.

Raphael squints. "You know, but you're still giving us that light versus darkness crap?" He shakes his head. "What's the matter with you?"

"The laws must be up-held," the loa says, matter-of-factly. "Come what may."

"Bullshit." B's eyes are like flint. "Your damn laws are outdated. The world isn't black and white. There are gray zones, Papa Legba. And this"—she points at the crowd—"qualifies as one."

"Gray zones?" the loa thunders. "Those are the reason we're here, child." His white eyes focus on me. "Isn't that right, Alexander?"

Muscles stiff, I feel like the running joke of the universe.

The loa rises to his feet, moving around the table like a lion, hunting an antelope. "You crossed a line when you fell for a witch. And not just any witch either. A Bishop witch, a descendant of one of the oldest bloodlines." He wrinkles his nose. "You upset the natural order when you fathered a child born of witch and hunter blood."

Whispers roar through the bar.

"A child?" Torres barks.

"What the actual fuck?" Draco hisses.

"Did you know?" one of the PAU agents—name's Luke, I believe—asks Carter.

"I…" Carter shakes his head, the shock of the news still rippling through him. "I had no idea."

The loa doesn't give a rat's ass about the hunters' gossip phone. "And as if all of that weren't enough," he says, sounding pissed, "you upped the scales by selling your soul for her, paving the path for the world's end." He inches closer. "Tell me, Alexander, have you not learned your lesson, yet?"

What lesson? It's not like I wanted any of this. I didn't wake up one day thinking: hey, let's fall in love with a witch, get her pregnant, leave her, and sell my soul for her. "You can't choose whom you love." My voice sounds alien to my own ears.

The loa laughs. "Never said you could, son." He narrows his eyes, his mood changing rapidly. "Doesn't make you less responsible, though."

"Enough." B is between us. "We didn't summon you to lecture Alex."

The loa straightens. "Restrain yourself, child." He tilts his head to the side, ogling her like a damn coyote. "You might be a powerful mamba, but never forget where your power comes from."

His thunderous voice startles hunters and demons alike. B, however, doesn't give a shit about his warning. It sorta makes her angrier. "You call yourself good, act all righteous and great"—she blows out some steam—"but you're just a puny little god. Too fucking scared to help us save the whole damn world."

"Scared?" The loa half-laughs, half-screams. "I am Papa Legba, guardian of the crossroads; I don't fear the demon nor the witch. But unlike you, I live by the rules of heaven and hell."

B's in his face. Two seconds away from smashing it. "You don't get it, do you? There won't be any heaven or hell left when the gate is opened."

The loa isn't impressed. He's not going to help us, I can tell.

Time for plan B. I push B aside. "You're right." Raphael casts me a sidelong glance, but I pay no attention. "This is my fault."

He flashes me a nasty grin. "Glad you're finally coming to your senses. Witches and hunters don't—"

"No," I blurt out, fully aware of what he's about to say. "Being with Manda was never wrong. I don't care that she's a witch and I'm a hunter. She was there for me when my kind"—I eyeball the other hunters— "turned their backs on me. She repeatedly saved our dumb asses, despite the fact I held a gun to her head. She traded her goddamn soul for mine. So yeah. I love her. Always have always will. If that's against some stupid law, then heaven and hell need a lesson in history. Or did you forget what happened when race defined your worth?" I have a million examples up my sleeves—slavery, Hitler, the senseless slaughter of Native Americans. Racism, no matter in which form, always ends ugly.

The loa crosses his arms. "What's your point?"

I force my spine straighter. "The only thing I truly regret is not trusting her. You see, I was so scared she'd go dark, I practically forced her into the demon's arms. So go ahead and put the blame on me. I deserve it. But you"—I look him in the eye—"will have to live with the outcome of this battle just as I have to live with what I've done."

"He's right," Raphael says. "Everyone will hear of the great Papa Legba, who refused to save the world."

The wheels in the loa's head start turning. He grabs the cigar, taking a few drags while considering his options. It takes forever and a day 'til he speaks again. "Fine." He reaches for the punched coffee, sipping it. "I'll help you, but under one condition."

I hate deals. "Which is?"

The loa moves closer. "You'll do whatever it takes to stop Amanda Bishop." His eyes are polar white. "No ifs or buts, Alexander."

"No," B yells, tears pricking at her eyes. She understands what the loa asks of me, that whatever it takes could be Manda's end. "We don't need your help. We can do this without you."

The loa smiles. "They"—he gestures at the hunters—"won't survive the first attack without Ogun's blessings. You know that as well as I do, my child. Why else would you have called upon me?"

"I don't care," B barks, slamming her hands on her hips. "He's not going to—"

I push her to the side. "Okay."

The loa eyeballs me suspiciously. "What was that?"

I've never liked myself, always missed the self-love Manda clearly had too much of. In this very moment, however, I hate myself to the point where I'd rather be someone else. "I'll do whatever it takes." I swallow some of the self-loathing, drying my mouth. "You have my word."

"Alex!" B digs her nails in my shoulders, shaking me. "Are you crazy? He wants you to—"

"We don't have a choice," I cut her off, unable to look her in the eye. I saw what Manda is capable of. Marching all these hunters and witches into a battle with her and the First Knight without protection is suicide. I can't let them die. Manda—the real Manda—wouldn't want that either. Why else would she have begged me not to hesitate? I didn't trust her once. I won't make the same mistake again.

B loathes me even more than I loathe myself. Didn't think that was possible, but damn. The hate in her eyes pierces my heart like the poison of a scorpion.

"Good." The loa steps around B. "Then we have a deal?"

I extend my hand. "We do," I assure him.

He shakes my hand, facing Raphael. "You may call upon Ogun, son."

Raphael lights the remaining candles—one black, one green. "Ogun, lord of war, come to us." He looks at B. "I can't do this on my own."

"I don't care," B barks. "I won't be any part of this."

One nasty look from Raphael changes her mind. She eats one of the grapes laid out next to the weapons, and closes her eyes. "*Ogoun, mèt nan lagè, vin jwenn nou.*"

Papa Legba's head falls back. "He's here."

Raphael pours a glass of rum, shoving it toward the arsenal. "Bless these weapons with your never-ending wrath."

"*Beni zam sa yo ak ou kòlè pa janm fini,*" B translates.

A fraction of a second later sparks fly across the table. A cloud of fire rains down on the weapons, a damn Fourth of July firework in the middle of a bar.

Raphael grabs the bowl with the charms, pouring the bottle of rum all over it. "Bless these charms with your magic and protect the ones who wear them with your power."

Like a priestess, B holds her palms over the bowl. *"Beni cham sa yo ak majik ou ak pwoteje yo menm ki te mete yo ak pouvwa ou."* Her eyes catch fire. Literally. They are two burning flames.

I sense the fear of the hunters behind me. Most of them have come face to face with mambas before. Yet I'd bet my Mustang, none of them ever felt that kind of power. The café has turned into a sauna. Energy jolts through the air. Feels like we're in the midst of a thunderstorm and lightning is about to hit. Only lasts a minute though. Then the flames extinguish and B is back to her normal self.

"Damn," she says, flinging herself back down on the chair. "That was—"

Her nose bleeds.

Jesse is by her side. "You okay?"

Shooting him a dark glance, she wipes the blood from her face. "I'm fine."

Raphael eyeballs his sister. He's without a doubt worried. I recognize the expression. It's the universal big brother look. "Sorry, I thought he'd use me."

Papa Legba, still inside B's mom, grins. "He seeks power, son. And your sister is—"

"Can we finish this?" she cuts him off.

The loa sighs. "As you wish." He faces me. "Don't forget your promise, Alexander."

How could I? I pretty much gave him my word to kill the only woman I ever loved, the mother of my son. "I won't."

The loa blinks. A second later, B's mom is back. I'm glad to see those light brown eyes again. "It's done," she assures us.

Raphael takes the bowl with the charms. "Let's get this show on the road."

They go around handing the amulets to the hunters when Carter walks up next to me. "You have a son?"

I just agreed to kill Manda. I can't handle Carter and his twenty questions. "Looks like it," I mutter, heading out to catch some air.

****

The sun slowly sets, wrapping the small town in orange light. Every second slipping through the hourglass is one step closer to the end. There's no delaying nightfall. When the last rays of orange drown giving birth to the silver of the moonlight, I will be forced to face my worst nightmare—the possibility of losing Manda. The question is can I honor my word? Am I capable of doing whatever it takes? Even if that means killing the woman holding the key to my heart? I search my soul for an answer. Except, the hollow black hole tells me shit.

Tired and drained, I gaze into the distance, watching, waiting, praying. I haven't heard from JJ, Bay, or Constantin yet. I keep telling myself Leandro will be okay. He'll grow into a happy young man. But I'm just lying to myself. Because even if they get him out of there, and even if we can stop the apocalypse, he might lose his mom. Possibly both of his parents in a single night. Yeah, I'm not naïve enough to believe all of us walk away from this in one piece. The knight has a legion, Manda, and the *First Grimoire*. Judging by our last encounter, Manda alone can take out half of the hunters inside the bar. Long story short, there's a good chance Leandro will be an orphan after tonight. And I? Well, I'll probably never get to meet my son.

"But he'll grow up knowing his parents loved him," Mrs. Lacroix says, sitting down beside me. I'm not surprised the mother of all mambas can read my mind. Being around Manda taught me no secret is safe around witches.

Casting her a sidelong glance, I'm not sure what to say. I mean, how can he know we loved him when we were never there?

"He's lucky to have you as a father," she goes on.

"Yeah." Bitter laughter crawls up my throat. "So lucky, his mother hid him from me."

She sets the silver bowl with the last charm down on the porch. "She wasn't trying to protect him, Alex." Her gaze darts over her shoulder to the hunter-filled bar. "She was protecting you."

I scrub my fingers through my hair, pulling hard enough to scalp myself. "I don't need her protection," I grumble, pissed at the world. "She's not my damn bodyguard. I mean, what the fuck was she thinking keeping my own flesh and blood from me? She never gave me a choice."

"She loves you," Mrs. Lacroix whispers. "Trust me; this wasn't easy on her either."

I stare at the darkening sky. "Fuck love." It only ever brought me pain and misery. Scratch that. It only ever brought pain and misery to the ones I love.

Mrs. Lacroix pulls the last charm out of the bowl.

It's a circular wooden plate with a pentagram carved into it. "Have a little faith," she says, securing it around my neck. "It's going to be okay."

I gaze down at my chest. Back in the old days, hunters used greenwood to burn witches at the stake. Mostly, because they wanted them to suffer a slow and painful death—fresh wood burns slower than its dried counterpart. Pretty ironic witches now use it to keep hunters alive, huh?

Chapter 41

Amanda

I rest my eyes for a little while. Over the course of the past forty-eight hours, I made sure I won't screw up the last ritual. I read the entries in the *First Grimoire* over and over. The words of a mad woman became my own. Up to the point where I could no longer differentiate between the voice of the book and my own.

"*You're going to kill him,*" roars through my aching head time and again.

Him, that's Alex. I caught a glimpse of the future, him begging me to stop the last ritual, me driving the cherub sword through his heart.

"*He needs to die.*"

In my vision, I had no issue ending his existence. He kneeled before me, telling me how much he loved me, assuring me it's the book not me. I laughed at him, thought he was stupid for not seeing the real me—the darkness I was fated to become—and offed him.

"*Just don't fall for his lies.*"

I didn't. I won't. Alex means nothing to me. Even now, when I sense his proximity, I'm numb to his charms. There was a time when one look into his malachite eyes made me wish I was someone…something else. Not anymore.

Fate

The season of the white witch is over. Masquerading as someone I'll never be ended when I understood why the book wants to destroy the whole of creation. You see, the world was always better off without humans, demons, angels, and gods. Born of light, we have become destruction. Once the gate to hell is unlocked, history will rewind. It's a new beginning. A fresh start. There'll be no one left to fuck it up.

"Amanda?" Clyde's voice wafts through the ajar door. "Are you awake?"

I sigh, tired of the demon's constant approaches. "What do you want?"

He moves toward the bed. "The sun is about to set," he says, flinging himself down next to me.

I gaze out the window, ogling the fireball. Its power slowly fades, giving darkness room to nourish. "I'll be there in a few." The gate is close by. It won't take us long to get there. The ritual itself doesn't need much setting up either. We're good.

"There's something you should know," he says after a short pause.

I snicker. "They're all here."

He squints. "How do you—"

"There's nothing I don't know." True story. The secrets the book shared with me, forgotten knowledge of ancient times, makes me the closest thing to all knowing there is.

Clyde folds his hands in his lap. "Then you know they have an army?"

"Yes." I prop my elbows into the mattress, pushing myself up. "But we have the book."

His gaze darts to the ancient tome, resting on my nightstand. "Does it...does it tell you things?" Clyde's dark brown aura suggests he fears my answer. Most likely because he's afraid I'll get to the bottom of his lies.

"It does."

He draws a deep breath, stroking his chin. "Like what?"

I shift closer. Our lips are almost touching. "Everything," I breathe into his mouth. "Absolutely everything."

His eyes go wide.

"Yeah, that's right." I trace his frozen jawline. "I know why you really want to open the gate, Clyde. But don't worry. Your secret's safe with me."

He yanks back, jumping to his feet. "We're leaving in half an hour," he says before he slams the door shut behind him.

"*Moron.*" He truly thinks he can win this battle. If I felt anything, it'd probably be pity.

Chapter 42

Alex

The full moon is high in the sky, fat and blood red. Its beams break through the crown of the trees, casting eerie shadows along the way. Setting one foot after another, I keep moving. The wind wails—a battle cry, foreshadowing what's to come. Somewhere in the distance, the hoot of an owl echoes. The animals of the forest sense danger. It's why the crows form circles in the sky.

The bloated blood moon accompanies me as I follow Berith's instructions, heading down a narrow path, supposedly leading me to the gate of hell.

The hunter inside me is on high alert, scanning my surroundings like a hawk, expecting a demon attack at any given moment. "They can sense you," Berith warned me. "Be prepared."

The best hunter couldn't be prepared for a damn army of demons. Not alone. Jesse was right. Legend's plan sucks. Sending me in alone to distract them is a suicide mission, but they don't give a fuck about me. To them, I'm just a traitor responsible for the end of the world. None of them will shed a tear if some demon rips me apart.

"It's okay to be afraid," my dad used to say. "Just make sure fear doesn't control you." I'm beginning to think he wasn't talking about demons and witches. The monsters out there are less terrifying than the ones we hide inside.

I spot the crossroad Berith mentioned and pause. The sky is clear, yet the stars are barely visible. Hope is out of reach, death treads on my heels.

C'mon, Remington. You can do this.

I'm not so sure about this. Taking a right now, means walking straight into my own hell. I'll have to face what I did to Manda, what my fear has turned her into. And maybe, Legend's plan works. Maybe I can stall the Knight of Hell and Manda long enough for the others to launch their surprise attack. But what then? Will I point my damn Beretta at her again? Will I pull that fucking trigger, sending the woman I love to purgatory? A place even demons fear?

Fuck life.

Fuck love.

Fuck me.

I'm the one who should rot in the pit. Not Manda. Never Manda. Sure, she doesn't pretend to be a hero like me, and maybe she *is* selfish and arrogant. Yet she's never turned her back on the people she loves. She didn't choose a fucking PlayStation game over her sister, never threatened to kill me because I'm a hunter. Amanda Bishop doesn't deserve that kind of fate. I do.

A branch snaps behind me.

Fuck.

Gun drawn, I spin, ready for the first fight of the night. "Show yourself," I order, index finger on the trigger.

Leaves rattle. A shadow steps out of the safety of a large ash. "Whoa, easy there, bro."

"Jess?" I keep my gun pointed aware demons can imitate voices. "That you?"

He approaches me, hands up in the air. Moonlight reflects off his hardened face. "It's me, Alex."

Holstering my gun, I inch closer. "What the fuck are you doing here?" He's supposed to be with B, entering the battlefield with the rest of the odd stop-the-apocalypse crew.

He brushes a loose strand of his untamable hair out of his face. "What do you think I'm doing?" He cocks a brow. "I'm not going to let my brother march into a war by himself."

The big brother wants to yell at him, kick his ass back to the edge of the woods where the others wait. A part of me, though, celebrates his arrival. We've been hunting together since forever. It feels right to face the end of our journey together. "Jess, you—"

"Don't." He shoves his palm in my face. "Don't even try to talk me out of this. We're brothers, Alex. We stand together, we fall together."

I smirk. "*Bad Boys* for life, huh?"

"Exactly."

"Legend's going to be pissed."

He pulls his brows to his hairline. "Do I look like I care?"

Nah, he looks like he enjoys the prospect of fucking with the Malleus dick. "What about, B?"

He plays cool, smiling lazily. "What about her?"

"Seriously?" I raise my brows. "You just gonna stand there pretending you're not worried sick about her walking into this mess?"

His gaze drops. "Does it matter?" Defeat lowers his voice. "She made it perfectly clear she doesn't want me anywhere near her."

"She's hurt and pissed." I meet his gaze. "What do you expect her to do? Throw you a 'thanks for threatening my family' party?"

"She hates my face, Alex."

Love drama takes a back seat when the apocalypse approaches. But what if this is our last brotherly talk? What if tomorrow he wakes up without me, forced to face the world on his own? I can't welcome death without knowing he'll be all right. "Listen," I say. "I've been where you are. So here's a piece of advice; don't be a coward. Go apologize. Make this shit right. It's not too late."

He sighs. "How can she forgive me when my own brother can't?"

I think of what B said. *Make your amends. Because some of us might live.* "You lied to me, Jess. And I get why you did what you did, but it's not your job to protect me. Just like it isn't Manda's. I make my own choices and I live with the consequences."

"I know." He draws a deep breath. "I'm sorry. Hell, I'd take it all back if I could, but—"

"What's done is done," I say, looking ahead. "Just promise me you'll make it right."

"How?" he asks. "How can I ever look Manda in the eye after what I've done?" He shakes his head. "How can I look you in the eye, Alex?"

"You—"

Cold steel presses against the back of my head. "Look what we have here," a female, high-pitched voice says. "If it isn't the Remington brothers."

Eyes wide open, jaw clenched, Jesse looks over my shoulder. "Shit."

"We've been expecting you," the woman cheers as a dozen red, glowing eyes stare back at us.

So much for Legend's ingenious plan.

Chapter 43

"Move," the red-eyed bitch orders, pushing the barrel of her shotgun against the back of my head.

"Relax," I mutter, determined to keep my cool.

The rest of the red-eyed dozen—seven dudes and four chicks—march behind us. One of them, he looks like Opie from *Sons of Anarchy*—long beard, leather jacket, biker boots—escorts my little brother. "Don't even think about it," he hisses as Jesse goes for his pocket.

"Chill," he shoots back, holding his empty hands up. "It's not like I'm dumb enough to mess with all of you." Liar. Hundred bucks say he was reaching for the herb mixture Mrs. Lacroix gave us earlier. Apparently, it can slow these mothers down.

We head down the narrow, overgrown path. The sky is an ocean of black wings. The red glow of the moon illuminating the crows' dark feathers. "They feel it coming," the bitch whispers in my ear, her sulfur breath beating against my neck. "It's just a matter of time before we take back what's rightfully ours."

I cast her a sidelong glance. "You mean before all of us, including you and your friends, perish, right?" I don't think Berith lied when she said the ominous final battle would end in a damn blood bath.

Red-eyed bitch throws her head back and laughs. "So you spoke to the princess, huh?" She waves it off.

"Berith is paranoid. Demons can't die. We can only be sent back to hell, dummy." Someone should tell her unwavering confidence has led to the downfall of empires before. I would, but she's still in her dream world. "And once the gate is open, we can come back any time we please."

Yay! The future reeks of hellfire and brimstone.

Jesse peeks over his shoulder at Opie-lookalike. "So you're not afraid of the final battle?"

"Nope." He cocks a brow, rocking a lopsided grin. "Can't wait to kick some heaven ass. Now"—he pushes him forward—"keep your mouth shut and move."

The scent of sulfur and burned meat wafts through the air. We're close. The meadow Berith mentioned is right ahead of us. Any second, we'll be two lambs in the midst of a demonic legion.

"Alex?" Jesse elbows me. "I truly am sorry. I need you to—"

"Don't," I bark, aware this is some crappy in-case-we-don't-make-it apology. "We'll talk about shit when this is over, okay?"

"Yeah," he grumbles, gazing at the beating black wings above us. "In our next life, maybe." It's almost as if I'm back at the bar, talking to B.

My lips part, but red-eyed bitch smacks me. "Quiet now."

We leave the path, stepping across an invisible power line. Electricity jolts through my bones, stiffening my muscles. My heart skips several beats. I can barely breathe. "What the fuck?"

Red-eyed bitch laughs. "Black jade." She points to thousands of tiny black stones scattered on the ground. "Keeps trash like you at bay."

I stopped listening to her about two seconds ago. My attention is torn between the First Knight's army—hundreds of demons, hungry for blood—and the rusty monstrosity across the meadow. The entrance to hell is an eight-foot tall iron gate. Its sharp spikes appear to pierce the damn sky.

"Welcome to the end, boys."

"Manda?" Terror fills Jesse's eyes. "Is that you?"

The girl moving toward us is just a shadow of Manda's former self. Black veins, pale skin, crazy in her eyes—hello, *Carrie*. "Jess." She snickers. "Glad you could make it."

The First Knight steps out from behind a tree, hauling a girl by the hair toward Manda. She's kicking and crying, begging and pleading, but the bastard doesn't care.

Neither does Manda. "Shut up," she barks at the terrified teenager.

"Wait." Jesse's jawline hardens. "Isn't that—"

"The Blairs' missing daughter." I recognize her from the pictures.

"Manda," Jesse starts, "don't—"

She snaps her fingers and Jesse's jaw freezes. "Sit back"—she forces my brother on his butt with a move of her hand—"and enjoy the show."

I drink it all in—the demons, the First Knight, the crying Blair kid, and Manda who isn't Manda. It's then I realize we're fucked. Seriously, we are *all* going to die here.

The First Knight rests a hand on Manda's shoulder. "It's time, love." He looks up at the monstrous moon. "We should start the ritual."

Manda winks at me. "Let the end games begin."

Whatever it takes, Papa Legba's voice thunders through my brain. "Manda?" She looks over her shoulder. "Why don't you take your issues out on the one person you truly hate?"

She rolls her eyes. "And who would that be, Alex?"

"Me," I say, spine like iron.

"He's just baiting you," the First Knight reasons. "C'mon, we've got more important things to do."

She's about to walk away. I can't let that happen. "I thought about accepting your mom's offer."

Good news: it works. Bad news: she's coming at me, murder in her blazing green eyes.

Chapter 44

Amanda

Alexander "jerk-face" Remington has some nerve telling me, the witch with more juice than Beetlejuice, he considered accepting Mother Dearest's kill-my-evil-daughter offer. And even now, with my hands wrapped around his throat, he laughs in my face. "Admit it," he chokes out. "You hate me."

Hate is nothing but a word children use when they don't get what they want. I am no child. The rush intoxicating my system is pure, unfiltered wrath. "You"—I tighten my grip around his throat—"don't know anything about me."

His face reddens. "You're wrong." He gasps for air. "I know you spent most of your life trying to convince your mother you aren't evil. And when you came to understand it's pointless, you spent the rest of it living up to being it." His gaze darts to the gate of hell. "This, all of this, is the rebellion of a little girl with mommy issues."

"Alex," Jesse hisses, about two seconds away from a heart attack. "What the fuck are you doing?"

I flash Little Remington a smile. "Signing his death certificate."

Fire blazes through my hand. I shut my eyes, picturing Alex flying against a tree. When I open them again, his body bounces off the massive ash, dropping to the damp ground like a puppet without strings.

That's enough, the voice in my head barks. *Focus on the ritual before you lose the power of the moon.*

I gaze at the sky. Hundreds of crows obscure the moon. A minute past midnight, the red giant will be useless to us. So why am I wasting my time on Alex?

He presses his palms into the soil, struggling to get to his feet. I could make my vision come true. Walk over there and stab the sword through his heart. It'd be a piece of cake. But the wrath inside my heart keeps me rooted to the spot. Death is too easy. I want him to suffer, to see who I truly am. "You"—I wave two faceless minions over—"bring him to the gate."

"Manda," Jesse objects. "Please…"

"Bring him, too," I order, spinning on my heels.

Congrats, Remingtons. You secured yourselves front row seats to the apocalypse.

Chapter 45

Alex

The creatures toss me to the ground, my head barely missing a rock. Then again, what's another head injury? Manda already broke a few of my ribs when she threw me against the tree. No fucking around, every breath I take hurts like a mother. I'm not sure I can stand on my own two feet. I had to do something, though. Coax out some kind of feeling. Wrath was better than no emotion at all.

The First Knight's demonic army circles us. They look like ordinary folks—teachers, nurses, grandpas, and occasionally a few thugs. If it weren't for their garnet eyes, you'd think we marched into some sort of high school reunion. But after years on the job, I know better than to judge a book by its cover. Those mothers might look fragile, but they can wipe you out with a movement of their damn pinky.

Jesse leans against the rock. "Just like old times, huh?"

I'd cast him a "WTF" look, but my facial muscles are too busy making pained grimaces.

"What?" he murmurs. "It's true. We've been through shit like this before, haven't we?"

"You and I remember our time on the job very differently, little brother." Zombies, pedophiles, witches, psychotic bokors—that's the sorta shit we made it through. My gaze shoots to Manda. She kneels before the book, a golden sword between her palms. An untouchable ex-girlfriend, possessed by the power of a bloody grimoire, hell-bent on ending the world? That's a little more than our usual crazy.

He shifts closer. "She almost killed you, Alex."

"She didn't," I shoot back.

He sighs, gaze glued to Manda. "Dude, do you really think you can bring her back from this?"

"I have to try." After everything she's done for us, I owe her that much. C'mon, she could have walked away when we lost the zombie cure. Instead, she risked her life to bring my brother back. Then when she learned I sold my soul, she could have easily left me to rot in the pit. She didn't. Now, it's time I pay her back. Even if it kills me.

Jesse's shoulders droop. "I hope you know what you're doing."

Not really. But does it matter?

"Bring the girl," Manda orders the First Knight's Voldemort fan club.

The Blair kid sobs uncontrollably as they drag her toward the gate. "Please," she begs them. "I didn't mean it. I never wanted this."

"What the hell is she talking about?" Jesse whispers.

I have no clue, but something stinks.

They drop her by Manda's feet. She flashes her a fake smile. "It's all right, Alison. We're not going to hurt you."

"Liar," the kid cries.

Manda looks at me. "I've been called worse."

The First Knight is by Amanda's side. "Let's just get it over with, love."

Manda cocks a brow. "Don't tell me what to do."

The demon frowns. "I was just—"

"You were just shutting your damn mouth." The ice in her voice makes the First Knight shudder. He, Lucifer's left hand, fears Manda. Can't say I blame him. Had she looked at me like that—as if she wanted to hang me upside down to gut me—I'd probably be afraid, too.

Manda shoves the sword under the Blair kid's nose. "Do you know what that is?" The girl shakes her head, tears streaming down her face. "It's the sword of a cherub," Manda explains, tracing the sharp blade with her index finger. "The only weapon that can kill a soul."

Did she just say the blade can kill a soul? That's impossible. Souls are indestructible. They're pure energy.

"Please," the Blair girl tries again. "I never wanted any of this."

Manda gets down on one knee. "Is that so?"

The girl nods. "I didn't know he'd kill them. I swear, I just wanted to be with my boyfriend."

I must have hit my damn head when she threw me against the tree. Because I could swear, the girl just admitted she had something to do with her parents' murders.

"What the fuck is going on?" Jesse clearly heard it, too. I don't recall him hitting his head.

Manda laughs. The chilling sound echoes through the woods, likely scaring every living and breathing creature in it. "Let me get this straight," she says, swallowing the bitter laughter. "You went to a crossroad at midnight, summoned a demon with a book you bought on eBay, asked him to free you from your parents' iron reign, but you had no idea he'd kill them?"

"Jesus," Jesse hisses. "What happened to the good old times when all teenagers did was get wasted and screw around?"

The kid averts her gaze. "I…"

"You"—Manda lifts her chin—"knew exactly how this was going to end. A deal with hell comes with a price." She eyeballs me. "Isn't that right, Alex?"

"Manda," I start, pushing myself up. "Please, she's just a kid."

"We were all kids once," she shoots back.

The Blair girl grabs Manda's ankles. "You don't understand," she cries. "They wanted me to be someone I'm not. All that talk about religion and being good"—she almost chokes on her tears—"they suffocated me."

Manda looks me in the eye. "Trust me, I know how that feels."

"I never wanted you to be someone else," I yell. Don't ask me why, but I need her to know that. "I didn't ask you to change, Manda."

"You didn't have to ask." She shrugs. "I saw the way you looked at me, Alex. As if I were worthless, rotten to the core." A lopsided grin tugs at her lips. "Guess you were right all along. Anyway"—she draws a deep breath, focusing on Alison—"you got what you wanted. Now it's time you pay the price."

Manda lifts the sword. "Start the chant," she orders the First Knight.

He and his minions gather around the gate. Each

holding a black candle, they speak words in an alien language.

The earth trembles, rattling the iron gates. Creatures with shark-like teeth snarl behind the barrier. Red, amber, yellow—eyes the color of an ugly rainbow stare back at us. Shadowy fingers reach through, rocking claws Freddy Krueger would envy.

"Where are the others?" I hear myself ask.

"They better hurry the fuck up," Jesse barks, never taking his eyes off what's behind the iron bars.

Manda rolls her shoulders back. "Don't worry," she says to the kid. "I promise it'll be quick."

In slow motion, the sword comes down. She's going to kill her and by doing so the beasts will be freed.

The demonic army kneels, completely focused on the ritual.

Whatever it takes. Well, that's now or never.

Chapter 46

Amanda

The cherub's blade catches fire. It's the only weapon mighty enough to destroy a soul. In fact, it can off any creature. Even gods. The weapon, once created to keep darkness away from humanity, will free it now.

"Please," Alison begs. "Don't kill me. I just wanted to be me." Pleading blue eyes filled with salty tears look up at me. They bring back unwanted memories. Flashes of a girl that would have understood where she came from and why she couldn't live in her parents' prison any longer.

Go ahead, the voice urges me, *end her suffering. She'll be better off dead.*

The chants of Clyde and his minions grow louder. A rush of pure energy jolts through my backbone into my palms.

Do it. Do it now!

An invisible force guides my hand. The blazing sword comes down. Any second it will slice right through Alison, capturing her soul, and releasing the creatures behind the iron bars.

"You'll be better off dead," I assure her.

Then I strike the sword down.

No, wait.

I am struck down.

What the fuck?

Malachite eyes gaze into mine. Alex lays on top of me, his weight keeping me down. "Sorry," he whispers, securing the blazing sword above my head. "I can't let you do that, Manda."

He's lost his last freakin' brain cells. Why else would he jump me, knowing I can kill him with a damn thought?

"Manda, listen to me." The pressure of him on top of me feels so familiar it scares the shit outta me. "This isn't you," he goes on. "You don't want to kill that girl."

Of course, you do!

Do I?

"How many times did you wish your mother was dead?" he asks, never once taking his eyes off mine. "She had no idea what magic and demons can do," he advocates on Alison's behalf. "The demon did that to her...to both of you."

Lies! We all have our choices. You chose to open the gate, remember?

I...I—

"Ma—"

Alex is off me, dangling a foot above the ground. "Enough." Clyde tightens his grip on Alex's throat. "You caused more trouble than I thought, hunter." He smirks. "It's time we get rid of you for good."

I get on my feet, head pounding like crazy.

Clyde throws him toward me. "Kill him," he orders.

It's the only way to be free.

The vision flickers across my mind. Alex on his knees, me driving the cherub blade through his heart.

It was always meant to end like this.

I lift the blazing sword, closing the tiny gap between us. Just like in my vision, Alex kneels before me. "You don't have to do this," he says, fearless.

Yes, you do. He hurt you, treated you like garbage. He doesn't deserve your pity.

I don't pity him. I—

You what? Love him? Dark laughter thunders through my brain. *Love is for children, Amanda.*

"Kill him," Clyde barks again.

Alex's malachite eyes stay on me. He doesn't care about Clyde, or the demons inching closer. "I…" He takes a deep breath. "I love you, Manda. I know I didn't always show it, but damn I do."

He'd say anything to get out of this alive.

"You don't know him," I yell, the pain in my head driving me insane.

I know he consorted with your mother. He said it himself he contemplated her offer.

But he didn't accept it. He had countless chances to kill me. Yet here I am, alive, and about to raise hell.

"Amanda," Clyde shouts. "Do it or I will kill your precious little boy."

Leandro. I gaze at Alex and all I see is that little boy's smile. The way he stretched out his arms, needing me to hold him. All I ever wanted was to keep him safe, to make sure he grew up knowing he's loved. Now, I'm killing his father?

He's not a father, the voice barks. *He left you pregnant with nowhere to go.*

"No." Alex never left me. "I was the one who walked away." I knew he was hurt when he had his gun to my head, just like I knew he would have never pulled that damn trigger.

Clyde grabs my arm, forcing me to face him. "You are mine. You will do as I say, or I make sure they tear your son into pieces."

Listen to him. Save your son.

An invisible hand guides mine, slowly bringing the sword to Alex's heart. "It's okay," he assures me. "I'll be fine."

Something wet rolls down my cheeks.

Are those—

Tears. I'm crying. How is that even possible? I'm darkness.

The tip of the blade penetrates Alex's shirt when a thunderous voice echoes off the trees. "I wouldn't do that if I were you." Across the meadow wearing her usual good-girl attire stands the Nun. Except she's possessed by an amber-eyed demon—another knight of hell.

Chapter 47

Alex

The tip of a flaming sword penetrates my chest. I'm sure it hurts like a bitch, but pain is the last of my concerns. I got through to Manda. I know because when she looks at me now, I don't see green flames. I see an ocean of sparkling emeralds. Berith is here. They didn't abandon us after all. Maybe there's still time to turn this ship around.

The demons form a guard of honor, allowing the Princess of Hell to pass through. Head up high, she sashays toward us. But where the fuck is the rest of the cavalry? Why is she alone? Where's her demon army? The hunters? The Lacroixs?

The First Knight meets her halfway. "Stay out of this, Berith."

"Or what?" She laughs.

The First Knight nods at his demons. They move in on the princess. "Really?" she mutters, unimpressed. A snap of a finger later, six demons are down and Berith still stands. "Is that all you got, Beelzebub?"

Beelzebub? Did she just call the First Knight Beelzebub? As in Lord of the Flyers? Shit just keeps getting worse, doesn't it? I mean there's a reason folks believe Beelzebub is Satan. The stories they tell about that creature are the stuff of nightmares.

"Shut up," Manda yells, startling us all. "Just shut the fuck up."

I have no idea who she's talking to, but I'm starting to fear for her sanity. Ever since I saw her at the B&B, she spoke to someone who wasn't there. Whoever it is makes her push the blade harder against my already torn flesh.

"Stop," Berith shouts. "You really don't want to do this."

Manda closes her eyes. When she opens them again, they're blazing. "Yeah," she says, smirking. "And why's that?"

Berith pushes past the First Knight. "Because if you destroy his soul, yours will perish, too. But unlike Alexander, you won't die." She raises her brows. "Darkness will claim you once and for all."

Manda laughs. "You're crazy. Why would—"

"He's your soulmate," Berith blurts out. "Destroying his soul means destroying yours. One-half of a soul can't exist without the other. You should know that, witch."

"I'm her what?"

"He's not my soulmate," Manda hisses, tightening her grip on the flaming sword. "He can't be."

"Why?" Berith sighs. "Because the smoke stayed black when you did the ritual in that tiny bathroom above the hunter bar?"

"You did what?" I bark at Manda, not giving a fuck about the blade to my heart. How could she have done the ritual without telling me?

"There's just one crucial detail you didn't consider," Berith continues.

Manda slams her hand on her hip. "What's that?"

"You're an untouchable." Berith comes nearer. "Immune to *all* magic, including your own."

Manda's gaze darts to the First Knight. "But…" She shakes her head. "I don't understand."

"I think you do," Berith objects. "C'mon, Amanda. You're a smart witch. I'm sure you can add one and one. Killing the kid isn't the endgame. It's just taking you one step closer to the edge, numbing you so you can do the real ritual. Why do you think he wants you to kill Alex?"

I understand jack.

Manda, however, puts the jigsaw together. "What is she saying?" she yells at the First Knight. "Tell me what she means."

"I have no idea." He shrugs.

Berith flashes him a wicked smile. "Sure, you do, Beelzebub. You know as well as I do what the last sacrifice really is. And it most certainly isn't"—she tilts her chin at the Blair girl—"the soul of that kid."

"Someone tell me what the fuck's going on," I demand. These goddamn riddles are getting on my nerves.

"Yeah," Manda says, slowly facing the First Knight. "You better tell me what she's talking about before I slam that blade into your heart."

The knight averts his gaze. He ain't going to tell her shit.

Berith flashes her an apologetic smile. You'd almost think she feels sorry for Manda. "Why do you think the book didn't want Alex dead?"

Manda's jaw clenches. "How do you—"

"It only shows you what it wants you to see. The last ritual you read isn't the real deal." She crosses her arms, eyeballing the gate. "There's only one way to unleash hell."

Manda's jaw clenches. "But…" The truth creeps up on her. "You used me," she yells at the Knight. "You and that"—her gaze darts to the evil tome—"stupid book used me?"

"Don't take it too hard," Berith says. "He's been planning this since the day you were born."

Manda stomps toward the Princess of Hell. "What's that supposed to mean?" Her eyes blaze like green hellfire, but she sounds more like herself than ever.

"Of course, he didn't tell you." Berith rolls her eyes. "Men."

Manda points the flaming sword in her direction. "Tell me!"

"Your birth was a big deal in hell."

"Why?" Manda laughs dryly. "Because they were looking forward to today?"

"No." Berith's eyes grow distant. "You see, every generation bears a gate keeper. A witch fated to keep darkness at bay. But you"—she drinks her in, eyes glistening with adoration—"you were special, Amanda. Born of the oldest witch line, blessed with powers unlike any we'd ever seen in a witch, and untouchable." Her lips curve into a half-smile. "The boss was obsessed with keeping you out of harm's way. It's why he sent his best and most trusted solider to protect you." She looks to the First Knight. "Isn't that right, Beelzebub?"

Manda is half-laughing, half-screaming. "The devil, as in Lucifer, sent someone to protect me?" She shakes her head in disbelief. "And why would he do that?"

"Because you're the only one who can keep those gates closed," I reply, finally able to answer a question. It makes sense, though. If Lucifer doesn't want to fight the final battle, he needs Manda safe so nothing like this would happen. Only problem? He trusted the wrong demon.

"I...I—"

"That's enough," Beelzebub aka First Knight thunders; his voice cracks the soil. "You signed a deal," he says, approaching Manda. "You're going to honor it. Or—"

She swings the sword. It cuts some of Beelzebub's hair. "Don't you dare give me orders." Her eyes are not the only thing on fire. Green sparks fly off her skin. "You made me sell my soul, blackmailed me into getting the book, and for what?" She narrows her eyes. "To free that bitch who promised you—"

"Shut up." Beelzebub stumbles backward. "Just shut up!"

"What bitch?" Berith asks, sounding pissed.

Manda's lips curve into a half-grin. "Tell her. Tell her why you really want to open the gate."

"How dare you?" He pays no attention to the sword, moving in on Manda. "If it wasn't for me, you'd be dead by now. All those times you sat in the attic, considering ending your pitiful existence, I was there for you. Not"—he shoots me a killer look—"your hunter. It was me who kept you sane."

Manda pales, making those black veins look even creepier. "The knocking on the wall...that was..."

"Me." He's inches away from her. "Who do you think freed you from your parents' constant fights?

381

Who killed anyone that looked at you the wrong way? That bastard in the alley who was going to rape you? The bitch at NYU?" His lips are so close to hers, they're almost touching. "I took care of you. What did he"—he tilts his head at me—"ever do for you, huh?"

"Y-you freed me from my parents' constant fights?" she stammers.

Beelzebub grins like he won the damn lottery. "You asked me to stop them, didn't you?"

"No." She shakes her head like a crazy person. "I never—"

"In the attic," he goes on. "Shortly before I pushed your drunk daddy down the stairs."

Manda gapes at the demon, unable to move or speak.

"C'mon." He traces her jawline. "You always suspected he didn't just fall. I would have killed Mommy Dearest, too, but I still needed the bitch."

"You...you killed my dad?" Her voice is as broken as she is.

Pride swells his chest. "Your dad, your sister's husband—he should have kept his hands off you—the asshole who tried to rape you in the alley, Jules who thought you weren't good enough for me."

Manda swallows hard. "What did you just say?"

The demon gloats. "I killed them all for you, love."

"No." Her spine is straighter than ever. "About Jules? What did you say about Jules?"

The bastard secures a loose strand behind Manda's ear. "The bitch came to me, told me I shouldn't date you because you were a Satan-worshipping whore." He laughs. "Can you believe it? She thought I was some kind of saint. Hilarious, huh?"

Manda yanks back as if someone just slapped her across the face. "De-DeLuca?" she stammers.

Pony-Boy? Why would she—

He snaps his fingers. A nanosecond later, he's the same dude who approached me, the hipster with the angled fringe and tight jeans. "Did you miss me, sugar?"

"Shit." Jesse's face is slightly green. "That's…that's the dude she dated at NYU."

Pony-Boy is Beelzebub? Amanda dated the First Knight of fucking hell?

Chapter 48

Amanda

Bridge DeLuca is Clyde? I had sex with a freakin' demon? Not just any demon either, the First Knight of Hell? This is a joke. There's no way I allowed a demon in my bed. Even now, as I feel the darkness inside me, I wouldn't screw a fucking bastard of hell. A mistake in the matrix is what this is. Any second, I'll wake up from this bad trip, laughing my ass off.

But I don't. I drift deeper into this world of horror and deceit as fractured memories coming back to haunt me.

****

I'm heading to the Bitter End to meet my not-so-blind date from hell, DeLuca. A blood-curdling howl echoes through the misty streets. Sulfur crawls up my nose. In my peripheral vision, I spot the red-eyed dog, a hellhound.

****

The diner is empty. It's just me, Joe's miracle cleanser, and the greasy exhaust hood. An icy breeze flows over the nape of my neck. Next thing I know, I hear Alex calling for help.

I walk into the storage room, coming face to face with the shadow of a gigantic hellhound.

"Amanda?" A hand lands on my shoulder, scaring

the living crap out of me.

I'm ready to fight for my life, but when I spin DeLuca smiles back at me.

****

DeLuca has me pinned against my closet, his tongue diving into my mouth. The kiss fucks with my mind and not in a good way. The bickering voice in my head screams stop. *I can't. I'm not in control. DeLuca takes over.*

His hand is inside my panties, feeling me up. "That's how you like it, huh? Rough and slutty."

Something about him creeps me out. I can't tell what it is, because a moment later, I watch a live-vision feed of Alex being assaulted by a hellhound.

****

I'm on the phone with him when I move into the alley beside Rick's Cabaret.

The demons walk out of the back entrance, coming at me.

I ask DeLuca to call B.

A few minutes later, my best friend is possessed by the Knight of Hell who saved me.

****

DeLuca *is* Clyde. How could I have been so freakin' blind? My stomach turns upside down, the taste of bile crawling up my gullet. "I'm going to be sick."

"You and me both," Alex grumbles.

DeLuca, Clyde, Beelzebub, or whatever else you want to call him pulls a grimace. "I gotta say I'm a bit disappointed, Amanda. You're so damn smart and yet you never once suspected anything." He steps sideways away from the tip of the sword, toward me. "Or maybe you didn't want to see the truth?"

The black pest coursing through my veins loses its grip. All sorts of emotions rush through me at intergalactic speed. Hate, fear, wrath, despair, self-loathing—I feel it all. "You're sick," I hear myself say.

He grabs me by the wrists, pulling me against his chest. "I remember you liking my sickness, sugar."

He tries to kiss me, but I pull back. "Don't you dare," I warn him, energy jolting through my hands. "You killed my father, pinned two murders on me, and tricked me into selling my goddamn soul." I spit on the ground. "Never touch me again. You hear me? Never!"

DeLuca's expression hardens. "Don't you get it?" He sounds desperate. "I did all of this for you, for us."

"Us?" I laugh hysterically. "There's never been an us."

DeLuca tilts his head to the side, studying me. "Is that right?"

"Damn right!"

He's in front of me, hands wrapped around my arms. "Then why sleep with me?"

My gaze darts to Alex.

"I see," he hisses. "I was the rebound, huh? Good enough to screw his hunter stink out of you, is that it?"

"Shut the fuck up," Alex yells, his posture screaming murder.

DeLuca ignores him. "Let me ask you this, did I ever judge you? Did I ever walk away from you? Did I leave you pregnant with nowhere to go?"

I say nothing.

"You were never good enough for him," he goes on. "He doesn't deserve you."

Deserve me? I can't stop laughing. After

everything I've done, I'm the last person to judge. "You're right." I look him in the eye. "He deserves better than me. And what is all this crap about doing it for us? Do you really think I'm that stupid?" I draw a deep breath, looking him in the eye. "This"—I point at the gate—"is all about you helping that Lilith bitch."

Berith's head jerks toward Pony-Boy. "You're helping Lilith?"

Chapter 49

Alex

Pony-Boy's chilling laughter rattles the leaves of the trees, his amber eyes glowing like molten lava. "Once Lilith is free, the two of us will rule alongside her. She promised me."

Berith laughs. "And you believe her?" She shakes her head. "You should know better than to trust the queen of mind-games."

"Shut up," Pony-Boy barks at the princess. "You're just jealous." He pulls Manda closer. "You and I, sugar, we're fated to rule this world together."

Manda's emerald eyes pierce mine. A half-smile tugs at her lips. Despite the *Carrie* look she rocks, I spot a glimpse of the old her—the defiance in her eyes, the warrior in her backbone. "We make our own fate," she says, wielding the sword.

The flaming blade is inches from Pony-Boy's throat when he catches it. "Sorry, sugar." With one swift move, he disarms her. "Killing me isn't going to be that easy."

Manda's eyes light up. Not with flames, but with the spark of fight I've been missing so gravely. "Didn't think it would be," she shoots back, lifting her hands.

Pony-Boy levitates above the ground. He isn't one bit afraid, though. Instead, he grins at her like the devil.

"Pots."

Manda freezes.

"Nwond."

Her hands drop and the demon is back on his feet.

I face Berith. "What the fuck?"

She sighs heavily. "Not only does he own her soul, she's infected by the book, too." She stares at the blazing grimoire. "He uses it against her."

Pony-Boy flashes me his brilliant teeth. "She's mine, Alexander. Always has been." Then he grabs her by the hair, shoving his damn tongue down her throat.

"Gross." Jesse gags.

Me? I'm less into puking and more into murder. I lunge forward, ready to kill the bastard. Berith, however, catches my arm. "Let go!"

"Don't," she warns. "You don't stand a chance."

I don't care. "I have to try."

"*Seenk ruoy no*," Pony-Boy whispers in Manda's ear.

She's on her knees in the blink of an eye.

Pony-Boy circles her. "You thought you were in control, that the book made you stronger than I am." He laughs. "But the book"—he extends his hand toward the tome—"is loyal to me and me only."

The *First Grimoire* slithers over the soil, halting in front of Pony-Boy's feet. "It's time," he says, picking it up. "You're going to kill the hunter and open the gate, or I will show you what real power is."

Manda shakes her head. "No."

"Yes." Pony-Boy scrubs his fingers through her hair, pulling her up. "Start the chant," he orders the Voldemort fan club.

The alien language roars through the woods. The

demonic army watches with excitement. Creatures behind the bars howl cheerfully, celebrating their soon-to-be-found freedom.

"Here." Pony-Boy slams the blade against Manda's chest. "*Mih llik*."

Like a robot, Manda stalks toward me, sword ready to pierce through my damn heart.

"Shit." Jesse pales. "This is bad."

You think?

Berith leans in. "Whatever you do, Alexander, don't get yourself killed by that sword."

"Thanks for the advice," I grumble. "But next time, tell me I'm about to be sacrificed before I walk into a battle."

Berith shrugs. "I wasn't sure. Now"—her gaze shoots to Manda marching toward us—"I am."

Manda is close enough to do some real damage with that flaming thing. Berith lets her head fall back, looking up at the feathered sky. "Time to party." A deafening scream comes out of her mouth.

Next thing I know, all hell breaks loose. Berith's army enters the battlefield. Without any warning, they attack their brothers and sisters, ripping heads off and hearts out. Hunters follow suit. They empty their magazines in the faces of mothers, fathers, sisters, and brothers—killing the vessels, but not the demonic essence. The red smoke escapes, merging with the night.

"Watch out," Jesse yells.

In the corner of my eye, I see the green flames of the blade aiming for my head. I barely manage to dodge Manda's attack. "Manda, you don't have to do this."

"I'm sorry," she says, taking another swing at me.

I move to the left. A little too late. The sharp blade slices through my upper arm. I'm no stranger to cuts, but fuck this one burns like a mother. "Manda—"

"Run," she begs, struggling to keep the blade away from me. "Run, Alex."

I scan the meadow. Amelia and Carter shoot their way toward us. Jesse used the initial confusion to engage in a showdown with Opie lookalike. Unfortunately, the demon has the upper hand. He has his bulky fingers around my little brother's throat, choking the damn life out of him.

I reach for the blessed hunting-knife in my back pocket. "Jesse," I shout, throwing it his way.

Like so many times before, he catches it with ease, slamming it right into Opie's damn neck.

Another demon—middle aged woman, probably a nurse or something—comes at him. I swear I'd help him. Only problem, Manda kicks me in the hollow of my knees, bringing me down. "I told you to run," she yells, crazed. "Why do you never listen to me?"

Propping my elbows into the damp soil, I push myself up. Pony-Boy is next to Manda. "*Mih llik*," he repeats time and again.

I try to move, but my limbs are rooted to the spot. Judging by the smug grin the bastard flashes me, he's responsible for my sudden paralysis.

Tears fill Manda's eyes. "Why the fuck didn't you run?"

"I'm not leaving without you," I reply.

Pony-Boy loses his patience. "*Mih llik*," he barks, eyes catching fire.

Manda's hands shake like crazy. Her face is a canvas of pain and misery. She fights the book and

Pony-Boy, but I can tell it's just a matter of time before she'll drive the blade through my flesh. And when that happens those snarling monsters go free and Manda loses her soul forever.

So, this is it, huh?

I'm going to die the death I always foresaw, hunting evil. I wish I was as excited about it as I was when I signed up for this job.

Chapter 50

I memorize Manda's smile, her eyes, her tiny freckles on the tip of her nose when voices flood the meadow. "*Men ansanm, kè nan senkronizasyon, nou mare pouvwa ou*," they chant.

Pony-Boy drops to his knees, pressing both hands against his ears. His face—a mask of pain and terror—shifts from his human form to something looking like Freddy Krueger, only ten times worse.

The Lacroixs march over the battlefield, secured by a bunch of PAU agents. B, Raphael, and their mom rock polar white eyes. "*Men ansanm, kè nan senkronizasyon, nou mare pouvwa ou.*"

Pony-Boy screams in agony.

Manda drops the sword.

"Alex." Jesse cups my elbow. "You okay?"

I'm bleeding, but all I care about is Manda.

"Alex," Carter yells as I move toward Manda. "Behind you!"

Jesse and I spin, just in time to spot a horde of demons running toward us.

I reach for my Beretta. Too late. A middle-aged demon dude lands a hit at my jaw. The impact sends my head flying to the left. Luckily, this isn't the first time someone tries to break my face. Shaking the pain off, I pull the trigger, placing a bullet between the mother's eyes.

Jesse wrestles a chick to the ground, sending her straight to hell by piercing the hunting-knife in her heart.

The meadow is a battlefield. Hunters fight demons. Demons fight demons. And the Lacroixs keep Pony-Boy on the ground.

Manda, too, fights. Not against us. With us. She throws red-eyed bitches through the air as if they're plush teddies.

"Alex!" Jesse points his Glock at me. "Down! Get down."

I duck and he fires, killing the teenage demon seconds away from stabbing me in the back. Literally. "Thanks."

He winks and shoots the next mother.

About two feet across from us, I spot Demon-Boy. He's lying under Hulk "the demon" Hogan, taking the beating of a lifetime.

Reaching for my knife, I stomp toward the skinny demon and his assailant. I slam the steel into the center of Hulk "the demon" Hogan's brain. He never saw his end coming.

"C'mon." I extend my hand.

Demon-Boy blinks several times before he takes my offer. "Why?" he asks, clearly shocked I helped him.

I shrug. "Because teammates have each other's backs."

He nods and moves on to his next fight. We both do.

The battle continues. Guns fire. Fists fly. Blood spills. Lives lost on both sides. No one is going to come out of this as a winner.

I kill two more demons, before I reach my little brother. "We have to stop this," I say, completely out of breath.

He looks around. "How?"

"I…" *Have no fucking clue.*

Chapter 51

Amanda

The meadow is a field of death and destruction, murder and mayhem. Bodies drop. Heads roll. Hunters scream.

What have I done? The voice in my head, *my* voice, chants on repeat. The book no longer speaks to me; it stopped when B and the rest of her family put DeLuca on ice.

Alex and Jesse are a few feet away under attack again. Some demons jump them. Five against two. This has to stop.

The book. The spell. You can end it.

My gaze shoots to the tome. If I can get to the "Kill a Knight of Hell" spell, we stand a chance. There's just a tiny problem. DeLuca's faceless minions protect the ancient spell book, and I'm no longer able to tap into the *First Grimoire's* power. It cut me off. I'm running on its last fumes.

Alex slices the throat of a demon. Another one is already waiting to kill him.

Fuck! I did this. I need to end it.

"I'll cover you." The Nun is next to me. "Go get the book and finish it."

"Why should I trust you?" I didn't trust Chelsea as a human; why would I extend the courtesy to her possessed-self? Trusting a knight only got me into a shit hole of problems.

She flashes me a smile. "Because he"—she looks at Alex—"does."

"Alex isn't the best judge of character." He dated me for Christ's sake.

The Nun nods. "You're right, but look around you. It's not like you have much of a choice."

The noses of B's mom and Raphael are already bleeding. B's magic is what keeps DeLuca on the ground. But as powerful as she is, it's just a matter of time before she loses her grip on him.

Men in suits, protecting my best friend, drop like flies. Demons off them, one by one. Amelia, aka *Pulp Fiction* granny, fights with one hand because some demon bitch crushed her other. The remaining save-the-world crew doesn't look any better.

"Let's do it," I say, gathering the remaining energy jolting through my poisoned system.

Chapter 52

Alex

In the corner of my eye, I catch Manda and Berith. Are they…*Shit*! What the fuck are they up to? The Princess of Hell speaks in alien. The air grows thicker, hotter.

Demons freeze.

The Voldemort fan club moves in on them in slow motion.

Berith lifts her hand, rooting them to the spot. "Go!" she yells at Manda.

Next thing I know, Manda makes a run for the *First Grimoire.*

"Hurry," the Princess of Hell urges. "I can't hold them for long."

A possessed twenty-something dude runs toward Berith. A large knife in his right hand, he's driven by murder.

I'm not sure what they're up to. If the demon offs Berith, however, the Voldemort fan club will take on Manda. I can't let that happen. I gotta do something.

I run as fast as I possibly can, praying I make it in time.

I don't. Pink Nail Polish does. She throws herself between Berith and the knife. A fraction of a second later, she drops to the ground.

"Akasha!" Demon Boy screams, catching his sister before she lands on the soil.

Red smoke escapes through her mouth. She's gone.

Demon-Boy rocks her like an infant, pleading with her to open her eyes. She won't. Not in this vessel, anyway.

I feel for him. Demon or not, losing a sister sucks. But there's no time to dwell on losses. Manda made it to the book. Some demons are on their way to her.

This time I do make it in time, throwing myself in front of her and the snarling bastards. "Whatever you're planning to do," I say. "Do it quickly." I won't be able to fight six of them for long.

Gunfire rings through the night. I look over my shoulder, spotting my little brother. He offed two bitches. Four to go.

A possessed elderly woman comes at me. She snaps her fingers, trying to take me out with magic. Except the charm around my neck actually works. It deflects the woman's power, sending it back to her. She lays on the ground with a broken neck.

Demon-Boy joins us. He alone takes out two. Leaving Jesse to battle a thirteen-year-old kid on demon steroids. I can tell he has issues hurting her. But eventually, after taking several hits to the face, he slams a blade in her eye.

I make my way to Manda. She's on her knees, touching the book. It catches fire, searing her hands. Her screams echo off the tress.

"Manda, stop!" She's going to kill herself.

A half-smile on her lips, she looks up at me. "Trust me." She pushes through the pain, turning page after page while the flames burn off her skin.

Her hand is nothing but raw flesh. I can't take it anymore. Before I get to pull her away, my brother screams like a lunatic. "B, watch out!"

I spin. Some demons made it past Carter's men.

"Hurry," Berith urges Manda.

She flips the last few pages. "Got it."

"Do it," Berith orders.

Manda draws a deep breath. *"Eerf uoy tes em ot emoc eeht nommus—"*

What happens next is one big blur. Jesse screams B's name. Out of the corner of my eye, I see a demon with a knife going for B's chest. A body drops. But it's not B's. It's Jesse's. The dumbass threw himself between B and the knife. The mamba's eyes change color as she spots Jesse on the ground. A second later, bone-chilling laughter roars through the woods.

Pony-Boy no longer holds his head. He has his disgusting hands around Manda's throat. "Told you it won't be that easy," he says, pulling her away from the tome.

Berith struggles to keep the Voldemort fan club under control, but with Pony-Boy back to normal, she can barely hold them.

"Boys," Pony-Boy shouts. "C'mon out to play."

A blood-curdling howl ripples through me.

My gaze darts to the edges of the woods. A dozen red, glowing eyes stare back at me. The creatures flash their sharp teeth.

Hellhounds.

We're so screwed. Hell, we're beyond screwed. We're dead. I remember what one of those things could do. Imagine what a whole pack is capable of.

The hounds paw the ground with their forefeet,

sending dirty flying over their backs. You don't have to be the dog-whisperer to know the creatures are about to attack.

"Go get him," Pony-Boy says.

The alpha hound kicks back its legs, coming at me. About two feet in front of me, it picks up speed, pushing itself up from the ground. The hound flies toward me.

I lie on my back. The creature's sulfur breath assaulting my face.

Pony-Boy hauls Manda toward me. "Time to end this," he says, as another demon passes him the sword.

He pushes the blade in Manda's palm. "Kill him. Now."

The hound gets off me. I straighten, aware there's no escaping death. The Lacroixs were only able to hold the knight so long. They can't help us now.

"*Mih llik,*" Pony-Boy barks at Manda.

She fights his mind-fuckery. But we both know how this will end.

I refuse to die on my back. So I get up, facing the woman I love, the one who will be my end.

"Amanda." Berith meets her gaze. "There's only one person who can open this gate. Do you understand? Only one."

A spark of realization gleams in Manda's eyes.
What the—
Sword dangling at her side, she runs into my arms.

"Amanda," Pony-Boy thunders. "*Mih llik.*"

She's shaking. "Take good care of Leandro."

She steps back, depriving me of her warmth. The moonlight reflects on a silver surface in her palms. *What—*

"No," I scream, recognizing the glow of my Beretta as she presses it against her heart. "Manda, don't—"

Bang!

Chapter 53

She shot herself. Manda put a fucking bullet in her heart. *No, no, no, no!* This isn't happening. She didn't—

"Alexander," Berith screams. "The sword. Take the damn sword."

What?

"You have to end this," she yells, struggling to hold the Voldemorts at bay. "Do it for her."

*End this...do it for her...*Manda took her own life to save me. She killed herself so I would live. And why?

I look from the blood on my shirt to Pony-Boy. Eyes wide open, he gapes at Manda's body. She lies by my feet, crimson pouring out of her chest.

He did this to her.

Emptiness possesses me. A moment of complete nothingness wraps the meadow into a clouded mist. Blazing gunfire and sacred chants drift into the background. Until—

Silence, not a single sound.

Numb, I pick up the sword. White flames burn bright, illuminating the darkness. The force of the angelic blade floods my system. I let it run freely, embracing its power.

"What are you doing?" Pony-Boy screams, fear in his amber eyes.

He knows time is short.

"Don't," he says, as I approach him. "I can bring her back."

I push the flaming blade through his goddamn heart. "No one can bring back the dead," I hear myself whisper.

Pony-Boy is on his knees, the fire in his eyes slowly extinguishing.

I pull the sword out, watching as the bastard's demonic essence merges with the blade. He ain't going back to hell. The sword captures his soul or the demon equivalent. Soon, the knight's body crumbles away. Until there's nothing left but ashes and dust.

"Alex?" a faint voice pushes through the emptiness inside me.

Manda? I spin. She gasps for air, blood leaking from the gaping hole in her chest.

I drop the blade, getting down. "Hey." I slowly lift her head, placing it in my lap. "You're alive."

She forces a pained smile. "I'm sorry, Alex. I never meant to—" She coughs blood.

"Shh." I caress her cheek, tears pricking at the corners of my eyes. "It's okay. Just relax, okay? We're going to get you to a hospital."

"It's too late." Manda reaches for my face. "But you already knew that."

"No!" I've seen her in worse shape. Back in Bakersfield when Walter shot her, she couldn't even speak to me. "You're—"

"Alex." She puts a lot of energy in my name. More than she has left. "It's all right. This"—she holds her crimson hands up—"is the path I chose." She looks me deep in the eye, suffocating me with that emerald ocean of love. "Just promise me…promise me you'll take care of Leandro."

I press her against my chest, holding her tighter than I should. "Why didn't you tell me, Manda?" This isn't the time nor the place, but I need to know. "Did you really think I couldn't love him?" I ask, my face wet. "That I give a fuck about what he is?"

She averts her gaze. "I knew you'd do anything for him, Alex. Even—" She stops herself.

"Even what?"

She exhales some of the pain torturing her. "Even give up the one thing you love most."

"Hunting?" I laugh.

She cocks a brow. "That's funny?"

"Yeah." I run my thumb over her cheeks, wiping tears away. "It sorta is."

Anger sparks in her eyes. "You—"

"Manda." I cup her face. "The one thing I love most in this world is *you*. It's always been you."

"I'm a—" A fresh load of blood crawls up her gullet.

"Hey, stay with me," I plead. "Manda, please…it's going to be okay. You'll be okay. Just keep those pretty eyes open for me, will ya?"

"My fate is sealed." Her body stiffens, fighting for another breath of air. "But you can get it right. I know you will." She pauses, struggling with the next words. "I've been waiting for you for all my life, jerk-face. And I need you to know I don't regret a damn thing. I'd get in that car with you all over." The light in her eyes slowly fades. "I love—"

"No!" I shake her. "Manda, open your eyes. Please, please, please…just—"

"She's gone." Berith drops Manda's wrist. "She's gone, Alexander."

"No!" She's not. Manda doesn't just die. She's a damn fighter. She'll come back to me. She always has.

"Alex." Strong hands grab my shoulders. "I'm sorry."

I shoot Carter a killer look. "Shut the fuck up! She's not dead, okay. She's just…"

What? Sleeping? Because she isn't. Her skin is already paling. Her body nothing but a burned-out shell. The girl I loved is no longer here. She's—

Dead.

In my peripheral vision, I catch a glimpse of the Lacroixs. They're headed toward us. Raphael and B, steadying my bleeding brother. The knife of the demon only hit his upper arm. But judging by his stained shirt, he lost a lot of blood.

When B sees Manda, she immediately runs to her. "Amanda," she screams, dropping next to her cold corpse. "Open your eyes. Please…just—"

Jesse is besides B. "Is she…is she—"

"Dead," I bark, unable to keep a lid on the wrath stewing in my soul. "She's dead."

"No," B cries. "You're a liar!" She shakes Manda. Hard. "I swear, if you don't open your goddamn eyes, I'll tell everyone how much you love Hallmark movies."

"Princess." One of Berith's demons bows low. "We have a bit of a situation."

I don't care about situations. Don't give a shit about the war that stopped raging in the meadow because Pony-Boy's legion vanished when I offed the bastard. Manda is gone and she ain't never coming back. Let the fucking world go up in flames. Let evil rule.

I. Don't. Care.

"Can't it wait?" she asks, gaze drifting from me to her soldier.

The demon stares at the ground. "We've been trying to locate H and T."

The princess' eyes widen. "And?"

"We can't find them," he replies.

Berith sighs heavily. "What do you mean you can't find them?"

"They haven't reported back." He eyeballs the hunters still alive. "And that's not all. The Malleus hunters and some of the others are gone, too."

"And you're only telling me now?" she thunders.

His gaze drifts over the corpses. "We were a little busy."

"What's going on?" Amelia asks, limping toward us.

Berith frowns. "Legend and some of your hunter friends are gone."

"And?" Amelia doesn't get it. Neither do I.

"And so are JJ, Bay, Constantin, and my two demons."

Wait, what? "Are you saying..." I trail off, unable to say the words out loud. It would make them real. A reality I can't handle.

Mrs. Lacroix squints. "She's saying it's hardly a coincidence."

Berith hunkers down. "I am sorry it had to end this way." She drinks in Pony-Boy's ashes. "Truly am. But I suggest you pull it together if you ever want to see your son again."

Leandro. I look at Manda. She trusted me to protect him and I swear by her grave, I will not disappoint her again.

"Where are you going?" Raphael shouts after me.

"Getting my son back."

Raphael blocks my path. "You're not going anywhere alone."

Demon-Boy is there. "He's not alone." He faces Berith. "With your blessing, I will honor the deal you made, protecting the witch and the hunter's son."

Berith smiles. "So be it." She turns to her army. "It's time for the rest of us to get back home." One by one, they escape from their vessels.

"Good luck, Alexander," the Princess of Hell says, before vanishing from the Nun's body.

I don't need luck. I have guns.

Chapter 54

Draco, Torres, Darryl, and Legend—those are the hunters missing. Child killers and bigots. We have no time to lose. There's no way of telling what they'll do—already did—to Leandro. "How much longer?" I bark at Raphael.

His pendulum swings back and forth over the map, trying to locate the missing. "Just a sec," he assures me, closing his eyes to focus.

"Leandro doesn't have a sec," I bark.

"Alex." Carter squeezes my shoulder. "I'm sure he's—"

"Don't you dare." I narrow my eyes at him. "You brought that Legend bastard here. And I swear, if anything happens to my son, you'll—"

"Got them," Raphael announces. "They're about ten miles down the main road."

That's all I needed. "No one is going to touch a hair on Manda's head 'til I'm back," I say to everyone still breathing. "You hear me?"

Some nod, some groan, but none is dumb enough to ignore me.

Jesse hands me my Beretta. The gun that took Manda away from me feels like poison in my hands. "Let's go get my nephew," he says, moving toward the narrow path leading out of the meadow and back to the main road.

"Stop." I seize hold of his good arm.

He casts me a confused look. "What are you doing?"

I point at his wound. "You're not going."

"But—"

"No." I sound like a damn beast, ready to rip some heads off. "I can't lose anyone else today."

He shakes his head. "You and"—he tilts his chin at Demon-Boy—"him against four well-trained hunters? That's suicide."

"Don't worry." Raphael pats my little brother's shoulder. "I'm going, too." My lips part, but he quickly shuts me up. "They have my brother."

Carter loads his gun. "I'm in."

He's the last person I want on my team. "N—"

"You can hate me later, Remington." He holsters his Glock. "First we need to get that boy of yours."

"I don't trust you," I hiss.

"Trust me," B says, wiping her red face. "I'll make sure he's good."

I could argue, but time isn't on my side. "Let's just go."

****

Manda is dead. Leandro is in the claws of child killers. Bay, Constantin, JJ, and the demons haven't been heard from since they left the Redrock Café. How the fuck did this happen? How did everything go to hell in a matter of hours?

"Alex?"

I look down at B. She's leaning on my shoulder, batting her damp lashes. "Huh?"

She draws a deep breath. "I'm sorry."

"For what?" She didn't sell her soul, driving

410

Manda in the bastard's arms. I did.

"DeLuca," she says, averting her gaze. "I…"

"It's not your fault." It's mine. All of this is on me. I fucked up the only good thing I ever had and did too little too late to fix it.

An awkward silence thickens the air inside Raphael's car. It's the kind found at funerals. You know when folks are sorry for your loss but don't really know how to express it.

Demon-Boy succumbs to it. "You guys know this is a trap, right?"

Carter looks back. "What do you mean?"

"Two hunters, one bad-ass voodoo priest, and two demons." He wrinkles his nose. "No way those bitches took them out without an inside man."

An inside man? An image of Bay flickers across my mind. He spoke to Legend shortly before they hit the road. Could he—*No!* He promised to protect Leandro. Swore he'd keep him safe. He'd never—

Never say never, Manda's voice roars through my brain.

B straightens. "We need a plan."

"I have a plan." Go in, kill the mothers, and take Leandro home. Only without Manda there isn't a place called home.

"I hope it's a good one," Raphael says, pulling into the driveway of an old, abandoned shed. Draco's car is parked near the entrance. "I have a feeling this won't be pretty."

"Something isn't right," B says, sniffing the air.

Demon-Boy nods. "Can't believe it, but I agree with the mamba." He ogles the shabby shed. Brown paint comes off. "We should split up. Just in case."

B nods. "I'll go with Alex. The rest of you, take the back entrance."

"You sure?" I ask her, well aware the front door is where death waits.

She forces a smile. "I'd rather die than let those bastards hurt Leandro."

I load my Beretta. After tonight, I never want to see this gun again. "Stay behind me," I warn her.

We all move in different directions. Raphael, Carter, and Demon-Boy toward the back. B and I right up to the front entrance.

"Ready?"

She nods and I push the large wooden gates open. The dim light of a candle casts shadows all over the place. Iron chains hang from the ceiling, haystacks scattered across the floor, but I don't see Leandro or anyone else for that matter.

"Careful." I pull B back. "Draco is ex-military. He loves booby traps."

"Seriously?"

"Wouldn't lie about it." Remember the transgender kid who had an unpleasant encounter with a wendigo? Draco used a damn bear-trap to catch him.

We head farther inside, watching our steps, aware they could be our last. B, on high alert, scans our surroundings. "Do you smell that?"

I draw a deep breath, but don't smell shit. Maybe my senses are as fucked up as I am. Maybe Bonnie smells ghosts. Whatever it is, I don't have time to dwell on it.

"I'm telling you," B insists. "I know that scent. It's—"

"Gasoline," I blurt out, glaring at the empty

canister on the floor.

B stops dead in her tracks. No, not because the place is soaked in a flammable substance and could go *poof* any second. She freezes for a whole other reason. About two feet away, next to a low burning candle, are JJ, Melinda, and Constantin.

They look like hell, bruised and barely conscious. Wanna know what's worse? They're soaking wet. Something tells me they ain't dripping with water.

Where the fuck is Leandro? Not here, that's for sure. Neither is Bay, or the rest of the hunters.

"Constantin." B rushes to her brother.

She's so fast, I can't hold her back. "B, wait!"

Too fucking late. Wood creaks. The floor gives in. B falls.

"Fuck," she cusses.

As long as she cusses, she's still alive.

"Alex!" She sounds a bit hysterical.

"Hold on," I shout, scanning the remaining floorboards with great care before I approach her.

"I'm not sure I can," she says. "Seriously, you better get me the fuck out of here."

Searching the shed one last time, I holster my gun, and move toward the hole. I understand B's hysteria. She's backed up against a wall. Across from her, about two seconds away from sinking its poisonous teeth into the mamba, is a massive white cobra. "Fuck."

"Get me out of here," she begs.

"I will." But how? That snake will strike before I even attempt to pull her out. "Just stay very still, all right?"

B shoots me a killer look. "Sure. I'm just going to stand around, waiting for that thing to kill me. No problem whatsoever."

"It won't kill you," I assure her. "Cobras only attack if they're scared. Don't move and you'll be okay." I hope Discovery Channel gets its research right.

I take it all in. Demon-Boy was right. This is a trap. I gotta get them the hell outta here before we all end like that poor kid in the bear-trap.

I get down on my knees, careful not to trigger any other booby traps. "Listen," I say, calmly. "I'm going to need some help to pull you out of there."

Fear clouds her cognac eyes. "But—"

"I won't leave you," I promise her. "I'm just going over there"—I tilt my chin at the cuffed and bruised rescue-Leandro group—"and get one of them to help me, okay?"

She ogles the cobra, standing taller than a tree. "Okay."

"Be right back."

"Just hurry."

I reach them without getting myself killed. I call that a win. "JJ?" I pull the sock out of her mouth. "Hey"—I slap her—"you with me?"

She blinks her eyes open. "Alex?"

I reach for my tools and work the lock of her cuffs. "You'll be all right." The shackles drop. "I'll get you out of here."

Her gaze roams the shed. The girl is totally out of it. My money is on drugs. "Leandro," she whispers. "They…they took him."

"Who?" I ask, freeing Melinda. Manda's sister looks worse than the others. She's got a bad shiner, cuts all over her, and several deep holes—cigarette burns. The demons who had her did a real number on her.

JJ struggles for composure. "Bay, he helped them."

I'm going to kill him. Actually, I'm going to kill myself. Because why the fuck did I ever trust him?

"There are others, too."

"Draco, Torres, and the Malleus dicks?" I ask, moving on to free Constantin.

"The Fords," she replies.

"As in the hunters from up north who kill their own kind?"

"Yeah." Her gaze darts to Constantin. He's conscious. "They surprised us. We didn't stand a chance. The charms Mrs. Lacroix handed out protected them."

"Mmmh," he grumbles.

Shit. I almost forgot to free him from the damn sock.

"I'm going to kill them," he barks, the second the thing is out of his mouth.

"You and I, both."

Melinda groans, slowly opening her eyes. "Alexander?"

"Yes."

She looks behind me. "Amanda?"

I avert my gaze.

"No!" She jumps to her feet. "Please, tell me she's okay."

"I wish I could." But that'd be a lie.

"Leandro." She digs her nails in my shoulders, sobbing. "They have him. I can't lose him, too."

Neither can I.

"Guys," B yells. "The cobra doesn't look happy. Unhappy cobra equals dead mamba. So how about you get me the hell out of here?"

Constantin is with her in a second. "Listen to me, little sis. I'm going to calm the snake and Alex will pull you up, okay?"

"So you're an exorcist and a snake whisperer?" Is there anything B's bro can't do?

Ignoring my question, he waves me over. "Help me."

I pull JJ up. "Get Melinda out of here."

"C'mon." She wraps her arm around Melinda's shoulder, slowly moving her toward the exit.

"Be careful," I warn JJ. "This place is a death zone."

"On my count," Constantin says.

I get down on my knees. "Ready."

He murmurs something no one understands. It doesn't really sound like Creole. More like an inhuman hissing.

"Now," he orders.

I seize hold of B's sweater. *This is too easy.* Draco didn't plan to let anyone out of here alive.

"Pull her up," Constantin barks.

I do as he says.

Something clicks.

The floorboard beneath the candle lifts on one side. The candle loses its balance, landing right on the gasoline. The fire spreads within seconds. Flames circle the hole. I barely manage to get B out of there before the flames swallow the white cobra like a hungry beast.

"Run," I shout at B and Constantin.

I don't have to tell them twice.

We make it out. Alive.

The fire consumes the shed within minutes, its flames raging high into the night sky. The bastards were going to burn us alive.

"C'mon." Constantin drags me toward the cornfield. "We have to get away from the fire."

Chapter 55

We seek refuge in the cornfield, running far enough to bring much needed distance between the fire and us. But some of us are weaker than others.

Melinda is the first to stop. Hands on her knees, she's struggling to breathe. "We have to find Leandro." She looks up at me. "Please, we—"

Headlights cut her off. They flood the field.

"Would you look at that." Draco slams the car door shut. "They all made it out alive. What a bloody shame."

Constantin balls his fists. "You—"

"Stop right there," Legend warns, stepping out of the car with Leandro on his arm. "We wouldn't want anything to happen to him, would we?"

Draco, Daryl, the four Ford brothers—Brian, Bobby Ray, Herman, and John—and Bay "the fucking traitor" jump out of their cars.

Leandro extends his hands toward me. My knees give in as I drink in his face. God, that boy is the spitting image of his mother. The pictures I saw didn't do their familiarity justice—same eyes, same smile, same spark.

"Dadada," he babbles on repeat.

He knows who I am. He's Manda's son. Nothing should surprise me when it comes to that boy. "Give him to me," I demand, voice low.

418

Legend's gaze darts from him to me. "You know I can't do that, Remington."

B is next to me. "Why?" She points at Leandro. "He's just a baby. Never hurt a soul in his life."

"But he will," Draco says. "Sooner or later, you all do."

Bay stares at his boots. There's so much I want to say to him, but what's the point? He made his choice. Now, I'm gonna make mine. I just need to know one thing before I kill him. "Why, Bay?"

At first, he says nothing.

"Manda trusted you," I blurt out. "She fucking trusted you."

"Bad choice." Daryl laughs.

JJ squints. "What's that supposed to mean?"

Legend frowns. "Did you really think he'd abandon the only hunters who know which demon killed his dad?"

Lightning hits. "You were never on our side, were you?" I knew it. I fucking knew it. Back in Winter Harbor when I first saw him sitting across from Manda, I had this sick feeling. One I couldn't decipher, one I eventually blamed on jealousy. But it wasn't just me being fucking scared Manda could like the asshole. It was instinct and I should have listened to it, like I should have when it told me Manda would never go dark.

Bay's shoulders hang low. "I—"

"You played us from day one," I bark, barely able to keep it together.

His silence speaks louder than any words.

"You're dead." I'm going to kill them. All of them. Hunters or not, by the end of this night they'll rot in hell.

Legend's hand circles Leandro's neck. "That's enough. Let's not sink that low, shall we?"

"Says the guy who has his hand around the neck of a kid," Constantin spits back at him.

"He's not just any kid." Legend meets my gaze. "You don't know what he's capable of. Even hell fears him."

"So?" B barks.

"We can't risk letting him live." He sighs. "We just can't."

I move closer. "You fucking asshole. His mother just died protecting you and your stupid friends. And you, you—"

"She was also the one who almost ended the world," he justifies himself.

I'm done talking. This ends. Here. And now. "I won't say it again, let him go."

"The answer is still no." Draco laughs.

I'm trying to come up with a plan. Anything that could get Leandro and hopefully, everyone else out of here alive. I don't know about Melinda, but Constantin and B could probably take most of the Fords out without much effort. They don't wear any protective charms. Only problem, the others do. One of which has my son.

Think, Remington. Think.

Despite Legend's hand around his throat, Leandro doesn't cry or whimper. His spine is straight, his eyes—Manda's eyes—are on me. He's a fighter. Like mother like son.

"Please." Melinda is on her knees. "I'm begging you, let him go. He didn't do anything wrong."

Draco grins like the bitch he is. "That child"—he looks at him—"should have never been born. He's an abomination. A freak. A—"

"Watch it." I'm already wandering on the edge. God knows I don't need a push to make the jump.

"Remington." Legend inches closer. "I get this is hard for you, but you don't know anything about this child."

I stare at my son. *My* son. I'm his father and I will protect him with my life. I don't have to know anything else.

"He's just a baby," Melinda cries. "He doesn't even have any powers yet."

"We can't risk it," Torres says, looking less thrilled than Draco. "He could erase our whole bloodline."

"So that's what this is about?" Bitter laughter crawls up my throat. "You're scared he'll come after you one day?"

"No," Legend replies. "We're scared he'll come after *all* of us."

"That's ridiculous," Constantin roars.

Draco crosses his arms. "Is it?"

"Yeah, it is," Constantin assures him. "Being born a witch doesn't make him any more or less dangerous than anyone else. Hitler was a human, wasn't he? So was Napoleon, Manson, Bundy, and almost every other serial-killer and whack-job who ever tried to rule the world." Constantin shrugs. "If your theory stands true, you'll have to kill every single child just in case it turns out evil one day."

"Bullshit," Draco shouts, hair standing on high ends. "Humans have a right to be on this planet."

"And witches don't?" B shoots back.

"No," they all agree. All but Bay. He just stands there like a fucking coward.

"Funny." Melinda rises to her feet. "Considering witches are the ones who protect the natural order of all things."

"Without us," Constantin adds. "Humanity would destroy this place."

Draco comes at Constantin. "Without *you*, this planet would be heaven, asshole."

"It's pointless." Draco pulls his gun on Leandro. "Let's just get this over with."

The second I see the barrel of the gun near Leandro's head, I lose it. "Wait." I inch closer, trying to get to him before he pulls the trigger. "Your beef isn't with him. It's with me. So go ahead and kill me, but leave my son alone."

Draco flashes me his rotten teeth. "How about I kill him first and then you?" He bends to Leandro's ear. "Say goodbye, Daddy."

The kid reaches out to me, smiling as if he doesn't have a care in the world. "Da...Dada..."

I extend my hand. Our fingertips connect.

"What the hell?" Draco yells as a green light bulb builds around Leandro.

Eyes wide open, he tries to pull the trigger but the gun malfunctions.

"Dada," Leandro repeats, struggling to get away from Legend.

The green light around Leandro quickly turns into blazing flames, searing Legend's hands. He drops him. I catch him inches above the ground.

Another battle ensues. The Ford Brothers march toward me. Constantin smirks, chants. Next thing I know, all four brothers are on the ground, holding their heads, screaming in agony.

JJ and B take on Daryl. "The charm," B shouts. "Take off his charm."

"With pleasure," JJ says, deflecting Daryl's fists like a pro.

She makes it close enough to rip off the protective charm. It dangles from her index finger.

B's eyes light up. "Take your knife," she orders him.

He complies immediately.

"Run it through your goddamn leg." I wish she'd said head, but she ain't no killer.

"Watch out," Constantin screams.

Legend comes at us. Something tells me Leandro's shield won't protect us from his hunting blade.

"No!" Melinda steps between the knife and us. It pierces through her backbone, killing her instantly.

Legend isn't done. He goes for another kill. This time, Leandro and I. I shield him with my body, waiting for the blade to hit a major organ. It never happens.

"I knew you couldn't be trusted."

Demon-Boy?

I peek over my shoulder. Demon-Boy caught Legend by the throat, dangling him above the ground. "You're not so mighty after all." He laughs, crushing the hunter's gullet.

And this is how the great Legend dies. At the hands of a lower-class demon, not standing a damn chance. Pretty anti-climactic, huh?

"You okay?" Demon-Boy asks, rubbing his palms on his jeans.

Leandro smiles at me. "Yeah," I say. "Thanks to

you, we are."

Demon-Boy shrugs. "Call it even."

The demon just saved my son's life; we're not even close to even. "I owe you. Just say the word and—"

"Hey." He flashes me a boyish grin. "That's what teammates are for, right?"

The fact a demon sounds so incredibly human would fuck with my mind if it wasn't for the fight that's still raging. Carter versus Draco. Constantin versus Torres. This should be fun to watch. Except it's not. Carter simply shoots the bitch between the eyes—he was most definitely aiming for the leg—and Constantin has Torres on his back and begging for mercy in under a minute.

JJ helps me up. "You guys okay?"

"O-kay," Leandro babbles, smiling down at the feisty huntress.

She isn't immune to his charms. "Hey, pretty boy." She grabs his small hand. "Looking just like your mama, do you?"

I'm all set to admit she's right when I spot Bay. He's still standing in the same spot, not moving a damn inch. "Take care of him," I mutter, passing my son to JJ.

"Sure." She holds him tight against her chest.

I stalk toward Bay, Beretta drawn. He doesn't even try to run. "Go ahead," he says when I aim at him. "I deserve it."

"Damn right you do," JJ barks.

My finger itches. He's a traitor. Almost got us all killed. He doesn't deserve to live. Then why haven't I pulled the trigger yet?

"Alex." Carter nudges me. "Look."

I follow his gaze. Leandro sits on JJ's arm, that same green light circling him. "Dada…Dada."

I lower the gun. Shooting Bay won't bring Manda back. But it will forever change the way my son looks at me. "Carter?"

"Huh?"

I turn away from Bay. "Get this son of a bitch away from me before I change my damn mind."

Carter grabs him by the arm. "My pleasure."

Chapter 56

The crows are gone, allowing the beams of the bloated moon to break through the massive tree canopy. At the end of this path lies my fate—a lifetime of regret and desire. Or should I say the lifeless body of the woman I love? Every step I take, every move I make reminds me how badly I fucked up. Some mistakes can't be fixed. This—not trusting Manda—is one of them.

I keep walking, drawing willpower from Leandro's shamrock eyes. He's snuggled up against my chest, holding onto my jacket as if he fears I might leave him. I won't make the same mistake twice, though. Leaving him will never be an option. He's my blood, my family. And I swear to every creature willing to listen I won't fuck this up.

"Dada." He smiles at me. "Dada."

I didn't know a heart could burst with pride and drown in sadness at the same time. But when he looks at me like this—like I'm his hero, his everything—I feel joy and failure at the same time. He'll grow up without a mom who gave up everything for him and still thought it wasn't enough. Without an aunt, a woman who raised him like her own, and died protecting him.

His tiny hand reaches for my cheek. "Dada."

I lean in, embracing his touch. "You're going to be

okay," I promise him. "Everything's going to be okay."

I find a pinch of sadness in his gaze. "Mamama," he mutters, pointing ahead.

My eyes are wet, my heart barely able to continue its rhythm. This boy lost more in one night than some folks in a lifetime. "I'll take you to her," I whisper, hugging him tighter.

Jesse's voice wafts through the old trees. "Alex?"

"Yes," I whisper, hoping the wind carries my reply.

He stands by the edge of the woods, next to Amelia, and Mrs. Lacroix. The closer we get the more dread I spot on their faces. I don't blame them. Constantin carries a body after all.

"Melinda?" Mrs. Lacroix gasps, clutching her hand over her mouth.

B runs into her mom's arms, sobbing like a toddler. "They're both gone," she repeats over and over. "I can't believe their both gone, Mom."

Mrs. Lacroix runs her hand over B's curls. "It's okay, baby girl. When the time comes, we'll meet them again." The mother of all mambas sounds so confident even I believe her.

"What happened to your hand?" Amelia asks.

I look down, seeing the burned flesh for the first time. It's probably from when I pulled B out of that hole. "It's nothing," I assure her, not feeling the pain.

She slams her hands on her hips, cocking a brow in good old Amelia-style. "Doesn't look like nothing to me, Alexander."

Part of me wants to reassure her I really am fine, but there's a question weighing on my soul. One I need an answer to right away. "Did you know?"

She squints. "Did I know what?"

I smile at Leandro. He fiddles with the buttons of my flannel shirt, looking calm and happy. "Did you know what Draco, Torres, and the Malleus dicks had planned?"

Shock widens Amelia's eyes. "You think I wanted"—she eyeballs my burned hand—"this?" She shakes her head. "It's no secret I was never a fan of your choices. But I would *never* hurt another hunter or"—she gazes at Leandro—"a child."

The Amelia I remember wouldn't. But how well do you truly know someone? Carter, a guy I trusted with my life, went behind my back inviting the Malleus bastards. Bay played us all to a point where I trusted him to protect Leandro. And Pony-Boy, the douche I hated because he had what I wanted, turned out to be the First Knight of Hell. So yeah. I don't believe Amelia was in on Draco's mad plan, but can I be sure? Nope.

Mrs. Lacroix nudges me. "Listen to your heart, Alex." She smiles at Amelia. "What does it tell you?"

My heart? It ain't gonna tell me shit. It's dying with pain and breathing with joy, mourning our losses and celebrating what I gained. My heart is as broken and whole as I am.

B's mom gently pats my shoulder. "You know you can trust her," she whispers. "Deep down you've always known. Or why would you have taken Amanda to her B&B?"

She has a point. Despite Amelia's stand on witches, I took Manda there. Why? Because I was certain she wouldn't harm her, for my sake. Why would she hurt my son then?

She wouldn't. "I had to ask," I say.

Amelia nods. "I know."

Jesse scans the survivors. "Hey, where's Bay?"

"Long story," B replies, a major frown on her face.

Leandro extends his small hands toward the meadow. "Mamama." He looks up at me. "Ma…Ma…Ma."

I draw a pained, fiery breath. "Let's go."

"Wait." B catches my jacket. "Do you really think that's a good idea?"

Taking a child to see his dead mother? Probably not. "I owe him that much."

"Mamama," he goes again, struggling to get down from my arms.

Raphael's hand is on B's shoulder. "Let them go."

Crossing the battlefield where we fought alongside our enemies for a world that's less than perfect, I tug Leandro's face against my chest, shielding him from the ugly sight of death.

Manda still lies there in a pool of blood, untouched. Her face too pale, her hair too tame, and her skin like leather, lacking the breathtaking glow. Yet even in death, she's the most beautiful girl I've ever seen.

Hunkering down next to her, I place our son in my lap. "Mama," he says, reaching for her.

Men might not cry. But fathers do. They sob for the future their child will never have, the joy that was taken from them, the pain it'll cause them for many years to come. "She loved you," I say, holding him tighter than I should. "She loved you more than she loved anything else in this world." *Even her own life.*

"Mama," he says once more, voice thick and cranky.

"Yeah." I caress Manda's icy cheeks. "She's your

mama, always will be." And something tells me even death can't keep her from looking out for our boy.

"I promise you," I say, squeezing her stiff hand. "He's going to grow up knowing how much you loved him, how much I love him."

Somewhere, deep inside, I pray she yanks her eyes open and says, "I know, Alex. We'll make sure he's loved, together." But the dead don't speak. At least, not to me, they don't.

The longer I look at her lifeless body, the more pressure builds in my core. Every bone in my body aches for her touch. Every fiber in my soul mourns her loss. Hell, I'd do just about anything to get her to call me jerk-face again, to hear her come back at me with some smart-ass remark that'll make my damn blood boil. I'd do anything for one last smile—a kiss.

Leandro gasps for air. I'm all too familiar with the pained look on his face. Seen it over and over in his mom's eyes. The boy inherited Manda's curse. He feels what I feel—excruciating pain.

For his sake, I focus on the good times we had. I remember the many nights we sat in my car waiting on Jesse, listening to music and arguing about the best bands. I see the fire in her eyes the day I pushed her against that wall and kissed her like a starving man. I feel her hands running down my back as I loved her for the last time.

Holding our son with one hand, I use the other to brush a loose strand out of her cold face. "I love you, Manda. I loved you before I even met you." Back then, I didn't know what that weird tingly feeling in the pit of my stomach was when I heard of the fearless witch from Salem, the one who put a no-more-hunting-or-wake-butt-naked-in-the-street curse on one of us. I couldn't decipher the anticipation building inside me as I thought about meeting her one day. I figured it was the thrill of the kill that made my heart beat faster. But it was love. A love that grew even when its seeds were doomed to wither. A love that was stronger than the fate of a hunter. "You were everything I didn't know I needed, and I swear to you, I will make sure our son knows every little thing about you."

I'm ready to kiss her goodbye when Leandro rocks back and forth in my lap. "Mamama," he says over and over, gawking ahead.

For a split second, I allow myself to hope. Manda cured a zombie. If anyone could find a way back from the dead, it's her. But it's not her I see when I follow my son's gaze.

A larger-than-life shadow floats toward us. I recognize the creepy top hat right away. Baron Samedi—the reaper Manda summoned to free Isobelle from purgatory.

What the fuck is he doing here?

Chapter 57

"Alexander." Samedi stops inches in front of Manda's body, raising his hat. "As predicted, we meet again."

Terror washes over me. Why is he here? Manda's soul is already gone. Is he here for someone else? I pull Leandro closer. "What do you want?"

Samedi reaches for a cigar, lighting it up. "I'm on the job."

I'm not in the mood for games. "Care to elaborate?"

He takes a deep drag. "My services are requested."

We didn't summon a reaper. At least, I don't think we did. "By whom?"

"By me," a husky, imperious voice answers, raising the hair on the back of my neck.

Whoever that is has some serious juice. So much so, the hunter inside me roars to life. "Stay right there," I scream at the obscured figure by the edge of the woods.

"Careful." Samedi grins. "You shouldn't piss him off. I clocked out and I'd hate to cut my free time short for you."

The gang gathers around me. "Who's that?" JJ asks, ready to fight.

The figure moves into the light. Dressed in a suit that costs more than my car, he steps over Pony-Boy's ashes. "I'm known by many names," he replies, smiling sheepishly. "The one you're most familiar with is—"

"Lucifer." Demon-Boy bows low, almost kissing the damn soil.

"Lucifer?" JJ rolls her eyes. "The ruler of hell wears Prada and looks like a younger version of Gerard Butler?" She snickers. "Yeah, sorry. Not buying it."

"Are you crazy?" Demon-Boy hisses, shooting her a shut-the-hell-up look. "Don't talk to him like that."

The guy—he really does look like Gerard Butler—waves the whole thing off. "It's all right, Jolene Jade. I—"

"How…" JJ's jaw drops. "How do you know my name?"

Yeah, good question. I've known the girl for years and had no idea what JJ stood for. She refused to tell me. *Jolene Jade, huh?* I sorta get why she kept it under wraps.

Prada flashes the huntress a mesmerizing smile. Seriously, if I were a girl, I'd probably have butterflies in my stomach. "I know a lot of things, JJ."

"Because you're Lucifer?" She seems to have a hard time with this and she's not the only one.

"I understand I don't resemble the images painted of me over the centuries."

"You don't," she testifies on all our behalf. Hoofs and horns that's expected when faced with the ruler of the infernal regions. Not Hollywood in Prada.

Lucifer inches closer.

"Stop," Mrs. Lacroix orders. "Not another step." Raphael, Constantin, B, and her mom are ready to rumble. Something tells me this is a fight they won't win.

"Mamba." Lucifer bows his head slightly. "I mean you no harm."

"Then why are you here?" She casts Samedi a disapproving look. "With him?"

Lucifer shoves his hands in his pockets and sighs. "As you might know, he's one of the few bending the rules."

"You mean breaking them." Constantin has balls of iron talking to the devil like that.

B is beside me. "Get Leandro out of here," she whispers, nodding at the path leading back to the main road.

"There's no need for that," the super-hearing devil says. "As I already said, I'm not here to harm that little boy or"—he scans the group—"anyone else."

Okay, I bite. "So why don't you tell us what you want?"

Lucifer's gaze darts from the gates—the creatures are no longer there—to Manda. "I'm here to restore the balance," he finally says.

"Yeah?" B crosses her arms. "And how are you going to do that?"

Lucifer takes another step in our direction. Literally, everyone tenses. "It came to my knowledge that things have gotten out of control while I was..." He pauses. "*Away*. For that, I must apologize."

"Apologize?" Jesse parrots. "Your knight almost ended the damn world. Sorry, doesn't quite cut it."

He draws a deep breath. "You're right."

Did Lucifer, the devil, the ruler of hell, just agree with my brother? And here I thought I'd seen crazy.

"I can't change what Beelzebub did." He scans the corpses, stopping at Manda's. "But what I can do is bring her back."

"How?" I ask, quicker than a bolt of lightning. He's Lucifer for fuck's sake. The stuff every nightmare is made of. Yet I am willing to listen to his offer as long as Manda comes back to me. There's something seriously wrong with me.

The King of Hell tilts his chin at Samedi. "He'll help."

Leandro wraps his arms around my neck. "Mama…Mamama."

I look from my son to Lucifer. What he offers sounds too damn good to be true. After everything, I should tell him to get lost. But what kind of a father would I be if I didn't at least try to bring Leandro's mom back? "Let's say you are able to bring her back, what—"

"Alex." Jesse taps my shoulder. "Don't do it."

"What do you want in exchange?" I swear, if he says *your soul*, I'll drive a knife through his damn brain.

Lucifer laughs. "What do I want?"

I nod.

"Nothing," he replies, amused.

"Yeah." Constantin bursts into laughter. "Right."

Lucifer blocks the others out, focusing solemnly on me. "By sacrificing herself, Amanda kept the natural order intact. She saved *all* creation, including myself."

I can't help it. His words blow through my heart like a damn storm. "So what you're saying is you'll bring her back because—"

"Because I owe her," he cuts me short.

Mrs. Lacroix ogles him suspiciously. "Is that all?"

Lucifer flashes her a wicked grin. "Of course, not."

There is a catch, after all, huh? Why am I not surprised?

Constantin draws to his full height. "Tell the truth, demon. Why would you really bring Amanda back?"

Lucifer glances at the spikes of the iron gate. "Because"—he exhales sharply—"there's a war coming."

"And here I thought we'd already fought it," Jesse grumbles.

A sad smile creeps over Lucifer's face. "I wasn't referring to the fight between good and evil, Jesse. I am talking about a war between evil and something *far* worse."

Everyone stops breathing. The devil talking about worse is bad. The devil's voice trembling with fear? The worst.

Not sure how long we stand there, glaring at him, unable to speak. But after what feels like forever, he says, "I'm going to need the best gatekeeper." He studies Manda. "She's the only one I trust to keep those gates shut. And it certainly doesn't hurt she's protected by"—he winks at me—"an Arrow who'd die for her."

I'm speechless.

Lucifer, however, isn't. "Bring her back," he orders the reaper.

Samedi frowns. "As you wish."

All it takes is the snap of the rogue reaper's fingers. A fraction of a second later, Manda jerks her eyelids open. An ocean of emerald roams the meadow. "W-what happened?" she stammers.

"Manda?" Tears of joy leak down my cheeks. I don't bother wiping them away. "Is that really you?"

She props up on her elbow, squinting. "Who else

would it be?" I've never been so happy to hear her snap at me like that.

"Mamama," Leandro cheers, almost jumping out of my lap.

Manda's eyes light up. She sits up, taking him from my arms. "You're okay." She's crying, too. "He's okay," she says to me.

"Yeah, he is." I swallow the remaining salt water. "And so are you."

She gazes at her chest. The wound is gone, blood still all over her. "I...I *am* okay." She pauses. "But...how? I—"

"You killed yourself," Samedi grumbles.

Manda looks up. "Oh. My. God," she barks, the instant she spots Lucifer. "What the fuck have you done, Alex?"

"Nothing, I swear."

She shakes her head. "Please tell me you didn't—"

"His soul is his," Lucifer says. "All deals made with Beelzebub are void." He smiles at her. "Including your own."

"But—" She looks confused. "Jack. I understand jack."

Lucifer flashes her an almost sweet smile. "I'm sure Alex will explain everything."

The King of Hell picks up the *First Grimoire.* "What are you going to do with that?" Manda asks, voice trembling.

The devil looks from the evil tome to her. "I will make sure no one ever touches this book again."

"Good," she whispers, shuddering when her gaze lands on the grimoire.

Lucifer turns to leave. "Until we meet again."

"Wait," Jesse yells after the King of Hell. "What about that war?"

"All in good time," he replies, merging with the night.

Samedi casts me an annoyed look. "Do me a favor?"

"What's that?"

"Forget I exist." Then he's gone, too.

Manda struggles to get on her feet. She's still shaky and Leandro's weight isn't helping. "Easy." I grab our boy, cup her elbow and pull her up. "You've been dead."

"And now"—she looks at her hands—"I'm not."

No. No, she's not.

B must have gotten over the fact Lucifer was the one who brought Manda back, because she literally jumps her. "I thought I'd lost you," she cries. "Don't you ever leave me again, you hear me?"

"I won't," Manda promises, hugging her back.

"Good," she barks. "Because next time, I'll kill you myself."

The mamba only lets go of Manda when Constantin pulls her back. "My turn, sis." He, too, hugs Manda as if he never wants to let go.

One after another, they welcome her back. Even Amelia has a nod and a smile for Manda.

"Where's Melinda?" she asks, looking around.

Silence settles over the meadow, thickening the air.

Manda looks me in the eye. "Alex, where's my sister?"

I hand Leandro to B, lace my fingers through hers—god, touching her never felt so damn good—and take her to her sister. "I'm sorry," I whisper.

Manda drops to her knees, holding her sister's body like I held hers not long ago. "How?" she chokes out, fighting ugly tears.

Throwing my arm around her, I gently tug her against my chest. "She saved our son's life."

"It's not fair," she says over and over again.

I hold her tighter, needing her to know she's not alone. I'm here for her like I should have been from day one.

I'm not sure how long we sit like this—her mourning the dead, me celebrating the living—but when the sun comes up, casting a beautiful orange light on the meadow, I lean down. "There's something I have to tell you."

She moves her head, facing me. Her tears have dried, but the pain is fresh and plenty.

When she looks at me like that—as if I were her savior and destroyer at the same time—I dread the outcome of this conversation. Amanda is smart enough to walk away from poison even if it's as sweet as our love. She's strong enough to remember all the hurt I put her through even when I offer her joy and happiness. But I'm neither strong nor brave enough to let her go.

Don't be a pussy, Remington.

Manda narrows her eyes. "What's going on, Alex?" She drinks me in, seeing beyond my skin into my soul. "I don't like that terrifying gray around you."

I force a smile. "Gray, huh? What does it mean?"

She sighs. "Means you're scared as hell."

That I am.

She shifts closer. "You're scaring me, jerk-face."

I laugh. "I missed that."

She cocks a brow. "Scaring the living shit outta

me, or your pet name?"

"Both," I answer truthfully. There's nothing I didn't miss about her. Why the fuck is it so hard to tell her, though? Why am I such a coward when it comes to her?

Manda cups my face. "Seriously, what's wrong?" I hate the trembling in her voice. It reminds me that even Amanda Bishop is vulnerable when I need her to be invincible.

Now or never, Remington.

"I'm sorry," are the first words that come out of my mouth. Not exactly what I wanted but it's a start. "I'm sorry I pushed you away. I'm sorry you thought I cared more about being a hunter than"—I look to Leandro—"my own son."

Manda sighs. "Alex, you—"

"Wait," I plead. "Let me finish?"

"All right." She shrugs. "Go on."

C'mon, you got this.

"I love you," I whisper.

Her face is a blank page. *Who scares the crap out of whom now?*

Doesn't matter. She needs to hear this even if she decides to walk away. I push through the terror clawing my gut. "When I found you in that alley, pinned against the wall by that bastard, I hated myself. I hated myself because all I could think of was doing the same damn thing to you. Pushing you against those bricks, hearing you moan my name…it's all I wanted." Her chest rises and falls rapidly. "You shocked and electrified me like no one else ever had. I didn't stay because I thought you couldn't handle yourself, Amanda. Fuck, I knew you could. But I also knew if I walked away, your eyes would have haunted me for the rest of my life."

Her hands drop to her sides. "Alex, I—"

"Don't, Manda." I caress her cheek, memorizing every line. "I get it. We're wrong for each other. Trust me, I've spent every single second since I forced you out of my life coming up with excuses why I shouldn't love you. But—"

She yanks back. "Alex—"

"Tell me," I say, holding her face firmly. "Did you ever feel that kind of attraction with anyone else?" I inch closer. "Did anyone ever hold you, and kiss you the way I do?" I whisper, our lips brushing.

"Alex—"

"I don't care what you are because I know who you are."

"Alex, I—"

"No one will ever love you like the way I do," I promise her before I kiss her.

It could be the last time I ever feel her mouth on mine so I make it count, savoring her taste, the softness of her lips, her scent.

She doesn't resist.

Her tongue finds mine, showing me just how much she missed me. I could die like this and I'd still be the luckiest bastard on earth.

The softness quickly gives way to the fire blazing in our hearts. Manda takes what she needs and I give her all I have.

"Alex." She's completely out of breath.

I can't handle "goodbye," but I have to accept her choice even if it kills me.

Resting my forehead against hers, I draw a deep breath. "Yeah?"

"I love you."

She went to hell and back for me; I don't question how she feels about me. "But will you stay?"

She gets up. I assume that's a "no."

"C'mon." She extends her hand toward me. "There's someone I'd like to introduce you to."

We head back to the others. They sorta look like they just watched a soap opera and now the characters have climbed out of the TV.

Manda doesn't care. She takes Leandro from B's arms. "Alex"—she smiles at the kid—"this is Leandro." She gives him to me. "Leandro, this is your dad."

He runs his tiny hand down my face. "Dada."

"Yeah," I say. "I'm your dada."

Jesse is next to me, inspecting his nephew closely. "Good thing he got his mom's looks," he teases me.

Leandro turns to Manda. "Mamama."

She kisses his cheek. "And her fine taste in music," she adds.

I lift him up. "Your mom's music sucks."

Manda cocks a brow. "Says the guy who tried to impress me with Led Zeppelin?"

"Hey, what did I tell about insulting Zeppelin?"

She rolls her eyes. "You're unbelievable."

I take her hand and pull her toward us. "Let's go home."

She frowns. "You don't even have a home."

"Sure," I say, looking from her to Leandro. "It's right here with you." The rest we'll figure out along the way.

Epilogue

Amanda

Bonnie bounds through the backdoor, fanning herself with some old newspapers. "Oh. My. Gosh." She looks over my shoulder. "What's Samantha Stephens doing here and where's my best friend?"

I put the salad servers down, facing her with a frown. "You don't think I actually made those, do you?"

She ogles the salads lined up on the kitchen counter. "Well, did you?"

"Of course not." I roll my eyes, smirking. "I mean, what's delivery for?"

B throws her head back and laughs. "Some things never change, huh?"

"Nope." But others sure as hell do.

I gaze out the window. "Dude." Jesse yanks the grilling fork out of Alex's tight grip. "You're ruining that yummy meat."

Alex sighs. "Says the guy who doesn't even know how to fry eggs."

Jesse flashes his brother a wicked grin. "You and I both know you're just jealous."

Alex shakes his head. "How many times do I have to tell you Mom and Dad were only trying to be nice when they said you make the best steaks?"

"That is not—"

"Enough." JJ disarms Jesse in a heartbeat, waving the fork like a sword. "You boys sit your asses down and let the real master handle this."

Constantin laughs. "I like this girl."

Raphael leans back in his chair. "You, brother, like *all* girls."

Carter smirks. "Kind of like Jesse, huh?"

"Hey." Jesse shoots him a look. "That's—"

"Not for the ears of a child," Mrs. Lacroix says, sitting Leandro onto the table.

B squeezes my shoulder, drawing my attention away from the odd formation in the backyard. "It's weird, right?"

Seeing them all at one table? "Yeah." Not too long ago, they would have killed each other. I guess an almost-apocalypse really does change people.

"So"—she pulls herself up on the counter—"how are you? And please, don't bullshit me." Her warning puts a smile on my face. She knows me too damn well.

"I don't know." How is one supposed to feel after almost ending the whole damn world, dying, and being resurrected by the devil himself? Guilty? Rotten? Like a damn failure? A bit of everything.

B looks me deep in the eye. "Amanda, you know none of this was your fault, right?"

My gaze darts to Melinda's picture sitting on Gram's old cupboard. She always tried to teach responsibility. *You can't just do whatever you want, Amanda. Actions have consequences and sometimes others pay the price.* Others included over five dozen FBI agents, thousands of innocents injured or dead during the quake, the Blairs, the sheriff, and that poor woman who left a daughter behind. Oh yeah, and my own sister, of course. And why? Because I put my trust in magic when I should have trusted my damn heart.

"I can't change the past," I say, leaning against the counter. Their blood will forever be on my hands.

B flashes me a smile. "Would you really want to?" she asks, cocking a brow at Alex and Leandro. They're playing in the grass. Baby-boy giggles like crazy when Alex makes funny faces.

"No." I'm selfish, remember? And this—Alex and Leandro—is everything I ever wanted.

Jesse barges in, trying hard *not* to look in B's direction. He fails, by the way. "Guys, what's taking you so long?"

Out of the corner of my eye, I watch B tense. "Here." I grab a salad bowl and push it against Little Remington's chest. "Stop bitching and make yourself useful, will ya?"

He mutters something under his breath and marches back out to the others. B never takes her eyes off him.

I pour my best friend a shot of bourbon. "So you gonna tell me why your aura switches colors like a damn mood ring?" From red to gray in the matter of seconds.

"Seriously?" She pulls a face. "You're reading me?"

I shrug. "It's not like I have an off switch for it." Even if I did, I wouldn't use it. I recall the days I only saw rainbows when I looked at folks. I hated not being able to tell what they felt. It was as if I had lost a part of me.

"So?" I push.

"Nothing," she replies too fast.

I study the pale pink glow around her, knowing she's trying to sell me bullshit. "That nothing's name is Jesse?"

"No," she barks.

I laugh. "So that's a 'yes' then."

She downs the tasty booze. "Shut up."

"Are you ever going to forgive him?" I hate the way they tiptoe around each other. Especially because my disappearance is what drove a damn wedge between them. Alex told me all about Jesse's let's-let-Manda-rot-in-hell stunt. Unlike B, I don't blame him. He needed his brother saved. So did I.

She says nothing.

God, why does she have to be so stubborn? "What would you have done if the roles were reversed?"

She looks at me, confused. "What do you mean?"

"I mean would you have chosen Alex's life over mine?"

"Of course not," she hisses.

I smile. "Then why are you mad Jesse did the same?"

B jumps from the counter. "I'm not mad at him," she says, throwing her curls over one shoulder. "I'm mad at myself. C'mon, what did I expect, right? He's a guy. Guys can't be trusted."

This isn't about Jesse and we both know it. B wasn't always the screw 'em and leave 'em kinda girl. She dreamed of a white wedding and chariots when we were kids. It all changed the day Gabe, the oldest Lacroix sibling, was arrested for rape. "Look, I get it. What G—"

"We should get back to the others." She jumps

down from the counter, grabs two salad bowls, and rushes outside.

Wanna know what else the past taught me? You can't outrun it, no matter how badly you want to. A lesson B has yet to learn.

Alex tickles Leandro. "Hey, B?"

"Huh?" she grumbles, still pissed I brought up her oldest brother.

"How's the Nun doing?" he asks, as JJ snatches Leandro away from him. She's sorta in love with our son. No kidding, the girl adores him. I can tell by the color of her aura—bright red.

B flings herself in a chair next to her mom. "She's her usual annoying self."

Looks like she got over her demonic possession rather quickly. "Want me to pay her a visit?" After Melinda's death, I had to transfer to Salem State University so Leandro could grow up in the only home he ever knew, but I don't mind driving to New York for a day.

"Nah." B props her elbows on the table. "She still thinks you're Satan's bride."

Alex circles my hip from behind. "She's not that far off the grid."

"You're such a jerk." I snort.

He pulls his brows up. "That's not what you called me at night." I fucking hate it when he's that cocky.

"Please." Jesse waves his hands. "Can you guys not talk about stuff like that when we're about to eat?"

"Stuff like that?" I laugh. "You mean sex? Something you seem to love more than anything else?"

He blushes. "It's just weird, okay?"

"Whatever," Alex replies, chuckling.

"So did you think about my offer?" Carter changes the topic. He wants me to work as a consultant for the PAU.

I cast him a sidelong glance. "Thanks. But no thanks." Every time the PAU gets involved, I end up dead. Granted, I made it back but there are only so many times one can cheat death.

Carter shrugs. "The offer stands."

"And I appreciate it, but hunting is"—I kiss Alex on the cheek—"his gig."

****

"Nothing Else Matters" by Metallica plays quietly in the background. It's Leandro's favorite lullaby. I've listened to this song about a million times, but never felt its lyrics the way I do when I look into those soft shamrock eyes, filled with love and happiness.

Leandro yawns like a tiger cub. Playing with a bunch of hunter slash witch aunts and uncles drained the little man.

I run my hand over his beautiful face. His rosy cheeks are softer than a feather, his brilliant purple aura as pure as his heart. "You're safe and loved, baby boy." I'm going to spend the rest of my life making sure of it.

The scent of lavender wafts through the air. Leandro gazes behind me, lifting his tiny arms, reaching for the ghost of the woman who raised him like her own.

"You see her, don't you?" He's blessed with more gifts than any witch child I've ever seen. He inherited my empathy, Melinda's ability to see beyond the veil of the living into the land of the dead. And then, of course, there's the green light bubble Alex told me about. The one that saved his life when the hunter tried to shoot him.

"Tell her I love her," I whisper, kissing his forehead.

"Love," he repeats after me, his eyelids slowly falling shut.

The door creaks open. Alex peeks inside. "Is he asleep?"

"Yeah."

Alex comes closer, wearing nothing but a towel. His chest glitters; his hair is wet. He rests his chin on my shoulder, circling my hips and pulling me against him. "I love you," he whispers. "Both."

I never get used to hearing him say it. Alex isn't the cheesy romantic type. He shows his love by being a jerk. But since the day in the meadow, he made it his life's mission to tell us every single day what we mean to him. It will take me a while to allow myself to believe this is real, to find trust in his determination to be with us. But I'm working on it, daily.

"We love you, too," I say, leaning my head back against his chest.

We just stand there, holding onto each other, while Leandro sleeps. We lost so much time with him neither of us wants to lose any more.

I tilt my head to the side, meeting his malachite eyes. "So what do parents do when the kids are asleep?" It's been three months since that night in the meadow. Three months since Alex gave up his old life as a hunter. And three months since we moved into the Bishop residence—the house I never wanted to step foot in again. Yet all of this is new for us. We have no clue how to raise a kid, or how not to strangle each other. But hey, we're trying. In the end, that's all any of us can do.

A mischievous grin spreads across his perfect face. "I can think of a few things," he says, tracing kisses down my neck.

I'd say each and every one of those *few things* have something to do with the hardness beneath his towel. "Sorry, jerk-face, you gotta be a bit more specific," I moan, giving him more access to my neck.

He spins me around. One arm wrapped around my waist, he pulls me against him like he owns me. In a way, he does. Alexander "jerk-face" Remington owns my soul. I knew that before we even met. He was the reason I waited every Sunday outside my house. He was the one I spoke to when my mother locked me in the attic, thinking I was evil. And he was the one who barged into my life on a black steel horse to save me from myself.

His thumb slides across my bottom lip. "More specific, huh?" He cocks a brow. "I thought witches knew everything."

"We do," I assure him, claiming his mouth.

I take my time. Tasting every inch of him. Savoring the feel of his tongue gently massaging mine. I died believing I'd never get to feel his warmth again. I came back certain I'd treasure every kiss for the rest of my life.

Breathless, he pulls back. "I love you, Manda." He places his strong hands on my butt, pulling me up. "And I'm going to spend the rest of my life proving it to you."

His hardness presses against my jeans. He was right. No one ever made me feel the way he does. His eyes alone have the ability to melt the walls I'd built so carefully around my heart. "You better start right now," I whisper, running my fingers through his wet hair. "We witches aren't exactly known for our patience."

A deep chuckle roars through the room. "No," he says, carrying me out of Leandro's room back to ours. "I guess you're not."

We make it to the bed. He lays me down and slowly undresses me. I feel his lips everywhere—my neck, my stomach, my breasts. He takes his sweet time torturing me with a love I never thought I was worthy of.

"Please," I beg, gasping for air.

He climbs over me, the look of the hunter in his malachite eyes. His hard thighs come down on me, his ripped stomach kisses mine. The heat of his hard cock pressing against my wetness drives me over the edge.

Just when I think he's going to release me, he stops. "Manda?"

"Hmm," I choke out, guiding his hard-on to where I need it.

"You're not going to get rid of me. You know that, right?" I don't know where the fear in his voice comes from, but I can promise you it's there for no reason.

"Who said I want to get rid of you, boy-toy?" Lifting my hips, I welcome him inside me.

He forgets all about leaving when he pushes deeper, sending me to another sphere.

What starts as a slow worshiping, quickly turns into possessive need. Love, hate, need, want, passion, fear—it's what we're made of. And I wouldn't want it any other way. Because for a destined love, you have to climb some fences, even if they're spiked with fate.

A word about the author...

A passionate reader and writer, Nadine is addicted to the dark side of the craft. She grew up with Marvel heroes and horror films. She loves stories that challenge gender stereotypes, religious beliefs, and tackle topics such as racism and cultural differences in an entertaining way.

Nadine has a BA in Comparative Religions and studied Creative Writing at the University of Oxford. If she isn't traveling the world, she's reading, writing, or watching movies.

www.ingramcontent.com/pod-product-compliance
Lightning Source LLC
Chambersburg PA
CBHW070752030726
47504CB00003B/526